A World To Discover

Barely able to believe their long incarceration was over, clutching each other and their bundles, the immigrants moved in the surging crowd towards the small speck of light which meant Freedom. They divided like water, glancing round every obstacle they came to, moved forward by their sheer might. In a flurry of noise they broke on New Zealand. Above the heads of the crowd, the sweet smell of fresh air drifted in to Ceci and Teaser, the speck of light growing larger, looming before them. Incredibly they had reached the end of their voyage. They had arrived safely at the end of the world. Behind them seas they had never seen, and ahead the Unknown. . . .

HEART
OF THE
HIGH
COUNTRY

Elizabeth Gowans

BANTAM BOOKS
TORONTO · NEW YORK · LONDON · SYDNEY · AUCKLAND

This edition contains the complete text
of the original hardcover edition.
NOT ONE WORD HAS BEEN OMITTED.

HEART OF THE HIGH COUNTRY

*A Bantam Book / published by arrangement with
St. Martin's Press*

PRINTING HISTORY

*St. Martin's Press edition published September 1986
Bantam edition / June 1988*

ISBN 0-553-27160-1

Published simultaneously in the United States and Canada

---

*Bantam Books are published by Bantam Books, a division of
Bantam Doubleday Dell Publishing Group, Inc. Its trademark,
consisting of the words "Bantam Books" and the portrayal of a
rooster, is Registered in U.S. Patent and Trademark Office and
in other countries. Marca Registrada. Bantam Books, 666 Fifth
Avenue, New York, New York 10103*

PRINTED IN THE UNITED STATES OF AMERICA

O   0 9 8 7 6 5 4 3 2 1

To my Mother and Father...

HEART
OF THE
HIGH
COUNTRY

PART ONE

Chapter 1

High above the ocean a giant wandering sea bird rose and fell effortlessly with the currents, soaring upwards above the trenches and ridges of the cold South Atlantic floor, heading on towards the polar ice-cap and the warmer Pacific waters beyond. Beneath him, the globe flattened out, its features sliding into place: the familiar dots of islands, shoals of migrating fish moving through the water like glass to vanish in deep chasms, clefts between sea mounts, darkened abysses of the ocean floor.

The bird turned its head at the sight of a tiny speck in the blameless ocean, a ship moving slowly, inexorably towards the ice-cap from the Indian Ocean then turning at an angle towards the Pacific. Lying on the current the bird watched this sight so rarely seen in southern waters. Unlike the war canoes of the Pacific Islanders, this bulky thing which seemed to be heading for Aotearoa had come around the wrong side of the Great Continent and had to it the feel of another, an alien hemisphere. The great bird wheeled and headed on, leaving it for Easter Island and the Galapagos beyond...

Below, long fingers of sun reached down and touched the *Grace* as she sat on the vast face of the sea like a brooch pinned on flat cloth. Like the picture of her which hung in a London office, she had a dignity which befitted isolation. A sailor peered up her long masts at the huge bowl of blue which had been lowered over them 'til it met the horizons. He shielded his eyes to look beyond her crafted front thrusting over bright water to the concave line of the earth's curvature, broken only in places by flints of light. He walked to the rear of the *Grace* to rest his eyes in the small patch of shade beyond her squared back...

Beneath him in a state room a lady drummed her fingers irritably on a writing desk. Nearly three months of what she regarded as "atrocious diet" had done little for her humour. Beyond her slanting squared windows she had been afforded the view of continually rising and falling mountains of sea, an ever-changing landscape to remind her they were somewhere towards the bottom of the world, as far away from Home as it was possible to be and that it had not been *her* idea. It was the immediate daily annoyance of being closeted indefinitely with one's spouse, the petty inconveniences which irked. For his part, she knew, the sooner the voyage was over and he had a chance to stretch his legs, preferably on a horse, the more his humour would improve. He would acquire 20–40,000 acres, occupy himself with it and, utilizing the services of some of the riff-raff below, doubtless turn a handsome profit. But there would be nothing for *her* to do... She watched him step to the window and peer up at the sky beyond and it suddenly occurred to her she did not know him very well... He now appeared to be staring at the minutest speck of a bird hovering high in the sky, wheeling, heading on, wheeling, turning, wheeling lower then beginning to descend...

"Albatross," he said pulling open her desk drawer and taking out a length of twine. She saw his pink fingers remove from her plate the greasy pork she had rejected for lunch, fix it firmly to the twine and leave the cabin. It was *amazing* how the man couldn't relax!

Picking at a cuticle she moved to the window. Now the bird was falling through the air towards them, getting larger the lower it came. As its great wings moved she could not fail to be impressed. Alone like them at the end of the world yet truly immense! *Surely* it was two yards across!! She caught the briefest glimpse of its eye as it passed her window then, whirling, filled it, its speckled breast and great wings between her and the light—turning its head to look down into the water their ship had disturbed then rising on the air and swooping again as if playing with them.

Beneath her feet in a space she did not know existed, two fifteen-year-old Assisted Passage girls pressed their noses to the iron grille of the airing space, thanking God for their daily ration of fresh air! Though they could not, in fact had never *seen* the sea, they could smell it and the light which slanted in to them through the grille was real daylight and all they would be allotted till the same time next day. Breathing it thankfully and hoping not to be called down before time, they filled their lungs. It was great to be almost level with the deck and breathing air! In their world, though they heard the runnings and shoutings, the dancing and music on deck, the walking and laughter— and interpreted it as best they could—their entitlements were limited to, sickness permitting, adequate food and being landed safely in New Zealand once the voyage was over. Beyond that they asked nothing. Now, crammed together with their dreams and fresh air, the girls Ceci and Teaser were gazing at the sky when suddenly the piece of pork hit the water below, making a new sound.

"They're emptying stuff," said Teaser, struggling to get to her large feet and thrust her bulk out of the airing space before they should get a drenching. "Give us a hand." Just as Ceci extended an arm for her to grip, the sound of great wings crashing into the water, thudding against the ship, overtook them. Shrieking, they grasped each other in the fear they were foundering on a rocky coast as suddenly a piece of taut twine rose rapidly into their field of vision, moved up and down before their eyes, sawing itself on their grating accompanied as it moved by choking thrashing sounds on the water line. Spray flew in on them. There were running steps. A man above shouted. In horror they listened to the sound of something very close to them being throttled, beaten and, as they cowered, knew for a moment the desolate terror in the eye of a great lonely sea bird dragged between them and their light. Against their iron grating it thrashed briefly, its breath coming short, the might of its wings beating hopelessly as water and occasional light flickered down to them ... With a triumphant shout from above they felt the bird's bulk dragged unwillingly away, saw it catch on the grating with its claws as its talons uncurled one by one and it was hauled upwards from view. Bump bump—up the wooden sides of the ship to thud on the deck above. It made no more cry, no croak or call ...

Sickened, they went below. Maybe they were better off in the dark, thought Ceci, dropping sadly on to the packing space she and Teaser used as sleeping quarters.

The entire hold of the ship would be filled with wool bales on its return trip but on the way out it was good enough for people. Sensing her mood, her dog Else came out from behind her clothing sack, muzzling its head into her hand. She took it on her chest, lay down and looked into its eyes. It was as if she could almost see her mother's sister, Aunt May, peering out at her. Was it some likeness of her own face reflecting there? Now it looked more like her own sister Norah. Thoughts like this made her sad for the dog had been a gift from May to Norah, and when Norah had died May had give her the dog as a keepsake. Norah and the sea! She always thought of them together! Norah on the beach outside the Sick Home, staring at the sea, wrapped in a grey blanket, the thick unruly plait down her back, stray hairs escaping from it. How clearly she could remember Norah, pale and intense, confiding she wanted to return to Clapham ... She could remember borrowing the money and bringing her home for the last time. Norah had been fourteen and she, Ceci, twelve. The people on the train had stared at them, moved their children out of the way as Norah coughed. She remembered Norah pushing Else towards her saying "Go on—make friends" or "Go away!" But Else had turned in anxious circles refusing to take her eyes off Norah, and as Ceci had sunk her fingers into the rough hair of the small dog's back, she'd felt its longing for her sister. They had arrived home to a deep silence. Two weeks later Norah lay dead and beneath the sofa the little dog grieved.

Yet on the voyage, almost unfed, Else had flourished, the lack of amusement below making her an instant celebrity and the only true diversion. She clearly loved disrupting Bible or sewing groups, would pick her moment then tear through, under legs, over stomachs, squiggling and squirming through every inch of steerage till Ceci would catch her and sit rubbing her head, scratching the rough hair, tapping the hard little skull with a finger and saying, "There now. That's enough."

"You're ever so lucky to have a dog," Teaser would say. She could not understand why Ceci "with a mother and married sister and that" should want to leave home.

"I mean you're not like me," she said.

"And what about you?" Ceci would ask.

But Teaser wouldn't elaborate.

"I've got my certificate from the clergyman same as everyone else!" she would say.

Teaser and Ceci had no complaints about the journey: it had been free and work was guaranteed to them. They could not expect to have the same kind of food as the people who had paid £42 for the passage or even put £5 towards it. Yet as the voyage had progressed, the lack of rain to replenish the ship's casks had meant stale drinking water had been rationed to half a pint a day and washing had become impossible. By now there seemed to be cockroaches in the folds of all their clothes and it took willpower and a round of jokes before they could eat the preserved vegetables or drink the water which tasted so sour it had to be swallowed with the mind on something else. They had become accustomed to certain areas of themselves being irredeemably dirty: their hair and finger nails, elbows... The ship's soap, guaranteed to lather in salt water, had not worked and because of the permanent stickiness it left, most preferred a generally "grey" look the darkness did much to conceal.

Though skins had become sallow and taut with dehydration, the lack of privacy and ever present smells in this place they shared with the pigs, hens and cattle kept for those above decks had caused tempers to fray and name-calling ensue, the fact it was the same for all held them together. But a sleeping girl's act of suddenly flinging an arm out on her sticky partner's stomach led to the pulling of long, exceptionally greasy hair. Not a change of clothing existed that had not been changed over and again and despite taking turns in the airing space above, the air below, especially since crossing The Line, had in truth become increasingly stale, foul and hot, and it could easily be understood why people became careful not to mention sickness. They had become superstitious about even grumbling and, hopeful of better lives in the future, kept up an easy acceptance one of another despite their dirt in an equality few would experience again. They changed names and plans... laughed when a fellow who'd cut his way into the supplies drilled a hole in a cask of brandy and got drunk. Even a disagreeable man who would not speak for weeks finally came out of himself and started a farming group for the older boys and men. While most of the Assisted Passage girls sewed on ship's cloth in small

groups, for her part Teaser teased and for hers Ceci kept
the steerage children spellbound with a form of "school"
as she, as a labourer's child, had received it on the Estate.
In the poor light without slate or chalk, gradually they
had come to her, those anxious peaky-faced children of
the poor: those who wanted to and those who were sent.
With knotted hair and faces ingrained with dirt, they had
joined in, poking fingers in noses and eyes and knowing
so little about anything. "For your dog," their parents
would say, forcing on her the barely edible scraps which
in truth their own children had twice rejected. "Can't
have you going underfed on account o' your dog!" Throughout the voyage the prayer of all was that there would be
no epidemic; that they would not become a "coffin ship"
forbidden to land till the disease had run its course...

But as night fell, when the sick moaned and fractious
children cried, the people in steerage longed to arrive.
Not for one minute did their gratitude to the Assisted
Passage Company diminish nor to the God who had thus
far preserved them; yet the thought of a good wash, dry
land, fresh air and a real change of clothes was so overwhelming that beside it the futures they had dreamed of
paled to insignificance. On the day the cry "Land!" was
heard in steerage, even the faces which had farewelled
them at Plymouth were hastily forgotten, so great was
their desire to walk on green grass again under an open
sky.

Barely able to believe their long incarceration was over,
clutching each other and their bundles the immigrants
moved in the surging crowd towards the small speck of
light which meant Freedom. They divided like water,
glancing round every obstacle they came to, moved forward by their sheer might. In a flurry of noise they broke
on New Zealand. Above the heads of the crowd, the
sweet smell of fresh air drifted in to Ceci and Teaser, the
speck of light growing larger, looming before them. Incredibly they had reached the end of their voyage. They
had arrived safely at the other end of the world. Behind
them, seas they had never seen, and ahead the Unknown.
Suddenly the square of light was fully on them. Eyes
pained, legs weak from the seas' roll and surge Ceci and
Teaser stumbled ffom the ship's bowels blinded by the

expanse of brilliant light. Rising around them on all sides were majestic hills, their sides shaven to a frightening brown barrenness as if burnt, their lines cruelly crisp on the hard sky. They tried to pause to drink in the sweet smell of dried grass on the air but were borne quickly on by the crowd, down the plank and, at last, on to the shore. Their eyes searched the hills. Where were the trees? The emptiness was unbelievable! Only the merest scatter of recently made wooden houses which could be counted in the turning of a head could be seen flanking the shaky jetty extending into the water. What a far cry from London, this landing pier with its uneven planks and scarce room to set a box down! Already a scatter of people had gathered on a slight rise to watch them come ashore, arms folded, staring rudely at the First and Second Saloon passengers as they left in carriages, their belongings behind them. Though they had arrived that self-same way themselves five, ten, twenty years back these New Land people glanced with disdain at the steerage folk before turning to study their recent companions, the red deer and livestock now ashore being penned. Once that was done and the boxes, trunks and furniture of the better off removed, they turned away.

Now alone on the quay the steerage folk waited. They had been told someone would meet them and take them to an Immigrants Barracks where they would stay until work was found for them. Awkwardly they moved from foot to foot in the unbelievable silence looking about. Nothing was to be seen but the dry brown sweeps of grass descending from a great height to the glass blue sea and above, a small cloud beginning its solitary passage across the sky as if it had decided to sail for Home.

Teaser winked at Ceci. It amused her to see her friend, despite their ridiculous position, pulling at her sleeves, examining her wrists as if someone were about to arrive and claim her. She had been just the same on board, calmly waiting out storms when the noise of wood, water, canvas and air clashing together had reached such deafening proportions the rest of them stuffed cloths round their heads. Yet here it was the Silence, Teaser thought, that stung the ears. Still, whether New Zealand meant indifferent glory or ruin she was ready. She had been ready to arrive the day after they'd left and now that they were finally here she wasn't going to be put off by a pokey little place like Lyttelton or an assortment of middle-aged women—let them think what they pleased!

Having asked directions, gradually the immigrants began to flow up the hill towards some barracks-style wooden buildings with deep verandahs within a paling fence. As they neared them they looked spartan in the extreme and immediately it became plain why they had not been met. The barracks were so full an official could have done nothing but apologize. Putting on a brave face they pushed in, past the resentful stares of those already there, struggling for space and forcing themselves through families and into corners. All around people spread themselves across bunks, using their children to block or claim spaces... They gripped the edge with feet and hands and everywhere the cry was the same: no room here!

The place was run by a Mr. Burden, a small sandy-haired man with a pink neck who did his best to disguise the fact that all would be done for the convenience of existing householders and landowners rather than the new arrivals.

As he moved amongst the crowded barracks giving the impression he did not want to touch anything, Ceci noticed people moving out of his way. He had told them to spruce up when Hiring Day came, adding that some of the young men could expect to be taken to a place called Addington where a rail head ended and there were rail yards and development going on. It was close by and had been occasioned by the laying of a railway line into the southern wilderness. New immigrants hurrying to establish themselves had formed a small suburb there which disgruntled former immigrants returning from other situations had helped to swell.

Other than that phrase "close by" Burden did not bother to draw a picture of the new country for them. There was no map, no talk of mountains, plains or rivers... Just the information that there was a place to the south called Otago, near the bottom of the island they were already on. Scots people could go there, he said, a touch of animosity in his voice as if he did not simply mean they could go there to find work... It was the citadel of Presbyterianism, he added, which viewed with a cold eye the Church of England Province of Canterbury

in which they were now fortunate enough to be standing.
If of course they were foolish enough to go there of their
own accord, he continued, he assured them they would
find the bald hills and icy streams "true Scots territory" in
a voice which managed to undermine any natural beauty
the place may have had. An uncomfortable feeling began
to shift through the barracks. *Surely*, animosities they did
not know at home could not exist here?

Waking with considerable trepidation Ceci realized Hiring
Day was upon them: the day that would decide everything. Around her the barracks was in turmoil, women
borrowing each others' hairbrushes, mirrors, pinning and
fastening their clothes, burrowing in trunks for their references, each anxious to outdo the other, to secure the best
job. At last their waiting would be over! Beyond the
window the first carriage had already arrived, a lady
being helped from it by a gentleman, carefully putting her
foot on the ground as if it were an eggshell. Looking
around, Ceci realized that Teaser was missing. Quickly
she ran to the cookhouse and on to the latrines, then
around the length of the paling fence but to no avail.
Teaser had vanished. Taking a hold of Else's string, Ceci
pondered. Teaser must have sneaked out last night. Something on the edge of her mind was trying to communicate
itself to her: it had been something to do with their walk
around Lyttelton yesterday afternoon. Carefully she recalled.
They had been up a steep dirt street, peering over fences
with the settlers staring back at them with slow glances
then . . . what? What was it, that sign of danger she could
not remember? Teaser had definitely vanished! Taking
Else by the lead, she quickly set off to retrace their steps.

Seeing a Parson's house she turned in at its gate and
hurried up the path. Although the bell push said "the Very
Reverend" she found little Reverend about the minister
and nothing Very. Between taking his pipe in and out of
his pocket, clearing his throat and offering to buy Else, he
confined his remarks about Teaser's whereabouts to the
observation that there had been a *great* demand for girls in
the last ten years though it was tapering off and they were
usually engaged or married within a month of arrival. He
declined to see anything untoward in Teaser's disappear-
ance, implying it was the way of the flesh and she would

probably end up doing better than the rest of them. If the
Immigration weren't looking for her, he said, the Church
wouldn't either. Besides, she was patently already *there*
and making a contribution in some form so he could not
see why Ceci . . . Her friend might already be in Christchurch—
eight miles over the hill and oddly named to his view, in
that it was a town of pubs, not churches, even if they *did*
call them hotels . . . Feeling disappointed, Ceci excused
herself and closed his gate and began slowly and thoughtfully retracing her steps to the Barracks. To the side of the
road she now noticed strange brittle plants which looked
like ravens clambering soaking from pools, standing miserably to dry. Beyond them were awkward cabbage palms,
odd ferns and grasses creeping between houses and down
into gullies. Pulled by Else she crossed to a tree whose
bark hung in strips above, its blue leaves making scratching
noises in the wind. Standing listening she inhaled the rich
aromatic smell, letting her eyes fall on the shiny, spiky-
leaved tongues beyond shooting from the ground . . . Strange
were the plants, she thought, that grew at the end of the
world where ministers even and Bishops had come.

Sudden noise brought her back and she became instantly aware of carriages passing in the street, their
clattering rumble shattering the silence. For a moment she
watched them roll down the hill, one after another until it
came to her they were going to the Hiring! Scooping Else
in her arms she ran but, as she did, the stream of
carriages was already returning past her, each seeming to
contain a smiling girl or girls . . . A hand she thought she
recognized waved: the trim of a lace sleeve which seemed
familiar flashed by: a box she half knew fell off, a voice
called . . . Suddenly the stream ended! Horrified by her
stupidity she continued down the deserted hill and turned
guiltily in at the Barracks gate. Immediately she sensed its
difference. The place was utterly silent. Only a broken-
looking dray, the sort used for deliveries, awaited, its tired
horse hanging its head. Tying Else to the fence she ran
quickly to the building and in at the door. Empty! Even
her box was gone! White faced, she spun. There at the
corner of the compound Burden's sandy head was leaving
by the small gate, seemingly trying to shake off a shoddy-
looking fellow who was following after him with an air of
dissatisfaction. Panting, Ceci caught up.

"Mr. Burden," she called, "my box—"

"Ah!" he said whirling on her. "The Trouble Maker who ran off when she was told to wait!"

Ceci stood frozen.

"This one," said Burden to the man, indicating Ceci.

"But I—"

"Don't waste my time arguing. You know the rules." He motioned towards the dray with the waiting horse to which the shabby man was already walking. Beyond him Ceci could make out the lump on its back which she now recognized as her box. She turned to look back at Burden but he was already walking away. Suddenly she felt terribly alone. Lifting Else in her arms she crossed to the cart and climbed on. It wasn't fair. They were supposed to have their work arrangements witnessed and in writing... She looked for the man but he had vanished again. Well, at least they were started. A cart like this couldn't go far...

"What do you fancy, Else?" she whispered to the little dog. Else sneezed, for the cart was dusty. "A large house with a garden? 'Nother hotel? You wait till we're settled!" She rubbed the back of the little dog's neck. Else sneezed again.

Ahead of them the man reappeared, crossed to the cart and without speaking or looking directly at Ceci got on, grasped the ribbons and delivered a resounding smack to the drowsing horse which sent it shuddering and reeling from the barracks compound.

Chapter 2

Ceci lurched through Lyttelton on the back of the fast flying cart, a mere impression of open mouths to either side of the street as she flew by. Even as she struggled for a hand grip they were rising into the hills which hemmed

Lyttelton in, grinding up a steeply dangerous track which jutted out over a cliff. Beneath her lay a beach, fleetingly pure, a beach on which surely yesterday land-hungry men must have scrambled ashore with boxes and barrels, dragged sails and tarps over them and crawled under to sleep. In the gullies running down to the beach she glimpsed giant ferns with stems like trees, tall flaxen topped grasses thrashing in the wind. Above the blue, blue sky and beneath it fold upon fold of brown hills crinkled and bald like wrapping paper. Coming on to the crest the wind knifed blowing away the sound of the cart's wheels. Holding on she turned to glance back across the immense belt of sparkling ocean ending at what must have been the edge of the world. On it, the dots of two tiny ships approaching were the only sign humans existed. So small and solid on the sea, they looked as if they had been glued there and could have been picked up between finger and thumb and slipped in a pocket. Turning her eyes from the wind she looked at the back of the man in front of her, at his stern, uncommunicative shoulders and dirty coat. The way the hat was impaled on his head was sinister somehow as he reared up against the sky, the clouds racing before him. As they swung around a bluff to begin their descent the loud sound of the horse's strained breathing, the crash of the wheels' jar, was worse than the wind when she'd turned her head into it.

In a sudden breathtaking moment the New Land revealed itself to her with an unexpected grandeur and immediacy in the form of a great sweep of unpeopled plain, larger than she could ever have envisaged. There at the foot of the hill it lay, bounded on the one side by the wavering coastline which vanished in a haze of yellow and brown and on the other by a chain of mountains spreading so far distant they disintegrated into dust. Only the glint of a river here, the tiniest smudge which could have been trees there broke its monotony.

Before her eyes had let go of the plain the man was bringing them fast down out of the hills past a clustering of poor sod houses so similar to their surroundings she had not seen them coming. With bricks made from chunks of earth, the grass, roots and all, still sticking from it, they merged with the yellow hills and, when she turned to look at them, were gone in the dust the cart raised.

"Where are we going?" Ceci called to the man. "Are you taking me to Christchurch?" She waited for him to answer. "Is it a big house then? Or a farm?" Patience counselled her to wait and see. The man could, after all, have been deaf and she told herself it was best to endure the discomfort of the cart quietly. It was almost as if he was deliberately hitting the dried clods of broken earth which lay in their way.

Her heart quickened as up ahead she made out the beginning of a town. Wooden buildings began to appear, asserting with lackadaisical confidence their disdain of any attempt to please the eye: the buildings of men, for men, bearing no female influence nor hint of wifely approval nor even those little signs, such as fences or gardens, that showed they were loved.

Though the outskirts were rough, the town itself showed elements of permanency. Yet she could almost feel the man despising it. As he deliberately hurried the tired horse past hotel and watering places it was as if he was trying not to see the boast of an utterly new town able to mount bookshops, clockmakers and jewellers.

Passing them Ceci sought about eagerly for the hotel, shop or office which was to be her home. Her eyes missed nothing. The way the town displayed its cutlery, china and plate was showy, as if having shipped them all the way out from the Old Country they were determined to set them in the sun... Yet after their long journey from distant shores they had a "lost" quality to them, these items which looked so commonplace at home.

Leaning almost out of the cart, Ceci stared at a group of women pointing in raptures at a lone roll of recently arrived taffeta. The look on their faces was of greed and innocence as they peered longingly.

Down a side street noise came from a large square where people in brightly coloured clothes clustered together, talking. The women had parasols and hats and were in high spirits as if there'd been a fête. "Down there please!" she longed to lean forward and call to the man. But incredibly he was going past it!

To her horror she began to realize they had passed the centre of town and were heading out again... the wide expanse of sky beckoning them on. The last store, which the man deliberately slowed to look at, was a blacksmiths-cum-ironmonger. On the edge of the plain with his baths, pans and springs, things he could make himself, his axles, ploughs, ovens and grates, he was obviously an important man. Ceci sensed the man driving her was trying to disguise the fact he was interested in the blacksmith's goods. Even from behind she could feel his eyes swivel to the edge of the head he would not turn. As if sensing he were the subject of amusement he whipped the poor horse up and hurried away from what Ceci was sure was the biggest town in New Zealand. They had left it behind—a mere smudge against the fading port hills... Even now her shipmates would be secure in Christchurch, unpacking in the servants' rooms of the hotels, the houses of its business people, she told herself grudgingly. And here she was, on the back of a delivery cart, heading out into the wilderness with a man who could very well be a maniac!

On and on they rolled into the plain she had seen from the hill, the occasional sod house giving way to shanties of split planks, rags and bent pieces of iron marking out people's claims. Small vegetable plots appeared behind the dwellings and children who jumped up and pointed at Else. Sometimes a woman would be there, with a quiet dignity going about the proprieties of life against a background of twigs and crooked awnings; or a man, surprised by them, lifting his face from a bowl, his chin covered in lather, razor in one hand and soap in the other.

Gradually the land took on a flat yellowness. Though the man had seemed bent on getting away from civilization as fast as possible, even now with nothing but tawny tussock and far hills concealed in dust he did not seem visibly at ease. Nor did he speak. It was as if he were playing an elaborate game with her, pretending she was not there. Well she'd go along with it! In fact by now she *couldn't* speak even if he *had* spoken to her! But she reckoned he wouldn't speak until they'd passed some personal point of reference on the landscape, somewhere he felt he belonged. Looking at him, she had a growing feeling they would come to have something in common.

Soon it became clear a larger track lay some way down from them, nearer the coast but going in the same direction, for over the flat land came the echo of calls as coaches met. Between the tracks the yellow grass waved, dust rose, and something that could have been the steel of an iron railway glinted. But they were now going away from the sea, cutting diagonally inland. She sniffed at the air, the dust lying thick in her throat. Straight as their track was, it was criss-crossed frequently by wheel marks giving the impression they were in the midst of dwellings yet none was to be seen. Even the mountains had vanished and in all directions the view was utterly flat, ending in haze. The poor horse struggled on.

Now, exposed to the sun and thirsty, she asked herself *why* she had come and subjected Else to this treatment. Why had that newspaper advertisement struck her as vividly as if she'd received a telegram with her name written on it? She had at once recognized it as an invitation meant specifically for *her*. It had been almost as if she *knew* her future lay in New Zealand. But had she been wrong? For a brief second the idea of "Going" which had seemed so life-giving reared up to mock her. Surely her family were now as distant as the ship she had arrived on. She looked at the back of the man in front of her and got a good hold of herself. At the time she had *known* she had made the right decision, she resolved, and therefore she would not let anything go against that now! Let the going be tough, she would get tougher. If it was work, she would work. She would endure and do and give all she must to this New Life and make it something worthwhile, something to be proud of and thank her parents for having once given her. Nobody would come between her and her determination to make it work! And if this man chose not to talk, or they had to go without a little drinking water, well, that was the least of her worries. All the same, she mused, rubbing Else's neck, the sound of a human voice would have made that much difference...

Finally a small scab in front of them swelled until it became trees and quite a solid building. Had the man driven straight past, Ceci would not have been surprised. But without a word he drove around the side, loosed the horse, dipped his hands in a wooden trough and, shaking them dry, vanished. Ceci waited in the cart staring at the newly made sign "Curton's Accommodation House, 1871." Awkwardly she scrambled down and flipped water from the trough into her face, held some in her hands for Else to drink. She looked at Curton's: it was really no more

than another thatch-roofed sod building yet whitewashed
it looked quite welcoming and she would not have minded being invited in...A notice nearby proclaimed that
Curton had secured this lease of 200 acres from the
Canterbury Provincial Government, was empowered to
act as a ford man at the nearby river, was licensed to keep
beds for eight travellers and shelter for eight horses.
Wandering around the back, she found several carts and
carriages, their freed horses using the shade of the sparse
stand of trees against which Curton had built. It seemed
they were on some sort of a main route for one of the
coaches was very large and could clearly take a lot of
passengers. She stood listening. By the sound of it they
were all inside eating! Was this the meeting place, the
local distribution point for the whole plain? Stiff from
sitting so long, she hobbled about, dust falling from her
skirt as she hit it. The earlier feeling of having arrived in a
New Land had gone completely. Instead a waiting had
come, a suspension between existences. Keeping the cart
in sight she wandered towards the strange trees from
which a deep scent like an incense or myrrh spread out.
These immense trees had a sadness to them—pushed,
broken by great winds, bound groaning in the fastness of
the plain. She looked up at their splintered barks. Poor
clumsily structured leaning giants, each one supported in
its midst great stands of dead wood. The trees looked
shipwrecked in the plain—almost as if they had been
washed there in a giant flood and left muddy and grey
when the water receded. She felt a pity and sympathy for
their lack of mobility, their broken stranded lives, and
wondered what names the settlers had given them. The
ground by them had an undug hardness to it and was
cracked, lifted in places by the crude roots as if ploughed.
Beneath her feet, like kindling catching fire, dead grass
crackled. In the shade it was almost chill. Tiny amongst
the trees Else stood, puzzled. She did not scud from one
to the other as she would at home. Disturbed by the lack
of smells dear to her, she was worried. Her nose found
neither dog nor cat, weasel nor stoat, squirrel nor even
fox. Only dust. Her ears picked up sounds in the dead
wood above: clickings and scrapings, the whirrs and pecking
tapping sounds...But the things of the nose, things that
mattered, she found not. She looked questioningly up at

her mistress and knew instinctively Ceci's mind was in some new place and she must wait.

Beginning to understand the man, Ceci sensed his absence was intended to convey something to her. Cautiously she walked to the doorway and peered in. There he was in the corner behind an enormous platter of food. Looking up he glared briefly at her dog—motioned with his knife to a bench where other women sat and got on with his meal. Almost at once a plump man was upon Ceci placing before her a similar meal of enormous portions, peering about the room as he did so. Slowly Ceci began passing bits under the table to Else as jugs of ale and water moved up and down, the women partaking of both. In this egalitarian society, it seemed, you ate the same food, same amount and no one told anyone else what to do because they were all equal! Never had she had such a large piece of meat in her life.

Suddenly the man rose, paid and walked to the door as if for all he cared Ceci could have ceased to exist. Worried, she stood then hurried after him, wrapping in her handkerchief the scraps for Else. She waved at the women but their heads were already bent to the board and they didn't see her go. Coming out into the light she saw he had already mounted and was impatient to be off. She ran to the cart.

"Where are we going?" she asked peering up at him silhouetted against the sky.

"The High Country," he said, turning the horse to the way.

Chapter 3

The High Country, she repeated to herself, feeling its ring, its lofty noble sound which had caused the man to speak for the very first time.

Gradually they resumed going, it seemed to her, further inland and away from the coast. From what the women had said Curton's brother held sway at the next river down, a wild and terrible crossing where most of them had been obliged to get off and walk. They said he had started there by pitching his tent on the river's edge and setting up forge at the very spot those taking their grain to be milled into flour at Christchurch usually forded. Imagine taking your grain all that way to be milled! Blacksmith and ford man, he had expanded and done nicely they'd said and a township was springing up round him . . .

If these rivers cut the roadless plain into sections how would it save them by going so far inland? They would still have to be forded and would be narrower but much steeper in the mountains; perhaps even with steep sided gorges unsuitable for a cart? Or were they indeed to proceed directly inland, head straight in through the summits by some secret pass? The chain of mountains now loomed like piled herring bones always beside them. How many ways in and out of them there must be! Whole kingdoms could be hidden there! Rich valleys trapped by rings of snows; places of fabled Eternal Spring . . . She was glad not to be alone! The experience of so much emptiness was frightening for there was nothing to eat! No shops selling food or farms growing it . . . A week there—a month— they would die! Else, sensing her fears began to whine and, despite the freedom of the open space, Ceci felt the need to hush her. Because of the man.

Was he simply averse to fording rivers where others did? Did he know of some better ford which perhaps didn't charge . . . ? Riding with him in silence she began to know his soul. He was a man who shunned others and needed no one. Yet he was not a settled man. There was something smouldering there, something dangerous she didn't know the name of. She was reminded of a tinker who'd once visited their house and whom her mother had sent away.

The barest suggestion of a track had faded away as the plains fell beneath them. They were rising. Below, Curton's river bed stretched unimaginable distances, its great rambling expanse of grey stones losing itself in the plain. For a while she thought she could still make out the

Accommodation House . . . but it was gone. Even the river didn't seem to move. Far down towards the coast the sun was glinting on something but there was no way of knowing what it was. By now she knew they would continue to ascend and make their own crossing somewhere higher up. With interest she noted she was not afraid to be alone with the man. Else had dozed. Running a finger over her small bulbous eyes, she felt love for the dog, for life, for things she did not know the names of.

Suddenly she awakened to find herself in the river bed. The sun was sinking. On the far side, it seemed half a mile away—the thin horse browsed. Else had awakened her, snapping viciously and baring her gums at the man who was trying to move the cart between and over the boulders, lifting its wheels, kicking away the stones. She rubbed her eyes and opened her mouth to speak but something in his face, the way he avoided her eyes, told her to say nothing and sit still. By now their silence had become cherished. It was not a thing to be idly scattered . . .

When she awakened properly it was to the wildest scenery. Savage, like nothing she had ever imagined; gaunt, in an intense, almost bitter light. So scared was she to see so much Nothing, even the sight of the man firm before her came to feel homely and safe. Hills rolled below, terrible in their emptiness. Hills and hills as far as the eye could see, a dead yellow brown with neither tree nor flower to brighten them, neither plant nor bird to give hope. Wasn't this their Spring, she asked herself? It was Autumn at home! To think of Autumn at *home* . . . ! The woods! The streets! . . .

They pressed on, hills yellow becoming brown becoming grey in distances unimaginable became purple and black, mauve against an empty sky. Ceci became aware of the man hurrying, seemingly anxious to reach some point by nightfall as if the hills had suddenly become unsafe. Increasingly worried by Else who lay panting in her lap Ceci drummed her fingers, the sun slanting in her eyes. Gradually, there on the worn-out grass, almost merging with it, she made out the smallest speck which grew and became a tent. The man jumped down, ran and stood silently before it. Ceci leaned forward to watch. Suddenly Else leapt from the cart and ran to the tent too, tail wagging. The man seemed to be coughing. Ceci peered anxiously. His chest shook as he stared at the tent flap, coughing deliberately to attract attention. Excited as she was, Else kept behind him.

Slowly the flap lifted and a wizened woman no more than four feet tall and dressed exactly like a man appeared. She seemed to have words with the man. At least, while he seemed not to say anything her eyes took in the girl beyond and she nodded over and again as if something were arranged. Feeling the subject of negotiation, Ceci scrambled down, shook out her skirts, started over and stood a short distance off nodding politely. Suddenly the man turned and passing Ceci in a wide loop, got his sack from the cart. Slowly Ceci crossed to the woman who lifted the flap and showed her a space within; wordlessly she probbed behind a wooden box with her foot indicating a china chamber pot, so ludicrous in its setting yet which so put Ceci in mind of Aunt May's forthrightness she laughed out loud. It seemed, as they were both female, the one was to care for the other. Certainly nothing had been forthcoming from the man. Ceci looked past the older woman at a square board lying by the tent door, doubtless meant for display, saying "GOLD BOUGHT MEALS." Suddenly she felt very content and good. She knew the woman accepted her and neither need bother the other with speech.

Beyond the tent, out of the shadows strange forms suggested themselves: tall raggedy men with long hair and beards who'd made the pass by night fall, with either a wild hungry disappointment in their eyes or a crafty complacency. They coughed quietly in the damp; crouched by their fires they eyed each other.

The woman said they were prospectors who continually criss-crossed the hills, slipping down mountainsides into rivers, clawing their way round crags into ravines, keeping their claims secret. She'd been in that same spot she said eleven years, since losing the two men she'd travelled, panned and lived with having all things equal between them. They had been carried away, she said, while she was behind a boulder relieving herself. She'd heard a rumble, stood up suddenly and seen a rain of boulders descending towards their shelter. Before impact the cliff had cleaved in two and the portion with her mates on had simply crumbled and moved off into the river bed and been washed down and away...Standing, the cold air rushing in her open mouth, she'd stared on what was now a bald cliff of rock before her, going down as straight as the side of a tree to the cold swirling waters below. Above the wide sky blew. After panning a few months alone, long enough to set herself up, she'd trekked in, bought a tent and supplies and set up at this crossing place, why she couldn't say. The men came and went. They knew her. She belonged. Apart from occasional trips in to buy flour, soap or candles she shunned towns and never stayed a night. "I do my bit," she said quietly. "This is the only store in these parts without rats."

Her flour runs were the life blood of the men.

No man came in her tent. They stood politely outside and coughed.

"That one," she'd say, "47lb of gold in two days. Nothing since but he can't leave."

She scratched a dirty hairy chin and sighed, "No more can't I..."

Clearly the men respected her. She alone knew who had gone where, who had frozen on which pass, hanged himself for hunger, stolen whose claim. Doubtless she allowed them credit; knew when not to ask and kept secrets for many. She could read a sigh or downcast face like a book and knew better than to show feelings.

Her dirty fingers poked into the embers the flax flowers, dead grass and dung, which she called her "yellow pine" or "buffalo chips" or the melodic-sounding "Kaladdies". By the faint light she was mending a coarsely patched pair of breeches, drying out some battered boots...talking quietly of days six years back when two men hurrying could start a gold rush; when "the boys out there" had fought and trailed each other; become so wild they'd been chained to logs, only to sober up, toss the logs on their shoulders and walk off laughing.

"Corky," she said, "carried his log two days. A whole half tree it was. Till it was bought off him for the timber."

Another fought for a woman. Challenged a man for beating his wife—held a long drawn out fist fight lasting all day but ending up winning the fight, the woman, and her six children.

"But they lived on together," she said, "and h·

another seven." The bully husband couldn't stand the disgrace of being beat and had left.

As evening became night her talk created a universe of strange and provocative-sounding places. Roaring Meg, Gentle Annie, Knobbies, the Styx, Rock and Pillar, Raggedy...

"Over Drybread..." she'd say, or "By Sugarpot" ... "Butchers Point" as if Ceci knew them intimately. "I could draw you a *real* map, if'n you could follow it... But what *we* call The Old Woman them down there call Leaning Rock..." she sighed.

"Are there no maps of this area?"

"This pass is Her Up There Pass. From people sayin' 'Went by her up there'..."

It seemed to Ceci she'd even less chance of discovering where she was amongst folk with "partickeller" names for everywhere... Names behind which rose careless frightening rivers knived into by sharp rocks; bleak tracks over treeless wastes where snow blew and mounted up taking man and beast by surprise; frozen swamps backed by great formations of impenetrable, unroaded rocks, their ways known only to hardy wanderers and flax cutters; to stern men making their way round great lakes to precious stands of timber in hidden places to return crossing the lakes on log rafts which would smash in gullies or be sold foot by foot for a long price to runholders or mining concerns. Names which conjured a region crossed only by men between work or dreams, men with empty stomachs and torn blankets, memories of wobbling wooden hotels where champagne flowed and dancing girls sang when times were sweet, paraded for them and their gold. Hotels which, she said, in the space of three years had been abandoned as the men moved on leaving only the wisp of remembered singing to whine in wiry grass thrashing on broken hills. The hotels' timbers had gone for fires. Their broken stone walls pointed silently upwards, mute witnesses to man's precarious hold on the land and his unloving use of it, second only to its grand disdain for him.

Lulled by the woman's voice, Ceci began to feel being overtaken by sleep. Her body began to sway memory of the boat and a man appeared before the bird like a dead bride in his arms, its great

wings drooping...She fought off sleep, knowing there
was something she must ask.

"That man I'm with—" she began. "Is he someone's
servant?"

"You a dancing girl?" the woman looked up.

Ceci shook her head.

"Then he's no servant."

Perplexed, Ceci lapsed back into silence. She remembered boarding, being swept up the gangplank unable to
turn round. She had felt her mother and Aunt May on the
quay below clutching each other, saying: "Where is she?
Is she on?" Then the crowd had pushed her into the hold,
Else squirming in her hamper. "Is that a chicken you've
got there?" Mrs. Purvey who had been set in charge of
them asked. The woman's voice merged with her dreams
saying she didn't think there was much future for dancing
girls. Folk had drifted over West over the mountains and
it was all "Red Jacks, No Town, Moonlight..." now. "All
our wild and dreadful men," she said sadly. "Gone over
there..."

Shy and withdrawn outside, the dreadful men hugged
their tussocky fires and dreamed on empty stomachs. The
night was cold. The light from the tent was as forbidden
and comforting as the soft sound of female voices. They
crept nearer for the warmth coming from under its side,
and the smoke, their occasional coughing audible within.

"Are you going West too?" Ceci asked, becoming
conscious—

"I'll stay, in case..." her voice drifted off. "Never
much for change."

The next day was even lonelier for the memory of the
tales spun by the woman; how strange and unexpected
these people were! Where could this peculiar man be
taking her?

Gradually the belt of hills flattened into a crusty
plateau. They passed along the edge of a vast lake, its
waters milky, open to the sky, reflecting rocks, clouds
and hills so strangely Ceci was overwhelmed by the
unnaturalness of the *light;* the feel that where they were
was wrong! The stunted trees, the parched grass and bald
hills, the lack of plants at the water's edge...They were
in some terrible dried out Sheol from which she would

not return. How could there be lakes without grass at the
edge, lying there like rents in a cloth? Around no birds
were soaring; the lake was flat water, cold and unwanted,
to which nothing came or responded; it seemed to burn
away the place it lay like poison. It was water which
mirrored the sky and threw back the sound of the horse,
the cart, the sound of their breathing. The man turned,
his eyes going far and away over the waters... Else drew
back her lips in a silent snarl. She did not like him.

As they journeyed on Ceci wondered would they
camp by the road? The thought both frightened and
exhilarated her for her life, already far from the bounds of
her control, was surely beyond the conventional laws
now. If they rested, for the horse clearly would not bear
another night's work, would he come to her?

As if cognizant of her thoughts the man pulled in and
released the horse. It turned tiredly away, too tired to be
really thankful. Else shook herself and waddled to the
edge of the silent lake. She sank her head to lap—but
raised it, finding the water bitter. Guiltily Ceci felt her
longing to be home. Home! A pain rose to meet her.
Briefly she saw her Aunt May peering down from the
window the day she and her sisters and mother had
stepped from the carriage and come to live with her in
London! Poor Aunt May bringing out odd plates one by
one... scrubbing away at her stains as if denying something worthwhile... May and she and her mother by the
river—Molly married and Norah dead. She had not come
all this way for nothing.

She looked across at the man kindling sparks, boiling
up an old can and throwing in a handful of leaves... In
the great silence the slow hum of his dung fire was
consuming, each occasional crackle, the sharp sound of
his stirrer hitting tin magnified as the smell of the burnt
pot spread out and the water bubbling through its holes
hissed. There was something friendly about him crouched
there against the horizon, his back to her, making tea for
them and not talking... Setting the brew half way between her and the fire the man crawled under the cart to
sleep leaving her to strain the scalding tin as best she
could. Having drunk she sought shade, but no sooner
had she dozed and awakened than the man was sitting in
the cart ready and waiting to be off. Eyes stuck with sleep,

she climbed shamefacedly dirty aboard for what she instinctively knew would be the last stretch of their journey. Wherever it was, a voice said, there would be no one to turn to: a frightening yet alluring fate.

They crossed, then joined with a good track travelling in their same general direction and clearly often used. It was an immeasurable comfort to have seen the cart tracks; to know she was near other humans again. Now she sensed an urgency in the man's pace; a resolution as if his thoughts were not with her or of her. It was as if she had become a thing accomplished allowing his mind to return to his own world, leaving her. Looking over his shoulder and over Ceci and Else as if to make sure none were watching, he turned round a spur and bore down on the roofs of a tiny settlement. At that moment Ceci was in no doubt. This was not merely a stopping place. It was the place the man lived.

Chapter 4

Moke looked the other way as Reg brought the dray careening into town. And town was a euphemism for Moke was little more than two stores, some tents, and a collection of shanties. The inhabitants had seen the girl clinging on in the back utterly worn out and, despite their dislike of strangers, were sorry for her for Reg Bowen was not generally liked. His appearance with the girl caused no little interest. He had not been out of Moke in twenty years—not since he'd run away at the age of twelve and a lot of good *that* had done him. The girl had to be an immigrant for no man would pass a daughter to Bowen nor had he been courting... That a man who could not string three sentences together should behave in such a bold manner was quite provocative. It was typical of the ill-bred scavenger that he should take it into his head to do something so—unlikely. Of course it was not *their* business, they reminded each other, lining up to watch. They looked at the girl's face, streaked with mud, the dust which clung in her hair, covered her in a fine film they could almost feel lining their teeth. Reg slammed up abruptly outside the store, jumped down and ambled with deliberate slowness towards its steps. Behind him his exhausted beast slipped its lead and dragged itself the last few remaining yards to the water trough. At that someone snickered and Reg spun and was back at the horse in seconds, forcing it up and tying in on a cruelly short length, aware of the indrawn breaths across the street. Ignoring them he went into the store. The villagers had seen the girl cringe. She'd soon learn a thing or two...

Their eyes turned hopefully as a cart with faded sign letters, *L—V—N Grain and General Feed*, came up the main drag.

"Ginger!" they called hopefully. He waved his hat, threw it in the back and slowed to talk to them. Hoping to provoke an incident they nodded towards Reg's cart but Ginger laughed.

"My, my, my," he said crossing to the horse. "Look at you!" Freeing her, he led her to the water.

"Shouldn't get yerself into these scrapes!" he said gently.

The inhabitants were a little frustrated. One day Ginger would get it, they told each other, but not today. The horse drank deeply, love in her eyes.

"There ya go, beauty," he said. "Better get you back before laughing Harry comes out." The horse backed up willingly and let Ginger secure her in her original place. Unaware of Ceci behind her box watching, he crossed to his cart, scooped some grain from a burst feed bag into his hat and brought it over...

"A bit o' this eh?" The horse snuffled her nose in his hat.

"Excuse me—" came Ceci's voice, peering around the box.

"S'truth!"

"This man I'm with—" she stammered. "Is he alright?"

Getting control of himself Ginger replied: "Oh they'll be carting him off tomorrow!" He gave her a broad grin.

She still stared at him, worried. Sliding his hand along the cart's edge, he patted hers.

"You'll be right," he said. "Give me me hat beauty." The horse blinked at him: she knew she was no beauty. In fact she was very plain, but she loved the tone in his voice. At that moment Reg appeared behind Ginger. "And a happy Christmas to you," Ginger said brightly. Ignoring him, Reg threw the flour sack into the back of the cart where it hit with a thud, just missing Else. Ginger saw Ceci snatch the little dog up as, without a backward glance, Reg took the cart off like a rocket, flinging Ceci on her back.

"Bastard—" Ginger murmured under his breath.

"Hey Ginger," called the store man from the top of the steps. "Make it four this week, eh?" But Ginger was watching Reg's cart barrel out of the village.

Clinging on in the back for dear life and feeling more than a little silly, Ceci saw fences and crude pasturage flash by. Why had this maniac waited until they were in a populated area to make a thorough fool of her by tearing along like this? Mouth set, he was bearing down on a boundary gate across the road which another man was already closing, actually whipping his horse up as the man meticulously bent and fastened the gate.

"Damn and blast the sodding bugger," she heard Reg murmur. Short of smashing into the gate, the horse managed to stop, its fear as palpable as Reg's anger which Ceci could sense directed at the back of the well-dressed man moving slowly away beyond the gate, his movements langorous with the insolence of wealth, his chestnut horse glinting, his garb of the best cloth. Clearly he was a man of culture and consequence, even at this distance she could tell his well cut jacket was velvet . . . Briefly she wondered about him as before her, Reg, livid to the point of destruction, wrestled the boundary gate open. Were it not for the element of danger in his anger—it would have been almost funny.

The gate behind him, Reg picked up speed, beating their way along the track as if fleeing humiliation and only slowing when Moke fell from sight. Apart from a weathered signboard marking an overgrown driveway with the word NOLANS, no other trails led from the track but shrubs had grown at its sides giving the impression it was regu-

larly used. As they returned to a more leisurely pace, Ceci
sensed them veering leftwards, cutting away and joining a
weak barely discernible trail, rarely if ever used other than
by the one or two conveyances that inhabited its end. She
knew at once it was where the man lived.

"Grim" was the word to describe Bowen's homestead. In
a dip between two hills where the road ended, it looked at
first sight little more than a broad wet ditch catching the
run-offs from higher land, its ground a sea of mud.
Though the barrier gate could be "walked" open, the next
gate, closer in, was permanently sunk ajar in weeds and
grass, stuck in the mud like a monument to a forgotten
wall. Beyond it, a dwelling, hovel kitchen and barn stared
disjointedly at each other while a dismal, shoddy feel of
neglect attended the untreated planks of a sheep run,
clearly more use as a home to beetles and lice than a
restrainer of sheep. From the worn posts, faded trails of
urine showed a time when things had been more lively.
Now death hung about. The pitiably rickety barn's door
hung open and inside with the dead hay, tangled wire
which could have been put to use outside just lay. Beyond
the barn, machinery which should have been inside slept
rusting in the mud.

Even before the cart came to rest in a rut, the air
around was filled with the wild hysterical slathering of
tethered dogs, nowhere to be seen, which grew guttural
and fierce as the man crossed to a wooden crate and gave
it a resounding kick. "Gerr-err," he shouted, the sounds
subsiding in nervous whines as the beginning growl in
Else's throat grew louder. He continued on to the barn
and vanished. Ceci waited.

Gingerly she got down and, taking Else in her arms
tiptoed towards the first building, the hovel kitchen. She
put her head in. It was like nothing she'd ever seen. Like
a small ice house or shepherd's croft, three of the walls
were stone, the fourth logging—as if the builder had tired
of the work or merely used the place to live in while he
built, or before having cause to build the main dwelling.
Inside was room enough for a man to lie down, though
what shelter the rush-thatched roof, now blackened from
cooking, would afford was doubtful . . . Smoke had stained
the walls so thoroughly a third possibility arose. The

kitchen may have been built separately to avoid the risk of setting fire to the entire dwelling had the original man cooked there! What a far cry from the tiled kitchen she had so recently left in that London hotel! . . . Her eyes strayed to the floor where lay a burst sack of rotten flour, weevils moving busily amongst its mildewing lumps . . . She knew in her bones there was no woman on the premises nor had been for a very long time. Nor was there point in looking for hens or a cow to be milked . . . On a blackened beam under the thatch stood a rain-stained, long-abandoned greyish tin. Climbing on a stump she reached up and carefully drew it down, putting her finger in and tasting soda! Well, at least she could make bread.

Crossing the muddy yard to the main dwelling, she laid her hand on the door. There was no sound anywhere nor sign of the man. It opened before her. Cautiously she stepped inside. The room, while not a sitting room, was clearly the only place to "sit." At some time in the past twenty years bits of paper had been stuck in places on the board walls. But there the comfort had stopped. With a start she became conscious of heavy breathing coming from a large winged chair facing on to the hearth, on the arm of which lay the large rheumaticky hand of a man of at least sixty. Cautiously she approached him, sideways on, but he remained staring straight ahead. Very aware he did not want to be spoken to she backed awkwardly past him and out of the door at the far end of the room, feeling him remain like a waxwork staring at the hearth, ignoring her. Gently she pulled the door in.

Beyond the door she fell into a filthy corridor whose floor had been wetted by yard water seeping in from outside. Clearly this part was an extension to the main room, added on some time later. The first door giving off it lay open. Quickly she looked in, then drew her head out again. It must have been the old man's room: a pathetic mess. Sad for an old man to have no one to care for him like this. Hastily she shrank from the next room—an utter pig pen—that undoubtedly belonged to the man who had brought her. She hesitated before the last room, its door closed. The corridor ended in it so it would be larger. . . As she opened it, to her amazement she found it had not only been swept clean, the floorboards, rough as they were, being spotless, but by the small bed a clean sack had been laid on the floor for standing on. In addition, beneath the ill-fitting window on a wooden crate no doubt intended as a vanity box was a tiny bottle with a sprig of green in place of a flower in it. Closing the door, she set Else down and shook out the bed sheets. Washed. But not ironed and very crudely patched. Suddenly her eye returned to the sprig of greenery in the bottle. She picked it out. Who had put this here for her? Holding it she moved to the window and looked out. There, the man who had brought her was walking from the cart to the kitchen, the fresh flour sack on his shoulder. Had he put the flower there for the girl who might come? Thoughtfully she went to fetch her box.

Ceci stepped into the room bearing Old Bowen's meal on a tray and hesitated, wanting to speak. Sensing it he rose, turned his back on her and leant on the mantel breathing heavily, stuffing his pipe. This was not the first time he had behaved like this, so she folded her mouth, and shrugged, mentally comparing the lumbering man with the board table, both of which had the same empty male heaviness to them.

"This tray—is your dinner," she stated.

Lighting his pipe he stared expressionlessly at the chimney breast.

She crossed to the window. Else was barking outside. Quickly the old man turned and got in a good look at her while the sight outside took her attention: a man was up their pear tree, meticulously filling a burlap sack with pears!

"Mr. Bowen—" she called turning. "There's a man—" But he was staring at the ceiling. She looked back. Now the man was climbing down, Else dashing furiously about him as he brushed ants from his collar, looking vacantly about as if there were something wrong with him. Sighing, she pulled a rag from her pocket. The room needed cleaning but it was a question of where to start. By the mantelpiece Old Bowen was now sending up clouds of smoke, making it plain he would not eat while she was in the room. As she uncovered the basins and prepared to leave she heard Else's barking get louder and louder until, suddenly, a sharp gun report rang out and the barking stopped.

She rushed to the door emerging into the light to see the small lump of Else quivering beneath the tree. Unbelieving, she ran to her, snatched her from the ground unable to calm her shaking and begged her to open her eyes again, to *move*. From the corner of her eye she sensed Reg going behind the barn, a gun on his shoulder.

"Else!" she whispered, desperately squeezing the dog to her but the head lolled showing the hole in its side and she saw the blood running on her wrist... in utter disbelief she realized Else was dead. Biting her lip she stayed still.

In minutes she found herself in the room staring at the old man who by now was up at the table. He had emptied the contents of the two basins side by side on to the plate and was eating them with difficulty if not annoyance, the flour rings to one side, the sauce to the other—and a clear space between them. He had not bothered to lift the plate from the tray and his chin was nearly on it. As if in a dream she stood in the doorway seeing all this, aware he knew she was there and *why* she was there, yet resisting her. She came and stood before him, in front of him, her feet sounding loud on the boards, the hem of her skirt in his vision. With all his force she felt him ignoring her presence. Unused to speaking first when it was clearly the other's turn, she began hesitantly.

"—That's sauce. It goes on top of the flour rings—"

He lifted a dry flour ring from the plate to his mouth meaning she should go away again.

"Mr. Bowen!" she burst out. "Your son just shot my dog!"

He looked up, centred his eyes very directly on her and spoke for the first time:

"I don't tell you how to eat your food."

Gathering herself to herself Ceci left the room and hurried to Else. She felt small against the dwelling which looked small against the hills. Like an insignificant speck she crouched, holding the dog she loved, rocking it, unwilling to bear the idea or accept the fact of being without her, of burying her, of having brought her to a place where she had suffered so much.

"I can't bear to see you go—" she murmured, wishing tears would not come into her eyes for the man to see. Else had loved her, given, taken pleasure. Was there not

something she could *do*? There would be no more times
lying, their heads together, making her room "home" . . . or
running the hills thinking of what lay ahead . . . A great
stone pushed at her chest ready to break out. She must
bury Else before the man cast his impure eyes over her,
perhaps smirking, desecrating their grief. Hastily she dug
a hole and laid the small dog in it, breaking her heart to
see dribbles of earth falling in Else's white hairs. The eyes
were already clouding, but the body so warm, the paws,
their suppleness and familiarity pervaded with the spirit
of Life. She felt the cold dampness of the ground with one
hand while with the other she held on to Else's paw and
could not let go. Her heart filled with the promises she'd
made to the little dog who'd been her best friend.

"I'm sorry—"

Becoming aware of the man standing immediately
behind her she swept earth into the hole, patted its
surface.

"Can't bury him there."

Spinning she leapt to her feet.

"I've *buried* her!!"

"Your business." He shrugged, continuing on past
her. Suddenly she was filled with doubt.

"Why can't I bury her there!?" she called running
after him, tripping on her skirt.

"Said you'd buried him."

"Yes but—had I better move her?" For some reason
she found she had snatched as his elbow as if they must
settle a matter of paramount importance between them.
The man pulled himself free.

"Always bury 'm again," he said looking at her sideways, "if he gets dug up."

For a moment she digested this, then shouted after
him:

"I'm leaving! Do you hear? I'll take her with me!" But
the man was still walking away, not even listening. "I'll
not stay another day!"

Back in her room she packed her box as if the world
were coming to an end. In went the work skirts, the
pinafores, her "good" but old-fashioned dress, the "suitable"
church hat, Bible. Down the side she stuffed the darned
socks and curling tongs and running to her "table,"
snatched up the sprig of greenery, opened the window

and flung it out. In went the china soap dish from the
floor, the iron, her Book of Household Remedies from
under the bed. There! It was done! She shut her box and
sat on it.

As her breathing quietened she was overtaken by the
urge to weep anew but forced herself to cross to the
window and take what she promised would be a last look
at the muddy yard and endless hills beyond. Gripping its
ledge she exhaled, breathing the place out, turned her
back on it and went to grasp her box.

Opening the door to the main room she noticed Old
Bowen in his chair staring at the hearth in the way she
now knew meant "Don't try and involve *me* in your life."
Indeed, she felt he *was* little more than a chair and it
certainly suited *her* to walk by him without attempting
speech even if, struggling with the bulk of her box, his
breathing *did* seem to grow stertoriously loud as she
passed him sideways on.

Reaching the broken gate she set her box down and
looked about. Close by Reg was slashing randomly at
undergrowth around the fence posts, very conscious of
her but pretending not to be.

"Will you take me into Moke?" she demanded, her
voice surprising her by its roughness.

"Got friends there have you?" he asked without looking
up.

"I want to leave now."

"Coach is Thursday."

She bit her lip. She might have guessed there'd be
only one coach a week!

"Got your fare?" he continued.

"How much have I coming?"

"You done how much...?"

"Two weeks. I've been here two weeks."

"You haven't got it then." he said, taking another
slash at the fence post.

She kicked her box furiously and sat on it.

"Whyn't you go out?" he said waving his arm vaguely around the horizon.

"*Out?*" she repeated.

"Walk about a bit. Get some air."

"How can I walk without my dog?" she shouted, the
words burning the air between them.

"Go on. Clear off."

"Alright I will! I'll clear off!"

He watched her walk briskly up the lane then resumed hacking. Suddenly her feet appeared again in his field of vision.

"*Why* did you shoot her?"

He shrugged as if to say, "What's the difference?"

"She was *my* dog! *I* want to know!"

Stretching lazily, he rubbed the back of his hip and drawled, "Got on me nerves," daring her with his eyes to challenge his absolute authority. He saw a look of disbelief cross her face, followed by disgust as if he were the most stupid ignorant person she had ever encountered.

"Is that all?" she demanded incredulously.

"You've a lot to learn out here young woman," Reg said pulling the sickle free and beginning to walk off.

Confused at the enormity of his act, Ceci wandered the hills, no more than a tiny thinking speck under a dead pan sky. Her eyes fell on the brown tired grass as she recalled in minced copperplate tones the advertisement which had lured her to New Zealand:

Unmarried women and widows of good character aged 15 to 23 required for domestic work in select situations. Satisfactory placement to be found within 3 days of stepping ashore... Unmarried women and widows of good character—Unmarried women and widows of good character...

She sat down against a large rock half way up the gully and began writing a letter in her mind, the light dimming around her.

Mother—

Else was shot this morning. By the man who got me from the Barracks. On account of her barking. I'm very lonely here. 4 months on the boat, the journey up, then not a word about "Are you feeling alright?" It was: "There's the kitchen—Where's the grub?"

The hills, the lines of the hills look alike but the light is different and the place has an emptiness I can't describe. It is a place where no birds sing. Funny how you get used to them—there don't seem any wild flowers either. I miss you all.

It'd take this letter so long to reach you and please God I'll be gone from this place by then! As soon as I've got my fare back down I'm leaving and looking for another job. I'll write to you then. So I won't send this.

Your loving daughter.

Returning over the hills in the dimming light, she longed for Else. Sheep stood in her way and would not move. Some lay, as if dead, forcing her to climb over them and when she did, they did not react. Bending she discovered they *were* dead. It was, she concluded, probably the way things were on a farm like this! Others remained bunched, flowed away from her and kept running and running, unwinding like a great ball of wool, then winding up again . . . as she descended through them to the dwelling, their fading white shapes moved around her like a sea of uneven ground.

Arriving she noticed her box had been put in. Then, to her horror, near where she had buried Else she made out some of the man's dogs yelping, scrabbling at the ground, as if disinterring something. An old dog was lifting its leg to urinate on the spot. Grabbing a stone Ceci ran down and was relieved to see they were beyond Else's grave which lay undisturbed. Still, she had better do something to cover it up. Crossing to the scrub fence she struggled to break off some sticks and, returning, planted them in the earth over Else's grave, unaware that she was being watched. That done, she crouched staring in the dim light at the man's dogs.

Hiding behind the barn the man from the pear tree watched Ceci approach the group of dogs and bend to see what they were about. To his horror he saw her slowly, hesitantly reach out a hand to touch one. Instantly his brother Reg came running at her, swinging a fence post as if to bring it down on her head. The man squeezed his cheeks, his mouth made shapes into the dark as Ceci's arms shot up to protect her head. Uselessly he covered his own—bit at the air. When he opened his eyes Reg was standing shamefaced, the post drooping in one hand, but

the girl had vanished. He watched Reg walk slowly back
to the dwelling, stumbling into the sticks the girl had
stuck into the ground smashing them to pieces under his
feet.

Slowly the strange man came forward from the darkness, agitatedly dragging a lump of old plough iron. He
drove a pole into the ground by the broken sticks—fetched
stones and thistles. Gradually in the moonlight, a strange
work of art emerged; its form a statement of pain yet
equally the spontaneous expression of a tortured mind.
Piece by piece the structure rose to the moon, crooked
and diligent, the light glinting obliquely off its glancing
planes . . . until the grave for Else was finished.

Chapter 5

Resigned in the short term, Ceci went about her work
avoiding Reg and counting the days. The old man continued unspeaking and though she occasionally thought of
him, she did not see the strange one from the pear tree
again. In her mind she associated him with the going of
Else and also the appearance of the sculpture marking her
grave which Reg had kicked to pieces causing Ceci to
wonder against whom precisely his anger was directed.

One morning, crossing the yard, she saw the man
burst from the kitchen with four hot loaves, drop one,
grasp it, see her, drop it again and flee. Amazed, she went
to pick it up and stare after him. Forgetting she wasn't
supposed to be speaking to Reg she called out:

"Who was that?"

Reg raised his eyebrows as if he hadn't seen anyone.

"The man who ran to the barn?" she continued,
taking a few paces toward it, listening. Suddenly Reg
came up behind her, took the loaf, opened the barn door a
few inches and flung it in.

"Who is he?" Ceci pursued.

"Who?" asked Reg indifferently.

"The man in there!"

"Brother."

"Why don't you introduce us?"

"What for?"

"So I'd—know who he is," she stammered.

"Who?"

"Your brother!"

"You know."

Ceci walked back to the kitchen, irked with herself for having spoken to him. Yet Reg followed as if he wanted to talk.

"Why doesn't he eat with us?" she found herself asking. "Where does he sleep?"

"Year round to year round he don't know he's awake or dreaming," Reg said. "The sheep are clouds. Clouds are sheep—takes his mind from the sky."

Ceci stared, amazed at his long sentence.

"Stays in the hills—won't come for 'is rations."

"He could take a leg off a dead sheep if he doesn't like coming down—" Ceci offered.

"Dead sheep?"

"The ones that are lying about. I didn't mean you had to *kill* one—"

"Lying about where?"

She pointed to where she had seen the corpses on one of her walks.

"Dumb sheep. Break their legs." Reg shrugged.

Ceci shook her head. "Not all of them—"

"*What?*"

"How could so many sheep break—" she began, quickly stopping as she felt his anger rise to the point he might shake her.

"Did you look?" he demanded.

She shook her head.

"You *should've* looked!"

"It was dark!"

"You imagined it."

Ceci considered lying, but told the truth.

"There weren't asleep," she said boldly, standing her ground. "And they didn't have broken legs. They were very thin. And dead."

He grabbed her wrist.

"*Where*!?"

"In the gully! Leave me alone!"

Throwing, rather than dropping her wrist, he stepped back, looked hard at her and began to walk in the direction she had pointed.

Panting she caught up with him, still in her apron, flour down the front and on her hands. Intent, concentrated, he strode on.

"Wait for me," she called, then hung back. Though it was his business and she wanted to see, she did not want to afford him another opportunity to be unkind. Carefully she made her way up to the rock from where she had "written" to her mother, with its commanding view over the dips and gullies. There he was below, examining the dead sheep ... turning them over ... deep in worry. She felt he knew she was up above, watching. Finally he climbed up and sat beside her, saying nothing, clearly without words. She wondered if conversation were possible.

"Why did you do that? To me—with the stick?" she began.

"Never touch a working dog, you hear?" he said slowly, staring straight ahead. "You don't hit 'em. You don't pet 'em neither."

Her eyes moved over the sky and back to him, taking this in.

"Do you mean that in their entire working lives your dogs never once get a pat on the head?"

He nodded. "Keeps 'em at it."

She shook her head at him.

"Start showing a dog affection and he's lost. Not like the thing that you had."

Her reaction was mixed. He had referred to Else as a "thing." Yet he was *talking* to her, in his own way trying somehow.

"So you just keep them—proving themselves, threatening, promising ... ?"

"Do their jobs."

"Is that the way you treat your women folk? ..." she surprised herself by saying. Reg stared hard ahead.

"You stick to breadmaking," he replied quickly. "Woman."

He got to his feet and stood looking down at her.

Something in the way he had said "woman" aroused her. She tested the water.

"You're talking a lot today."

"Lucky for you that I am," he replied, turning and heading back down towards the dwelling. Inside herself Ceci stepped back. That last remark had been said in a very cold voice and nor had the look in his eyes been kind.

Following him back down the hillside she saw him wrench a post from the ground and fling it as far away as he could as if the post had been her and he regretted their recent familiarity. Then he picked up a stone, bounced it in his hand and hurled it far far towards the horizon. Having spent himself he walked on towards the dwelling, slamming the door neatly as Ceci approached.

Then and there she decided never to speak to him again unless she could possibly help it. He was thoroughly rude, probably illiterate, and seemed to take delight in drawing her out, then being deliberately abrupt. From now on she would stay in her kitchen, do her job and finish working the month out. Then they could get by without her! Look where it had got her taking an interest in the rude creatures! And the next time either of them acted up they could expect a bit back!

Cramped in the hovel kitchen that night, she was priding herself on her new found resolution when Reg came in, clearly wanting to talk to her. He had brought a pair of shears that needed oiling as an excuse, but hung back in the doorway, eyeing the lard tin, waiting to be invited in. She continued stitching.

"Those sheep," he began from the door.

"Not my worry if you lose all your sheep," she sang out gaily.

"If a handful die," he muttered defensively, "it's not the end of the world."

She bit off the thread, turned Old Bowen's collar over and began to tack it back on to the shirt. Reg shifted on his feet—plainly wanting her to comment on the sheep situation.

"I suppose you know what it means when sheep won't eat," she said in a voice of utter reasonableness, though already she could feel him beginning to grow furious. "It's common knowledge."

"Can't you work quiet?" he snarled, clearly longing for an explanation.

After a pause he added:

"Well?"

"I'm not talking now, am I?" she replied. "Just because you feel like a conversation doesn't mean everyone has to talk."

"So shuddup!"

"In fact I wouldn't be talking at all except—apart from you—there's not a living soul in miles that speaks—and I don't want my jaw to freeze up!"

The confidence and defiance were too much for Reg. "Just 'cos you 'aven't got your dog to talk to," he sneered, hoping to unseat her. "Only took one bullet—"

Instantly she was on her feet. "AND YOU WON'T HAVE ONE BULLET *LEFT* BY THE TIME YOU DONE SHOOTING YOUR PRECIOUS SHEEP!" she shouted, knowing she'd won. "You'll see who's laughing then!" She felt Reg begin to crumple. "Look at you!" she went on. "Don't know how to use a knife and fork or be friendly! Great hulking thing and you want to know what I'm talking about but wouldn't think to say—"

"Been chewing on something upset you?"

"—do tell me what you *mean* about the sheep, because we haven't heard of what you're talking about over here!"

"Lot of lip tonight," said Reg.

"Well let me say one thing," she flared. "We've had farms at home where sheep have begun to die because they wouldn't eat because it *hurt* to eat. Because their mouths were sore and their tongues all blistered and—"

"Rubbish!"

"*Our* sheep got some disease—"

"They would."

"And it went from one end of the country to the other—and on to France. It was a sheep plague. And they shot them. *All* the sheep that had it. *And* the ones that didn't. All the sheep in those parts got shot. And that was *hundreds* of them. *Thousands!*"

"Likely story."

"And they dug great massive pits to bury them!" she went on, aware of a dangerous look coming into his eyes but unable to stop herself. "The stench of the burning hung in the clouds for weeks. It's got a name. *Foot* something."

"Get on!"

"You'll love it! Chance to shoot defenceless animals."

"Load of rubbish."

"*You* wouldn't know because *you* don't get papers sent out and the only newspaper *you* ever get to see has been chewed by everyone from Te Anau and back—*if* you can read it—"

"Who the Hell here wants to know what's going on over there?"

"So next time you look at them—" she said, beginning to pack up her sewing as if the interview were over, "look between their toes too because—"

She noticed he had taken down the hurricane lantern.

"Oh. So you don't believe me?"

Half way out of the door, he turned to her:

"Joking—I'll flog you."

She managed to flick him an indifferent look to leave with. Though fighting was alien to her nature, she was clearly aware this was her first victory over Reg.

Let him talk big and run at her with sticks! He and Old Bowen were people of a kind she had not known existed: dangerous dumb animals that could not be talked to, reasoned with . . . There had been nothing in her experience which could have prepared her for their lack of imagination or mental facility; their inarticulation so dangerously combined with the absence of that basic consideration called "manners." Thinking of it—manners prevented clashes. Without them people were raw and each encounter potentially volatile. Even growing up on Lord Knevitt's estate as a child of virtually a servant, she had been amongst essentially cultured people—civilized. People bound by forms of behaviour, their ways circumscribed, predictable and safe. Even the kitchen staff had been cordial with each other. But here? She was angry at herself for not having imagined it would be like this. Because they spoke English she had expected similarities yet had they had bones through their noses, feathers in their hair, in truth they could not have been more surprisingly different.

On the face of it, she realized, she was living in a situation she was totally unable to influence and for the

first time in her life, none of the skills she had been taught
could be brought to bear. These two, as far as she could
see, were without not only manners but the simple
kindnesses behind them. It would not do to let feelings of
impotence numb her. She would have to rethink the way
she was with them, to protect herself somehow from
being flushed out by their rudeness. In her room she tried
to be honest. If the man Reg was so repulsive what was
his attraction? Was it that he seemed to be speaking to a
part of her neither she nor anyone else had granted
recognition: the simple female animal within that he felt
did not need to prove itself or be literate or do other than
rely on him? In exchange for which he would provide?
This kind of thinking was dangerous, misleading and not
to be encouraged. He was out there now struggling to
provide, to come to terms with what had happened to his
sheep. Let that be his affair! From now on she would take
care to protect herself better from his influence. There
would be no more running after him in that pathetic
fashion, asking why she shouldn't have buried her dog
there! The idea that you could look up to men was
ridiculous. It was a childish desire for a dependent state.
Why, the man clearly had no answers for anything. Never
would she cower before him again. From now on, as long
as it lasted, she would see to it things would be different.

The next day as she transferred clothes pegs from mouth
to line she was well aware of him watching her, lingering
on the edge of the yard, shifting his hat from one hand to
another.

"Yeah—well. I'm thinking of packin it in," he began.
"Sheep."

She bent, picked up a wet cloth and shook it until it
cracked loudly.

"Sheep's hard," he said.

She folded the cloth at its corners and carefully secured it to the line.

"It's a hard life," he repeated. "Sheep."

Deliberately ignoring him she moved behind the cloth,
began to hoist Old Bowen's nightshirt sideways on like a
flag and secure it with the prop. "Supposed to put your
strong-woolled ewes to your fine woolled-rams—" he

went on, peering at her between the sheets slapping against his face in the wind.

"Well he mated the well-woolled hoggets as two tooths, didn't he? Should have let them run with the wether flock and looked again."

The way he pursued her through the washing she could almost believe he thought she didn't hear him!

"Wethers are getting past it . . ." he mumbled, by now standing close to her. "Shoulda planted turnips, fattened them up."

Bending, she picked out the worst she could find in the tub of washing, shook it on his boots and moved off.

"Like to jack it in—" he began, following her between the sheets. She glimpsed a frown of concern on his face as she took a shirt from the tub and shook it violently.

"Do nothing for themselves. Sheep."

"They eat," she replied, looking away. "Some of them."

A half awareness he was being taunted flickered on Reg's face but was overtaken by the urgent need to speak. Anticipating he would want an answer she quickly put more clothes pegs in her mouth.

"Dip'em and crutch 'em," his vocabulary took her by surprise. "Eye-clip, ring 'em—"

"What?"

"Shave off their behinds," he explained, making her instantly angry she had asked.

"If you're looking for sympathy because this place is in such a disgusting state—!" she exploded.

"No hay baled," he pleaded. "Grass covers burned off—"

She put the washing down. *"That is not why they are starving!"*

All pretence over, Reg stared at her coldly.

"I'm selling them," he announced.

"You're not," she stated, shaking her head as if confident the last say would be hers; as if addressing a child she knew would obey words behind which lay common moral duties.

"I'm not seeing everything I've ever done pass off like that!" Reg's voice began to rise in a childish crescendo she recognized as appealing to her on the grounds of things being not fair. "Early mornings—late at night. The one mad, the other stuck in his chair! Who do you think puts food in their stupid mouths? Nobody thinks of *me*!"

"If you sell those sheep—" she began.

"I'll have a man out and make an offer—"

"Oh well—he'll see of course," said Ceci indifferently. "But because *you've* been unlucky—"

"Muster and separate the worst—" Reg went on.

"Well you won't have a friend left to speak to..."

"Don't you preach at me!" he exploded. "I'll make sure everyone knows it was you brought the disease out with you!"

Well that was an amazing idea he had there.

"They'll probably burn you at the stake," he continued.

"How could I have brought the disease with me?" she asked unconcernedly, letting her arms fall to her sides, facing him.

"Knowledge of it," he protested. "Same thing—"

She lifted her chin in a way she knew would infuriate him and began to hum. So that was it. It was her knowledge he feared. He had handed her a weapon that could be used again and again and he would always cringe before it. How terrible to have to go armed into conversation, to have to fight to win the chance to be heard. She was angry with him for bringing her to this stage and to these alien ways she did not want to learn.

She glanced over at him; now he was frowning as if she was the *one*, the *only* thing on the entire place he might not hit and his fingers were itching for a fence post. On second thoughts judging by his gathered brows it would be better not to say any more now... Allowing herself the last luxury of raising her eyebrows as if to say, "Well if you've nothing to add I'll be off out of here," she picked up the empty washing tub and swung her hips off towards the kitchen with it.

A little later, just when she felt she was succeeding in putting Reg firmly from her mind, he suddenly lurched into the kitchen as she was clearing up after a meal, basining the one untouched portion that should have been his. Quickly she untied her apron and hung it on the back of the door as if to leave.

"Ahum," he said to her back.

Turning, she saw climbing from his pocket a small

pup which he plopped on the table. Too quickly joy and
delight leapt to her face, hastily withdrawn as she reminded
herself not to trust him with anything he could smash.

"What's that then?" she enquired in a hard cold
voice.

"What does it look like?" he replied. "Wooden spoon."

Determined to match him blow for blow she went on:
"You shot its mother or something?"

"You bin drinking?" he returned, not to be outdone
and clearly preferring this way of speaking.

"I can see *you* have," she frowned. "And you missed
lunch."

"You like it?"

Surely he didn't expect her to tell him? He, who was
so devious when asked a direct question!

"What?"

"The wooden spoon."

"And what am I supposed to do with it?"

"Make a pie," he snarled, pushing past her and out
of the room. For a moment she believed he actually felt
she should have been grateful!

"I suppose you told your father about the sheep?"
she called.

That made him stop.

"We haven't spoken in a while," he said, swaying
back towards her.

"How long a while is that then?" she said, holding
her ground on the kitchen steps.

"Twelve, fifteen years." Was this fact or a bit of
insolence? she wondered. That he would make a revelation to her was most unlikely. If he were drunk she was
wasting her time.

"You tell 'im?" he asked, stale fumes reaching her on
his breath.

She shook her head and he nodded as if to say
"good."

"But I know my duty," she added, stepping back into
the kitchen. As he came on to her doorstep she could feel
him fighting down the urge to grip her throat, getting a
control of himself then remembering something he had
planned to say:

"You want to marry me?"

She was so aghast she asked honestly:

"Doesn't it make any difference to you whom you marry?"

"Long as you do your job—" he said. Well this was incredible!

"And we'd just go on living? Here?"

He shook his head, proud to announce his thoughts: "A provisions store."

"And I'd be a storekeeper's wife?" she asked, more struck by the incredibility of their holding a proper conversation than by his proposals.

"Anythin' wrong with that?"

Unable to help it, she found herself laughing. It peeled off her like dead skin, as she leant shakily on the wall watching Reg, who at first didn't know how to take it, become aware it was not he or the idea of the store which was the subject of amusement; it was the *relief* of being spoken to directly. Watching her, his face took on a second degree of amusement, becoming by default pleasant, almost friendly. He sent a small laugh out himself but quickly pulled it back.

"There's money in a thousand sheep," he said earnestly. "Long as you kept your mouth shut. Well?"

Suddenly she was struck by the meaning behind his words.

"If you think by telling me to shut my mouth and asking me to marry you—" she began.

"There's a buyer arranged to look at the sheep—" he said over her voice. "You'll stay indoors—"

"Will I?"

"Will you?" he asked, his face saying she would if she knew what were good for her.

"You seem very sure of things."

"I am!" he replied with a firmness she had never heard before.

"Well if you think by giving me a puppy you can fix things like that...!" she burst out, livid at his presumption that he could so easily contain her.

"Nothing that can't be fixed."

In two strides Reg was upon her and had grasped the scruff of her neck and flung her like a sheep for shearing on the table. Even as she reached for her skirts and struggled to get up he had flicked them up and knocked her back, her head hitting the table with a bang. She was pinned down by an arm across her throat, a knee between her thighs and a hand on her left leg. In a minute he was on her, his own gasping and writhing so shocking she was momentarily mesmerized as by a snake. As knowledge of what he was doing sank in, she strained with all her might to keep him out, struggling and tossing yet unable to move her hips. There was no possibility of resisting the intrusion. With horror and pain at the last minute she kept still, feeling him tear, then squirm into her. A sensation of tightness, burning and bruising as if she had been punched and winded at that exact spot spread in a dull ache through her lower belly. She screwed up her eyes. Now he was pulling out of her... leaving a searing ache, stickiness and the totally unwelcome and disturbing feeling that she wanted him to come back again.

The muscles of her arms were almost too weak to draw her to a sitting position but as she pulled herself off the table she saw at the window the face of the "idiot" brother, Jock, watching in horror. She passed her hand across her eyes. Letting go of the table and standing, she was conscious of a throbbing pain in her lower groin and ache in her bowel. Everything had changed. She had been introduced to a fact of life she had never considered before: the reality underlying the relationships between women and men. The man had hurt her. Easily. His strength was greater than her knowledge. She wanted to be comforted yet, because it was him who had done it, and done it deliberately and without her permission, she could not go to him for comfort. The conflict between what had been perpetrated and how confused it had made her feel, drawing her to him yet making him seem repulsive, hurt more than anything and made her want to cry. She saw him leaning on the door, looking at her as impartially as if she were a sack of grain. "You shouldn't have done that!" she shouted at him, finding she couldn't trust her own voice, quavering and strange in her ears. He shrugged as if totally unaffected, yet she sensed in him a pleasure almost akin to her own when she had discovered the weapon of Knowledge. The fact that he was glad he had hurt her was written all over his face, as was the awareness she would remember he could do it again. This ultimate weapon which the man held, would, his look said, ensure she watched her every step from now on.

Awkwardly she lowered herself on to a chair, leaping upwards from the pain of sitting.

"That's how it's done," he said slowly. Keeping her eyes down she shook out her skirt. "I'm leaving," she said. It wasn't what she'd wanted to say.

"Know where your box is," he replied calmly.

"When do I get my money?" she asked, hating the humility in her voice, the hurt she could feel showing in her eyes.

"When I pay you," he said.

"That was a *stupid* thing to do!" she screamed thumping the table, unable to adequately express her anger at the injustice, the outrage.

"So where'll you go?" he asked calmly, seating himself in what had been *her* chair at the table. Limping to the door Ceci realized the logic of his act. What he intended. The man was a sheep breeder. That meant he knew about running them together and dealt with Delicate Matters as a fact of his daily life of no more significance than her cooking was to her. Already she could see him reaching a bloodied arm into a struggling ewe's privates to draw out the lamb, uncaring of her, thinking he knew it all and no secrets of the female animal were barred from him . . . She felt she *hated* him for this knowledge.

"*It might not have worked,*" she said, summoning all the disdain her damaged voice would carry.

"Then I can do it again tomorrow," he yawned, rising to leave the room.

How could she had been so *stupid*, she told herself! A man who dealt with everything physically, of *course* he would do that! It was as if a new world had been opened to her. Never had she realized how *easy* the act was to do! In the days that followed she wandered further from the homestead, moping and overcome with feelings which got in the way of her former decisions and certainties. The incident itself had not struck her as so terrible. Removed from its social element a "rape" lacked colour. The fact it had happened at all suggested they had somehow become equals before for they had not been "strangers" in that moment and in some ways it was done as an act between equals. Though she had put it from her mind as much as possible the effect lingered on so that she felt her confidence waning. How terrible that a woman could be got at through her body like that! . . . This sense of a whittling away going on inside her persisted with more force than the early awareness of learning new and ugly ways of surviving in this socially dangerous climate. What was the point of all the hard work her parents had put into her; all the kindnesses they had taught which had become second nature? Why lovingly raise children so meticulously if others could come along and cut their names heedlessly on their bark?

Increasingly depressed by these thoughts and unwilling to approach the man again for her pay, she went walking. From what she had read in the Book of Household Remedies her position was far from sanguine. Though it was too early for her stomach to swell up she did not like the way it was feeling. Or the way the man had taken to looking at *it* before looking at her face when they met. Of course he may only have been doing this to worry her but if she could only have that "circumstance" again then she would know she was alright!

Longing to find a kind human to talk to she wandered back towards Moke, stopping in confusion where their cart had swerved at the weak crossing of tracks unable to decide which was the way that led to Moke or even if she was at the right crossing. Now she was aware that where previously she had enjoyed the open country, there was the feeling it was dangerous to be alone . . . As she pondered, the sound of an approaching horse reminded her of the newfound sense of shame which prevented her from wanting to meet decent people: she felt unaccountably dirty, unready to be seen. Quickly she leapt into a bush, squeezing herself into a ball but as the horse neared and passed she recognized the man Ginger who had been kind. Unable to help herself she ran from the bush, waving her hand, shouting after him but biting her lip when he turned and cantered back.

"Hallo little immigrant!" he said cheerfully.

She stood frowning before him—arms down—afraid to speak lest she burst into tears, for the look on his face was so kind, so very friendly.

"Which way's Moke?" she asked, carefully controlling her voice.

"Now there's a question," Ginger grinned back, delighted to have run into her.

Was he teasing her? Ceci's eyes flashed hurt, making her look disgruntled yet vulnerable—in a word, attractive.

"You want to come with me?" Ginger said, patting the front of his horse. Without moving from the spot, she pointed the way he was headed.

"So it's that way? It's where you're going?" she frowned seriously up at him.

Taking a good look at her earnest face, Ginger noticed her eyes were filling with tears as if she needed a good cry but daren't open the floodgates.

"What's the matter...?" he said, sliding from his horse.

"I just want to know where—that—horrible town is—" she insisted in a high wobbly voice, stepping away from him.

Instantly sensing her dismay, he reached out a hand to her and she started to cry and fell into his arms sobbing and howling. Ginger juggled with her, trying to get one arm around her shoulders and with the other wrench a handkerchief from his pocket, then seeing how filthy it was, force it back in. Suddenly she shook her shoulders fiercely and ducked out of his arms. But a stillness had come over her. "Now do you want to come into Moke with me?" he asked gently.

She shook her head. After all, what good would it do?

"I'll go back now," she said, sniffing loudly, turning to go.

"Shall I come and see you tomorrow?" he enquired.

"No." Her voice came out harsher than she had intended.

"I—I don't want anyone seeing me—" she blurted. For a moment Ginger looked distinctly offended, then he softened.

"Ah well there you are then—" he said sadly, getting back on his horse. But she had already begun to run back up the track and away from him.

Moving off, he thought about it. He knew nothing about the girl except that she'd been seen in church once and not his church at that. Being Catholics, his family and their kind had to make do with a covered trestle table outside a barn. There, every Sunday on a freshly starched sheet they celebrated Mass in the field—except when it rained and they went inside. It was said their small community could be singled out from the rest of Moke by starting the Day of Worship with mud on their shoes and ending with straw on their knees. Yet they were accepted in all fields except marriage and though individuals might have strong leanings towards each other, when it came to the altar they found the line firmly drawn.

"Ginger!" a voice rang out as he clopped by.

There, slightly off the track, a man, Old Nolan himself, was leaning on his cart waiting for an able bodied youth to happen by. Drink, rather than age, had been his undoing and despite having a good patch of land it was said he delighted in allowing things to return to their original condition. Now that a sack of swedes had burst in his own driveway and sent its contents bouncing about the road he was speculating on it rather than gathering them up.

"There's a lovely boy!" he said as Ginger got down, crawled under his cart and began to roll out the swedes to him.

"Was I after telling you true as St Thomas was martyred I'm castin' about fer a son-in-law?"

Under the cart Ginger grinned safely. Weren't half the Catholic community?

"Me daughter Maureen divil take the larrikin..." said Old Nolan, aware that the news would have to be a surprise given that his daughter, the last to leave home, was not "going out"... He watched Ginger crawl out, the last swede in his hand.

"...but I'll not be mean to the boy who'll wed her." he said guiltily. "And a foine girl she is. A foine foine gorl! Exceptin' this."

Suddenly he became aware of Ginger giving him a strange look yet at the same time had the impression the boy had not been listening to him at all. Surely he could not be in love himself?

The sound of a horse coming from Moke made both turn their heads.

"And who's *he* off to cheat out of a half farthing?"

said Old Nolan, clapping his eyes on the District Buyer, with his money roll, his dogs and gun and a speculative look in his eye. "Good morning to you Sor, a *lovely* day..." Stepping forward, Nolan reached for the Buyer's horse, but the man steered round him with a look that said "Would I be drawn by you?" and rode on.

"Devil take 'em," said Nolan. "Come in for a drink."

But Ginger shook his head and continued staring thoughtfully after the Buyer...

Chapter 6

There was no doubt in Reg's mind he was doing the right thing. He had started the day early, well away from the homestead, shooting the worst sheep and driving the remainder down towards the paddocks. Any bad ones that turned out later could be locked in the barn, he decided, because he wouldn't be shooting near the house. He had not seen much of the girl lately but was confident she'd see sense. Before him now the sheep milled in the paddocks, thrusting against the old timbers, cracking them, sending up clouds of dust. Where the fences had broken, his dogs rushed in at the mob, yelping and snapping, their teeth bared. It was a scene of great activity such as the dogs had rarely seen. Looking down on it, Reg felt how his life might be were he a busy, successful farmer...

Returning from her wanderings Ceci paused on a point on the hill. The barking of the dogs carried clearly to her. She could see what was happening but did not want to go down again. As her eyes passed over the valley she made out the form of a man on a horse picking his way almost insolently towards their gate, pausing to look, moving on. When it dawned on her who he was, she began to run down the hill, determined not to let Reg succeed by force of threat in silencing her. But the closer she got to the Buyer, the less she liked the look on the man's face and the more uncertain she became of the reception she might receive.

In response to a warning bark, Reg spun, saw her, fell backwards over a sheep and swore as it shot off. In the next minute seeing the Buyer he was shouting: "Take your loose morals and clear off!" at Ceci in a tone which made the Buyer turn at once and stare at her.

"Got a lyin' tongue on 'er—" he went on, striding towards the Buyer, offering his hand.

Ceci shrank away then ran to the house.

"Mr. Bowen!" she shouted. "Get out here!" but the door did not open. She ran around the back, only to find Jock forcing the face of the abandoned puppy into a bowl of milk and muttering earnestly determined it would feed. Quickly she ran back again, to see the Buyer and Reg, now on the far side of the paddocks, Reg attempting to act big.

"Give you 800," the Buyer offered.

"Me entire farm?"

"Look lousy half of them," Ceci heard him saying. "Probably got footrot."

"Can tell you're a buyer!"

Suddenly, pulling up his trousers, Old Bowen opened the front door and gazed in amazement at the activity.

"What's going on here?" he demanded, outraged.

"Shuddup!" called Reg without even looking at him. He grinned at the Buyer as if at a private joke. "Puttin 'is face in!"

"You're not sellin' none of them sheep—" bawled Old Bowen, stumbling down the steps, warning on his face.

"Mad," Reg murmured.

"He's not mad!" Ceci shouted hanging on to the fence but ready to run.

Reg turned, furious.

"I warned you . . ." he said, raising his hand but she was already off, running towards Old Bowen, darting behind him as Reg pursued.

". . . followin' shearin' gangs round till you can hole up somewhere—" he shouted for the Buyer's benefit. He reached and snatched at Ceci's wrist and hauled her off towards the barn.

"Geddin there!" he growled, throwing her in and

bringing the bar of the door crashing down. In the darkness she struggled to get to her feet. The air was close with the stench of sick animals, their movements weak as they fell against her. Finding her feet she rubbed her shoulder and started pushing at the door, confident it would give. She could hear the men outside shouting over the din of the healthy sheep.

"They're not in good condition."

"Only eat 'em once."

"750 pounds."

"You said 8."

"Smart to sell," she heard the Buyer say. "Can't run the place."

Reg wouldn't know whether to take a remark like that as a compliment or a negotiating tactic!

"Yeah well—" she heard him saying in a confused tone.

Sliding a stick through the door she managed to start raising the bar.

"So that's it. 600. Take it or leave it."

"Waidda minnit!—" came the voice of Old Bowen over them but his only reward was a casual glance.

"This is *my house!*" he shouted.

The bar began to slide up.

"He hand that lot on to you?" she heard the Buyer say clearly.

By now she could see Reg nodding.

"Don't look like he got much feel for sheep. Don't look like they've never amounted to—"

"I got stud sheep out there I know by name—!" Bowen was bawling as with a mighty heave she raised the bar enough to free it from the catch. Jubilantly she burst out but only to see the Buyer and Reg shaking hands and beyond them Old Bowen bowed over the fence, trembling.

As the man left with the sheep, Ceci accepted her helplessness in the situation but at the same time advised herself that was not the only area in which she had failed. So taken up had she been with affairs between herself and Reg she had neglected the two most needing care, Jock and the puppy. That she would have allowed a man's cruelty to her to decide the way she would treat a helpless puppy was unthinkable! The sight of it sneezing in the saucer of milk and blinking up at Jock had impressed itself on her, making her feel ashamed. She would have to do better, she told herself. She would have to care for those worthy of it, give them her attention and let Reg go his own way. Jock, she could sense, was outside the kitchen now, half wanting to come in. He could probably smell the food she was preparing. She sensed he liked her and that she reminded him of some "safe area" in his life...

He was certainly making himself known. The *winga wonga winga wonga* of his jew's harp crooned through the door crack to her...

"Come on in—" she called. "It's alright..."

He responded by playing an even louder burst of music but didn't enter.

"Come and eat where it's warm—" she tried again, talking at the door frame. "I'll put it in a basin then will I?—"

The music stopped in anticipation of the basin.

"Alright I'm putting it on the stoop—" she said, moving towards the door frame.

Expectantly she bent, placed the basin on the stoop and hardly had her arm drawn back from it than a muddy hand shot forth, grabbed the basin and bolted.

As she watched him run, she became aware of Reg walking stiffly towards her, wanting to talk but uncomfortable about having to. She almost sensed he was hoping she'd make it easy for him. Entering the kitchen he stood—arms hanging—looking at her. She was determined to do nothing to help.

"Thought about yourself then?" he asked.

Well she certainly had but she wasn't going to tell him!

"Could come with me," he added.

"You really disgust me!" she burst out, inflamed at the realization he would take the money, leaving father, brother—herself—

"Put the banns up day I went to town," he went on.

"May our God in Heaven—damn you—to Hell!" she burst out, horrified to hear the words coming from her own mouth.

"Don't know what you're making such a fuss about," he said, genuinely surprised. "Said you could come—" He finished in a petulant voice.

"You bloody"—she sought a word and, finding it—shouted, *"animal,"*! hating the image she was creating of herself, and herself for degenerating to his level of the raw animal in man; snarling and unrestrained, the only one he could deal in and in which he was the more skilled.

"Come here and think you know so much 'cos you've read a bloody paper couple of times—" he jibed, safe on home ground, visibly relaxing.

"I suppose you're going to leave that barn of them, locked in?" she hurled. "You're—*disgusting*!"

"And you're—" he said, losing pace, fumbling for appropriate words "—a—a—dirty piece of tripe—"

"Some country this!" she sang out. "No wonder you have to advertise for people!"

That was a good one.

"Look what we get!" he returned.

"Better than you deserve!" she shrilled.

His voice rose in derision. "The dregs!"

"Shut up!" she burst. "Shut up! Shut up! Shut up! Shut up!"

"What a lady!" She saw him grin. "Plenty more where you came from I bet!"

How could he grin when there was nothing funny?

"You ought to be *branded*," she railed. "There ought to be a *stone* around your neck with your sin written on it! People should be warned—"

"And it won't be you that does it," he said, turning to the door, "because either you come with me—"

"I wouldn't go with you if—if I were on top of a burning building and you had the ladder—I wouldn't if—"

"Suit yourself."

"Get out of here." She felt her breath coming short. But Reg turned and took two steps towards her.

"You want sortin out again?"

"No," she said backing away.

"It's all the same to me—" he said advancing. "Attract my attention—pickin' holes—"

"That's not true!" she pleaded, at the same time seeking desperately the word that could make him desist.

"What you came out for, isn't it?"

"Please!"

He let go her wrist and her eyes became hard as his. He had *wanted* to hear her plead; to know she subjugated herself before him. He had no interest in her or her body, she now knew, and with shock she realized that for both reasons she hated him.

The barn door bolted and padlocked, the paddocks emptied, Ceci stood resolutely on the kitchen step watching Reg on saddled horse with saddle bags, leaving. A light rain had begun and apart from the occasional whine of Reg's waiting dogs, the place was already eerily silent. Old Bowen watched from the back doorstep in his slippers, waving his fist and shouting, "Never mind me!" at the departing back. "I'll make me own dampers!"

Reg brought his horse around and paused before Ceci, giving her a good long look, then drew from his pocket a thing which he threw at her feet. She did not need to look at it but kept her eyes firmly on him. Slowly he turned and moved off, his dogs cutting to and fro, uncertain as to their future.

"Remember the Prodigal Son!!" she shouted as he got to the gate, but he didn't react.

"You'll be back," she bawled. "Glad of the husks the pigs leave!"

He would probably take her literally and believe she wanted to keep pigs, she told herself, letting her eyes sink to the thing in the mud; the heavy barn door key. Already his hat was growing small beyond their bit of hedge. She looked at the old man staring back at her across the yard's muddy ocean from his private rock, the doorstep. Quickly she stooped, grabbed the key guiltily and slipped it into her pocket, and entered the kitchen. He would have to be told, she realized, and this would be difficult to do for so hurt was he by what he saw as Reg's betrayal, each time she had approached asking if she might talk he had shaken his head and the sight of tears coming into his eyes had made her withdraw. Left to herself she would worry anew about whether she had understood correctly the advice concerning Women's Things given in her big Book of Household Remedies for though it counselled against alarmism, she was beginning to get a bit worried.

It was strange to have proper meals, everyone sitting at

table together. To Ceci's left Old Bowen struggled to cut his meat, to her right Jock.

"Your brother's gone," she said, adding, "He's not coming back. I think." She assumed Jock had taken this in for he had been in the house several times without encountering Reg and the way things were looking he might even take to sleeping there again.

"Is your meat alright Mr. Bowen?" she asked turning to him. He seemed to be trying to remember how to deal with intimacies of this sort and as he frowned, Ceci wondered if she had gone too far in making herself so familiar with the old man.

"This meat is tasty," he said, making it sound like a statement from a primary reader.

"Oh." They ate on in silence.

Concentrating hard, Jock knocked his glass over, sending a stream of water running towards Old Bowen.

"Garrh!" he shouted as instantly Jock scrambled back from the table as if expecting a clout. But Old Bowen put down his fork and covered his eyes.

They resumed eating in silence with much self-conscious swallowing and staring at the board until the sound of horses' hooves could be made out in the lane beyond their dwelling. Who could this be? As the horse turned into their yard, Jock, who could stand it no longer, leapt up knocking over his chair, grabbed his plate and rushed off through the inner door with it. Transfixed, Ceci and Old Bowen listened to footsteps crossing the boards and awaited the tap on the door. Though Old Bowen did not call "Come in" the door slowly opened to reveal a middle-aged man in dark clothing, an expectant energy on his face. With dawning horror, Ceci recognized him to be the Minister of Religion whom she had seen on her only visit to Moke's tiny church. She got to her feet at once, conscious that Old Bowen was deliberately not standing.

"Get out of here!" he called. The Minister entered, saying enthusiastically:

"I come to make things right in the sight of the Lord—"

"Young Mr. Bowen has left now Sir. Permanent," Ceci squeaked.

A frown crossed the Minister's face. It was twenty years since he'd visited the Bowens' homestead and though he had that day intended to discuss rather than perform a ceremony, he could not stand facts once set in motion coming to nought. It was quite against the natural order of things and besides, he had a reputation for tidying things up, making them work in the long run.

"Fetch me a draught to quench my thirst, would you?" he asked Ceci, all but patting her on the head as she scuttled past. "Now, now, now," he went on. "This will never do."

Old Bowen stared at him.

"Can't have an unmarried girl staying on here—" he shook his head.

"Then she can go!" snapped Old Bowen. "And if you've come out here to sympathize with me on accounta my son—"

"You should marry that girl yourself," the Minister pointed out, adding, "Since the beginning of time they've— accepted the unacceptable—to have a place—"

"You got the wrong address!" Old Bowen's voice continued on, still heavy with sadness. "When I was a young man," he said, "the Lord blessed me with two sons. A keeper of sheep and a tiller of soil—"

"You'd be doing the girl a favour," the Minister insisted. "You've your other son to provide for and she won't stay otherwise."

Gradually the import of his words dawned on Old Bowen.

"You so hard up you go out peddlin' these days?" he asked.

"It would be easy for you to marry her," retorted the Minister lightly. "Same name after all."

Old Bowen shook his head.

"If she's a woman of good character," the Minister urged. "Given your obligation—why would you possibly object?"

Re-entering the room Ceci was instantly alerted to the changed atmosphere, the men eyeing her expectantly as she offered the water to the Minister.

"Now if you wed him—" he began blandly.

Could it be that to a Man of God her condition was instantly discernible? Appalled she gasped out:

"Who—who says I even want to *stay* here—?"

The Minister frowned at Old Bowen.

"I hardly know Mr. Bowen," she went on. "We've hardly spoke two words together since I came."

The Minister put her flustered and defensive tone down to embarrassment.

"An act of charity," he whispered, pulling her aside. "He needs looking after. And his barmy son—"

Scarce able to believe her ears Ceci pulled back from him.

"Marryin' you won't make *no* difference at all!" assured Old Bowen, his tone hovering ambiguously between insult and a guarantee of safe conduct. "Nothing to worry about from me girl."

Could the Minister not see this man he was proposing to espouse her to did not even know her name?!

"Done well for yourself," nodded the Minister.

Slowly confusion gave way to dismay followed by repugnance then thoughtfulness. It was obviously all the same to Old Bowen who had turned his back, stumbled towards the window and was now staring out. Nor was there any doubt she could fulfil the contract scrupulously in terms of looking after him and poor Jock but...

"No one lives for ever my dear," the Minister confided, pinching her arm. "You're a comparatively young woman—" She stepped further away, shaking her head. But as he looked at her, waiting, she was overwhelmed by the terrible vision of herself, very pregnant, in torn clothing, standing alone in a circle of women, all pointing at her and bending to pick up stones. Suddenly Old Bowen's back seemed very safe and secure...

"Alright," she said in a small voice. "I mean, *thank you*."

The Minister ordered her to look about for Bowen's first wife's ring, fetch Jock to be witness and get herself organized.

"You won't have to pay for her now!" he joked to Old Bowen, receiving for his troubles a look that could knock him over.

"I can be fair!" Bowen growled, wondering how he could lift the floorboard where his money was kept without the Minister seeing.

"And how much'll *you* be charging?"

"Well they do say marryin' 'em is cheaper than hirin'!"

the Minister went on, unable to bring his levity under control.

"And while you're here you can put your writin' skills to use," Old Bowen frowned. "You step outside and write me will. I'll not have that boy come back and—" his voice began to rise dangerously.

"Your wife'll come first—"

"I'll have it in *writing*. So set it down! The land to my wife—on condition that she's to see tò the boy."

"We use the word 'maintain'—"

"*See to* you fool! Anyone'd understand *see to*—"

Turning his back to Old Bowen the Minister began to write. No doubt the old boy wanted to get at his purse! He had no need of a will yet would not be pacified without one on account of his anger at the departure of his son.

"Your boy can witness them both together—" he said cheerfully.

"You take it with you, do you hear?" Bowen urged, replacing the board carefully under his chair. "You hand it in and get it lodged—"

Quickly he stood up as Ceci re-entered the room, coaxing in Jock who looked as if he were expecting a good thrashing. She had glimpsed Old Bowen kneeling before his chair.

"Nobody spoke agin it in town," said the Minister to the three of them, "but does anyone know any reason why these two people should not be joined in holy matrimony?"

As if sensing something about to happen between his father and Ceci, Jock's mouth unleashed a stream of incoherent babble, making Ceci recall his face at the window as she had seen it after the rape. Pressing her lips together, she saw his mouth bite at the air.

"Shuddup!" Old Bowen barked. "This is a solemn occasion."

"Good. Well—" said the Minister, moving smoothly into the practised words. Over her head they floated—honour and obey—death . . .

They drifted past Jock, now picking his nose—and out of the door and over the hills. For the briefest moment she felt the pain of realizing these two men who had at first struck her so strangely were now her kin.

"My family," she whispered, the gentle caring face of her mother sliding from view to be replaced by the staring face of Old Bowen. The anxious smile of her deceased sister flickered and went out as the form of Jock now fidgeting by the door moved swiftly across the light, blocking the elder sister who had watched over her. She saw the ghost of herself pausing in the open door, waving wanly to her, caused to leave by the magic of a few words. Whether Reg had put her in a Difficult Situation or not, he had made her pay dearly for it with her time . . .

Vaguely she became conscious of the Minister trying unsuccessfully to cheer Old Bowen by suggesting he "might not feel so old now." He seemed hopelessly unaware of any of the true feelings in the room. Old Bowen turned briskly away, the distraction of the wedding gone, his thoughts back with his son's desertion which had caused such pain.

Ceci's heart went out to him as she approached. Though the Minister had gone he lingered by the window like a trapped fly.

"Can I help you Mr. Bowen?" she asked, but his eyes filled with tears as he beat her away with his hands, stepped around her and went out quickly. This was the first time he had left the room in her presence. Did it mean it was now her room too?

Chapter 7

Wagers as to whose sheep the close-mouthed Buyer had driven through town that afternoon finally looked like paying off when Reg Bowen was seen coming out of the store with a rusty dish for panning gold. His waiting horse looked more like a pack animal than a mount, and the sheepdogs milling between his legs and snapping at each other highlighted the incongruousness of the grey blanket, pick, coils of rope and supplies plainly indicating an intention not to return to sheep farming. His face was sour and unwashed and it was possible that he had been "off the place" some time already without their knowing. Their curiosity was further heightened when they saw him heading out of town on the fork used only on Sundays which lead nowhere but the little church! Why, they told each other, the man couldn't even go panning right! What a pity it was he should choose a Thursday to clatter by and not a Friday or Saturday!

As the few curious souls waddled after him, they saw him reach the church, lean across from his horse and tear something from the notice board, crumple it into a ball and fling it away. Quickly they hurried forward, glad that Reg was cutting around the back of the church and heading over to the mountains and away.

The first to arrive snatched up and uncrumpled the paper. Wedding banns between Reg Bowen and the Immigrant girl!

The news spread like fire through Moke burning every name it touched, raising endless possibilities. They had already married and the girl was waiting outside town! They had sold their land! The girl had seduced Reg, caused him to murder his father and hence they were fleeing! Perhaps she was a thief or a whore? Could they not have sold their land to emigrate to Australia? There was no limit to the rumours the sight of Reg's departing back provoked.

Shown the much smoothed piece of paper Ginger shook his head and, leaving his Grain and General Feed cart in the middle of the road, went and rapped firmly on the Minister's door.

At once the man's discomfort showed. The fact that he had allowed his enthusiasm to overtake him had impressed itself on him on the way home, though he did not want overly to blame himself. It was, after all, customary to pay a visit to intending couples before the ceremony to find out their particular requirements and he had intended to *see about* the marrying, not to perform it. Yet he felt his cheeks beginning to flush.

"Did this girl marry?" Ginger demanded, waving the crumpled paper in his face.

"Well yes—" the Minister said awkwardly.

"Who?"

"Reg Bowen," shrugged the Minister as if to imply "Who else?"

"And he's left her already?" Ginger pursued.

"Mr. Bowen is with her now," said the Minister, his discomfort receding with the awareness this was *not* one of his flock and he could push the door on his face any time. "Now if you will excuse me . . ."

"Are you trying to tell me she married Old Bowen?" Ginger persisted, aghast, holding the door with his hand.

The Minister nodded. Ginger stood, looking again at the paper.

"Since when was Old Bowen born in 1840?" he shouted at the closing door. "Is he 33 years old?"

Lying in bed, Ceci stared at the ceiling. It was very quiet without the sheep. The candle beside her passed a wreath of light on the rough wooden box on which lay the wedding ring. She picked it up, turned it around in her fingers, frowned, put it on and looked at it. With a strange expression she took it off and put it back by the candle, which she blew out. Was she really married? The idea stretched into the distance like an endless tunnel. She, the Old Man and the idiot. Oh, she hated herself for saying that. Her eyes caught the barn key blinking on the window sill in the moonlight. Was there really any need for Bowen to know the full extent of his son's betrayal? Sitting up, she pushed her feet to the floor. She would go to the barn and finish the matter off once and for all.

Moving down the corridor she paused outside Old Bowen's door which had blown in. Though his room had no window, her candle picked out the shape of his back curled against and, she assumed, facing the wall. "Whaddayou want?" he said gruffly. She knew he had intended to be polite with a woman on the place but that the habit of years had come first and he felt intruded on. She shook her head meaning "nothing."

"Everythin' alright?" he enquired.

"I came—to say good night Sir." she replied.

"Good night then girl."

She pulled his door to and passed on her way. Half sitting, Old Bowen heard her steps head for the main room, and cross it. He heard the front door open.

Ceci struggled with the heavy key in the padlock until it cracked open and she could heave the bar up. Entering the barn the stale air almost put her candle out as she stood listening to muffled movements. Gradually she made out the shapes of maybe 30 or 40 sheep, standing amongst the bales of loose hay, observing her. Carefully she caught at an old fence post lodged in some coils and began to wrench and tug at it; her own shadow frightening her in the dark. Suddenly the post came free—sending her flying backwards on to her candle, putting it out.

"What do you think you're doing?" came the voice of Old Bowen in a pool of light at the barn door. "Setting fire to my barn?" The sight of him standing there in his nightshirt released in her the urge to scream and rush about. Picking up the post, she raised it above her head.

"Killing your sheep for you!" she replied.

"Give that here!" he said wrenching the post off her. "What are you?" He began to propel her towards the door with his hand.

"But they're *sick!*" she pleaded. "You don't understand! He put them in here so the buyer wouldn't *see!*" Struggling she fell amongst the sheep.

"Like a rabid dog! Get out of here," he said gruffly, pulling at the neck of her nightgown, shaking her like a fish.

"Look at their *mouths!*" she shouted. "*Inside* them!"

As Old Bowen raised his hand to hit her he was struck by the force of her words. Letting go he dropped to the ground, passed her his candle and forced open the mouth of the nearest sheep. Then he crawled to the next, then the next.

"Aaargh!" he sighed out as she stood above, watching.

"Go to bed," he said, rising, taking the candle.

From the door, Ceci saw he had taken a large knife from his belt.

As she crossed to the house and trudged wearily to her room, her whole body ached with the events of the day and sorrow for the old man out there killing his sheep.

Peering from the window she saw Old Bowen's bent form dragging a small number of dead sheep behind the barn, then returning, rubbing his neck. He pushed the

barn door in, wiped his knife clean on the jamb, then, as
if struck by a thought, instead of returning it to his belt,
stuck it in a post and turned towards the house with the
tiredness of years of struggle. She saw his hand clamp
down on the nightshirt blowing around his knees and as
if he did not want her to see him looking broken, saw him
straighten his back and make a show of looking impassive
before opening the door. Quickly she hurried to stand by
the mantel. As the door creaked in and his laboured
breathing filled the room, she was moved by the urge to
comfort him somehow.

"I'm sorry," she began.

"You done nothing—" he said, his tone suggesting
his main concern was how to get past her and go to bed
without being intruded on. Also, she sensed, he did not
like her being the last one in the main room at night.

"Git to bed."

"I don't want to go in there," she said truthfully,
turning with the white face of a child afraid of the dark.

"Git you a blanket," he mumbled.

When he returned she was sitting in his big chair,
biting her knuckles...

"I'm sorry about the sheep," she said.

"Most of them cut-offs."

"Cut-offs?"

"Stole."

She was so amazed she couldn't stop looking at him.

"See I'm what they call a cockatoo," he began. "That's
a squatter between stations. Year in year out they been on
at me to sell. Both sides," he boasted. "But I'll not
budge!" He spread her blankets on the floor, sat by them.

"Why?" she asked.

"Settler's mind, girl!" he said proudly, his face gradually
lapsing into thought.

"Clean musterin'."

"Pardon?"

"Only way to control scab. You got a situation—
broken fences, herds gone to straggle, it's bad for your
neighbours. So it's worth twice what it's worth to buy you
out."

He looked up cannily at her. "Worse condition your
place gets in more you're likely t'be paid for it!"

"How long is it since you had a conversation Mr.

Bowen?" Ceci asked politely. Ignoring the question, Old
Bowen looked into the fire and nodded slowly: "I been
here a *long* time," he said.

"My wife," he began, as if opening a stiff door to the
past. Leaning forward Ceci listened amazed as slowly the
story of Old Bowen tumbled from him late into the night.

They'd married because people married. Because they
were of age. He hadn't thought about it one way or the
other. Hadn't looked forward to it or regretted it. Hadn't
not looked forward to it either, mind; it was just the next
step. But living with her—he'd become aware of something in her seeking him out. He'd found this odd,
amusing, even a threat. Something he had not reckoned
with so he'd ignored it. But as time passed and he slowly
tied up a suffering in her with his poker face, he'd begun
to feel sorry for her. He almost wished she'd married
someone else. Change himself? He couldn't. From her
actions, her *good*ness he knew that love, whatever that
was, existed; that she loved him. That what she wanted
back from him was the trivia of expressed commitment.
At one level, it was a battle. She trying to make him say
nice things—be nice . . . He wouldn't budge. Wouldn't be
told how to behave. She'd no right to expect it. Besides,
he said, she knows I love her. I may not show it, but she
knows.

She had become ill. Small pains became larger. She
began to waste. During the four years it had taken her to
finish up she'd become thin and silent. Now, a limit
having been set on her days, she viewed her husband
differently. No longer was there any point in hoping for
there was no time for the hopes to come true. Perhaps she
hated him. Or hated herself for her own ideals, for believing that if she gave him all the love she had—which to her
was all the love in the world—she could warm him over
like an old brick; heat him, bring colour to his cheeks.
Perhaps even from her sickbed she'd looked at the life she
had "thrown away" on him, on other lives she might
have had.

She had become a stranger to them all—in itself
terrifying to the household for she alone had made their
lives possible. The one child, Jock, simply wasn't making
out. The other, Reg—following his father—had few

words. Alone in the room—neither would speak to the other: it had been she who had carried messages between them . . . tied up the ends. They were not aware of the fact that she was the vital link but when she had gone, Old Bowen paused, *it* had gone. Had there been a time for Reg to finish "growing up" before she'd died—perhaps there would have been hope for them. She couldn't have gone at a worse time. He shook his head. Suddenly the house was empty—three strangers rattling in it like peas in a pod with no one knowing where the next meal would come from. He, incapable of grasping the feelings of the two boys or talking them around what had happened, had continued rock-like, showing nothing.

Seemingly finished, Bowen stared at the fire.

"Tell me about her going," Ceci said softly.

Finally she'd gone into a trance, he continued. Scared out of his wits, he'd sat by her bed. He took her hand— spoke her name, terribly quietly . . . Nothing. He'd sought her face. "You can hear me," he'd said, "can't you?" But the hand lay limp. "Listen," he said urgently, "I'm sorry." He'd begged her not to die, to forgive him, for his hardness, to say she forgave him. He told her then all the things she had ever wanted to hear . . . And he'd wept. But her hand lay limp, her face unmoving. "Forgive me," he repeated, sure she could hear. Glancing up he'd seen the boy Reg in the doorway.

"Do you want a drink Mum?" the boy called.

"No," she'd said clearly without opening her eyes. "Watch over your brother for me." As Reg crossed to his mother's bed Old Bowen had risen, his thoughts coming down like a blade narrowly missing Reg. Sometime during the night she'd passed on, Bowen said. He had not approached her again.

From then it had taken four or five years for a pattern to come. Lost in the fact that he could never know if his wife had heard but rejected him; had *not* heard and had gone to her death unaware of his sorrow and regret and of the fact that he *had* loved her; or had finally thrown him out of her heart for eternity—he was confused. Had he made her die with bitterness in her soul? Had she actually become the unthinkable, a person capable of a spiteful end? Or had she merely endured, pretending to love him . . . ? These things he would never know kept him in his chair. In any case, his voice dwindled away, Reg had avoided him. The boy was always out, taking over, running things. A case of too many cooks, he said. He'd let him get on with it. Old Bowen stared at the dying fire. Once established, he said, it was a silence neither broke.

"He wasn't going to be the first to speak 'n nor was I!"

In its darkness, dark things grew. Speaking fell away. There was no reason to speak. There was nothing to say. And this was the shell which Jock had evacuated for the only truth he knew: the wind turning the grass, the rain coming down, smoke always rising to the sky...

Ceci felt a deep sympathy for the old man.

"If you loved her she would have known—"

"She would?" He turned to her incredulous.

"Even if you said nothing, she'd still know."

"Is that true?" his eyes glinted, the hoar going from them, making them young and vital.

"Yes," Ceci nodded tiredly. "I'm quite sure she knew you loved her. Even if you acted bad."

Old Bowen sank back, a smile of peace suffusing his face as the stone which had weighted his mind for years rose to the surface and broke like a bubble. She caught him smiling.

At that moment a great sense of healing came over Ceci, as if her whole journey had already proved worthwhile. This man had accepted forgiveness from her, on behalf of his wife, as if women were all of one bone. As if they were a mystical commodity he looked up to and revered yet could never expect to understand. Yet even as she was conscious of having eased away and explained, taken the pain from him, she could feel the ghost of the other woman, frozen for ever at the age of 30, not smiling or nodding but looking down on her 15-year-old wisdom which flattered itself it had discovered some great Female Identity. She felt it mocking her for being pleased with what she had done and for glowing with the comfort she had created in the old man.

"Shall I tell you my name?" she asked, allowing tenderness to show on her face.

"Your name is 'Wife,'" he said, turning suddenly on her. "Thank you!"

Instantly Ceci repented her forwardness and began to draw back the hand he was reaching for.

"A good woman," said Old Bowen, "refreshes the soul."

As if there were two Ceci's in the room, she stepped back and watched horrified as Old Bowen drew her to him, laid her unresisting body on the boards and eased himself on top.

"We are married!" she told herself. "He has the right! You made him feel 'welcome' by listening to him!"

But *surely* one could be kind without...

Staring at the wall ahead, he was moving over her with the assurance of an oft performed, unforgotten act. Totally tense, she lay, keeping him out but as he forced his way in she felt a sudden slackening in his thrust as if he had encountered an inexplicable contradiction. In the next moment he was moving off her.

"I see you are not—a woman of good character," he said as, his voice riven with disgust, he stumbled from the room.

The next morning the sun rose on a still house. The memory of the preceding night which seemed to have dragged on 'til dawn was so embarrassing that Ceci couldn't bear to look at it. Every time it arose she said something out loud to make it go away again. Clearly the old man had bitterly regretted telling that tale of his wife's death, confessing to his own fears and weaknesses! It had been immensely personal. There had been degradation, remorse, betrayal and despair on his face as he'd stumbled from her. Worse still, he probably thought her remark about women knowing when they were loved was a pack of lies and she probably a gold digger! Awkwardly she hurried towards the kitchen. There was nothing for it but to make the breakfast and give him his on a tray as when she'd first been there. He would probably relapse into total silence now and it would be largely her fault.

Crossing the yard, on impulse she went to close the barn door. If she and Bowen were to make a go of it, despite everything, it was as well to be thorough. Peering in she saw the sheep he had not killed huddling mindlessly in a corner and drawn in by curiosity advanced, bent down and forced open the mouth of the one nearest to her. Only the faintest trace of blisters was evident on its gum. Surprised, she moved cautiously to the next, then the next, even dragging one that wouldn't stand to the door to get more light on it, pushing her fingers deep into its mouth, forcing it open. Only the scars...! Whatever it was had definitely cleared up!

Overcome with relief she filled her lungs and rushed behind the sheep waving her skirts and whooping, making them run out into the open baa-aaing. Suddenly the hills looked brighter; she threw back her head, spun in a circle. But a twinge of guilt stabbed! How much of this situation which had disenfranchised Reg and near broken the old man's heart had she been responsible for with her reading and newspaper knowledge? As she stood being honest with herself, a white fluttering like a flag above caught the corner of her eye. In the draught from the barn door she saw Old Bowen's night shirt caught on a beam... and beneath it his feet, legs and privates hanging in full view. On the floor lay the bales he had kicked away in his great haste to rush to his end.

In silence she stared up at the blue face and the body, now looking more than ever like an unloved shell a man had left behind. That a man could show such deep regret at having broken a silence puzzled her. Had he continued to hold it would he still be alive? Struggling to cut him down she saw how his great weight had made the rope eat into the beam: a mark that would always remain. As the kitchen knife ate into the rope, the sound of it tearing in the emptiness of the barn was sickening. Bit by bit it snapped and unravelled, pulled down by the great weight of the body, the knife eating through the rope as it stretched 'til the cut appeared along an eight inch length and with a SNAP finally the body plummeted down.

Laying him in his grave she covered his face with a cloth. The scars on his neck told their tale but still it would be best to leave the sawn rope knotted around the beam in case... Not that anyone could accuse *her* of heaving Old Bowen on high but in case Reg came back or the Minister fetched a constable...

"Dear Mother—" she began, sitting on the hill. "Things have taken a turn for the different here—"

Her eyes strayed across to the simple grave that she had made for Old Bowen, to the jar with two flowers in it.

"I put some flowers in against the back wall which Jock has painted white," she wrote, wondering how she would ever phrase it, if she could bring herself to admit her condition ... "Jock isn't such a bad stick but he takes watching..." Frowning she ran her hand protectively over her protruding stomach. It was no good. There was no way of saying it. "Even cut down to size, there's more to running this place than I thought—" she went on. "I have decided for the time being not to send this letter but to wait till I...till..."

Sighing, she breathed out. It was unlikely anyone would ride over the hill and propose marriage to her. So till what? She had better settle down to the fact she had earned herself a stigma and that the road ahead would be long and very lonely. Listening to a slight wind that was beginning in the hills, she pushed herself to her feet. It was no good worrying about these things. Putting her cares aside she set off to look for the puppy that Jock had lost. She had not written once since leaving home. Soon, now that she had an address, she must summon courage to do so. Yet the thought of opening a letter in her mother's hand, full of news of London and love and life, made her eyes smart. Scarce could she bear to read about all of them and of the things she had lost.

Chapter 8

Once Ginger had settled down to the idea of marrying Maureen, the wedding followed fast. Since being a small child he could remember seeing her every Sunday kneeling with her family, growing bigger before his eyes.

When she started wearing a mantilla he noticed and when she moved from her sisters' handdowns to her mother's cast-offs he also saw, for often during the Priest's sermon the tiny congregation in the field found they had little to think of beyond who was wearing what and who would be ready to wear whose whats soon...

Really, as his mother put it, he was grown now and once you married you didn't look back. Nor could she, as a married woman, say it made much difference who you'd wed...

Maureen was the only Catholic near his age in Moke, only a couple of years older. She had been a fact of Ginger's life, his mother pointed out, not an unknown quantity; the girl was quiet and hard working, she insisted. At that Ginger realized he must've stopped noticing her for as he remembered Maureen, she was impetuous, noisy... always the girl who led them on and encouraged the younger ones to jump over people's fences...

Ginger's mother knew better than to mention to him that as Maureen was the last to leave, in all probability Nolan's land would be his, for she knew talk of this kind was wasted on the young. Nonetheless, as he was from a large, land-shy family and the Grain and General Feed business, good as it was, was difficult to "share" amongst so many, marrying Maureen would seem a natural and wholesome progression. The sense of honour which had prevented Ginger informing his mother of Maureen's "condition," though in charity she would certainly have overlooked it, also forbade him to consciously examine it himself. Maureen had already had her privacy eroded and for his part he would try to make it up to her, not torment her further. As he began to look at her, she had been overcome with a sort of shyness, blushed and hung her head. No one had ever done that for him before and he sensed in it a pathetic animal gratitude he could not refuse.

Yet thoughts of the girl Ceci nagged at him. Despite his mother's assurance "they were all the same underneath" or the general feel in Moke that strangers looked exciting until you knew them, he could not account for the inexplicably powerful draw he felt towards her. It was like stones in the pit of his stomach being dragged towards rapids. As he sought to come to terms with a decision he was not ready to take, news of Ceci's marriage threw Moke into such a state of loquacity simple mention of her name became impossible without complications of the most severe nature. The name "Bowen" was everywhere and though the Minister longed for the people to forget, for a while all other matters became very small beer. To his delight, the eight day wonder was suddenly eclipsed by gossip touching more accessible people: two of the Catholics—Maureen and Ginger—were soon to be married . . .

Back at the homestead Ceci held a watchful brief. Apart from a visit from the Minister's boy bringing the copy will she had seen no one. She had explained to him the details of Old Bowen's death and his eyes had widened accordingly and showed him the grave, saying she had prayed over it. As Autumn drew close, she knew she must brave "town" and buy supplies. "Autumn at Home," she sighed. The woods of Surrey, knee-deep in golden leaves, squirrels scuffing about! She, her two sisters, and Mother walking there—glad to be out of London for the day— reminding each other of Autumns in their beloved Cheshire on the Estate where she and her sisters had started life. Autumn, she sighed, looking around. Only a faint withering in the grass could be seen here, a change in the crispness of the sky. . .

Taking Bragge, the pony, she set off for Moke. Refreshed by their recent scandal, heads began to turn and eyes narrow as Ceci moved along, feeling word spreading ahead of her and closing in behind. So used had she grown to the fact of her bulging stomach she had overlooked it, thinking only of the pony and hoping it too had not been stolen. Yet now it could not have been clearer it was her stomach, not the pony, people were staring at. Grasping the nettle she urged the pony bravely towards the store, determined that this was one small battle with Moke *she* was going to win!

Inside the store four young girls pressed their noses to the single square window, peering with deep satisfaction at the men coming and going across the street. It was no accident the girls were there for today was Mail Day, the day when newspapers and magazines from Home drew

in the able bodied from outlying stations and grasslands,
a sight no right-minded young girl would be wanting to
miss.

"There he is!" shouted Miss Faye as Ginger appeared
across the street. That he had married "that ugly lump
of a Maureen" had in no way diminished his status in
their eyes. On the one hand they could disregard it and
on the other, it inflamed their ardour. "Ooh!" Miss
Faye added, pushing her friend Miss Monahan aside
sharply to get a better view. Beyond the window Ginger skipped lightly down the two steps of the building
opposite.

"Mm!" Miss Gregg agreed, her elbow reaching deep
into Miss Faye's side.

"A little perfume in affairs of the heart," breathed the
storekeeper, Mr. Sweetwater, "goes a long way..."

"What's he *doing*?" asked Miss Drummond, craning
to see around the man standing in the middle of the
street, blocking her view, seemingly offering his con-
gratulations to Ginger. Yet Ginger was squinting up the
street past the man towards the entrance of Moke, as if
he had seen something coming. The look on his face
suggested he wanted to go forward and help someone.
It was almost as if he was forcing from his mind known
facts in order to make room for a dream he wanted to
believe.

Stepping into the store, Ceci missed the half step
and, to the intense satisfaction of its occupants, fell forward. As she righted herself, not knowing the store's
layout, she turned abruptly into the packing box area
behind the door, aware of a snicker from the girls by the
window. Instantly she reddened, crossed to the table
which ran the length of the store and, keeping her back to
the girls, began to pick up and discard cloth remnants.
Immediately Sweetwater was upon her, his moist lips
rubbing together in excitement as he made up his mind
what to say.

"Good morning," said Ceci quickly, forestalling him.
"Is your wife here?"

"Alas alas!" he said, swaying his hands. "The peren-
nial bachelor but not, I assure you, ignorant of *ladies'
needs*!" Ceci moved quickly nearer the girls, feeling repulsed by the man's aura, yet sensing their hostility.

"We have everything—'particular'—" he went on, trailing faithfully and proferring napkins and bandages, his fingers somehow indecent paddling amongst them. Frowning Ceci began to assemble baby needs, pins, bandages, powder. Suddenly Sweetwater took her elbow, whispered in her ear: "You'll find ready cured bacon a great time-saver!"

Totally amazed she stared at him.

"Nutmeg graters?" he hissed intimately. "Toasting forks!"

As she struggled to pull her elbow away, light from the door was blocked by men, stepping in, looking for their wives. Instinctively Ceci turned hoping to know someone yet reminding herself in the same breath this was unlikely for she knew no one but Ginger in Moke. Looking, she found the men eying her like a stray she-animal. As they stepped out of the doorway she crossed to the till where Sweetwater began to tot up her purchases.

"Mrs—ah—Miss—ah—" he began. Again Ceci heard the snickers off. Blushing and near tears, she struggled to unknot her hankie and bring out Bowen's money.

"Let me do that," said Sweetwater leaning forward greedily to snatch at it but succeeding in knocking over her purchases which spilled on to the floor. Covered with shame, Ceci bent to gather them up. Behind her she heard the shop door go, footsteps approach and pause behind her as she grovelled on the floor.

"Give the lady a box, Sweetwater!" came a familiar voice. "Wake up!"

In the next minute Ginger was kneeling beside her, reaching under the table to retrieve and hand her a wad of cotton. Intensely embarrassed to see him handling her intimate things she flushed furiously while behind him the girls at the window stared scandalized. How *dare* he! Ginger helped Ceci to her feet and stood clutching the baby things to his chest while Sweetwater brought the box. Keeping her eyes down Ceci counted the money out as Sweetwater wrenched the items from Ginger's arms, the two men vying with each other to pack her purchases in the box. As Ginger held the door open for her and she moved through, Ceci felt the cold scowls of the girl by the window striking her back like little stones.

"I could deliver this for you," he said, holding on to the box.

"It's very kind of you," she replied, "but it'll go in the sides."

For some reason Ginger continued staring at her.

"We're neighbours—" he began, ignoring the whispers even Ceci could hear.

Carefully fastening the saddle bags' straps, she eased herself up on to the pony. Even the girls could see the desire on Ginger's face to help her—yet if she were prepared to ignore her condition in public, how could he draw attention to it by giving her a leg up? They saw him run quickly for his horse, gallop after her up the street, rein in alongside and proceed with her, from the height of his taller mount, smiling warmly down.

No sooner were they out of town than he began to question her.

"How could you marry an old man like that!"

Ceci stared ahead. "I can marry whom I like, can't I?"

At once Ginger regretted having said it and looked about wondering how to start over but his desire for the truth drove him on.

"If you'd just tell me *why* you married him—"

"He asked me," she said blandly. Ginger frowned ahead. In the pause before she had replied he had clearly seen her deciding what to say and what not to say. He felt personally violated at the idea of her and Old Bowen in bed, him dragging his folds of thin flesh over her, scratching at her with his ribs, his hip bone poking in...

"Were you in love with Old Bowen?" he demanded angrily.

"I—I'm not an object of—of—" Ceci began, but ran out of words. "Why can't people just—*leave me alone*!?"

For a while Ginger said nothing. Then:

"At least I didn't say you were after his property!"

As Nolan's signboard came into view, he slowed up. It would hardly do to ride past it, past *home* he should say, in the company of this woman, arguing fiercely. The blood was thundering in his veins and he felt scarce responsible for any words which might slip from his mouth. The general feeling of confusion had communicated itself to even his poor horse.

"I have to get back—" he said gruffly, turning his horse

towards Moke. "If you want anything, come by the Grain and General Feed, Fridays—"

She glanced quickly at him and saw a look on his face that quickened her. Rather than be left staring after him, she urged Bragge on, knowing from the silence that he had remained on the spot and was watching her go. She did not turn but made a point of raising her head high and moving lightly off as if she hadn't a care in the world.

Before long she was planning what she'd say next time they met, reminding herself she hadn't told him Old Bowen was dead and concluding that made him very bold in his behaviour. He'd been very direct with her, and somehow they had been like flints striking on each other's stones, flashing against Moke's drabness, ringing out. She had not failed to notice the eyes of the other girls on him: he seemed to be the town favourite. Yet, apart from when he was angry, surely he was the most ordinary man she had ever met? Wasn't that ordinariness, though, wholesome, and wholesomeness desirable? The way he moved, laid his hand on the back of a horse, smiled, all were affirmations of the values of quotidian existence. He was the sort of man, she mused, who could bind up a small child's knee without her crying...

From a hilltop, gnawing alternatively on a stick and his knuckles, Jock saw the small form of Ceci come into view, turn at the weak crossing of tracks and disappear under a canopy of trees. He did not see her grip the pony's mane, gasp, lean forward biting her lips, and bent double reach the ground to crouch, waiting for the pain to pass. Tense with expectation Jock waited. This was the part he liked best when people vanished under trees and he had to wait for them to reappear. It seemed this time he waited an eternity but finally she emerged and with joy he began to rush down the hillside to surprise her by arriving first at the house.

As she entered with saddle bags banging on her knees, the sight of what he had done prevented her collapsing in a chair. He had "set" the table! Dishes were cramped close together, knives mistaken for forks, spoons upside down... Pleased and amused she had just decided to leave them as they were when Jock burst into the room.

"Thank you for setting the table!" she exclaimed

making him go pink with pleasure, stick his tongue self-
consciously out and begin to rub his head in a circular
manner.

"Go and wash your hands, there's a good boy," she
went on for they were as usual covered in earth which, if
she did not make him remove, he would speedily convey
to his mouth along with the bits of grass and sticks that
found their way into his food. Jock stood beaming. He
like the way she talked to him, especially during meals
when she would tell him things both knew he did not
understand but which were a way of sharing because she
liked him. Sometimes she would touch his wrist to get his
attention and when he looked up she would be speaking
her very soul directly into his face as if she actually hoped
he *would* understand what she was saying.

"I met a really nice man today!" she sighed in exactly
one of those tones. "But apart from that—it really wasn't
such a success, my 'day in town'..."

Jock stared at her, keenly aware that something was
wrong.

"I had hoped to meet a woman at least," she admitted.

In the early morning, a shawl round her nightdress, Ceci
sat awkwardly on a hard chair. Lying in bed, turning,
sitting, lying again, she had been unable to get comfortable and finally swinging her legs over the edge had
discovered the surprising fact that the bed had been wet.
To the sound of boards creaking she had crossed the small
space to the window and stared out at the lightening sky
and the fingers of the sun beginning to touch the base of
their hill. Now peering from the outer door she let day
creep into the room and reach towards her. The world
was unbelievably quiet, its stillness unbroken by insect or
bird. The grass was without dew, dry and upright and in
this space before the awakening of living things, she
waited. Gradually, as the sun began its long climb up the
sky, her pains became more regular till she was in no
doubt that the time was upon her.

"Jock!" she called, limping towards the barn and
opening the door. "Come quickly."

Instantly awake at the sound of her voice, he dropped
down from his nest in the hay and ran behind her back to
the house.

"Baby," she gasped, pointing at her tummy.

"You," she motioned at him, "run. Village. Anybody. Anybody! You *say* it! Baby."

For a moment Jock stared horrified, realizing he must understand and do something or this woman he loved would be cross with him.

"*Say* it," Ceci pleaded, tears in her eyes. "Baby! Baby! Baby!"

Cautiously Jock opened his mouth and bit at the air. "Baa—Baa—" he began.

"*Baby*! Come *on* now!" she said, squeezing his hands. Then came the miraculous, almost inaudible, whisper: "Baby."

"Good! Good!" she shouted, hugging him, holding his shoulders, making him say it again.

"Now run to the—"

He started to run.

"No wait!"

He stopped.

"Listen."

Slowly and calmly she repeated it.

"Keep saying it all the way, Jock. Baby! Baby! Baby!"

Gradually he joined in.

"Baby. Baby. Baby. Baby," they chanted together.

Quickly Ceci guided him to the door still saying it and pushed him through. To her relief she saw him begin to run with incredible speed, the urgency of his mission written in his bent head and his awkward gait. Relaxing the control she had kept on her face, she allowed herself to crumple.

On ran Jock like a gazelle, his mouth making the movement "baby baby baby," his eyes potent with responsibility. He had an ungainly run, as though one leg was shorter than the other, though it certainly wasn't.

As the last gate on their land reared up before him he prepared his energy to climb up and over it when to his utter horror he saw on the other side a large, well fed, powerful looking man in a velvet jacket, waiting calmly on a massive mount, observing him.

"Open the gate," said the man, taking in the frightened staring eyes and muddy forearms caught up in the brambles and torn wire.

"Open the bloody gate, Idiot," he repeated, using

"idiot" more as a Christian name than an insult. Jock dropped to the ground terrified and crouched. At that the man cantered alongside, stood in the stirrups, reached over and flicked at him with his whip at the same time making guttural noises in his throat. Jock curled himself into a tight ball aware that something was going very wrong in his life. Then, as the whip found him, leapt up and ran back the way he'd come. Back to the gulley, back to the gulley's river, through the water to his hiding place, a crevice in a rock marooned midstream which he crept into, shutting his eyes as tightly as he could.

Back in the dwelling Ceci waited. The mid-day sun, now high in the sky, fell on the empty yard, its gate standing open. A fly buzzed noisily past and was gone. Any moment now, she told herself, someone would appear over the hill coming to help her—perhaps an older woman who would become a friend. Already she had assembled the things the Book of Household Remedies said would be required and spent time puzzling over many of its references. That "delivering women" should not be allow to squirm or roll about in case they crushed or strangled their babies was obvious but her confinement had not been nine months to her way of thinking, nor was she at all clear what the "afterbirth" meant except that it came up to forty minutes after the birth. Slowly she let her mind wander Home where it would have been so different! Her mother would have been with her longing for the birth and there would have been gifts of clothing, advice, tales of frightful experiences from older women who were quickly told to shush.

With the afternoon, the pains came and went. When there were none she regretted having sent Jock to disturb the people of Moke on her behalf but when pain returned she cried out, longing for someone to tell her what to do, or to make the pain go. Alone as the room darkened, she felt Moke had rejected her. Gritting her teeth, head bowed, she knew a kinship with women since the beginning of time. When it came to it, they were alone. They crept off into caves or alleys, frightened and unfriended, and came back smiling with or without a child. When their time came, nobody wanted to know...

Evening became night and a grey dawn followed to

find her arched on her bed shouting in the knowledge none could hear. The pain in her back so intense, so searing she was convinced something was wrong, yet as she tried to reach her hands behind her, her great bulk blocked her and memory of the words in the Book of Home Remedies about rocking and squirming made her grip the bed's edge and keep still. How long she laboured she did not know. Pains rushed in then left as if stolen and her eyes would plop shut, her mouth fall open and she would be asleep only to be rudely awakened when they rushed back again, shoving her exhaustion aside and making her scream. Terrified of rocking in either direction she clung desperately to the bed's edge wishing the child would come out. At a tearing sound that she heard, rather than felt, with a great sense of relief, the child rushed forth, but so weakened were her arms when she let go of the bed's edge she could scarcely push herself up. As she did so she caught sight of it lying between her legs, slippery and alive. Carefully she lifted its face, wiping it so it could breathe, and, tilting it over the bed's edge holding it by the feet she swung it gently to and fro like a thurible.

"There you go," she said nervously, "like that." As she frowned anxiously the baby made a little coughing noise. So far so good. She propped it on her own feet and reached for the scissors then hesitated. Would it hurt either of them when she cut? Taking a deep breath she shut her eyes, cut, and felt nothing. At least she had done that right, she thought with relief. But what a mess they were in!

What a way to start life!

Standing well away from the badly messed bed, Ceci held the baby to her in the silence of early morning. She was afraid to move, afraid to make even a board squeak. What should she be feeling? doing? At Home people brought flowers, told you how you were feeling, that you were happy; they joked you into the correct way of starting out as a new mother. Her only feeling, she realized, was relief that the child was normal, that she had done it without hurting either of them too badly. What would happen next or whether it was even over she was unsure, for despite the reality of the child in her

arms, she felt as pregnant as before and in no manner
ready for the next stage.

Convinced that nothing more was going to happen
she was standing worrying in the grey light asking herself
where the emotions people talked about came from and
wondering if they would suddenly arrive when a tugging
lurch in her abdomen made her quickly lay the baby on
the floor and run behind the bed to squat anxiously.
Conscious of its presence in the room as another being
and embarrassed at her animal behaviour, she kept one
eye on the baby and rubbed at her belly. Suddenly there
was a wrenching plop and a large lump like a piece of
dog's meat detached itself and fell to the floor. Backing off
it in horror she realized *this* was what the Book meant by
an "afterbirth."

For a long time she sat on the step holding the baby
telling herself over and again it was real and reminding
herself that in all those months no one had used the word
"baby" to her or prepared her in any way for the outcome
of her condition. In the merciless quiet of early morning
she examined the two thoughts which had burst into her
mind on seeing it for the first time between her legs:
firstly relief that it was alright and second—No, she could
not bring herself to say it . . . it was just too terrible—a
sense of *failure to have produced a girl*. How could she, who
had grown up with girls, who *preferred* little girls *think*
such a terrible thing?! Where did the thought unbidden
come from?

She looked at the baby who was looking up at her, its
hard blue eyes studying her with as intense an interest as
she was thinking about it, almost as if it felt she had
already wronged it by being unaware of its existence
before it was born. It was making no demands she could
try to respond to "instinctively" and the concentration in
its eyes frightened her, making her wonder if she was
holding it right. Conscious that she felt neither qualified
nor efficient she sat very still and wondered.

By the time Jock came home the "right" feelings were
beginning to come. She felt pleased with herself, in fact
joyful and wanted to get an air balloon with a long
streamer behind it announcing the birth and sail across
Moke and possibly clear down to Christchurch with it!

She certainly wasn't about to be cross with poor Jock standing in the doorway covered in mud, head hung like a whipped dog.

"Come and look!" she called to Jock, taking his hand, pulling him into the room and across to the little padded box on the table.

"Look. Baby. *Baby*!"

Jock's mouth worked as the familiar sound "baby" triggered a half memory of something that had gone wrong. He picked sticks from his hair awkwardly. Ceci lifted the baby up.

"Isn't she sweet?"

Jock looked at her curiously but not with disapproval.

"Say hallo Jock! She's pretty, isn't she!?"

She jigged the baby on her hip as if she'd had her for months, trying to take Jock's hand to introduce him to her but he put it behind his back and stood shyly biting his lip.

Chapter 9

Calvin Laird picked fluff from his velvet jacket, confident that the rumours he had heard relating to Old Bowen's departure from this world were probably true. He had made four preliminary trespasses on the land without being shot at or seen. Apart, of course, from the Idiot whom he had only seen the once cowering by the gate. The other times Calvin had remained motionless in the shade while Jock stared an infuriatingly long time at a bush from which came the sound of a bell-bird. As his man led his horse towards him Calvin noted with approval its shining coat. That was good, he told himself, for today he intended to get in close and take a good look at the dwelling and anything that might recommend itself. It was always a good idea to look affluent when trespassing.

But if rumours concerning Old Bowen's other son, Reg, were true the place might even be empty.

Singing to herself, Ceci hunted through the bean plants for any bean she might miraculously have missed since picking them clean. Her fingers ran through the stalks and the heart shaped leaves, up and down the poles playing them like a harp but finding nothing. Apart from two marrows lying like bloated dogs on the dry soil, their leaf-work shrivelled away, the garden was well and truly finished and winter would soon be upon them with the seeds Reg had bought for root vegetables still unplanted. Poor Reg. The memory of finding those seed packets with their bright colours on them saddened her. They had been in his bedroom—the carrots and parsnips, broccoli and silver beet he'd got in for her arrival. Poor Reg. It was difficult to believe he'd hoped they'd make a go of it.

She crossed to the large orange pumpkin—grown from an isolated pip in the marrow packet—and crouched, tapping it with her knuckles, listening. Pongg! it resounded hollowly in the quiet afternoon. Pongg pongg! she did it again. Suddenly she became aware of someone watching her and with a terrible start looked up and saw quite close by across her low wall an enormous man on a black mount observing her closely, knowing he had the upper hand. Getting to her feet she wanted to say something about his trespassing but felt so stared down as his eyes moved past her that she lost her tongue. Now he was surveying her dwelling as if she wasn't there; as if all he looked at he would own. Turning, she ran around the house past the clothes line of baby rags and inside where she slammed and bolted the door. Creeping to the window she peered out. Now the man was casually moving his mount a little this way, a little that, and surveying her garden and roof with insolence tinged with amusement . . . Had she not known for sure it was Bowen's land she could have believed this was a bailiff come to throw her off.

Holding her baby as if ready to flee, Ceci crept into the shadows, then returned to the window. He was still there, now staring at and through her house, his very eyes coming in through her window and directly at her! Hastily she withdrew. From now on she would have to be very careful: they'd all have to be careful. There was something vaguely familiar about the man though she could swear she had never seen his face before.

"I don't want you wandering so far away in the day time, do you hear?" she said to Jock that night. "You stay near the house."

Jock looked at her, knowing she was trying to tell him something and to not tell him something at the same time. Ashamed of herself for not having gone out and dealt with the man directly she held the baby to her and watched Jock pulling at his ear. Before the rape she would never have let a man terrorize her like that, she realized. She was waiting for her courage to return. Here they were, the three of them, locked in a house that a good gust of wind could blow down and she had no courage left! How ridiculous it was!

"We're to have the baby christened," she said as the first crisp winter morning came. "Do you hear? Look at me! That's right." Jock looked up from the table where he was quartering crab apples. In the bedroom the baby began to cry. "Now I'm going to sort you out some decent clothes—"

The knife in his hand, Jock rose.

"It's all right. I'll get her." Ceci said, hoping Jock wouldn't sulk, for although he loved getting the baby he was in such a mess with the crab apples.

Picking the baby up she returned.

"Jock, what have you done with the apples?" she gasped, seeing on the table before him all the cores and bad bits but no sign of the actual quarters! "You've thrown the wrong ones away!"

Jock grinned, delighted at his joke, scooping the quarters from his thighs and putting them back on the table.

"You little devil you," she said fondly, rubbing the top of his head and handing him the baby.

In all, Ceci thought as she washed the apples, the three of them got on exceedingly well together. She had never asked Jock what happened to the little puppy but he was clearly enchanted with Baby.

When Christening Day came he stood on the doorstep in Reg's cut-downs and looked quite smart. Though he fidgeted with his collar as if it were full of ants and his hair was severely plastered down, he would certainly "do."

"Now don't you touch anything lad!" called Ceci, going to harness the cart.

As they rode gaily towards Moke, Ceci sang at the reins while Jock beside her clasped Baby. She was filled with love for them both.

"Not too tight dear," she called. "You'll crush her."

This was too difficult for Jock to understand so she stopped the dray and gently, to his consternation, loosened his arms. Surely Moke would marvel at the baby, she told herself, at its head and little feet... If God sent babies into the world with His blessing who could accuse her? Never had she felt more joyous or as if a whole new chapter of her life were beginning than when the first dwellings and shanties of Moke began to appear.

By chance she had hit church-going and before her twenty-five families all neatly turned out were heading the same way. They got in a good look at she passed, currently starved for a scandal, reaching out to her with their eyes and tongues. Even at the cost of desecrating their church, they sincerely hoped that was where she was going and that she'd enter. Indeed where else *could* she be going? But the cheek of the woman to drive down their Main Street with her brat and the Idiot on a Sunday!

Coming to a stop outside the church, Ceci took the baby and urged Jock to get out of the cart and stop staring. Boldly she went up the aisle, turning to lead him, noticing frowns fade as if people were thinking she had a bit of bounce to her. Truly that day she felt the world had been made specifically for her. The sun streamed in through the bright glass windows on the crowd, larger than usual this morning to welcome the new Minister and doze through his inaugural sermon.

Squeezing into a bench Ceci saw at the other end the girls from the store who had snickered when she was buying the cloth. Across the aisle, Sweetwater was busily turning, taking in what everyone was wearing, nodding greetings and trying to get in individual "looks" of personal commitment. Well behind her, though she could not see him, the man on the dark mount who had frightened her moved his head slightly to ascertain if it were she and briefly the look of utter boredom left his face to be

replaced by one of close interest. Next to him a smart lady
inclined her head to get a better look at Ceci while
children in front of her turned around to stare openly and
a line of nudging spread like a ripple through corn, the
congregation whispering in each other's ears, determined
then and there to settle the matter of who the Idiot was
and who had fathered the baby.

As she settled down, Ceci began to feel sorry for the
new Minister who could not find the beginning of his
notes. The man to her left gobbed loudly into his handkerchief and the woman in front winced. All around the
older men's resentment at having been dragged to church
to hear the Minister, in their eyes not a proper man, witter
on like a poet and show everyone up and make a right
fool of himself to boot was clear as could be.

"God gives daily opportunities to love—" the Minister finally began.

"Been a bit of loving there alright!" a woman muttered
too loud, making Ceci flush. Realizing he had started at
the wrong place, the Minister stopped abruptly and shuf-
fled his papers again, looking for a better entry point.

"Is it nearly finished?" a child whispered.

"Aha!" said the Minister, launching into his sermon
anew, at the paragraph comparing Man, the Pioneer of
the Spirit, with Man, the land pioneer... "As a faithful
woman's fruit is brought forth gratefully." He stopped
again. This was a fine image he had coined yet for some
unaccountable reason the congregation were laughing. He
checked his notes, found he had been in order and
continued. "Her crops bending to the scythe, as a woman
before her husband..." Suddenly the snicker cut him
short again! This time he raised his head and took a good
look at the congregation. One person seemed to be looking
at him with interest: a young mother clasping to her a
recently born child.

"How good it is to see parents so solicitous for their
offsprings' spiritual life—as to bring them so young to
fellowship—" he beamed, wondering if a direct personal
approach might be of more value with a congregation of
this sort who experienced difficulty in concentrating. Yet
to his surprise, even that harmless remark caused a giggle
and as he cast his eyes across the turning heads, it
seemed not a tongue was left still! Suddenly Jock, ever

sensitive to atmospheres, decided to bolt and pushing past those next to him, treading on feet, knocking hats, to the delight of the event hungry congregation, he tore straight down the aisle and out of the door. Now watching the *back* of his people's heads the Minister saw Ceci rise, dip her head respectfully to him and, carrying her baby, walk with dignity down the aisle after Jock.

The entire congregation had turned to watch her leave. Some were even standing. Before she reached the door her baby began to bawl, shattering the vestiges of any ideas the Minister might have had to resuscitate his sermon. Desperately he nodded to the lady organist who plunged her fingers deep into the keys, working "Nay But I Yield I Yield!" so loudly the congregation were obliged to turn and face front. Gradually, pulling at collars and scratching necks, they resentfully started to sing.

Standing outside and waiting for the service to finish, Ceci saw a small group passing on the street and cutting across a field towards a barn, their missals and scarves giving them away as Catholics. Straggling along, unworried by the time of day, they waited for each other, joked and called out. Down at the road's fork she could see their priest galloping in, knowing he was late for his appointment with the tiny community and struggling to pull vestments from his saddle bag as he rode. As the crowd flowed from her own church, Ceci did not see Ginger and Maureen crossing the field with their baby, a little girl they were taking to be baptized after Mass. But as Ginger turned to check the youngsters behind him, engaged in their weekly inter-faith stone throwing, name calling battle, his eyes lit on Ceci, standing holding her baby and waiting. His steps dragged and he stopped. Maureen turned and saw Ceci too and flushed, keenly aware that at that moment Ginger's thoughts were not with or of her or their little girl but on the creature outside the Protestant Church.

As the crowd passed between him and Ceci his view was blocked by people scrambling into carriages and flowing out into the street. Then he saw Ceci hurry over to the Minister and extend a hand.

"We were wondering if you could see your way to christening 'Olwen' while we're here," she began.

"Ah, Mrs. um—Mrs.—" said the Minister, still feeling

hurt by the small groups who'd closed up on him as he'd approached to introduce himself. "My dear Mrs.—"

"Bowen," Ceci put in. "And this is Jock."

"Good. Well. Mr. and Mrs. Bowen. Yes," said the Minister, noting the crowd now surrounding them. Carefully he eased a passage through them and back into the Church.

"Mr. and Mrs. Bowen," he repeated, "and the Godparents?"

Ceci hung her head.

"No matter," he replied gently, removing his cape and preparing himself for his very first christening in Moke.

"—I baptize thee Olwen Bowen in the name of the Father and of the Son—"

As the words washed over her and Jock stared fascinated at the pouring, splashing water dancing in shafts of sunlight searing the windows, Ceci's belief that she had never felt happier communicated itself to even the Minister who caught what he perceived to be the beautiful smile of a young mother's radiance at the christening of her first-born. This, he told himself, he would always remember: the look of acceptance on the face of this girl when he'd welcomed her small daughter into the Family of Man.

Returning home in the cart Ceci found herself humming quietly. Olwen was quiet too and Jock stared contentedly out over the hills. It was only when she had arrived home and opened the creaking door of their dwelling that she found herself wondering whether Ginger had been in the Church that morning and if he'd seen her and Jock and the baby? Now that she was established, she told herself, someone would tell him and with a bit of luck he might even come out and visit. He could even have been staying away because he wasn't sure if things were "convenient" . . . For sure by now he would know that Old Bowen was departed . . .

Winter came to the High Country, at first in stray white flakes, drifting down, then in great clouds blowing and settling over the hills, covering all in an undulating white blanket from which only the tips of fence posts protruded. In the shelter of hills, fast blowing snow storms moved over, leaving small strips for the sheep to huddle. When the wind changed, these vanished...

From within the dwelling, Ceci looked out on the winter landscape. The barn and hovel kitchen lay like stones in the snow. No birds, nothing moved. Behind her a fire, which could use more fuel, burned weakly drying out the peat, badly chopped logs and snapped branches stacked beside it. Nearby on a makeshift rack her child's nappies, little more than rags, clung in the scant yellow light glimmering through the window from a leaden sky. Above in the darkness of the eaves could be made out mutton curing, bunches of dried nettles hanging. The only sound was the wind which blew so hard it lifted the door and sent the rags stuffed there scudding across the boards, followed by stray flakes of snow. In two places the sky could be seen in the gap between wall and roof, and in places by them, icicles scratched beams, scraped at the thatch in the wind. It was a far cry from anything she had known before.

Days passed on leaden wings; mornings spent preparing for the afternoons and afternoons waiting for the day to be over. At times Jock's incapacity caused her to lose her temper though she would be instantly ashamed of herself. When the weather was bad he lay wrapped in rags on the floor sleeping, like a dog by the fire, but if Olwen cried he would leap up, lift her from her box and bring her quickly to the fire and begin to pile peat on. This would usually put the fire out, so frowning in concentration he would remove the peat and apply the best of the dried wood or the kindling till Olwen gurgled delightedly as the flames flared, encouraging him to throw on more. By the time Ceci would come rushing in from beyond, all the morrow's kindling would be gone and several of the nappies could be on fire.

"Look what you've done! Stupid creature!" she'd shout. "Isn't it enough I have to climb on the roof and fix it? Chop the wood! Oh hoh hoh hoh hoh—" and she would drop down sobbing, her rough cracked hands scraping at her face. "Look at my hands! Thick with grease and splinters!" she'd cry out and Jock would stare at her, feeling sorry. Then: "I shouldn't have shouted at you Jock," she'd say hanging her head. "I'm sorry I really am." And Jock, who understood her feelings more than her meanings, would know she had not meant any of the anger.

"What about that fine friendly Ginger?" she'd say dropping on a chair beside him. "Show off in front of the village when you're a figure of—of—But come and help? Oh they don't want to *know* I'm alone out here and it's winter! What have I done that's so terrible?"

The fact that she was exposed to more than the elements was brought home one silent afternoon when a wandering man without horse tried to force his way through her door, shouting against the wind that he wanted to see if she had "things to sell", pleading he was half frozen and offering to make himself useful "if'n she'd allow." He would not come to the window for her to see and his voice sounded rough.

"Go to the barn," she shouted. "I'll bring you food—" But carrying it to him she was afraid to enter. Conscious of the candle picking out her neck and chin she peered into its darkness.

"I heard about you," came his cracked impure voice, "at the last place."

"They'd say anything to a man like you—to get rid of you," she said nervously as his hands reached forward for the food and he sunk his stupid crafty face to the bowl.

Returning to the dwelling she feared for all of them and for their pony. What would stop a man, having eaten, taking the pony and going on? Quickly she urged Jock to fetch Bragge in but as her voice rose impressing on him the urgency of her request his panic grew until, disturbed by her unaccustomed lack of calm, he kicked over a chair, walked to the table, looked at her then deliberately swept the china bowl off it to crash to the floor. She was amazed! Instinctively she picked up a switch and ran at him to give him a good smacking but he leapt the chair, flung open the door and rushed shoeless into the snow. Biting her fingers she waited, wiping a pane of glass, peering through at the mass of grey, listening to the knocking of the wind and chiding herself that apart from everything else she was a fine landowner to be cooking for strangers with her own *child* a stranger!

Distressed at emotions she could not chart, she hurried to fetch Bragge in herself, creeping towards the shed anxiously, listening to each icicle crack. Back in the main

room she warmed Olwen's feet in the pony's breath,
while it slowly relieved itself on the floor, its warmth,
sounds and smell somehow comforting... As she began
to nod, the door cracked violently open and a flurry of
snow blew through the room. Spinning she found Jock,
face mauve, feet cut by ice, torn and bleeding. Quickly
pushing the table against the broken door she sat him
down and rubbed his feet with lard, hot tears of guilt and
shame for being angry with him splashing on to the floor.
Above, Jock stared at their stew pot hissing on the fire
and clasped Olwen. He was oblivious. The past was
forgotten... Outside the wind gathered itself for a fresh
assault on their house.

Chapter 10

Spring came with bird movement, life thrusting everywhere. Over the brow of the hill a lady on a fresh bay
appeared wearing a well-cut velvet riding dress and gloves.
On closer inspection, her face suggested a good, quiet,
hurt woman with breeding and class but a woman who
accepted rather than challenged. Her eyes passed over the
shabby dwelling below and she turned her horse, moving
down through the fresh foliage towards it.

Arriving, she stood on the step, wondering whether
to tap with the handle of her crop, remove her gloves and
knock or knock with gloves on. The decision seemingly
caused her some distress for looking about for a bell,
vague irritation registered on her face. As she paused, a
loud crash came from within and a shouted:

"No—!"

Knocking before she might overhear anything un-
seemly the lady leaned forward listening to a sudden
silence, then running steps and to her amazement instead

of the door being opened widely, the sound of a bolt
slamming into place.

"Who is it?" came a timid voice from within.

Embarrassed at having to describe herself she toyed
with various words.

"A—neighbour?" she offered.

At that the bolt scratched back and the face of the
girl, amazement writ large on it, appeared in the crack of
the door. Pushing her hair back the girl opened the door
wide and saw the woman hesitate as if uncertain about
entering. Wiping her hands on her skirt Ceci backed into
the room:

"Do please—won't you—come in?" she said, irritated
at herself for the servile tone she had slipped into and
determined, as the woman entered, to keep a better grip
on herself. She saw the woman was waiting but what for?
It had been so long since Ceci had seen anyone, especially
a Lady, she could hardly remember the social niceties.

"May I take your hat?" she asked, the words ringing
hollowly. "Will you take tea?"

Torn between dusting of the chair, taking the Lady's
hat and dusting the table to lay it there, Ceci was in an
obvious tizz. She saw the woman was clearly not at ease
and looking as if she was worried about sitting *any*where,
touching *any*thing in her less than spotless dwelling.

Quickly she boiled some water, dabbing at her hair
and examining her sorry fingernails which attested to a
hard winter without male help. She tried urgently to rub
the stains off the cups but it was too late and accepting it,
she carried the tray in. The woman, now seated like a
waxwork, turned to her and explained. She was from the
next property, or station, she said, donning her gloves
and drawing a map in the dust on the table top indicating
with pointed fingers and fine hands where her land
joined Ceci's and the way she had ridden down one side
of the boundary, clear around the bottom, up the road
headed to Moke, and in from that side.

"Is there not a nearer way?" asked Ceci. "If our
properties join?"

"*This* property—" the woman began, making Ceci
clearly aware she did not refer to it as "your property"
"—is—well—has always *been*—" She decided it best to let
the matter drop.

"*Nobody* comes here," Ceci sighed, meaning it more as a question than statement.

"How then do you manage?" asked the woman, shifting on her hard chair.

"Pedlars."

"How—if I may ask—," her voice faltered, "do you—'settle with'—them?"

"Sheep."

The woman's already suspicious face frowned a question.

"They slaughter 'em, keep half for themselves." Ceci shrugged.

"Half a sheep's a lot for a packet of seeds!" said the woman, unintentionally slipping into a conversation.

"They have to catch 'em too," Ceci smiled, "and they don't always."

The woman cast her eyes across the lines of preserved mutton and dried vegetables hanging in dark sooty corners and took in, in their journey, the daylight coming through the roof. Ceci watched her looking—a mixture of pride in survival and shame at her memories of how proper houses looked—yet she could not help warming towards the presence of another human, a sane one and, what's more, a woman. She filled her cup again without asking while the woman, knowing her staring was not resented and that the girl liked her, pulled off her gloves, took the cup gingerly and indulged herself in a thorough scrutiny of the entire room.

"It was a hard winter," Ceci said.

"It often is."

She could not read the meaning behind the woman's words but suddenly as if coming from another world, she got to the purpose of her visit.

"My name is Moira. Moira Laird."

"I'm Ceci."

"Ceci . . . ?" she queried, as if first names were of no consequence in a society where only second names implied ownership.

"Bowen," Ceci stammered, resenting the interrogation.

"Bowen," repeated the woman thoughtfully.

"I'm Mrs. Ceci Bowen," said Ceci in as firm a voice as she could manage, flashing her ring at Mrs. Laird, her face saying "I'm a decent married woman, this is my place and that's an end of it."

"To come straight to the point," Mrs. Laird began. "Eleven days ago our cook hanged himself. There is no point in explanations." She brushed away the irrelevance of the idea, missing the frown gathering on Ceci's face. "We are also without a maid which, as you may imagine, is quite awful."

Suddenly Ceci found herself looking hard at the woman.

"The size of our station," she went on, "means we have a large seasonal staff of working men with big appetites. Now Calvin has been down to the Immigrant Barracks," she said, dismissing the futility of the situation with a wave of the hand, unaware of Ceci's eyes narrowing, "but there's a shortage!" She threw her hands out.

"Of what?" Ceci asked, resenting her talking about people as if they were cattle.

"Cooks," Mrs. Laird said. "And we cannot continue! At times I am even *alone* in the house," she sighed, "when Calvin is away. Usually we have a housegirl too but—"

Ceci began to feel angry.

"To come *straight* to the point—' Mrs. Laird went on as if she had not been straight enough already, "we knew you were here—"

"And you were wondering if I'd help out!" Ceci finished for her.

"To tide us over till the next lot comes in," Mrs. Laird nodded, "the next ship . . ."

Ceci crossed, moved to the window and kept her back to the woman.

"I'd pay very well," came the voice from behind. "*Any*thing you asked. And there are clothes you can cut down—"

"And what's wrong with *you* when it comes to cooking?" Ceci said spinning on her.

Taken aback but no stranger to rudeness, Mrs. Laird stuck to the point.

"It's too small a world for us to—disagree," she said gently.

Instantly Ceci felt shamed.

"I thought you came to visit as a neighbour," she mumbled. "Would you have come here otherwise?"

Mrs. Laird hesitated. Obviously she would not have.

"Would you have helped at 'my time'?" Ceci demanded, pointing at the baby.

"I'd have had you brought up to the house, certainly I would!" Mrs. Laird retorted.

There was a short silence during which Mrs. Laird's hands traced the tumble-down state of the dwelling.

"It can't be easy for you living like this!" she said. "You don't intend to *continue. Surely!?*"

"*This* is my *home*. I *like* it!" shouted Ceci, dismayed to hear her voice rising so childishly. "I *own* it!"

Hastily Mrs. Laird got to her feet.

"I'm a married woman. I'm not a servant!" Ceci announced from the doorstep, confused and saddened at her own outburst, watching her visitor reach her hands up to grasp at her saddle as if anxious to flee the place.

"Mrs. Laird—" she called, desperately running towards her, "as a *neighbour*—I'll help you."

"Why *thank* you Mrs. Bowen," said Mrs. Laird sliding from her horse, warmth and a look of relief suffusing her face.

"How *kind* of you. How *very* kind!" she hurried towards her, a hand outstretched. "*When* can you come?"

Filled with joy at the friendship, the other woman's acceptance and the idea of going, Ceci bubbled:

"My stepson has—special requirements..."

"I'm sure we can fit him in," said Mrs. Laird, barely taking in the meaning of the words.

As luck would have it at that moment Jock chose to appear around the side of the barn, the usual complement of mud and straw in his hair. Seeing Mrs. Laird, he stared fascinated.

"Are you going to come over and say hello nicely?" Ceci called to him. Shyly Jock came forward, the tip of one finger in his ear, amazed at the sight of Mrs. Laird in her smart clean clothes.

"Mrs. Laird, I would like you to meet my stepson— Jock Bowen," she said, deciding Mrs. Laird's reaction was vital to anything that might happen between them.

"Hallo dear," Mrs. Laird said enthusiastically to the grown man. "Are you a good boy?"

Warmth flowed over Ceci as she squeezed Jock's hand.

"Go and wash, Jock," she said softly. "It'll take a couple of days to get him ready."

"Shall we say Monday?"

So overcome was she by Ceci's generosity in falling in with her plans she could do no more than shake her hand up and down as if to say, "I can't tell you how grateful I am!"

Bright lights streamed through the open door by which Ceci knelt, re-sewing a button on Jock's fly, fastening his belt and tucking in his shirt. A packed carry-all was on the floor and behind her the room was spick and span, every pot and basin polished and shining and Jock, like a boy on his first day to school, waiting in his "church-going" clothes, hair well parted and plastered down.

"Get some nice clothes for you up there my boy and *no* mistake," said Ceci, a pin in her mouth. "Turn around now." Behind her on the table lay a small pile of folded baby clothes and beside them a box, Olwen asleep within.

"You'll do," said Ceci bending to kiss her. "Now not five minutes now," she called to Jock as he ran through the door like a child going on holiday. "Because they'll *be* here! Walk about but don't touch anything."

Carefully she started to re-fold the pathetically worn pile of baby bits and torn towelling which passed as nappies, trying to conceal their poverty.

"Don't know what she'll make of these!" she said remembering Mrs. Laird's smartness. "Still, we are as we are!"

In his clean clothes, being careful not to touch anything and to step around puddles, Jock hovered obediently in the centre of the track, his eyes wandering from side to side until suddenly his attention was caught by a bird moving in a bush top. Motionless he stared into the leaves, so absorbed that he did not see a carriage rounding the corner and coming into view. Fifty yards off the driver quietly brought the carriage to a halt, tucked his whip under the arm of his velvet jacket, got down and began to creep silently forward, at the last minute running and taking Jock totally by surprise, laying about him with his whip and driving him off the path. As Jock leapt into the bushes the man spun. Where was he? Where was the Idiot? He looked around, listened for frightened breathing and started to pace clicking his whip to his boots. Click, click. Pace. Pace. Pace. Click. Spin. Click click pace pace. Spin. Aha! The Idiot was in the bush! Determined to frighten him more he stood with his back to the bush, clasping and unclasping the whip behind him and listening as the breathing grew louder and louder and as it climaxed, spinning and thrashing wildly at the bush in a spasm of rage.

"Come on Jock—on parade," Ceci called from the doorstep, turning to run back into the house for a thing remembered. Every nerve in her body was excited at the prospect of going away. Hearing the coach rattle to a stop she burst through the door again to have her excitement snatched away and replaced by utter amazement on seeing who was driving the coach. It was the man who had stared at her house and frightened her so badly that day! There he was, looking down on her from the seat above, doing nothing to put her at ease, his stern manly face expressionless.

"Are *you*—'Calvin'?" she asked, curiosity giving her the courage to speak first. He barely nodded.

"I thought—Calvin was Mrs. Laird's husband—" she began, seeing his eyes pass idly away from her and across her boxes, implying that what she had said needed no reply and she was actually keeping him waiting.

"Well I have to wait for Jock!" she announced, folding her arms, making him shift in his seat. "I'm not leaving without him!"

Turning on her heel she marched towards the barn to begin her search of the wash-house, the stables and any other corner he might be hiding in for the sheer joy of being found by her. Really the man had an infernal cheek when it was *she* who was doing *them* the favour! Turning, she saw he had actually descended from the coach and was already loading her boxes as if they would leave regardless when the coach was loaded! And now he had gone into her house and was coming out with the box with the baby in it!

"Mind!" she cried, running at him. "Put that down!" To see a man handle her baby, swing it above his head in the air made her insides twist in a new way and she was sure he'd delighted in doing it! She would certainly make sure he didn't do that again!

Frowning she went into the house to make up a bed for Jock on the floor. It was just too bad he should vanish like this: he could have gone anywhere! At times he followed rabbits, birds... Sighing, she left a homemade sausage, a jug of water and a mug on the table, brought out a knife and tested the blade for sharpness, hastily replacing it with a blunter one.

"Ridiculous!" she said under her breath. "Where is he?"

"Probably waiting at the gate," came an indolent voice from behind her and turning she saw the man was actually leaning in *her* doorway, propping himself on the frame and looking directly at her. He had spoken in cultured, not unconcerned tones and there was a certain arrogance to his stance which attracted her. She took care to cover her surprise with sternness.

"Well I'll have to come back every day so if you don't mind catching my pony—"

"We've horses—" the man drawled.

"I'll take my pony," Ceci insisted, "if you don't mind."

As the man removed himself from her doorway she caught a hint of annoyance mixed with power in his eyes. Following him out she climbed on to the water-butt, then on to the roof and began shouting for Jock:

"Jock!? Can you hear me?! You *be* here tomorrow! When I get back! You *wait* for me!"

She listened carefully to the sky.

"If you're not here—I'll come back every day to feed you! Do you hear?"

Again she waited then scrambled down. "It really is too bad," she said to herself, thinking of him.

Hiding in the bush he had been whipped into, Jock heard the coach approach and tried to shrivel into a smaller ball in case the man should get off and menace him again. As the coach drew closer, he saw the terrible legs of the man and his leather boots with the hard heels on them at the front. As its window passed he glimpsed sideways on the face he loved going away from him, out of his life. Then the last terrible thing, the pony, running behind on a long rope. Coming out of the bush he stood shaking, hurt and abandoned, in the middle of the track as the coach receded from view.

Within, Ceci pressed her face curiously to the win-

dow as the coach reached the main track and turned left
instead of right. She was going away from Moke for the
first time. For a while they continued along on the flat
before turning abruptly again at what she guessed to be
the boundary to her property and gradually the track
began to rise to higher land. Now she could appreciate
that the gulley she had come from was no more than a dip
between hills for all around the High Country rolled on in
undulating folds, like an elevated plateau. As the coach
crested one such ridge, a working man on a horse rode
towards them and came alongside.

"Take her in, Sam," said Calvin changing places with
the man, handing over the reins and easing himself carefully on to the other horse. To her amazement, from the
window Ceci suddenly saw him observing them from a
hill. How very rude, she thought, having collected her on
behalf of his mother, to allow her to arrive unaccompanied like a kitchen servant. Doubtless the coach was
under control but for all she knew, he had somehow
managed to abandon her in the middle of the wilderness.
Quickly she swung to the other window as the coach
straightened out and saw before her a sight which took
her breath away. Suddenly—in all this wilderness and
straggle—a sweeping driveway beginning out of nothing
and within its curves, the unbelievable: a lawn. Weeded,
mown, rolled—in every way perfect. On the extremity of
the curve sat the house, Hexham itself: two-storeyed,
gabled, and made of finely pared wooden planking, its
windows shining in the sun, its roof tiled, a real brick
chimney and a verandah-porch partly enclosed with lattice—
over which creepers climbed, draped themselves, and
bright plants bobbed in pots. To one side was a well-
established and maintained garden to include young fruit
trees and currant bushes. Ceci viewed it all, aghast.

Holding her baby on her hip, mouth open in wonder,
she stood on the highly polished wooden floor, breath
indrawn, surrounded by graceful antique furniture while
before her Mrs. Laird in soft clothes waited in a shaft of
sunlight. She saw the girl swaying, and led her through a
doorway into a large room.

Once again Ceci was stunned. That grand old fireplace! The floors graced with white embroidered Kashmiri
mats, a wine-red weathered Afghan carpet, sideboards,

Old Imari bone china, silverware...Watched by Mrs. Laird she plopped on to a piano stool, one hand to her face.

"What's the matter?" said Mrs. Laird.

"It's just—it's—so *beautiful*," said Ceci haltingly, defeated.

"Did you live in a house like this once?" Mrs. Laird asked.

"I helped clean one!"

"We had our 'effects' sent out," Mrs. Laird continued.

"It's so—" Ceci grasped at the air with her hands to pluck words which did not come.

"Of course the garden was established before we bought, though not the lawn," Mrs. Laird nodded. "Around 1850–56 I think. Acquired in '62 and divided. It used to be 40,000 acres this run—We took over in '66...The place seemed 'right.' Calvin's very proud of the lawn."

Ceci rose, a grin on her face.

"Show me the kitchen!"

Overawed, she stood in the room allocated to her. Far too large for a servant's room, it was more like a room planned for or lived in by an elder daughter. Again, the refined furniture—the rugs and pictures. She crossed to the window to look out then turned abruptly to examine a satin lined wicker cradle put there obviously for the use of her baby.

Evening found her in the large, well-equipped kitchen, a mound of scrapings and peelings before her and to one end of the long table, bread and piled clean bowls awaiting. Behind her pots simmered and boiled. A little flustered and unaccustomed to cooking for so many, she was giving herself constant advice.

"Right," she said touching the vegetable peelings. "Keep that for the pigs. Save one for Jock." She popped a pie into the cupboard. "Nearly ready there." She lifted the lid on a pot. There was a knocking on the outer door. Pausing, hair stuck to her forehead, escaping steam burning her arm, she dropped a pot lid. Appreciative noises were coming from without. Wrapping a cloth round her arm she called:

"Alright you can come in—"

The men started to push in, big and dirty, dissolute, simple or shifty looking.

"Just two of you!" she burst out, inspiring the two already inside to push the door on the faces of those beyond.

"And take off those boots!"

"Can't go without boots," said the bigger man, a ruffian whom she sensed disliked taking orders from her.

"You make a chain and pass it out," she went on over cries of "let us come in" and hammerings on the door. As she turned to the stove the ruffian deliberately slid his filthy hand along her arm. She spun, catching him round the face with her cloth.

"Right! Outside you!"

With sullen ill-will he left the room.

"Ready?" she said to the other one. He nodded and plates, dishes, pots of food began to flow through the door.

"Put the slops in the bucket," she called, "and bring the plates back scraped clean and rinsed."

"Last one didn't make us!" came a rude shout from beyond as the men dispersed towards their "cookhouse" with the food. She had a mind to shout: "And wash your hands," after them but felt it might be unwise. Cautiously she closed the door, eyeing the bolt, then turned and sank utterly exhausted at the table. She let out a long sigh and through half closed eyes became aware she was the object of someone's scrutiny and looking up saw a clean and serene Mrs. Laird at the inner door composedly watching.

"Well done," she said.

"Oh I forgot you!" Ceci leapt up, at once the servant. She began to hustle a tray.

"Will you eat with me?" Mrs. Laird invited.

"Oh I couldn't take another step!"

"It's only the season." She shook her head. "We don't usually have so much in hand. In fact," she went on, "I have never seen half of them before!" Was she trying to make a joke of the amount of work? "I think they just come for the meals!"

Ceci was amazed.

"Doesn't your husband—?"

"My husband," Mrs. Laird paused, "was caused to— pass on—a considerable time ago—"

"What about Calvin? Will he eat?"

"I'll—deal with—him—later," she said, a change coming over her.

It did not take long for Ceci to get into a rhythm at Hexham and soon it was as if she had always been there. In some ways it reminded her of life on the Estate where people did their jobs, got on with it, and enjoyed whatever benefits existed. But whereas on the Estate duties were carefully apportioned to different people, here it was she who did everything within the house and the labouring men apparently who did everything outside. They had no permanent stake anywhere and, it seemed, drifted across the country like leaves sticking where they would, working or not working, and not expecting to form permanent ties. It looked as if the men were the responsibility of the foreman, Sam, though Calvin was obviously the overseer, but while he held the whip hand, she had never seen mud on his clothes or the sweat of a decent day's work on his brow. He moved silently about, his lack of speech stopping just short of being rude so that at times she wondered if it was indifference or ice or whether his politeness was a way of protecting himself from involvement with less interesting people such as she and his mother. Did he believe this was the kind of treatment their status decreed? In the small details, he could not be defaulted. It was in the larger things he failed. There was an enormous part of him like desert, on the edge of which Ceci hovered, unable to see across or determine what lay at its centre. Were there the remains of things eaten away by the wind, or simply nothing? She had read in the *London Gazette* that the desert was full of houses that had fallen to pieces and returned to sand, once the people who had lived in them had gone away. Like relationships that were no longer inhabited they had become empty and the wind had passed over them once. Then again. And then again. And one day, they were not there. But looking at the sand, people could speculate that once there was life . . .

She did not realize how prophetic these fanciful thoughts were, but put them down to the refined surroundings of Hexham, chiding herself that in the entire time she had been in Bowen's gully, she had not given a single thought to the *London Gazette*.

Usually she rode down looking for Jock and taking his supplies in the still hours of the afternoon, it giving her pleasure both to leave the Big House behind and return to it. Sometimes she encountered Calvin on the way. "Come on Calvin—move out of the way," she would say good naturedly, wondering what it was about her that clearly amused him. "I'm riding over to look for Jock."

"Will I accompany you?" he would ask, turning his horse, moving apace with her.

"No, but if you could indicate a shorter route I'd be obliged. Why go all around when our lands join—"

To her surprise, Calvin had dismounted at once, pulled the pliers from his pocket and made two neat snips in the wire and fastened it back. This was a quite uncharacteristic act, she knew, for previously the sight of a single loose fence attachment which had allowed the wire to trail a few inches from the post had caused him to be angry beyond all measure, though his fences went on in waves and waves unchallenged, across the hills.

"If you'd care to cross through here," he had said, "that being *your* land and follow that crest down to the gully you will see the *place* inside of ten minutes." Something in the way he said *"place"* gave the impression he found the dwelling quaint.

"I don't see what you find so funny!" she said indignantly. "Or why you'd go to all the trouble of riding around—"

"Your late—*husband*—" Calvin interrupted, "was known to *discourage* visitors." He paused, making it difficult for her to know whether he was teasing her about her husband or being sarcastic. "With a shotgun."

"Was he a good shot?" Ceci asked.

Calvin shifted slightly on his horse. "We chose to ride around."

Ceci laughed, delighted at Old Bowen's bloody-mindedness, now her own, and turning her pony through the gap looked back at him, so dignified, exactly like something from Lord Knevitt's china cabinet! Did he think he was a Doulton Cossack!? She felt a deep grin creep across her face. Calvin remained imperturbable, sideways on.

"Will I come with you?" he asked in a deep voice.

"*You* can ride around!" she joked, tossing her head and cantering off down the incline.

Arriving, the shoddiness of the dwelling hit her each time anew. As she moved towards its open door, calling for Jock, a glance told her he had been recently there, trampling her seed beds.

Moving into the room she saw the makeshift bed hadn't been used and apart from a muddy footprint on the table there was little sign of his presence yet this was not surprising for in better weather he often stayed away for days. What had he been climbing on the table for, she wondered, looking up at the rafters. Aha! He was collecting feathers again, she realized, seeing them carefully hidden there. Getting down, she knocked over a chair and, stooping, saw half the sausage she had left under the table and crumbs everywhere, clear evidence that Jock, not rats, had done the gnawing and dropping.

Laying the bundle she had brought to one side, she gave the table a good scrub before putting on the old tablecloth Mrs. Laird had insisted she take. With pride Ceci smoothed it out and set the food on it, the pies, three hard boiled eggs and a fresh pitcher of water. Standing back she looked at the eggs, cracked the shell of one and half eased it off to give him the idea . . . This was certainly a vastly superior spread to what he was used to! Taking the broom, she swept the room clean and went out to straighten and water her seedlings.

Before leaving she climbed on to the roof, looked in all directions and, mustering all the force and authority into her voice she could she shouted: "Your food's on the table." She peered again around the horizon. "And *wash* your hands!" she shouted at it, confident he could hear.

From the top of a hill Jock happily watched her going. He liked their new arrangement and took his food to all his favourite places to eat. Particularly he liked to see her climb on the roof and shout and when his name echoed around the hills in her voice he felt inordinate pleasure! Now he watched her riding back up the new way she'd discovered, the blurred path he'd long known leading to Hexham. On an impulse he began to run parallel, just out of sight, scrambling up cliffs, ducking under roots and keeping her in view, but when they came in sight of the fence where Bowen's land ended, he instinctively drew back and turned away. This was where he lived. This was where he belonged. This was Home.

Chapter 11

In her heart, Mrs. Laird thought it one of life's crushing injustices that she had not been at the Immigrant Barracks the day Ceci had landed. The girl was extraordinarily skilled in the kitchen, drawing on a vast repertoire of dishes which, frankly, Mrs. Laird in all generosity of heart could not imagine where she had learned. The way she carried herself from room to room, her natural easy grace and familiarity with the names of artists and the makes of better brands of china was disconcerting. Perhaps it was nothing for one in her station to be able to talk of Constables and Gainsboroughs but to be able to pin the right name on the right painting meant either a love of art or enforced visits to galleries. In their occasional conversations, the girl was likely to come out with ideas and references quite removed from her probable background. Indeed, Mrs. Laird herself had been brought up to relate to art only insofar as she could make appropriately stimulating remarks to her husband's visitors, to encourage them to say something really stunning. Her curiosity was frequently primed when she saw Ceci, in dusting an item, turn it over, look at the base for a name and fade momentarily into nostalgia. Obviously the girl had at some time been in a situation where she was allowed to move with relative ease amongst the accoutrements of a better class person. It was just a shame that that was where the breeding stopped for once the splinters and grime had gone from her fingertips . . . Well, let us just say, it was unfortunate . . .

Returning from the dwelling, Ceci guessed Mrs. Laird would be in the upstairs room and decided to sit with her.

Of late she no longer went daily to the dwelling but,
attuning herself with Jock's ways, went twice a week
leaving more food and spending more time there in the
hopes he would appear. Now she tapped gently on the
sewing-room door and entered. Mrs. Laird looked friendly, approachable, doing the accounts which Ceci knew she
did not enjoy, puzzling over them, adding up figures and
scratching them out on bits of paper. Beside her on the
table lay a pencil snapped in half and behind her the small
cradle with Olwen asleep within. Glad of the excuse, Mrs.
Laird nodded at Ceci, got up, took Olwen, crossed to the
window and began to jig her. Looking at her it was
impossible not to sense her sadness as, with the force of a
long dead habit, she spread one hand across the baby's
back, the thumb supporting her neck, and with the other
made a seat for her behind. Why, Ceci asked herself, had
Mrs. Laird brought the cradle out from England with her?
She caught a softness on the woman's face, a melancholia,
as she turned half aware of Ceci kneeling, examining the
cradle. Ceci crossed and joined her at the window and
together they stared out. Below, Calvin was angrily pulling up a small weed that had sprouted in the gravel.

"He can't stand anything that isn't perfect—" Mrs.
Laird murmured.

"He's proud of this place—" said Ceci.

"It's all he's got!" burst Mrs. Laird, not realizing until
she had said it the terrible truth that there was something
important lacking in his nature. The two women leant
forward to peer down on Calvin as he stooped over the
weed. *What* was he, Ceci asked herself. Handsome, yes.
Intelligent, strong, reserved, proud—all these things—
yes. But beyond that—nothing came *out*. There was no
indication of the person inside, of what he was *really* like.
As Ceci, Mrs. Laird and Olwen looked down unseen on
the Man of the House, sensing it, Calvin looked up.
Seeing them he let his eyes pass quickly over them without acknowledgement and rose, walking away out of their
sight.

Hexham put Ceci in mind of poor old Lord Knevitt's or
the Earl as she should rightly have called him. The dear
old man! She remembered how he'd sneaked her, all of 5
years old, through a cold stone passage of uneven flags,

dying flower arrangements, things which belonged in neither pantry nor sheds and into his study. There were the shells he'd "brought back" from foreign shores, stones, strange iron devices and canisters which had an interesting smell. He had shown her a padlock from Tibet. Did she know Tibetans made tea in a butter churn? That *that* etching was actually Cairo though the writing was French... that that was how the men dressed *there*, he'd explained. And *this* was called Japanese Lacquer...

The good old man had talked about whole villages of Chinese women who never married because they tended silkworm larvae; of the bread of Central Asia, flat like snowshoes; the colours on the ice when the day began in Arctic wastes; of men chasing the fabled unicorn, the narwhal; of many shocking and strange things she instinctively knew she must never repeat to her mother, her playmates, or *anyone*! When footsteps sounded she had stood behind a screen and witnessed Lord Knevitt's chastisement: "Dinner *was* announced. Don't talk to yourself."

How his wife had disliked that room! The book-lined shelves; the notebooks piled on the floor on expensive mats which should have been straightened and shaken; the dirty cups that could be seen under the sofa; his pine cones, clocks, pressed flowers, stuffed birds, maps and broken globes! The compasses, sherry bottles and telescopes on his cluttered mantelpiece! The muddle of a mind so fascinated by life it could not cut down a thistle without enumerating its "medicinal properties." He had been a really grand old man, thought Ceci, looking up. A real hereditary gentleman!

As Mrs. Laird observed Ceci, who was sewing opposite her, she noticed a soft smile spread on her face and felt the atmosphere of comfort and acceptance between them.

"Don't know that clothes *mean* much to Jock," Ceci said, "but there's no harm in him *having* decent things..."

"Take some hens when you go back," suggested Mrs. Laird. "Start a run."

Ceci nodded, pins in her mouth. The thought of hens at the dwelling and how Old Bowen would have liked them scrambling about, jumping on and off his chair, amused her.

"There's a bit to keeping fowl," continued Mrs. Laird, a curious remark to come from her for Ceci was sure she'd never had to handle a hen.

"What I'd really like," Ceci confided, "is a cow. Funny to sit here fancying a cow. I'd really like one!"

"At home one would never even think of it," said Mrs. Laird modulating her voice skilfully to strike the right balance between decorum and cordiality, and re-introducing her needle to her sampler to indicate the subject had gone far enough.

"The more you can do out here for yourself..." agreed Ceci, bending her head to her stitching.

Mrs. Laird nodded at the unfinished thought, then, driven by her own curiosity though aware of the impertinence, laid down her work and set about nosing out the circumstances of Ceci's marriage.

"Long periods with nothing to think of—" she began. "One has heard, of course, of interest in the—'older man'—in wedlock. Not that I've experienced it myself..." she left it floating.

"Did you know him?" Ceci asked lightly.

Mrs. Laird shook her head. What an extraordinary question. How could she possibly have had any truck with a person in Bowen's Gully? She bent to her work. After a pause observing her, Ceci began:

"What was your husband like?"

This genuinely flummoxed Mrs. Laird. She stared intently at a curtain, shaking her head.

"Like father—like son," she shrugged. "Which, unfortunately, women find attractive." She looked guardedly at Ceci wondering whether in fact if the girl had "noticed" her son...

"My mother embroiders," Ceci said innocently. Mrs. Laird looked up, amusement bordering on the rude hovering on her face.

"Not *samplers*?" she queried.

"Pillowslips, cushions."

"For sale?" asked Mrs. Laird.

"For her—room—" said Ceci, conscious of the fact that her truthfulness in describing her mother's situation as a "room" would not have escaped the older woman's notice.

"Were your family in service?" asked Mrs. Laird sharply.

"We were attached to a Lord Knevitt's estate in Cheshire. My father was Head Groom," Ceci replied honestly.

"Is that where you learned to ride?" pursued Mrs. Laird.

"Heavens no! Mother wouldn't let us *near* horses after the Estate!" She quickly changed the subject. "Did *you* want to come out here?"

"Can't go back now. Calvin won't let me." Mrs. Laird shrugged, reminding herself that, however tempting it was, she must not talk about personal matters. "You were saying you were attached to an Estate," she prompted.

"My father was Head Groom," Ceci said quickly. "He was kicked in the leg by a horse. They settled him in a small pub in the Dales, but he didn't do much. Two years later, a blood clot slowly making its way up—"

Mrs. Laird eyed the girl, talking quickly, head down possibly to hide her emotions.

"He was sat by the window, looking out over the forest, then he said: 'Lin—I'm dying—' My mother join d her sister in London. My elder sister went into service. The middle one died of consumption, and I left."

It seemed easier to say it all in a rush.

"Why did *you* leave?" she added.

Mrs. Laird was taken aback both by the fact and the content of the question.

"Man's greed—the urge to conquer—" she stumbled "—to establish themselves . . . which usually means destroying something else . . ." her voice trailed off. That had been quite a profound sentence, she told herself. But was it true? So often with this girl she found herself saying magniloquent things. It was as if her mind, like a convalescing muscle, were suddenly beginning to invigorate.

"I wanted to work with children out here," said Ceci. "But it clings . . ."

"What?" Mrs. Laird said, allowing herself the usage of the common word.

"Being a servant," Ceci shrugged.

For a while they stitched on. This was the first time

Ceci had told another person out loud about her father's death. The kick of a horse! The phrase had not done it justice. Though she had been no more than eight years old, that precise kick had engraved itself on her mind. It had changed their lives for ever!

Her father had been leading Miss Immelda, Lord Knevitt's youngest daughter, to be "helped down." Her face had been piqued, not with cold but with anger because that disgusting child of the groom, Ceci, for whom she had several punishments in store, had seen her fall from her horse.

"Get me down!" she snapped.

"Yes, Miss." Her father had stood sideways, ready to help her down.

"My crop!"

He'd looked around.

"Over there, fool!"

It hurt and infuriated Ceci to watch her father stepping after the crop deliberately thrown by the nine-year-old girl. As he bent to pick it up, Ceci had seen Immelda draw something from her lapel. Returning, her father had stood before the horse, his face concealed by its steaming breath rising in the cold November afternoon. He did not see Immelda plunge the hat pin into the horse's ear. Ceci had seen. Unaccountably, to his way of thinking, the horse's leg shot out, knocking him down.

"Calvin has decided on a party," Mrs. Laird informed, recalling Ceci from her reveries. Was there no limit to the use they would make of her, she wondered, at the same time reproving herself for having "done very well" out of them.

"I'll be happy to help," she smiled. "You've been good to me and Jock."

At that moment the other party to Mrs. Laird's generosity sat mesmerized by the sunset eating one of Mrs. Laird's pies, oblivious of the ants lovingly carrying away the pastry crumbs beneath him. As he lifted the pie to scratch at a spider on his ear, it broke against the side of his head, sending chopped meat showering over his shoulder and into the grass to the further delight of the little things. The sun was sinking slowly, its great golden eye slipping down with that marvellous certainty that so fascinated Jock at the exact same spot it had vanished the day before, a place where the folds of two hills met. As he stood, part of him wanted to walk towards the dark purple spot where the sun had gone, but the lengthening shadows told him, though the sky might be fire-red, he should heed the order of things and return now to his lair.

Up in the Big House, the women of Hexham made ready for the party Calvin did not want.

"*I'm* exhausted already!" said Mrs. Laird. She was in fact seated holding Olwen and her entire contribution to the activity so far had been to wear a full length apron. Ceci took Olwen and sat down and Mrs. Laird rose.

"It's things like this they don't think of when they drag you out here!" she sighed, knocking over a pot of cream.

"Look what you can do when you have to!" Ceci put in.

"I once made bread in this kitchen," the lady confided. "I thought I'd won the Derby!"

"Would anyone eat it?"

"Well of course he complained," she went on, referring to her husband. "Though where else *would* one learn to make bread but a book?!"

Ceci nodded in sympathy.

"Don't misjudge me," Mrs. Laird continued. "I'm the first to admit times have changed—"

"The sauce is burning!" Ceci called. Rather than remove the sauce, Mrs. Laird backed away from the stove. Ceci got up to relieve her. "Calvin asked me to stay on and break in the new cook," she said grasping the saucepan with a potholder. Behind her Mrs. Laird flinched. She did not like Ceci referring to Calvin as "Calvin."

"I can only apologize for his horrible cheek," she said, her voice two degrees cooler, glaring at Ceci's back. Competent or not, it was time the girl went home. Even in the circumstances that had obtained, to have tolerated the presence of a servant living as a household member for so long had been a clear oversight for which they were now paying. She smiled with difficulty, as her thoughts pursued each other in meaningless circles. Suddenly she became aware of Calvin in the doorway, frowning at the smell of burning sauce. Quickly she ran to him.

"I want you to be *especially* careful and make an effort

with the Pinn-Herriotts tonight," she begged, making his
nerves jangle. He resented his mother directing his ways
and could not resist taunting her. Quickly he looked past
her at Ceci, her back to him at the stove, and said in a low
voice:

"Why go to town when you can shop locally?" He felt
gratified to see his words punch, shake and wind her. She
took a quick gasp of breath and reminded herself he could
not possibly have meant it. What a preposterous idea! It
was *typical* of him to make a hurtful remark and disappear. Would she never learn his ways of changing the
subject? Wondering at the silence Ceci turned from the
stove to find Mrs. Laird looking as if all her jewels had
suddenly been robbed!

It had not been lost on Calvin that Ceci, like himself, was
a person who could accept responsibilities, executing them
without the need of constant applause. He sensed they
were two people of equal power and independence, and
remembered with pleasure their confrontations on the
path when she had asked him to move out of the way.
Had she delayed or hovered, or expected kindness or
shown rage or attempted conversation, he would not
have been pleased. Equally had she attempted to inveigle,
interpret him or read his behaviour as in some way
pertaining to her, he would have closed up at once. But
with a toss of her head she had been off down to her
dwelling, as if for all the world he had ceased to exist.
This he liked very much. It was the certainty that she
would ride away from him each time, remain her own
person and not seek, as women did, to decant herself on
him, that made him feel infinitely safe and free for the
first time to take a tiny step towards making a friendship,
or as he saw it, "letting go."

Not that he would permit the beginnings of friendship to show on his face. The sensation of even imagining
letting go was without precedent in his life. No man being
swung across a chasm on a rope would loose his hands
simply because there was something below... Vaguely he
remembered from the nursery window watching children
his own age playing with each other, letting go, and
getting hurt for it. Worst of all, they'd lost face. But *he* had
been smart enough to hold himself back, which continual-

ly fascinated others while avoiding the danger of expo-
sure. Even though he was vaguely tempted to make
friends, in truth he could not see what people *wanted* with
them.

His mind returned to that first time he'd seen Ceci in
her garden. She had been realistic about its confines,
methodically checking her beans, tapping her one pumpkin. That sight had stayed with him. There, on the top of
the world, she had been getting on with her own life
without fuss or bother, involving no one. They neither of
them needed people, he mused, or the intrusion of people
wanting those sticky messes they called relationships.
How pleasant it was, beset by vicious conventions, to
meet a contractual person who did not continually interpret his behaviour in light of her own needs and aspira-
tions. As long as he could remember his mother had
ascribed to him motivations and desires he did not pos-
sess. Living under the same roof with a person who
refused to take the care to observe one truthfully was
frustrating in the extreme. He knew what she wanted!
Had she not made it abundantly clear, reinforcing it over
the years? If occasionally he hurt her with his behaviour,
surely the cause of the hurt was not he but her own
foolish beliefs and the selfish attitudes she used like
hammers to smite him with and bamboozle herself! In the
last resort her attitude was a trespass, he consoled himself. Indeed the woman deserved what she got. Never
would he stoop to acting out female-imposed roles nor
make it easier for them by explaining he was not any of
the things they wanted or insisted he might be.

Mrs. Laird moved cautiously around checking everything. Candlelight, chandeliers, adjoining doors open.
Everything was perfect. Soon the place would be full and
this would be an evening to remember! Her mind went
back to her young days in Huntingdon and Calvin's own
father! What a handsome, handsome man! She could still
see him standing beyond the grand piano. How thrilled
she had been! This was the man the people spoke of as a
person going somewhere. His eyes when he turned had
not belied the report. Dark, burning with a fierce intensity, they passed through and over her as if approving her
for some pressing mission. Her mind fleeted out on to the
verandah with him. The chill May air, the smell of damp

from the rhododendron bushes... She turned, shutting
the door on it.

In the main room groups of well-heeled, expensive,
incompetent people, gentlefolk and interesting bachelors,
maiden sisters and "academics" who had ridden considerable distances and were putting up at surrounding stations were milling and exchanging murmurs with the
Cloth, sizing each other up greedily. Through the group
Mrs. Laird noticed a natural but glowing Ceci moving
about discreetly with a tray in her hand, Calvin introduc-
ing her as "our dear neighbour, Cecille Bowen" when the
need arose, but fortunately not associating with her. Murmurs of "Widowed did you say?" could be heard by Mrs.
Laird as she passed into the hallway. Perhaps it wasn't so
terrible her having been introduced as a neighbour. It did
at least explain why she was sharing the role of hostess,
indicating a silver tray of hors d'oeuvres here, sweet
biscuits there... Guests could not be expected to believe
with her bearing that she was entirely from the kitchen,
especially in that dress—one of Mrs. Laird's own which
she had cut down—and it went some way to explain her
indifferent manner towards them. There was no substi-
tute for breeding which this girl plainly hadn't got. Yet
when all was said and done it was an excellent spread and
the remark "They must keep a wonderful kitchen," which
she had overheard, had gone no little way to please her.
What was Calvin up to? Aha! There he was by the
window, his back to the room, staring out as if he were
completely alone. She moved to stand by him, linking her
arm lightly with his. He did not react. Her fingers could
have been a moth he had not felt. She sighed, used to it.

"It quite takes me back Calvin—the mingling—" she
breathed, prodding him somewhat sharply to get his
attention. "Why don't you talk to the Pinn-Herriott girls?"

"What?" said Calvin turning rudely.

"Over there dear. The Pinn-Herriotts," she repeated,
her voice patient. Slowly Calvin slid his eyes in the
direction of her discreet nod. There they were. Two sisters, charmingly got up in white muslin, mincing affection
for each other. He scathingly took in their thin noses,
tightly curled hair and useless hands. He felt he could
vomit.

"Miriam plays the piano quite beautifully," chatted his mother.

"So?" he said coldly as Miriam gave a nasal laugh.

"And Pinn-Herriott has a *lovely* run," she went on bravely.

"Not child-bearing hips," said Calvin staring from the window.

"I *beg* your pardon?" Mrs. Laird was shocked. "It's bad enough we *came* here! Without going the whole hog! The Misses Pinn-Herriott—"

Calvin pulled at his ear. "If Pinn-Herriott were worth anything he wouldn't have come."

"—speak Greek *and* Latin—" continued his mother.

"They hate it out here. And he was on the way down." How deeply did he have to hurt her before she would leave him alone?

"Well what about that one?" she persisted. Would she never quit this infernal pestering? The idea of sharing his life, in itself repulsive, was doubly so when enlarged to include not only a female person but one requiring conversation, dresses, even to occasionally *touch* him or cling to his elbow in public and worst of *all*, attention. Visions of married people he knew hammered at his mind. The women wincing, mincing, milling and cloying around their men, enforcing them to mindlessly act out humiliating roles. The men grinning, nudging each other as if maintaining one of these useless creatures were a "natural development" and never daring to admit in their cowardly way the whole thing was a big stupid lie. How he despised them! Women "needed" attention because they were allowed to have it. Even the kitchen women and cooks who were otherwise competent had constantly to let you know they were in the house clamouring for approval! Who could be bothered with persons who did not know their own worth?! Were women mere shadows of people? At times everything about them repulsed him.

He had to find some way to get around them, to settle the situation in *his* household, in the fastest, most efficient manner. It *would* go away, he was sure of it...

Coming back from his reverie he found his mother staring into his eyes as if she had been waiting for some time.

"I asked you," she said with laboured patience, "what you thought about that one?"

"Can she cook?"

"You're not even *looking* at her! It's the Turbot's Amelia!" she snapped.

"Probably can," Calvin yawned. Mrs. Laird ran her eyes over the dumpy pasty Amelia who was trying to disguise the fact she was picking a spot.

"She is rather awful," Mrs. Laird sighed.

"I don't know," Calvin teased her. At times when she stopped forcing her ways on him she was quite companionable. Looking across at them, Ceci saw Calvin smile gently at his mother as if they were sharing a moment. Not expecting humour from him, Mrs. Laird took it perfectly seriously.

"What pleasure could there be in a woman like that?" she demanded earnestly looking up at him.

"Are women for pleasure?" he asked passing through the doors onto the verandah just as the dancing was about to begin. Quickly Mrs. Laird followed him out, behind her the sound of music tinkling tinnily from her Victriola Polyphon as a young man cranked. Calvin did not need to look round to know who it was. Even standing behind him she felt his hackles rise.

"Well I worry about you!" she said defensively.

"Don't."

"I—I don't—think you even *like* women!"

Calvin stared across the lawn.

"What's to like?" he asked. Apparently it was going to take more than the odd remark to dislodge her tonight. He turned his back on the lawn, lent on the verandah, folded his arms and stared very hard at her.

"I said what's to like?" he repeated. Mrs. Laird was frightened, though of what she didn't know.

"I refuse to take responsibility for *that*!" she gasped.

"I am not getting saddled with a useless remnant of your idea of the world order! I apologize for my frankness."

That should do it.

"If you'd gone back for a *proper* education—" said Mrs. Laird, taking the bait marvellously. "Cambridge—"

"I'd have sat on my arse waiting for someone to help me up!" Calvin savagely replied watching her back slump as the starch went out of her frail bones, and she shrunk, shrivelled before him.

"You would most *certainly* not have spoken like that before me!" she burst out, almost in tears.

"Shut up, mother," he said softly.

"Down! Down! That's where this family is going!"

"Where else?"

Mrs. Laird straightened herself. "It's a wonder you can still use a fork!"

Stepping sideways to look around her Calvin let interest then fascination play on his face as if he were suddenly taken by the sight of a woman so attractive all other considerations paled. It was an expression which cost little to wear and one which he was sure would bring good returns. Ready to forgive all, Mrs. Laird spun to peer into the room amongst the dancing couples. She had to know whom Calvin was observing with that same burning intensity she had seen in his father's eye the night he chose her. *It was not, surely* it *could not be* . . . There against the wall, watching the event but clearly bored by it, was Ceci, seated in a male way, legs too far apart, almost "chewing grass" . . . You could put a pipe in her mouth, Mrs. Laird thought, looking up at Calvin and realizing with a horror that undermined the very essence of her being, that Ceci was indeed the object of his scrutiny. And it was not an appreciation of her innate usefulness she saw playing on his face. *That* she could understand! It was *desire*! Trembling, she summoned her last reserves of energy, turned and spat up at Calvin: "Get in there and dance with the Pinn-Herriotts!"

Dropping the expression which had cost him so little to wear, Calvin stepped off the verandah and out into the darkness.

For a few moments Mrs. Laird remained leaning, peering across the lawn. The light from the large windows flooded it but there were dark areas in which Calvin could be standing. She could not run after him or call. The idea was quite impossible. Turning on her heel she marched quickly back into the room, nerves making her close the verandah door, her hand fidgeting with the curtain. Nor could she stay in this room without people reading the expression of her face, she thought, hurrying to the hallway. She must find something to do! Something to lift, perhaps a plate of biscuits, and carry from one place to another. Looking up Ceci saw her hurriedly lift a plate of biscuits, catching the rim of a glass and sending it bouncing to the floor. Quickly she hurried over.

"Let me help you—"

"I can manage!" snapped Mrs. Laird. In amazement, Ceci stepped back.

Calvin stood outside in a long finger of shade, the lights and music reaching towards him followed by a high pitched giggle, the tinkle of a glass breaking, total silence, then everyone talking again. His face flashed revulsion. Disgusting drunken people! Standing fuming he was possessed of an intense, an overpowering desire to be elsewhere, to get away. Hurrying around to the stables, unmindful of his lack of jacket, his inadequate frilled party shirt, cummerbund and dance shoes, he took out his horse and rode into the sultry air, sensing there was a storm to come.

Inside the house Ceci watched Mrs. Laird and was sorry for her. People were asking after Calvin and a gap seemed to have opened up around her as she fumbled for an answer.

"He—he's attending to a guest," she murmured, covered in shame.

As Calvin rode he saw the lights of a carriage coming towards him. Late arrivals! He quickly turned his mount through the gap he had cut in the boundary fence between his property and Bowen's and in bursts of moonlight made his way down to the old dwelling. Arriving, anger at the sight of its imperfections tore at his mind. It was thrown together without any consideration, barely fit as a byre for pigs! That he who worked so hard, strove towards perfection, should be confronted with such a sight... The pain of persisting in a world where he, alone and unrecognized, gave all he had, tore at him. Engorged with rage he leapt on the roof and began to tear at its beams and wrench the thatch this way and that. He got hold of a beam and pulled—pull pull pull!—till it cracked, till the roof began to come apart in his hands.

Crouched by the barn, Jock watched with fear as his Home was destroyed. He saw the terrible Being drop from the roof, kick open the door and enter. Quickly he fled.

Inside, Calvin looked around savagely. Through the

gaps he had made he could now see the sky above, a big clear patch with distinct stars in it. He punched a poorly attached window dislodging it from its hinges, kicked the chairs on to their sides till only the board table and a particularly stalwart armchair remained standing. Taking the broom he knocked hams from the eaves and brought down the dark sides of mutton, fighting back the urge to defecate there, to use the filthy, fly-covered rat-infested byre as a dunny! On he went, breaking and destroying till his rage was spent and he stood heaving, surveying what he had done.

Outside Jock ran on through the night, fleet of foot and not needing the moon to guide him on the blurred track towards Hexham and Ceci. As he ran, his trousers slipped lower and lower on his legs, till finally he climbed out of them and threw them away. On he ran, the rhythm of his pounding feet matching the pounding of his heart. Without realizing it he crossed the boundary fence and slowing, found himself at the entrance to Hexham and beyond him saw the lights pouring on to its lawn.

"Where's that naughty Calvin?" asked Amy Pinn-Herriott. "Shall we look?"

"No. Ask his mother," said Miriam Pinn-Herriott, more circumspect in these matters, nodding towards Mrs. Laird who was peering from the window as if trying to make out something curious on the lawn.

Distracted by the light Jock drew nearer the house. With its curtains drawn back the sight was so enticing he could not resist and, minus his pants, he walked happily forward hearing music and seeing the nice lady he had met before pressing her nose to the glass and peering out at him. Suddenly it came to Mrs. Laird with a terrible clarity exactly what she was viewing. Quickly she swished the curtains across the french door but not before the Pinn-Herriott girls had glanced past her and seen with amazement the vanishing buttocks of Jock, frightened by the suddeness of Mrs. Laird's gesture. They stepped back, looking at Mrs. Laird as if she had somehow contrived this effect especially for their benefit. Mrs. Laird grimaced. Never in her life had she been exposed to such ridicule, such public torment. *All* she had endured this evening had been attributable to the Bowen girl. It was her presence which had encouraged her son to behave in such a wilful, an outrageous and utterly unmannerly fashion. Apart from dealing with the girl, tomorrow she would most certainly deal very firmly with Calvin.

The next morning hearing sounds below Mrs. Laird hastened from her bed and found Calvin casually wrapping cold cuts in a cloth as if nothing had happened.

"How *dare* you walk out of your own party!" she began.

He spoke without looking up. "It was *your* party."

Angered, Mrs. Laird snatched the food from him and began to rewrap it. "You don't do that kind of thing! Give it to me!"

Calvin sighed, leaned his huge indolent frame in the doorway and watched her fuss, drop things, knock his water bottle over.

"And you stay *out* of the kitchen!" she snapped. "Remember who you are!"

Calvin began to pick at a small wart on the back of his hand.

"I'll be glad when she's gone!" he heard her mutter. "Really I will."

"You've never liked any of the staff," he yawned.

"I don't *have* to! When they're *staff*!" she shouted, spinning on him righteously.

At that Calvin approached her angrily, making her tremble involuntarily and hold out his lunch bundle before her as if anticipating violence.

"Well you don't know where you are. Do you? A situation like this!" she pleaded.

Calvin wrenched the package from her hands, turned and stalked from the room. Running after him she caught hold of his elbow and shouted in a hoarse whisper, "You have no idea of the strain I've been under!"

"Mother, you make me sick," he said in a deep voice.

Instead of backing off, hurt, as he had anticipated, she rose magnificently to the occasion: "And you, Calvin," her voice rang out nobly, "may find yourself having to choose—!"

Suddenly with fear she realized the prophetic truth in those heat-of-the-moment words! How could she not have realized it *sooner*! It was imperative that she start making arrangements for the girl to go at once—yet contrive to make her attention seem innocent. As she worked towards this end she was surprised to encounter no hostility from Calvin.

Chapter 12

"You can't leave on a day like this!" Mrs. Laird said carefully, looking out at the leaden rain. "Stay over!" Ceci looked up.

From the woman's face, it was impossible to read her meaning. Calvin put a restraining hand on his mother's wrist.

"We must respect her decision," he said. He turned to Ceci. "You've been extremely kind to us. May I?" He poured her more tea.

His mother glared at him.

"Only being neighbourly," said Ceci, ignorant of the nuances. She took a slice of lemon which somehow riled Mrs. Laird, dropped it in her tea and smiled up at Calvin.

Mrs. Laird sought desperately for an entry point. Although things were going very well she must not be left out.

"We—we've become such—friends—" she stammered. "The house'll be quiet without you."

She was amazed to hear herself say this.

"But I'll be glad to be back," said Ceci.

"That's very natural," Calvin said, inclining his head towards her.

"You must visit—" interrupted Mrs. Laird, seriously disturbed by Calvin, who never talked at breakfast.

"And Olwen," said Calvin earnestly. "You must bring her—" Calvin had no use for babies whatsoever. Mrs. Laird frowned. Had she been tricked? What was happening?

"She's been comfortable here!" said Ceci, smiling at him. "She's had a nice time."

Calvin reached for a piece of toast. "Good for the chest—a dry house," he remarked.

By now Mrs. Laird was so badly out of her depth she did not bother to conceal it. The girl clearly was not impressed by Calvin, yet something was afoot.

"I don't suppose you'll find time to come and see us at *all* now!" she gulped, in retrospect feeling her tone might have been over-clear. Before her Ceci ate her breakfast as if she had all the time in the world. Well, their cook was already in the kitchen and that was that!

"I'm taking more than I came with," Ceci smiled at her in the hallway.

"Well you wouldn't accept any—any—" Mrs. Laird could not bring herself to use the word "money." Ceci leaned forward and embraced her.

"Goodbye Moira," she said. Over her shoulder Calvin saw the name jar.

"You will be—looking forward to the rest!" said his mother, stepping back, face pale from the exertion of being kissed. He grinned.

"I must get the place in hand before winter," Ceci said moving towards the door. At last she'd nearly gone. Two more steps and she would be over that lintel and out of her life forever!

"Now don't forget," she said with tears of relief, "any time you're—over this way—" Ceci looked out on the rain.

"I've to get the fowl settled in. Garden'll need work."

Calvin flicked his eyes from Ceci to his mother knowing this kind of male talk from a woman enraged her and seeing Ceci notice it. Unable to help himself he winked at her in amusement.

"And Jock's new clothes of course." Mrs. Laird ran on, feeling something she did not understand scuttle past.

Calvin strode out into the rain and began to load Ceci's boxes and cover them with a tarp. *Not even wearing his cape*! Following Mrs. Laird's frown Ceci turned and saw the water streaming off his head as he carefully knelt, fastened the tarp, climbed up front and nodded impersonally to her to join him. How brave he was! How very courteous! Ceci held Olwen forward for Mrs. Laird to give a last kiss then, clutching her to her chest, bent double and ran through the rain to the open door and scrambled in. Before she had time to wave they were off into the rain, leaving Mrs. Laird blinking and shrivelling against stray drops in the doorway.

As the coach slooshed along, rain ran in streams across the window and through cracks in the door, the sound of it beating on the roof like bullet fire. The wheels squeaked and groaned as they lurched sideways in ruts, squished mud up into the bushes, spraying it from the track, or ground roughly on stones. Ceci could make out nothing of the journey but that they were descending, going the long way around. At a sudden jolt to the right she guessed they had met up with the main Moke track. It seemed softer now, muddier. Suddenly they stopped. She wiped the window to look out. Calvin had walked to the nearby hedge and was dragging out dead branches, returning with them and bending down. Craning her neck she lowered her window to find they had sunk in mud. Pushing the window all the way down she called: "Can I help?"

But Calvin stood up abruptly and shut the window on her and in doing so brought his face quite close to hers, perhaps by accident. It made her flush. From the safety of the window she watched him kneel in the mud in deep concentration, forcing branches under the coach wheels, trying to rock it, frowning with serious commitment to the job and indifferent to the water running in rivulets down his neck, the discomfort to himself. A curiously tender look hovered on her face as she looked down on his boy-like concentration.

Through the rain the dwelling finally lurched into view as the coach rocked to a stop. Wiping the wet pane clear, Ceci was unable to believe the sight before her. What had the rain done? The wind? Where was the roof? Leaving Olwen in her box in the seat, she fell from the coach and ran to the dwelling clutching her mouth while behind her Calvin stood watching with polite concern. He saw her bite her fingers, rush into the house and vanish from view then reappear in the doorway, blanched, her face shredded. She looked wanly at Calvin, rushed past him to the barn and vanished within, then reappeared

again and ran to the centre of the yard where she stood
shivering.

Calvin drew close, every word, every action planned.

When she began to cry and shake with sobs he
waited the briefest minute then reached forward and
tentatively took her by the shoulders, holding her at arm's
length. Ceci pulled back.

"Why did I *stay* so long!" she gasped.

"You weren't to know there'd be a storm—" he said
casually.

"Saw it blowing up! Everyone did! And where was I?
Showing off at your party!" Calvin shook his head in what
Ceci took to be either embarrassment or the absence of
any emotion. Assuming he felt personally responsible she
sought to reassure it.

"It's not your fault," she confessed. "I don't know
where to start."

Calvin's eyes slid towards the coach.

"Better come back."

"Jock! Help me look for him!"

While she searched the barn, Calvin, bored, wet, and
waiting for it to be over, went up the lane certain that if
anyone found Jock it would be he and having a pretty
good idea where Jock would be hiding. Taking his time he
ambled towards the original bush he had whipped Jock
into and in which, wretched and ragged, Jock shivered.
He had seen the coach and the Man at the front and was
frightened. Now to his horror, instead of being gone, the
Man was returning towards him, the dreaded whip clicking
against his boots. In the next minute the whip was poking
the edge of his bush separating the branches, holding
them back and revealing the unbending face of the Man
looking directly in at him with a terrible authority, commanding him to remain there.

Back in the dwelling, Ceci knelt by the dead hearth,
muddy, rubbing her red eyes with the heel of her hand.
Perhaps the smoke from a fire would bring Jock back. At a
sound she looked up. It was Calvin standing in the
doorway, the rain hammering down behind him.

"No sign of him," he said.

Ceci sat back on her heels. "If anything's happened
to him I couldn't live with myself!"

As Olwen started to cry she stumbled to her feet and

lifted her up. She turned, half hoping for guidance from Calvin.

"Better come back to the house," he said.

"I'll stay till he comes!" she replied, shaking her head grimly. "Even if it snows!"

Calvin shrugged as if to say suit yourself. But his eyes narrowed.

"There's *one* person you're not thinking of," he said, staring pointedly at the baby clutched to her shivering chest, his implication clear. Torn between guilt and anxiety Ceci bit her lip.

"*I'm* leaving now," he added, stepping out of the door. She ran a few paces after him.

"Please help mend the roof," she pleaded.

Calvin turned to her frowning censoriously. "You take other people's lives very lightly," he said.

"But I don't know where to *look*!" she begged.

"This place isn't *fit* for a child!" Calvin thundered. "Get on the coach!"

"You mean—*leave* him?" she gasped.

"He's not your responsibility!"

"He *is*!"

"Then why didn't you come over every day?" Calvin accused.

"I left *food* for him!" she defended herself, "a *lot* of it!"

"But you didn't *come*!" he threw at her.

Now Ceci was pacing. "There seemed no *point* in riding over every day."

Calvin nodded sarcastically from the door. "Too busy with your own life..."

Ceci started to beat the floor with her fist.

"I try so *hard*! And everything goes *wrong*!"

He observed her dispassionately. "Your new clothes will mildew. Your child get sick!"

"I can't *help* it!" she pleaded. "I can't *help* it!"

"If that's what you want!" Calvin said from above her. "He's obviously gone!" Although his voice was intense, Ceci could sense it was directed away from her, and looking up she found him examining his nails.

"Take down the hens," she said tiredly. "The boxes. I'll wait."

Without looking at her Calvin walked straight from the house.

A hurricane lantern cast a lonely splash of light against the wet stones. Up above the sky rumbled, threatening fresh draughts of rain as, through the darkness, the form of Jock limped dragging itself towards the house to peer cautiously through the windows. Seeing movement he ducked down then rose slowly again. Yes, it was she, her back to him, face in her hands, rocking. Fearing there might be other dangers he crept on all fours to peer in at the base of the open front door, the light shining on the crown of his head where it was bruised as if he had been struck by or fallen against something. Seeing all was well he moved soundlessly to sit in his accustomed place and was resting his eyes on her when suddenly from her deep grief she looked up, saw him sitting there and gasping, ran full force at him giving him such a fright he nearly bolted. Quickly she controlled herself and pulled back saying gently:

"It's alright Jock. It's alright."

Wet to the bone, Calvin turned the coach in at the gate of Hexham and left it to Sam. Shaking rain from his hair, wiping it from his neck and stamping his boots he strode into the hallway where his mother, in an obviously better humour, called to him from the top of the stairs.

"Everything go alright?"

"How was dinner?" he asked, walking straight past her without looking.

"Burnt. Gravy cold. No sweet," her martyred but cheerful voice followed him. "Still—it's nice to be back as we were."

In Bowen's Gully the rain poured down, screen after screen of it moving across the gully in great curtains, pouring into the dwelling, gathering on the floor and collecting against the walls. Damp, muddy and wretched to look at, Ceci and Jock drank from hot mugs, staring wordlessly at their miserable fire. Ceci reached across, took Jock's hand in hers, tiredly glad they were together again. Now relaxed, Jock stared into the kind flames as Ceci's eyes wandered the room, taking in the damage, the missing legs of mutton. Had someone been living there?

A tramp? A vagrant? On the point of dozing she heard a new sound which utterly terrified her: the baby *coughing*. In deepest horror she ran to Olwen's box listening to the whoop-whoop-whoop of a serious cough beginning. How could this final terrible thing have happened when it seemed that everything that *could* happen *had* done! She lifted the child—terror on her face—listening to its COUGH COUGH COUGH and walked the room with her, frantic. Finally, when the coughing stopped, Ceci lowered Olwen into her box, bending her legs to fit her in and biting her lip at its crude wooden sides. She shook her head at the gaps between the "cradle's" planks where the wind blew and the torn petticoat and sacking lining which before she had gone to Hexham had seemed so fine. Now after the cradle she saw it for what it was: a pathetic broken crate Olwen was fast outgrowing.

Seeing how unhappy Ceci looked Jock climbed from his seat, crossed to her, slipped his jew's harp from around his neck and held it out as a present. Worried, she shook her head and continued looking intently at Olwen. Recognizing she was staring at the baby with its half opened eyes and wheezing breath, Jock tried to amuse Olwen by swinging his jew's harp on its neck string in her face but Ceci gently moved it away.

Evening became night. Ceci looked at Jock, sleeping like an animal before the fire, one arm sprawled, the fingers caked with mud. She had propped Olwen on cushions against Jock's back, out of the draught of the door, and was keeping a watchful eye on her and listening to her seared breathing filling the room. Finally she got to her knees. "Show me to do what is right—before Winter!" she prayed, raising her head to look round at their ruined home.

By morning bright light streamed down and the rain had stopped. Her boxes were still piled wet through where Calvin had unloaded them in the middle of the yard the previous night but as she knelt, feeding the fowl through the sides of the wicker hamper, she was resolute.

"You stay there 'til I make a run," she said. Behind her weak smoke curled through holes in the roof and within, clothes dried on string and goods were piled wherever the floor was dry. The main thing was, she told herself, Olwen's coughing had stopped and if Calvin would just bring her pony down as agreed she would be able to get into Moke and see about a couple of things. But even as her resolve strengthened, storm clouds had begun to gather and rumble above, harbingers of another deluge to come. Quickly she picked up the hens and ran into the house.

The weather then unleashed itself on them with a fury. Never had she experienced such relentless rain. Before her eyes, whole sections of the roof gave, slithered diagonally to the floor crushing chairs and whatever lay in their way. Beneath the table she and Jock crouched: she with the hen hamper in one hand and he nursing Olwen as rain beat on the table and mounted over their feet as if it would never stop. It rained and rained. Shivering, Ceci looked at Jock. It seemed not to bother him, as if he had switched his mind into a kind of acceptance. As Ceci wrested Olwen from Jock, held her to her chest, she felt heat radiate from her tiny forehead, and with dread laid her hand on it.

Though the afternoon brought fresh wind, it was not good drying wind. Nonetheless Ceci dragged their bedding out into the yard and began to peg it up. Frowning with pegs in her mouth she was asking herself if there was any point in the exercise when out of the corner of her eye she saw Calvin, good to his word, turning in with his mount, her pony Bragge following behind. Holding her head up, she finished pegging, wondering how to word what she had decided to say.

"I've nothing to offer," she said crossing to him, "and I know you've taken staff, but I'll come back in any capacity"—she looked up at him—"for the time being."

There was no trace of expression on his face as he looked down on her.

"Till I'm sorted out," she continued, searching his face and his horse for some sign of reaction.

"With your dependents?" he enquired.

"Yes," she nodded, chewing her lip.

"*Any* capacity?" he asked, like one interviewing a labourer.

"Uh, huh," Ceci nodded.

At that he leant back in his saddle. "Are you proposing to me?" he enquired languorously. She hung her head. How awful it sounded. Was that what she had actually said?

"If you like." The words fell awkwardly from her mouth and floated up to Calvin sitting motionless above.

"Well remember it was your idea," he said softly. For a moment Ceci paused, puzzled. Although the words were in themselves harmless, *something* was wrong and there had been a peculiarly menacing ring to them. Perhaps it was best to clarify it.

"I don't think you care for me at all Calvin," she said flatly.

She found him looking at the horizon. "I never expected to be swept off my feet," he replied, adding sŏttŏ vŏce, "by a *woman*."

That was more like it, Ceci thought! A bit of banter. A smile spread on her face as she folded her arms before him.

"Being 'neighbourly' I suppose," she grinned.

Calvin suddenly looked down at her. "We're well met," he said intently.

At that moment Ceci had the strangest sensation of having been there before; of having stood looking up at his horse, hearing those very words in that order and being as confused by them then as she was now. She almost knew the words he would say next.

"What did you think I was saying?" the words came.

Surely he was proposing to her without even getting down from his horse! The safest thing was to say she didn't understand.

"I don't know."

A flicker of impatience crossed Calvin's face. "When would you like to start?"

Again recognizing the words, the sequence, the fact that he was speaking to her as if they were the only two of a particular kind of person on earth, a strange feeling came over her. He was, she knew, being frank and honest with her as no one had ever seen him before. She knew that he was aware she realized he was laying himself open and that this, for him, was an intensely personal moment even if disguised by indifference. Then came more words she recognized, this time from her:

"Doesn't it matter who you marry?" she asked softly. "You could be talking to *anyone*! This is *me*!!"

"You were waiting for someone special?" he asked. "Some particular person in your...carefully planned existence?" His eyes moved over her shattered dwelling, taking with them her sense of things having happened before.

"I—I just wouldn't want to do—the wrong thing for—the right reason," she stammered.

Calvin's horse stepped sideways as if impatient to be gone.

"I'll come back once," he said, peering at her but allowing his horse to continue moving away. "If it's Yes— yes. If it's No—I won't raise it again."

"You don't care either way do you?" Ceci called after him.

He half turned to face her. "No," he replied and in the next moment was gone. Slowly Ceci re-entered the house and began the long day's think.

As evening came, doubts preyed on her mind and, prior calm gone, she paced in confusion. Olwen was clearly ill, the earlier respite being no more than a quiesence. Nor was whooping cough an old wives' tale; it was a killer! A dry house would surely benefit Olwen, but wasn't marrying more than a job? Did there not have to be *cherishing* or a fondness there or did that come as a result of an *intention* to love. What about those women throughout the history of the world who had married in accordance with their parents' wishes, especially Royal people, without for one moment considering the question of whether they liked or felt drawn to the man? Possibly Calvin was shy. It could not be easy to ride down and propose to a virtual servant even if she *had* accidentally put the words in his mouth. It must have taken courage. But what could he possibly *want* with her? Was he sorry for her or feeling perhaps on behalf of his mother a family responsibility for having kept her so long from her home that it had fallen into such a condition? That must be it. If only there were someone she could *ask*! When Calvin returned if she had no answer he would take it for No and it would be *her* fault, *her* responsibility if Olwen and poor Jock suffered as a result of her choice.

Lost in her thoughts she did not see Calvin appear at the door until the sound of Jock leaping up in terror, sending a chair flying and a cup crashing down, made her spin. It also instantly cleared her mind for her.

"Stop that! Jock!" she screamed. "I've had enough!"

Amazed, she saw him crawl on the floor, backing away and whining as if he wanted to get out but feared passing Calvin. Ignoring him Calvin stepped into the room and quickly Jock ran for the door but Ceci got there first and blocked his way.

"We can't go *on* like this!" she pleaded. "How am I to lead a normal life? *You're* coming with *me*! *I'm* not stopping with *you*! If you run away this time!—" Her eyes filled with tears. "I'm *sick* with worry!"

Hands in his pockets, Calvin leaned indifferently on the hearth watching.

"What's the matter with him?" he enquired.

"Oh," said Ceci apologetically. "You haven't met..."

Polite interest arranged itself on Calvin's face. "So it"s Yes—" he yawned. Ceci nodded limply. "Mind you don"t hurt the poor beggar," Calvin went on.

"Get a rope," Ceci said abruptly.

"Leave him here," drawled Calvin crossing over, reaching a hand to loosen her grip on Jock but finding she shook her head fiercely and kept a good hold.

"You're just sorry for him but you don't know him," she gasped, hanging on in a shamed way.

"Well there's no need to be so brutal!" Calvin snapped.

"I can see I'm disgusting you—"

"You surprise me, yes."

"Well never mind that. Get the rope."

Angrily, Calvin kicked the door and stepped out into the dark, while behind him Jock began to bite and snap at Ceci's hands, holding his wrists.

"For *God's sake* Jock!" she implored. "What has got into you?"

He bucked and thrashed anew as Calvin appeared with the coil of rope.

"I think you're being cruel to him," he said in measured tones.

"I'll just—lock him in—till he knows where we live," Ceci said, struggling with Jock who by now was foaming at the mouth. "Help me Calvin!" But Calvin stood yards off, watching her struggle with the rope.

"You can't lock him in!" he said, his voice suggesting the distaste of a man of culture for vastly primitive things.

"If I don't, he'll run away," Ceci begged. "It's for his own good."

At that Calvin stepped towards her, and threw Jock to the floor like a felled pig. As Ceci watched he knelt on Jock''s chest and began efficiently tying him up.

"I don't know what's *wrong* with him," Ceci lamented. "He seems *afraid* of you."

"Just having a fit," came Calvin's dispassionate voice.

Ceci knelt beside him. "I'll have to undo him," she gasped. "He's hurting himself!"

Instantly Calvin lunged forward, hoisted Jock on his shoulders and staggered past her and out the door with him, watched by Ceci, a mixture of relief and exhaustion on her face. She could not explain the feeling of deliverance that came over her as she saw Calvin's broad back with Jock's feet waving over it disappearing from her shattered dwelling. She had the sensation of an immense weight being lifted from her chest. Quickly she turned and gathered Olwen in her arms.

As the coach ground over the stones of the main track, Ceci began to have doubts. At her feet, Jock thrashed mercilessly, on the floor, his animal noises of snuffling terror soon setting the baby off.

"For God's *sake* Jock, it'll be al*right*!" Ceci urged. "Be *quiet*! It's al*right* Olwen—!" she begged, rocking the screaming box on the seat, her voice barely audible. Up front, Calvin could hear the tumult above even the juddering of the wheels. Unpleasant as it was, it was something he knew how to resolve. Ultimately. Suddenly there was a loud thumping on the wall.

"It's no good Calvin. You'll have to take us back!" Ceci shouted, clawing at the closed window. He stopped the coach and got down.

"This is the best for *all* of you," his impersonal voice came to her through the glass.

"But what about *love*!" she threw at him, amazed to hear the words come from her own mouth. Suddenly Calvin snapped.

"Alright! You had your chance!" He began to turn the coach round. Ceci panicked. Of all the stupid times to mention love! What had they to return to? Now Calvin was struggling with the horse, furious to have been argued with, furious that she had put her finger on the one fault in the scheme, perhaps even furious at himself for having been made aware of it. She had destroyed all they might build on!

"Back you go!" he shouted as she struggled to lower the window.

"*Help* us," she pleaded, meaning only help us rebuild the house.

"You got yourself into this!" Calvin roared in a tone which implied he was washing his hands of her altogether. Why couldn't he speak kindly? She hadn't intended any harm!

"But I don't *know* you—" she explained, pleading.

"Will you obey?" he shouted, bringing his face close to hers. Shuddering, she sank back in the coach feeling confused and terrified at what he thought she had agreed to. What *was* it he was so convinced she had promised him that he was now angry with her? Never had she felt in such danger in her life as then, with the coach rolling darkly on through the night towards the life she had chosen, towards Hexham.

In the quiet of the country, Mrs. Laird heard the coach coming and laid her needlework aside. Good. Calvin was back. Where he had been she had no idea but doublless he'd tell her. Descending the stairs she hurried towards the back door and was turning to the kitchen entrance when suddenly her ears informed her that the coach had chosen to arrive at the front! A visitor?

Preparing a smile she opened the door and stepped out into the shaft of light, at once recognizing their coach and vaguely conscious of a pale face shrinking away behind the glass. Suddenly the surprise on her face became consternation, then incredulity and utter rage on recognizing Ceci. A mask of angry colour rose but drained quickly on looking up to the driver's box and seeing battle and resolution in the eyes of Calvin above. She backed away and leant on the wall. Calvin jumped down and pulled open the carriage door for Ceci to get out and after a minute reached and roughly grabbed her wrist. Ceci Bowen was back at Hexham.

Chapter 13

Out of respect for his mother's wishes, Calvin waited for her to depart for England before installing Ceci as Mistress of the House. Almost immediately he had sent for a doctor for Olwen, for which Ceci was eternally grateful. The doctor diagnosed infantile pneumonia and showed strong approval of the comfortable quarters in which Olwen was housed. For her part, Ceci set time aside to spend with Jock who, ignoring the space allocated to him in an outhouse, had scrambled into a disused stye, dragging timbers and branches over to disguise its roof and cover its entrance. Occasionally she saw him, dog like, peering out but he seemed content. He had hours when he ran free, only taking care to check that the coast was clear before making the dash across the courtyard and into his eyrie. Herself, she had been returned to her old room, Calvin continuing in his.

She felt deeply sorry for Mrs. Laird who had taken to eating in her own apartment. Her eyes, when she glimpsed her in the corridor, were as often as not red from weeping. Sounds of things being thrown emanated from her room and frequently she would ring her bell with a fierce abandon for one of the two maids who had arrived with the cook from the Immigrant Barracks. Ceci would hear these girls pass her door, giggling, as she and Teaser had done. Apparently they had been forbidden to communicate with her, for when she addressed them they looked the other way. Despite all this, though, she felt at home in the big house.

When Mrs. Laird left, she took with her the baby's cradle, a last destructive act against herself for now that Calvin had committed himself to marry, no child would come to that cradle other than through Ceci. As Calvin smirked at the cradle in the hallway, Ceci guessed it had been his and that he was heartily glad to see it going out of the house.

When she departed, Mrs. Laird left in her room a variety of clothes she could not fit in even her voluminous trunks. Though she had told the maids to "help themselves," they disregarded much of it, and raking through the remnants Ceci came upon a large tent-like nightdress of sky blue pale cotton with little white dots on it, exactly the sort of cloth, had she dared imagine it, she would have liked for a smock for herself while pregnant with Olwen. As things were, she had cut her clothes open, patching them with bits of curtains and sacking. She passed the cloth through her fingers. Hardly worn. The sleeves were long and bunched at the wrists into cuffs and the collar had a gentle rounded shape. Smocked across the top, it would still make a lovely maternity robe. But perhaps she was being premature she told herself. He had not married her yet. Carefully she folded the nightdress and carried it to her room.

The wedding took place in the house, the minister arriving coincidentally on the same day the doctor was attending for his final check on Olwen thus enabling him to act as a witness. In the circumstances it seemed natural there be neither music nor dancing and Ceci put the lack of festivity down not to Calvin's natural astringency but his sense of expediency. However she found herself thinking that at least Reg had put a flower in her room. After the minister and doctor had gone Calvin nodded at her as if the matter were closed and strode off to his summer house. Ceci went to her room and drew down the nightdress. Should she start sewing now? There was no sign of a trousseau and surely Calvin would expect her to have *some* reasonable clothes . . . Sitting with Mrs. Laird's remnants draped over her knees she wondered if she should go to his room that night, but decided better perhaps to wait till she was invited.

Despite his new station in life Calvin did not take on more staff. In fact after his mother had left he relieved the cook and housemaids immediately. "Better on our own," was how he put it.

There were no more parties and no more guests. He rose early and went out while she tended to Olwen and resumed her duties in the kitchen, finding much time on her hands in which to think of her past.

If Immelda could see her now, Ceci thought, reclining on the sofa in the absolute stillness of the house . . . Immelda who used to waylay her and perpertrate untold cruelties on the frightened child she had been! Looking back with an adult mind, Immelda had disliked—no, hated—her for two reasons, both to do with their fathers. First that Immelda's own liberal minded father, without waiting for legislation to come in, had converted a barn into a school-room for the children of the Estate and shared his own children's tutor, Mr. Lovely, with them. How well she remembered that dear man bending down, spelling things out in the mud with a stick for them and the anger on the face of Immelda waiting in the house beyond for her lesson and seeing her tutor dawdle and delay on the path with them. The other reason Immelda had hated her was the fact that her own father as Head Groom had taught Immelda, Francine and Althea to ride. She had had to accept instruction from a common man and had bitterly resented the glancing touch of his leathery hands helping her up and down.

She heard again Immelda's imperious voice. "Do you know what my name means?"

"No."

"No what?"

"No *Miss*."

"It means *Go Gather Honey*!"

Ceci looked at the golden balls of the four hundred day clock following each other around in a pointless circle. She'd like Immelda to meet her now, she told herself. No she wouldn't. She'd still be every bit as frightened of her.

Moving out into the garden Ceci gathered roses and laid them in a basket. All were traditional, no doubt Mrs. Laird's choice, and the collection of rose bowls she had left behind were truly "English." Lovingly Ceci arranged the blooms, setting the bowl in the centre of the dining table where its colours were reflected in the deep polish. Already in her mind's eye she could see Mrs. Laird's huge summer nightdress as a gently pleasing afternoon wear. The sleeves could be bunched then allowed to run like gloves from elbow to wrist. Given her narrow waist and the smallness of her bodice, the skirt could be gently full and there would even be cloth enough left over for a sash, she thought, glancing across the lawn to the summer house where Calvin was working. She thought hard about the neckline. In the middle of the most beautiful summer countryside with no one to see them, would it not be permissible to drop it a little and let the sun at her throat? In fact if she were to take some of the old lace from the curtain cupboard a modest yet attractive top could be effected. Going to her room she happily set about pinning and sewing, baby Olwen taking her first few steps across the rug beside her, falling and getting to her feet, down and up again and bumping into her knees. Were it not for the fact that the dress were to be a surprise she would have sewn downstairs for it pleased Calvin to see her working. She knew this by the way his eyes flickered towards her and away again as he passed through the room, always careful to move them off her before she could look up, but she'd know he had been looking. Sometimes a slowing in his footsteps gave him away; other times his reflection in the french cabinet showed him to be turning to her. At these times she imagined his face to bear an expression of gentle affection, perhaps even approval as she bent over her needle. When the dress was finished she would carefully hide it, she told herself, and await the right moment, a moment she would build towards, being certain the meal she presented was special, the flowers particularly well arranged, and everything the way she felt a man in Calvin's station would wish it to be. It would then be easier for him to make conversation, to talk to her and make a beginning in what they had committed themselves to: a life-long relationship of love and friendship with each other.

The Special Afternoon came. The room was arranged to perfection and a dish she was quite confident he would not have seen since leaving England awaited him in the kitchen. He had returned early from his day outside. Hastening upstairs to ready herself, she heard him kick off his boots, wash and attend to the other facets of his toilet as he always did preparatory to eating in a hygienic manner. Quickly she donned the dress and hurried downstairs, carefully positioning herself in a pool of late afternoon sunlight by the great windows, hands nervously before her. Calvin's footsteps sounded in the hallway. The door opened. He saw her. For a moment he stared straight at her as if stunned. Then: "You look ridiculous," he said quietly. Ceci fled to the kitchen. Feeling deeply hurt and confused she drew forth the food she had prepared, arranged it on the tray, and putting an apron over her shame carried it to serve to the Master of the House, seated at the table as if nothing had happened. Quietly she moved about uncovering dishes, placing serving spoons within easy reach of his hands. When he had finished taking food she served herself and sitting opposite, watched him begin to eat. Not a muscle on his face moved. He could have been eating cold rice pudding. Anxiously she frowned. "D-do you like it?" she asked. Immediately a faint gathering of Calvin's brows was detectable. She chewed her lip, fidgeting with her knife and fork. Perhaps she was being a bit silly. Obviously he liked it or he wouldn't be eating it.

"I—I mean—" she began again.

Calvin picked up his plate and walked straight from the room.

Time grew over this and many other small hurts. In her generosity, she assumed it was natural shyness or a lack of experience on Calvin's part which prevented him inviting her to his room. Perhaps the fact that she had been married before made him fear comparisons. But who with? Old Bowen? She sensed in Calvin a deep hurt that she wished she could make better. Perhaps given that she had the more experience, it was up to her to make herself more available. It could even be that this was what he was waiting for or expecting. Was he even perceiving her keeping to her old room to be a rejection of him? Hastily she took out her needle and began to work on Mrs. Laird's discarded underthings, her vast quantity of petticoats, satin, silk and taffeta . . . which the departing maids had not found in the old cupboards or had been unable to stuff in their small trunks. Before long she had fashioned herself an attractive yet demure nightdress which, she recalled honestly, was of a more modest mien than many a lady's evening dress she had seen as they tripped in and out of balls and functions at the hotel she had served at in London.

Stitching on, she wondered if the time was right to approach Calvin. With Olwen he seemed at ease, his hands lifting her up as she ran about the house colliding with his legs, with chairs and tables. Olwen had brought new smile lines to Calvin's face. Watching them play, Ceci began to get up the nerve to approach him in her new nightdress. There had been no bad atmosphere between them for some weeks, partly because she had managed almost to vanish into the furnishings, an attitude he seemed to thrive on. It looked as if they were settling into a way together and perhaps it was necessary to go to him before their separate arrangements became *too* established. On the night he retired early, she wondered if he were giving her an opportunity to do just that! Slipping into the nightdress she pinned her hair, touched her throat with lavender water, tiptoed around the banister and along the corridor to Calvin's large room overlooking the grand lawn and listened. She knew he was not asleep. Cautiously she opened the door and peeped in. There he was, sitting at his dresser, his back to her, clipping protruding hairs from his nostrils. Cautiously she stepped in. At the sight of her in his mirror he returned the scissors to the table, waited, then turned:

"Take that disgusting thing off!" he said with a trembling voice so full of anger she felt covered in shame. Of course he did not want her to take it off! He wanted her to cover up at once! Clutching Mrs. Laird's finery to her she fled the room.

With his near perfect memory, his strong will and his head uncluttered by trivia, Calvin went about his daily life. The fact that the hands and all who visited Hexham treated him as the epitome of normality heightened sensitive Ceci's feelings that it must be *she* who was in the wrong. There was no one to discuss him with nor anyone to reassure her that she was not all those things his treatment of her suggested she was. Nothing she did seemed to influence or change him and as he continued with his granite exterior it was she, open to him, who became eroded . . . No longer were the small marker flags she had previously used to navigate others, warning of their shoals and chasms, of any use; nor was the whole way of a woman's life based on sending out signals and listening for their echo to detect the *real* person behind a stern frame of any avail. He was like a large stone lying on a river bed that she dived at time and again to try and get under and lift to the surface but always found too heavy, always gave up to return exhausted from her task . . . Beneath the waves of her life he lay, cold and unloving with neither desire nor need of her. Why then, she asked herself, did she so desperately still want to please him?

At night she lay awake in her lonely room as the wind passed over Hexham: a wind which had blown for days without passing human habitation, would pass on over their small scab of privilege on the upland carcass to blow itself out in snow caps, the West Coast or the sea beyond. Whatever happened, she told herself, nothing would change her life and no one would come. She would stay tucked away in this huge house with its silver and Imari, its wine red Afghan carpets and Bokhara rugs and Kashmir, hidden behind velvet drapes and surrounded by wealth.

As time passed, without speaking a word, Calvin managed to convey to her that she was an object of shame and revulsion; that her idea that another person would want her was based on the grossest form of vanity and that if she wished to save the minimum of self-respect she should avoid exposing herself needlessly to or trying to attract the attention of others. Desperately she held herself in check trying to win his favour and to curb whatever it was in her that annoyed him so that they might be alright!

Chapter 14

Olwen awoke. The sun was streaming through her window. Pushing the blue curtains aside she peered down on the stable courtyard below. There, looking up at her, was her very best friend in the whole world! Quickly she slid off the bed, slipped her bare feet into her leather sandals, reached up and turned the big handle and crept quietly along the corridor to the head of the stairs. She paused for a moment, her tongue touching her upper lip. Good. Both were still asleep. Carefully she went down the stairs and out of the door, keeping to the side of the path on the grass verge which was wet with the promise of another hot summer's day. Her sandals left marks on the grass as she skipped and darted away from the house being careful not to tread on the gravel path. Being six meant she was allowed to get out of bed without waiting for someone to give her permission to do so though in fact she had been doing this since four, always managing to get back and be lying there when her mother's worried face appeared around the door jamb.

This was the time of day she liked best. The house behind her lay still with sleep and the low sun picked out the sparkles in her unbrushed pale ash hair as it fell over her nightdress and rippled down her back. She ran between the outhouses to Jock, waiting for her, grinning hugely with anticipation and standing aside to let her scramble into his shanty first.

Awakening early, Ceci opened the door to Olwen's room and saw she wasn't there. Realizing at once where she had gone she hurried after her, afraid Calvin would find out first and be angry. Softly she padded down the stairs, sped through the kitchen and out the back door. "Olwen!—" she called outside Jock's shack. "Olwen!" Within, Olwen heard the muted tones and frowned. They were playing her favourite game, jousting, and she was winning. Balancing a pencil on the back of her knuckles she ran her hand along the ground till it came to the stone representing a wall. Breathing carefully, she let her hand "jump", raising an elbow and flicking it out to keep the pencil on an even keel. Jock gasped in excitement as she soared safely over. "Olwen!" came the cry again. She looked at Jock, put a finger on her lips.

Outside as Ceci paced, arriving labourers glanced over at her, knowing exactly why she was there, that she was afraid of Calvin and that she had no power in the house. They heard from within Jock's mounting hysterical giggles indicating that he was winning; that the pencil balanced on the back of his knuckles was managing to stay there as he galloped his hand across the floor towards the stones and prepared to leap. His panting grew louder.

"Sssh!—" Olwen frowned, but Jock couldn't stop. "Olwen!" came Ceci's voice, now at the entrance to their tunnel. Sighing in exasperation Olwen rose, stooped and crawled out of the entrance way.

As Ceci took her daughter"s hand and led her past the labourers and back into the house through the kitchen, she was aware that her days were threaded with secretive acts, innocent things she did not want Calvin to discover, become angry about and blame her for. Living in the shadow of his anger, she was prepared to feel guilty even for the simple fact of her existence. Examining the condition of every item, she carefully loaded a breakfast tray to take to Calvin in his summer house.

The summer house was a circular wooden tea house near the rose beds with a verandah, once favoured by Mrs. Laird and to which after her departure Calvin had had glass windows added. Now, with lawn chairs stored at one end it contained no more than a table and a few shelves and had become a small "office" for him, a place separate from the house. From the outer paintwork to the inner the tone was white. White painted chair, Calvin's billowing white shirt. Seated there, he bent over a large ledger, his face heavy with thought, solemn and undisturbed. All was silent but for the ticking of a sedate clock he had brought down from the house. 6.25 a.m. Hearing stumble-hurry steps, his face tensed. The door creaked slightly. He knew that would be Ceci peering through the gauze, his breakfast tray balanced on her knee. He did not turn. She managed to open the door and enter.

She stood holding the tray, the utensils glinting in the morning sun, the boiled egg looking back at her, thinking what to say though to say anything was dangerous.

"Good morning Calvin—"

With measured authority he turned, an absence of expression other than guardedness on his face meeting the caution on Ceci's. Each balanced on the edge of unnatural nakedness as Calvin moved his ledger slightly and Ceci came forward to unload his tray. Speaking to the back of her head he began his onslaught on her irresponsibility in regard to Olwen:

"See that you remove that symphonium before she gets any older."

"One of your mother's favourite things that music box," said Ceci softly. "Be a pity to put it away—"

Was he, she asked herself, disturbed by the balance in his household changing now that Olwen, whom he had always encouraged, was striking out on her own?

"Also her greatest weakness!" Calvin snapped.

"It's a—a—nice piece of furniture," Ceci pleaded.

"Frivolous."

Though there was no point in saying more, she was aware that Calvin was not through with her.

"Did you cross the lawn?" he asked.

"Yes."

"Don't."

With the tray dangling from one hand, Ceci began to walk back the long way around the gravel loop, scrunch scrunch scrunch, viewed by the hired hands roused for their day's work, trickling in and turning to stare. There she went, head down, tray dangling; they nodded, knowing she'd had a rollicking. She was no better than them, their eyes said, but was trying to be.

Calvin stared at his untouched breakfast, hearing the scrunching scrunch fade. By the time Ceci reached the kitchen the scruffy line of hired hands ready to eat were falling in from different directions to collect their utensils, pannikins, and food to carry to their mess. Head down in thought, Ceci passed up the line not really seeing it. As she entered the kitchen, the men's eyes followed her and as the door closed they looked at one another and grinned.

Within, Olwen was waiting at the long table, elbows out, ready to watch her mother relay food to the first two men allowed in. She saw the ruffian Harry enter, a man she disliked but had nothing to fear from as he would not dare come near her. The fact that she could tell her Father had not been wasted on Olwen *nor* the workers and knowing she could have her way at Hexham, though she occasionally took advantage, she generally disregarded the men.

"Where them eggs! Where them eggs!" she began, repeating a phrase she had often heard. As Ceci turned

from the stove to smile at her, a large pot of scalding eggs
in her hands, the man Harry glanced across at Olwen to
see if she was still looking then pushed his thumb gently
into the small of Ceci's back. Her mouth tightened. She
too glanced at Olwen who was fortunately looking away.

"Let *me*," said Harry loudly as if meaning "let me
help you." Reaching his arm around her as if to ease the
pot from her grip, he succeeded in pinning her against the
stove, still keeping one eye on the child.

"This is the last time you come in this kitchen!" Ceci
whispered with intensity, worried that Olwen might hear.

Harry put his face near to hers and breathed on her.
She recoiled.

"And I'll report you," she gasped.

"You won't," said Harry pulling back with the egg
pot as foreman Sam entered to lift a load from the table.

"Just gettin' the eggs," he called at Sam's back, leaning towards Ceci, his foul breath caressing her face. Startled, Olwen saw and began timorously to fiddle with the
handle of the parasol lying next to her on the bench.

"Where them eggs!?" came a voice from outside as
Harry pushed his bloated form towards the door with the
egg pot and Sam re-entered yet again.

"Come on Harry! Move it!"

Ceci saw Harry slow in the doorway, look at the
foreman as if to say "You are no one. Remember it." She
saw Sam's eyes inwardly give way and sink. The poor
man was *useless* with the men, she told herself, looking
away rather than have him know she had witnessed his
disgrace. Getting her breath back after her own encounter
with Harry she gripped the stove's edge and was frowning
down at its surface when he looked up.

"You alright Missus?" he asked, noting her pallor.

"Yes thank you Sam," she said tiredly.

Without a word he angrily lifted the plates of bread
slabs, and withdrew from the kitchen.

Sam entered the shed on the tail end of a dirty joke
Harry was telling which stopped immediately, not because
Harry feared censure but because he did not intend to
share himself or his jokes with the Foreman or create a
convivial atmosphere for him to exploit.

"Later," he said, meaning he would finish telling the
joke later. Around him the men shrugged ill naturedly,

glared at Sam, on their faces the frustration which so readily turned to anger and dislike of him.

Sam handed the plates of bread and as they began to circulate, men picking slabs and passing the plate on, he motioned an "over here" to Harry which Harry ignored. No one had seen, the men being busy cracking their eggs, pouring tea and passing mugs, so Sam crossed and spoke directly in Harry's ear:

"You're riding for a fall."

"You see anything?" Harry asked insolently.

"She'll tell," said Sam, well aware Harry knew what he was talking about.

"She's scared still of 'im!" Harry scoffed, raising his voice to draw in the men around.

"Harry reckons women lead 'im on!" said one of them obligingly. The men began to snicker. Harry played to it.

"All that good hump going to waste," he joked.

Somebody growled—rrrRuff!

"If 'er husband don't *want* it," explained Harry. Sam began to feel himself sinking.

Briefly it occurred to Sam to report Harry to Calvin, who would surely never believe Ceci to be a woman of loose moral standing, but ultimately his courage failed him. Desperately he sought some phrase which would bring the men to heel and force them to treat with respect the Mistress of the House whom he knew in his bones to be a good woman, but he could not find one.

Bored with waiting for her mother to serve their breakfast, Olwen left the kitchen, ran across the lawn and climbed on to the summer house verandah. Quietly she pushed the door open a crack and peeped in. Her father had finished his breakfast and pushed the things aside. With an impish smile she tiptoed up behind him, reached and put her hands over his big eyes.

Slowly Calvin covered her little hands with his, his face gently solemn but before she could say "Guess who this is?" he asked without turning:

"Where were you when I got up this morning?"

Instantly her face dropped and she slid her hands back over his shoulders. Rarely was he cross with her but she knew his tone presupposed a guilty answer. Quickly she ran round the room waving her arms like a butterfly, then came back and blew on the back of his neck hoping he would have forgotten. He exploded and spun on her.

"Where did you learn that?" he said in a deep tremulous voice. Olwen's mouth popped. Now she didn't want to say anything at all but he held her wrist firmly.

"Ha Ha Harry . . ." she began, eyes round as a kitten.

"On you?!" Calvin gasped, livid. Olwen shook her head.

"On Mummy," she said, raising her eyes to see if perhaps he was angry with Mummy instead. He muttered a strange word and breathed hard. Carefully she slid from his arms as the sound of her mother tinkling their breakfast bell across the lawn provided a welcome excuse to flee from the summer house and run.

"Mummy what's a barster?" Olwen said, slicing the top of her egg with a silver spoon. She liked breakfast with her mother. The big table always properly set, the stiff linen cloth grazing her knees, the salt cellar glinting . . . Ceci frowned.

"A *barster*," Olwen repeated, knowing she had found a word of some substance. She rested the tip of the silver spoon on her lip, observing her mother.

"Shall we go out today?" she said.

"What for?"

"See Daddy working."

Ceci looked down repressing the phrase: "That's not at *all* a good idea!"

Oh it was so difficult to walk a tightrope between them, Ceci thought. To try and raise the child so that her behaviour would not anger Calvin, yet at the same time instil in her a respect and affection for him.

"We want to please Daddy, don't we?" she asked gently.

Olwen gave her egg a mighty whack with the spoon and exhaled. In the morning light, she looked so ethereal and pure it was impossible to imagine how conniving she could be . . . Suddenly a way of killing two birds with one stone presented itself to Ceci.

"We *can* go outside today," she said triumphantly. "We'll do Art! *Just this once mind.*" Olwen smiled up at her, pleased to have got her way while Ceci anxiously examined the extent of the misdemeanour she had planned.

She certainly could not tell Calvin Jock had a cold without getting into further trouble yet clearly something had to be done about it.

Shaking out the table cloth to the hens, her mind returned to the incident in the kitchen. There was no point in reporting Harry to Sam for he could only repeat it to Calvin and Calvin would either blame her for causing it or retreat into an even deeper, more disapproving silence on account of having been bothered. Any appeal she had made to him in the past had brought anger until finally she had learned the lesson that anger would result on any occasion she chose to attract his attention by seeking guidance or expected him to "lend himself" to her in the form of offering an opinion... Returning to the kitchen she took some money from the housekeeping jar and secreted it in the folds of her skirt. She did not see Calvin in the stable beyond, saddling up his horse. Where was Olwen picking up words like "bastard" Ceci asked herself.

Observing Calvin saddling up at a time when he was usually in his summer house, it came to Sam that against all the odds the Master had found out. This certainty was compounded by the rage on Calvin's face and when Sam was foolish enough to be caught observing him, it came as no surprise that Calvin should cease saddling his horse and beckon him over. Again and again as he listened to Calvin's instructions, Sam cursed himself for having been the last to leave the quarters that day!

As following Calvin's instructions he rode along, Harry's swag behind him, despite the weight of authority his action carried, he dreaded what he had to do. Coming up on the men he found Harry in the centre of the group: a situation promising danger and a certain amount of ugliness. Stopping a few yards off, he made whistling noises to get Harry's attention. Instantly Harry knew. Pushing the men aside he swaggered slowly over, determined to make a good show of it.

"It's all there," said Sam, producing the swag and dropping it at his feet. "Paid ter the end of the month."

Harry produced a wicked looking knife from the back of his belt and began cleaning out his filthy nails with it.

"Pick it up and give it to me," Harry said, adding in a voice so low the others would not hear: "Then I'll leave." Sam got the message very clearly. If he did not bend down and offer Harry his swag, he would have to throw him off! But were he to bend down, doubtless Harry would knee him in the throat. For once Sam decided to stand his ground.

The store in Moke was deserted as Ceci and Olwen entered but hearing the bell, Sweetwater hurried out.

"My dear *ladies*," he enthused.

"Some lemons and a jar of honey please Mr Sweetwater," said Ceci quickly.

"We *surely* haven't taken cold?" he enquired, a look of utter scandal on his face.

Nothing was forthcoming from Ceci though her mouth tensed.

"Is this—'Art'?" Olwen whispered.

"Never you mind about this," she said. "Oh—and some watercolours. Do you have any? A drawing tablet . . . ?"

Covered in confusion Ceci stepped from the store. Olwen knew exactly what lemons and honey were for.

"You're not supposed to buy things for Jock. With money," said the child smugly. "I could *tell*!!!!"

Ceci urged Olwen to mount quickly so that they could leave Moke and return to Hexham but Olwen wanted to delay. They hardly ever came there and when they did, hurried in and out without speaking to anyone almost as if they had no right to be leaving the station. Her mother, she noticed, did not seem aware of people observing them. Suddenly a call made her turn her head.

"*Hallo there*!" came the voice of Ginger, leaning in the doorway of the grain store, an accounts book under his arm. Without thinking, Ceci smiled. She had heard long since he was married but as he hurried towards them and laid his hand on the back of her gelding, she could not help but think he had not changed at all.

"My my my!" he said, looking up at her. "So here you are!" Olwen noticed a look of youth come into her mother's face and one of the prettiest smiles she had ever seen. In fact her mother was blushing.

"So how come you never visited us then?" asked Ginger.

"How come you never visited *us* out in the gulley?" Ceci retorted.

"Couldn't have you thinking I was after your water rights!" joked Ginger.

"Afraid of being shot at more like!" Ceci replied.

Ginger turned to Olwen:

"Hallo poppet!" She looked at him strangely and scratched her face.

"What a fine lady your mother is, eh?" he went on. Olwen had never met a man like Ginger before and was not sure she approved of him.

"Your mother used to be 'the Bowens' Girl'," he informed her.

"Well," shrugged Ceci from her horse above. "I'm 'The Lairds' Girl' now."

"You come up!" Ginger urged her.

"I couldn't do that," she said quickly, her face draining of colour.

Ginger looked up concernedly, wondering if he had been misunderstood.

"Come and visit. The both of you," he explained. "You tell that man of yours I asked."

But Ceci shook her head.

"I—I don't see how I could," she stammered.

"Couldn't tell 'im you been in town or you met me or what?" asked Ginger perplexed.

Ceci twisted awkwardly on her horse quite unable to find the words to explain a situation she did not herself understand.

"Oh not that! No—just—it's just—"

"You see the sign 'Nolan's' as you go by on the main track?" Ginger went on. "You bring that man of yours up and have a drink. *Enjoy* yourselves!"

He gave her horse a quick pat and saw a strange look spread over Ceci's face.

She swayed on her horse, the word 'enjoy' having hit her like a punch in the stomach. As her hand reached for the saddle to steady herself, she frowned down, looking at Ginger as if she were recovering from a long illness or struggling with the memory of a loss.

"You come up! Be sure now," he said firmly, deciding the best course would be to leave her. "*Right* then." He slapped the back of her mount, nodded and walked off.

*   *   *

Leaving Moke she allowed their horses to follow the track that led to Bowen's Gulley, meaning to stay on the crest of the hill and take slightly longer to return home. Olwen moved on ahead, curious, pointing at the broken fences, deliberately riding her pony over the old gate which had fallen down, letting its hooves splinter the weathered timbers. Finally as they rose on a small bluff, she saw the broken dwelling lying in the dip below.

"Look!" she shouted. Following her hand Ceci made out the old homestead to which Olwen was cantering down the incline.

"Olwen!" she called after her. "Come back here!"

"I only wanted to *look*," she protested, her small frown making Ceci feel thoroughly unreasonable.

"Come on," she said. "Let's go and look!"

With Olwen leading they approached the dwelling Ceci could scarcely bear to look at for the memories it evoked. Its roof had grown moss; gangs of tall nettles stared back at them over the low stone wall and·beyond it in the dried mud of the yard were the footprints and wheelmarks of Reg, Old Bowen and the Buyer—all hardened, all telling their tale. The door of the dwelling, as she had left it, hung on to its secrets, closed. Ceci stood by the gate drinking in the eerie and strange feeling as Olwen rode to the centre of the yard, jumped down and ran to the door.

"Look!" she called turning to her mother, ready to go in and explore. But her mother's face was so pale she left the door and ran back to her.

As they rode up the hill together, Ceci knew Olwen would return to the croft and explore, if not now, then when she was a little older. The thought of its door being opened, the light shining once again into the dark room and reaching towards Old Bowen's chair disturbed her beyond all measure.

"We'll do Art now," she said, spreading the water-colours and little painting tablet on the grass before them, tipping water into the lid of her canteen and looking around for something other than the dwelling which they might paint.

"I can't see *anything*!" sulked Olwen, annoyed at not having explored the dwelling properly. "Who lived there?"

"A princess, I·expect," said Ceci tiredly offering to replace the dwelling with a story.

"Daddy says you're not supposed to tell me stories—" the child said reprovingly as Ceci dipped her paint brush into the water and began to mark in the hillsides, the lines of the horizons and the great sky which looked down on them in the landscape they were trying to capture.

"Start with a line like this—" she began.

"There's nothing here!" shrilled Olwen, the irony of her words striking Ceci. How strange that in this spot where so *much* had happened to her a small child could see nothing to distinguish it from any other place!

Chapter 15

Having sent Sam out to get rid of Harry, Calvin pondered his saddled horse and the day's interrupted routine. Alone in the deserted stables he whistled for Gyp and began to look around for the wilful Collie his mother had so thoroughly spoiled. She had become useless as a sheep dog. Secretly Calvin had continued to lavish on Gyp the odd fondle when none were looking, in the belief his affection for the dog was a thing unknown. He gave his special whistle twice then swung on to his horse intending to pick up with Gyp on the way. Usually when she saw him against the horizon she would manage to be there, scuttling between his horse's legs, pawing the ground and looking up at him.

The day need not be entirely wasted, he told himself, for there were always things to be done in the farthest reaches of his property. Water was one of their most pressing problems and for some time he had been thinking of digging large water tanks to take advantage of the occasional heavy rains which fell as they had done that summer he had acquired a wife. Moving along he found himself thinking of her. Why had it not occurred to him that marriage would change their relationship? Or perhaps, he should say, that she would attempt to create one. It had certainly come as a shock when Ceci had started behaving differently towards him, getting in his way in passages, asking things and wanting answers. Looking back, he had gone through a ridiculous ceremony to get people off his back, to relieve himself of the discomfort of being pestered by eligible women, forced to render them court and to rid himself of the obligation to "maintain the goodwill" of cooks who tended for the most part to be female. These prerequisites to his freedom had been satisfied—the departure of his mother being an added bonus—yet the price had been not inconsiderable. He had attached to himself a formerly level headed girl who had become something of a stumbling-block, and riding the farthest reaches of his property he found himself wondering how it had not occurred to him at the time that being married actually meant being in the constant presence of another person. All in all, he thought, it was just possible that at the time he should have thought of a different way out of his predicament.

As he moved across country on his hack Calvin became aware of one of his hands riding urgently at him, cutting him off. The man came up shouting, his arm describing a great arc then stabbing back at the hills. As he list_ned, Calvin's face engorged with blood.

"Bastard!" he murmured.

He directed the man to fetch a spade then return to his duties and rode off attempting to block a great tide of passionate anger with the cliff of his face. Leaving the trail he made for the outcrop of exposed rocks near their boundary that the man had described and there, just as he had been told, lay his dog Gyp, her throat opened from ear to ear, and beyond her on the fence the cutting knife which had been issued to Harry. Stricken, he dropped from his horse and stood observing the glazed eyes of the dog while in his chest a crushing anger grew.

Returning from their excursion Ceci squeezed lemons, measured out honey, poured in water from a steaming kettle.

"I know who that's for!" piped Olwen, appearing in the doorway.

"Pick some flowers for the table," Ceci said, keeping her eyes off the child.

"*I* want to give it to him."

"Never mind about *this* Olwen!" she begged, already late with the labourers' meal and not wanting the matter of Jock's cold raised before Calvin. "Go and gather some of those small white flowers you like and arrange them on the table."

Glancing up Ceci saw the knowing look on the child's face and sensed it would not be past Olwen to manipulate the situation.

As she hurried across the courtyard with the steaming pitcher and some clean nose rags, she looked nervously about her. The sound of a horse approaching on the path caused her to stop guiltily before Jock's hut but it was only one of the hands. Rounding the corner he rode straight at her.

"Found Gyp with 'er throat cut Ma'am," he burst, sliding from his horse to stand before her.

"Not *Gyp*," Ceci gasped, distressed on account of both the dog and Calvin.

"It'd be Harry," went on the man.

"Harry?" Ceci repeated.

"I'm sent for a spade to bury 'er," he said, crossing to the shed.

Ceci watched him ride off astounded. The reference to Harry mystified her but she was heartbroken on account of Gyp. Gyp had been close to Calvin in a way barred to her. She imagined Calvin standing over her, moved by the same sentiments she had experienced at the death of Else.

Jock smiled at her, a long stream of snot running from nose to chin.

"This is for drinking, not dropping moths in," she said, setting the pitcher down. Jock wasn't cruel to moths but she knew he liked being cautioned by her, that it made him feel safe.

"Don't fling that in the corner," she ordered. "Give it here."

She reached her hand for a dirty nose rag. Jock drank from the glass she had poured with the concentration of a child. Warmly she watched, pondering that he and Olwen shared a special state of grace Olwen was already leaving but Jock never would.

If the Bible were true, how Man must have welcomed

the Fall, she thought, gently wiping Jock's nose. How he must have longed for Knowledge and Degradation, for any way of escaping the boredom of Eternal Purity. In the arc of light Jock looked at her with utter contentment. They knew each other so well, she thought. Dear Jock! If Calvin did not exist Jock would certainly be the happiest man she'd ever known...

Taking the alien thought of Calvin from the hut with her, she realized he would stay away from Hexham till all signs of emotion had removed themselves from his face. Possibly he would not even return till all the lights were put out.

Calvin sat in the darkened summer house, his blank face reflecting the moon. Behind him and across the lawn, a light went off upstairs and a light came on and went off downstairs as the front door opened. A cloak over her nightgown, Ceci stepped on to the lawn and tiptoed across to the unlit summerhouse, its white paint cold to the moon. Certain Calvin was there, she paused on the verandah and very softly opened the door to see him sitting in his usual place, his bent back to her, staring. Filled with compassion she crossed and stood behind him wanting to put a hand on his shoulder. Thinking better of it she came and stood in front of him, then knelt in order to place herself within his gaze which fell to the floor. Quickly Calvin turned his head away, rose and walked past her and out of the hut.

Entering the drawing room with mud on his boots Calvin poured himself a port and stood, the cut glass decanter in one hand, watching its warm droplets of colour move on the velvet curtains in the yellow light. He became aware of Ceci appearing like a moon in the doorway and briskly turned his back, but she entered and went to sit in her usual chair, observing him. At that, Calvin replaced the decanter, turned on his heel and walked out of the room with his glass. Alone, Ceci looked about then rose, moved slowly to the sideboard and poured a glass and stood leaning there in thought, gently sipping at the drink. Suddenly Calvin reappeared in the doorway, saw, and rushed at her shouting: "Are you totally mad?"

He snatched the drink away and poured it on the floor. She stared aghast at the spreading puddle.

"Must I get a doctor to you?"

Brutally he forced the glass top back into the decanter almost cracking the stem. Ceci stepped back in horror, watching the port sink into the wood, hardly daring to look up at Calvin as he left the room. Was this outburst intended to drive her away because through his grief an avenue had finally opened up, allowing her to get close to him?

Her heart heavy with pity for his need to carry his burdens alone, she hurried upstairs and into the room where he lay on his bed wide awake, eyes boring into the night.

"Calvin," she began, crossing to the bed, tenderness and sympathy overwhelming her former caution as she looked at the back of his head, reached out and, without thinking, laid her hand there. Calvin recoiled as if stung, turned a burning face to her. Alarmed, she withdrew her hand, holding the charred fingertips.

"What are you trying to do?!" he demanded in a voice so fierce and out of control she was for the moment afraid.

She had tried to *touch* him, she told herself; she had done no wrong! Hurriedly she moved to the window and stood looking out 'til gradually a sense of understanding came over her: Calvin was mad. There could be no other explanation for it. To touch a person in grief was surely no crime: it was a thing that normal people did every day yet Calvin would have none of it. She had half known this for a long time but never examined it consciously, she told herself, struggling to remember the word which Ginger had mentioned which was vitally important.

"Nolans on the other side invited us over," she began in a steady voice feeling his anger building up behind her. She had known he did not like to be touched just as well as she now knew it would be against his will to hear what she was about to say:

"Shall I tell them we'll go?" she demanded, spinning on him. "We'll go and *enjoy* ourselves!"

"Get out," Calvin said in a deep hate-filled voice, but Ceci did not move. She leant on the window staring at him and nodding, absolutely certain she had discovered his weakness, the weakness he had used like a stick to beat her over the head. As she stared, all traces of fear went from her eyes and Calvin seemed to retreat before her. Without either of them moving she felt she had invaded him to the point he was now backed up against a wall and shaking. Resisting the temptation of an uncharitable rejoinder she walked quietly past him and out of the room. Calvin, she suddenly realized, was afraid of her.

Striding into the drawing room Ceci pulled out and cranked up the symphonium and slapped on a metal disc. She pushed back the chairs sending them dancing to the walls and kicked the carpets away. As a rich waltz filled the emptiness of the night, she began to dance and dance as if in someone's arms, her left hand resting exactly where his shoulder should be and her right arm outstretched, hanging delicately by the fingertips from her invisible partner's hand. Her head hung back swaying, eyes shut, mouth in contented smile as her face moved from side to side as if resisting caresses. Round and around she went as the sounds of the sweet music filled the room, gown swirling, hair flying. She did not see the door open a crack, Olwen peep in and, amazed, crawl to sit on a small pouf, hands clasped around knees, to watch.

Suddenly Calvin appeared at the door and in two strides was at the machine, trembling in rage before it, looking from the machine to the whirling image of female beauty and back again. Head thrown back, with a blissful smile Ceci danced on while Calvin wrenched the lid, almost snapping it, removing the disc and stood holding it. But Ceci continued to dance, face bewitched by her invisible partner, now seemingly trying to kiss her eyelids. Finally she dropped on the sofa in a peal of laughter, exhausted, to find Calvin standing before her.

"What in God's *name* are you doing?" he growled from a place deep in his throat.

"For the joy—the romance—I've never had!" she gasped breathlessly.

"Control yourself."

"—the *love*!" she threw at him, seeing him clench his fists. "Joy! Enjoy! Joy!" she jumped up. "There! I've said it!"

"I can't believe this," muttered Calvin pacing the boundaries of the room.

"I won't *drag* you to Hell if you *look* at me!" she shouted at him.

"Oh you *disgust* me," Calvin said wiping his mouth. "What are you afraid of? Damnation?"

He turned to the walls. Quickly she went to stand behind him.

"Someone has done you a great wrong Calvin Laird," she said firmly.

"I'll get a governess for the child," he said.

"You've been taught some terrible doctrines," she went on, aware at the same time Calvin did not believe in any doctrines at all.

Suddenly her sense of exhilaration left her.

"Why can't we be *friends*?" she pleaded, her mind coming back to the terrible centre of her existence. "We've got so *much*!"

"*We*?" he shouted.

"Well *you*!"

Calvin whirled on her.

"Do you think we're here to—*enjoy* ourselves?" he demanded as if the issue were important.

"I'll clean the house from top to bottom to make you *happy*," said Ceci, "but you're *never* happy!"

"Did you think you could make me happy?" he asked in a way which made her feel smaller than she'd ever felt before. "Apologize in the morning," he said from the doorway.

Ceci flung herself on the couch and stared mutely ahead. Her moment of freedom from Calvin had been very short-lived: now she was back in his shadow. Suddenly Olwen poked her face out from behind a chair and stood up. Ceci groaned at the sight of her.

Rather than wallow in self-pity Ceci took stock of herself. Even if she were a piece of refuse washed to the furthest extremities of her husband's existence, surely she could find space somewhere to continue on with dignity, setting her own boundaries and knowing peace of mind? There was nothing to be gained from lifting the layers of her hurt or examining the pain underneath.

Immediately following the incident of her dancing,

Calvin had displayed new forms of silence: silences which meant he accused her, silences which implied that as far as he was concerned she did not exist, and Grand Silences which cancelled out entire parts of her world. His silences became difficult and dangerous to tread. Into them, she would drop little slivers of sound and listen for an echo but the more she listened, the more she heard something she did not like coming towards her. Gradually, though, it went away and Calvin resumed the semblance of friendship when it became necessary for them to eat together for Olwen's sake.

After some weeks during which his manner had ameliorated, she had almost convinced herself her dancing was forgotten when the true cause of his improved humour was made known to her.

As she sat musing over the contents of a letter from Home she did not see a carriage pause at their gate, nor its driver descend and address the person within nor, over the voice of her child, did she hear it turn on to their drive or come to a halt outside their portico...

"If London Granny is sick," Olwen reasoned wisely, referring to Ceci's mother, "she could go and sit in Granny Bath's garden..."

Briefly her parents' eyes met, the twinkle of a beginning smile between them at the impossibility of the suggestion.

"Sam found three more traps yesterday," said Calvin loudly as if deliberately struggling to make conversation.

"Makes me homesick reading all this," Ceci said folding the letter.

"Up the top end," he went on, having seen the carriage rounding the bend.

"She goes on about how *lucky* we are to be here but sometimes..." Ceci sighed, letting her voice trail off. Glancing up she found Calvin looking at her as if something crucial were about to happen. At that moment the door bell rang and Calvin got to his feet with unaccustomed speed.

"How many London cousins have I? Bella, May—" Olwen was chirping as he left the room.

"Florrie and Tring," frowned Ceci, her mind on who was at the door.

"*Tring!*" Olwen sang out.

"Terence Edwin," Ceci corrected.

"I'm the eldest!"

"You're the *second* eldest," her mother said, dimming her voice to a halt as she listened to steps in their hall. A woman appeared in the doorway. Ceci could not believe her eyes. She struggled to get to her feet noting Calvin's hand in the small of the woman's back, the woman leaning hard on it·as if resisting being propelled into the room. In her early thirties with an unfortunately shaped mouth and grey angora shawl Ceci could no more believe the woman was there than that Calvin was actually touching a woman. In the second it took her to realize his act was an introduction to some new politics, she knew the woman would come between her and her child as surely as she was intended to stand between her and Calvin.

"Miss Robertson—your charge—Olwen—" said Calvin in a firm voice, eyes filled with self-confidence and no little pleasure at seeing Ceci so overtaken by the event, coming as it did after that rare occurence, his smile during breakfast. Had it reminded her of the wink that had slipped out unbidden the day she left Hexham in the rain? Ceci stared at the woman unbelieving, shock and betrayal weakening her knees. She was aware of Olwen frozen beside her, looking to her for reassurance; aware of the rays glinting off the silverware becoming suddenly unreal.

"I'd be obliged if you'd fetch down my bags Mr. Laird," said the woman to Calvin in clipped grim tones. "That driver fellow looks—*most—unreformed*."

Horrified, Ceci realized the Change had arrived.

Chapter 16

With the advent of Miss Robertson, a chill reformist wind blew through the house. Colours were toned down, pictures removed, the books Mrs. Laird had left ("idolatrous rubbish") swept from the shelves and Ceci's days filled with dismay. With this pall descended the smell of suspicion, attaching to the slightest relaxation, instantly labelled "idleness." She must be forever dusting, polishing, for "time spent in idle pursuits was time removed from the service of God" ...

Man had, she was told, been put on earth to convert his time (by labour) to surplus profit to be reinvested, more speedily bringing about the ultimate "ordering of the Universe" (which, it irreverently occurred to Ceci, better planning might have taken care of). God wanted, she was told, a tidy universe; a place where his minions clocked in and out in reformed quotidian bursts, reliving the energizing logic of the Age of Steam. Those who were smart enough to realize What God Wanted would know that "emotions" were post-Fall stumbling blocks, deliberately strewn in Man's way. Man was lucky (as *Paradise Lost* had pointed out had she been wise enough to study it) to have been given the chance to regain Paradise by the relation to God of *work*. If Man or in this case woman chose *not* to work, the alternative was only too clear.

"You are not here to enjoy yourself," was the One Grand Message cascading down via Miss Robertson from those great watersheds of reformist thought: Luther, Calvin and Wesley. "Enjoyment," she was soon informed, was a danger second only to the friendships and human emotions that led to it. "Distrust your deepest friend," was what Baxter preached, informed Miss Robertson, (explaining he'd meant "your wife,") ... "who would lead you from service to God by enjoyment..."

Pondering Miss Robertson's diatribes to which she was daily subjected it occurred to Ceci the woman was uniquely suited to the Puritan way for as one shunned by society on account of her looks, base usefulness was an area in which she could excel. Moreover, her appreciation of power was considerable. Where was the man or woman who, once having invited her into their house, could fly in the face of her "good example" and criticize? But while Ceci could admire the skill Miss Robertson brought to bear, she could not help pitying her for needing to barricade herself in. Doubtless the woman had a more winning side. What had caused her to so mercilessly shut herself off from those prepared to see beyond her physical looks to the real person within? Briefly Ceci thought she must have had love as a child. Had it been very terrible for Miss Robertson when that love stopped?

For her part Miss Robertson did not anticipate any particular problems in the Laird household. She could see it was a case of a man who couldn't handle a wife and had sent for a governess, ostensibly for the child, but really to see the woman didn't get under his feet. The reputation had gone before her of being able to make wilful young women accept the reality of life without love—or, as the men usually put it— "constant attention." Having trodden that road herself, the way was not unknown. She remembered Mr. Laird talking about "her charge's" upbringing as if that were paramount without even acknowledging her true role in his household if he'd even known it . . . Was it possible the man had not thought his way clearly through before engaging her? That would mean she must take time before playing any major cards for Mr. Laird was a *rather* nice man and distinctly handsome . . . Tucking her secret mirror into the jacket of her Bible and adjusting her collar till it looked particularly stern, she congratulated herself for having been born amongst Protestants in the Puritan Age for in Catholic countries where moral fibre played a poor second fiddle to Beauty she would never have known her many victories. Power, in the end, she mused, afforded more pleasure than love and the older she got the more she could see it. It was *hated* more, more *sought after*, a thing *envied* and *crawled to* and she could not deny feeling it surge within her as she kept women from their men, made men dependent on her to do this for them. Indeed the greater became her influence in most households, the more the women had to subordinate themselves to her to get anywhere *near* their husbands.

In Miss Robertson's presence, Calvin seemed to flourish. No more was he pestered by Ceci and apart from the odd encounter with her when he took particular care to avoid any reference to the household or acknowledge anything she might say concerning it, it seemed he could finally congratulate himself on having found a female who could take orders, get out of his presence and execute them. Never had he caught *Miss Robertson* lingering or staring at him, nor did she sigh or look hurt, nor was anything in her appearance aimed at him. Indeed the way the woman dressed was praiseworthy for its almost military annihilation of character. Indeed, he told himself saddling up his horse, there might be something in the woman that was worth taking a second look at. As he pondered, Ceci ran out of the house at him.

"Calvin—" she began.

"See that?" he said indicating a broken trap of poor twine fibre lying in the corner. "Local poacher. Certainly not Harry..." He turned to mount his horse ignoring the breathing he could hear searing his back, the tears he had seen flash in her eyes.

"I can't *bear* to be in the house with that woman another moment!" Ceci burst.

"Until you take a leaf from her book," Calvin said turning to her sternly, "you will remember your position in this house is no different from hers."

Returning to the house, Ceci hesitated outside the drawing room door listening. From within came the voice of Miss Robertson, faint but clear, reading aloud from a book.

> *"It was well you escaped her net!" said Christian. "It was like to have cost you your life!"*

Gently she turned the handle the merest fraction so she could see in. There directly in her line of vision was Olwen in a sad grey-black dress with white color, hair drawn severely back with a solitary bow.

> *"You cannot think what a flattering tongue she had," said Faithful, "promising me all manner of content!"*

Ceci could see that her child was asleep in the winged chair, mouth open, yet at the window Miss Robertson continued reading gazing periodically across the lawn.

> *"But not the content of a good conscience, I trow!" said Christian.*

Horrified, Ceci understood the words she was hearing.

> *"...All carnal and fleshly content."*

went on the voice. Drawn into the room, to her amaze-

ment she realized Miss Robertson was in fact staring hard
at Calvin who was crossing the lawn towards the summer
house, presumably for an item he had forgotten. The
woman was bobbing from side to side, straining her
head to see as he moved behind the roses and went in
through the screen door. For a moment the reading stopped
then:

> *"Thank God you have escaped her!" said Christian.*
> *"The abhorred of the Lord shall fall into her ditch. Her*
> *steps take hold of Hell!"*

As the summer house door opened and Calvin emerged
again the reading ceased and Miss Robertson stepped
back slightly to reposition herself behind the curtain.

> *" . . . Adam had three daughters—The Lust of the*
> *Flesh, The Lust of the Eyes—"*

she began in a fast tremulous voice, glancing towards the
room door and in that instant seeing Ceci observing her.

"I do not allow intrusions!" she fired, deeply conscious of having been caught staring at Calvin and ignoring her pupil.

"Give me that disgusting book," said Ceci.

"This," said Miss Robertson advancing on her, "I
doubt you would have had the inclination to acquaint
yourself with it—is *Pilgrim's Progress*! The epic of man's
struggle through the world of sinful pastimes to the
Celestial City."

For a moment it occurred to Ceci that the Celestial
City Miss Robertson was struggling towards was Calvin.
She extended her hand for the book as if she had the
authority to demand it, as if she expected Miss Robertson
to hand it over, grim showdown on her face Miss Robertson
stood her ground.

"That book is not suitable for children," said Ceci.

"Have you read it?"

"Isn't it about a man living in a place which is to be
horribly destroyed?"

"The City of Destruction. *This life!*"

"And his wife and children cling to him yet he *leaves*
them there."

"To seek his salvation! One of the greatest pieces of literature—"

"If I remember rightly, it's the work of a tinker, written in a prison cell!"

"*Reformed.*"

Ceci laughed aloud and went on: "When he's safe it occurs to him it might be nice to have his wife and family with him, doesn't it?"

At that, Olwen woke up and saw the two women facing up to each other, Miss Robertson's head drawn back like a swan about to strike. Instinctively she knew she need not worry about falling asleep in class for something bigger was afoot. Suddenly both women looked at her.

"Can we do—'Art'," she asked coyly.

Miss Robertson's face bulged.

"You are responsible for this *wantoness* in a child so young!" she fired at Ceci, fumbling fiercely at her book for a quotation on a particular page.

"I have hindered you, my children,—"

Ceci made a quick grab at the book but Miss Robertson spun away.

"If you remove this book," she said fiercely, "you will be instructed to return it to me. Olwen! Get your father!"

"Stay," said Ceci. The child moved to the door and hesitated.

"I can see you're not a—happy woman, Miss Robertson," Ceci began, "but..."

"You are like a bog for men to fall into!" Miss Robertson shouted at her.

"This living on the brink of being eternally Damned all the time—" said Ceci understandingly.

"You resent me holding a candle to you!" interrupted Miss Robertson. "You, unable to withstand the temptations wealth has put in your way! For the likes of *you* poverty was created!"

From the doorway Olwen saw her mother stare up solemnly at the taller woman then say quietly: "You'd like to live in a house like this." She saw Miss Robertson shudder as if a great wind passed through her.

"God has created stewards for his wealth!" she

thundered. "To watch over it and bring order to the world! Your upright husband—"

"What a hypocrite you are!"

"What is happening here is predestined!"

"I'd like you to leave this house."

"I'm sure you would!"

As Miss Robertson turned on Olwen she ran from the room giving Ceci the chance to take another lunge at the book. Skirts swinging, the women wrestled over it as if they were wringing a goose's neck together.

"It's people like you, trapped in your cycle of sin—" gasped Miss Robertson, her breath coming short, "repentance—atonement—relief—renewed sin!—repentance—atonement." Suddenly it occurred to Ceci Miss Robertson was referring to that scourge of Reformists, the Catholics! She was even accused of being one!

"I'm not a Catholic!" she burst out. Affronted by the very word Miss Robertson lost her grip on the book for one sweet moment letting Ceci know victory. As she whirled away the woman pulled herself up.

"You're one of them!" she snorted disdainfully. At that moment Calvin appeared in the door with Olwen peeping around him and the smile of victory fled from Ceci's face. She handed the book back to Miss Robertson and walked quietly past Calvin and Olwen from the room. Lingering in the hallway she heard Miss Robertson apologize briefly yet sincerely to Calvin for wasting his "valuable time" before despatching him from the room with a speed which amounted to ejection. She saw Calvin amazed reappear in the hallway, his polished riding boots pointing neatly at her.

"Make her *go* Calvin!" Ceci pleaded. "Get *rid* of her!"

"She object to your touching spirits and dancing?" Calvin asked snidely.

"She won't let me *near Olwen!*" Ceci begged. "She's unhealthy."

Calvin tossed his head as if the matter were of the greatest indifference.

"Work," he shrugged. "Make yourself—*useful.*"

At every turn, Miss Robertson drove home her advantage. In encountering Ceci in the kitchen the next day, apart from ignoring her position as wife of her employer, she tried by decreeing it to deny even the fact of Ceci''s sexuality, her vulnerability as a fragile female amongst true red blooded men.

"Mr. Laird tells me you object to skinning a deer—" Miss Robertson remarked in a tone reflecting surprise at Ceci's reticence.

"Certainly I object to working in the outhouse with twelve men!" Ceci retorted.

"And why is that?"

"Because it puts me on a level with them and I'm the Mistress of this house. Besides they'll think I *want* to be there!"

"And *do* you?"

"Of course not!" Ceci snapped.

"Then there's nothing for you to worry about, is there?" Miss Robertson said glibly. "*I* obey Calvin without complaint!"

How much more of this woman could she take, Ceci asked herself smouldering from the discomfort of hearing her own husband described to her face by his Christian name when tradition had it that even a wife referred to her husband as 'Mr.' to third parties. Her power over her own child had been eroded to the extent Olwen took account of every reprimand she received. As she attempted to steer a course between Calvin and Miss Robertson, what kind of a mother did Olwen find her? Indecisive? Guilt ridden? Weak?

"Olwen," she called gently as the child moved past the kitchen door. "Run this in to Jock for me," she said holding out the pitcher of lemon and honey.

"I don't have to," stated Olwen.

"Here," Ceci urged, gently extending the pitcher towards her.

"No!" said Olwen putting her hands behind her back. "Coz he's dirty," she recited as if reading a lesson. "And seeved in sin." Seeved? Did she mean conceived?

"Come here," Ceci frowned at the glaring child. "*What* did you say?"

Tossing her head Olwen walked out of the room leaving Ceci clutching the pitcher and biting her lip. She took a deep breath in.

She would outlast Miss Robertson: of that she was *sure*.

*   *   *

Chapter 17

Ceci mounted her horse, tossed the ends of her bright red shawl over her shoulder and paused on the edge of the lawn. Calvin, she knew, would be in the summer house and Miss Robertson and Olwen in the drawing room "studying." Taking a deep breath she turned her horse and galloped it in a straight line across the lawn for the gates.

Miss Robertson paused in her reading to look at Olwen. The child seemed not to be listening but staring into the deep polish of the table seeing there the reflected movement of the clematis leaves beyond the window. Suddenly a bright red streak tore so vividly past, they both spun in their seats. Eyes round as saucers Olwen saw her mother, hair flying, lips reddened, shooting across the lawn as beyond it the door of the summer house burst open and her father came out and stood there and she heard Miss Robertson say in a voice thicker than the thickest gravy:

"To cause emotion to rise in the breast of a man, to mislead him from *God's work* is an unforgivable sin!" Her chest rode up and down as she looked out at Calvin examining the hoof marks on the lawn and staring after Ceci as if he would personally like to deliver her a good thrashing.

Ceci turned through the cut in the wire onto Bowen's land and decided not to give them one more thought! She made herself sing and for a while kept up the bravado.

> Jog on jog on the footpath way
> And merrily hent the stile-a
> A merry heart goes all the way
> Your sad tires in a mile-a . . .

she sang, remembering that the verse came from Home and for the first time wondering what it meant. Slipping from her horse she lay on her red shawl looking at the sky 'til the loneliness of the place overwhelmed her and the relevence of the chant she had sung hit home. Rising, she tucked the shawl under the reins and headed on towards Moke.

Leaving Bowen's land with the intention of visiting Ginger she began to feel queasy. Should she have come? Carefully she pinned up her hair, took out the hairpins and repinned it. Already she regretted the shawl's bright colour and the lipstick she had used; only the fear of being afraid to go on forced her to move forward.

Turning in at the cracked signboard "NOLAN" she reminded herself Ginger was married, feeling relieved and embarassed at the same time. While no one could accuse her of pursuing him which she certainly wasn't doing, at the same time, to visit a married man's household without her husband or child was strange behaviour surely, particularly coming in the middle of the day. Would her visit be taken as a statement of disloyalty to or rejection of her own husband? She forced her horse on up their driveway. The Nolans had clearly never heard of Wesley she thought, glancing at the base of fence posts eaten away by white ants. Where the driveway finished and the land began was an open question and a far cry from Calvin's dutiful wire sentinels, conquering hill after hill. Rounding the bend she came on the house for the first time, a large untidy structure in clear need of maintenance. Bars of the balustrade were broken, a window was cracked, it had been years since the place had seen a lick of paint and by the look of it, a burglar could have gained entry in a multitude of places. Before the front door the earth and remains of plants had been trampled to a flat finish and a child's cardigan hung caught in a rose bush. There was nothing to suggest work in progress or any indication that repairs to the guttering, the roof, or split weatherboards had ever been contemplated. Somewhere a child was hammering a stone on a flat piece of tin, a sound which would have driven Miss Robertson *mad*!

As Ceci approached the door she was struck by an awkward thought. Suppose Ginger were not there? What possible explanation could she offer to his wife to arriving at exactly the time of the midday meal? As she hestitated the hammering stopped and a child tore past her dragging a clothesline with pillow slips and underwear still attached straight through the dirt. Her eyes sought vainly the doorbell. Gathering nerve, she began to tap on the door with her fingers. It swung instantly open to reveal a shoe and a sleeping cat. Loud noises, applause and clapping were coming from a room further in and as she stepped in, a small child pulled at her back:

"May I use your red shawl off the horse?" she asked grinning. "That's Kevin's boat."

Looking again Ceci saw the shoe had a hairbrush in it, and a piece of paper caught like a sail in the bristles.

"They're in there," said the girl before running out again.

Ceci called nervously then a little louder, then feeling uncomfortably like an intruder in the house walked towards the room from which the noise was coming. The door hung slightly open to reveal a boy of 7 doing a conjuring trick with folded tea towels watched by an assortment of children, an old man in a stained armchair; a standing woman, babe on hip... and Ginger at the table! If any room was a contrast to Hexham this was it. Rarely had Ceci glimpsed, even in the fleeting seconds it took her to realize it, a sight so like the nesting hole of small animals. Folded clothes were piled on chairs, homemade toys lay on the floor with cups and rattles as, silent but for Ginger's chewing, the entire room waited for the boy to bring his trick to a climax.

"Excuse me," said Ceci quickly.

Instantly their eyes were on her, Ginger's widening with wild incredulity and unmistakable joy while his wife's sunk in embarrassment at the state of their room.

"Lawks!" she said clutching her mouth. "Looks like we've bin dragged through a hedge!"

"Ah!" said Ginger getting to his feet coughing crumbs, his trousers beginning to slide as the small girl streaked through the room in Ceci's shawl and a pile of ironing went over.

"I—I was passing," Ceci stammered.

"Let me fetch you a chair," Ginger grinned, lifting a chair from the wall. Instantly Ceci noticed it was dirty.

"Glad you came," he said glancing at his wife, who was still unaware who Ceci was and motioning to Ginger to re-fasten his flies. "My wife Maureen."

"You must wonder at us!" said Maureen, untangling her hair, ready to apologize for what was obviously their usual way of life.

"Only four's ours," said Ginger. "Michael and Kevin—Come here Michael. Twins. Elizabeth there with your cape."

"Told her to give it back! . . ." murmured Maureen. "That's my Dad."

The old man leaned forward.

"And baby Faith," said Ginger, motioning the child on his wife"s hip.

He wiped his mouth and looked as if he were about to leave.

"You weren't—going out were you?" Ceci asked nervously.

"He comes for his lunch," explained Maureen smiling nervously at Ginger who at that moment was staring at Ceci with a mixture of pain and desire on his face.

"You stay! I'll be back," he said looking at her. "We'll get this place cleaned up and you have tea with us."

Ceci smiled, convinced he didn't mean it.

"How about it Maureen?" he said, motioning to the pile of ironing.

Maureen nodded and sat at the table, trying to brush the crumbs off while the children ran from the room to continue their game outside. Ceci saw Ginger come up behind his wife, put his hands on her shoulders, bend and kiss the top of her head then straighten out looking ashamed.

"Mind my hair!" she flinched. "S"all greasy!"

She looked down as Ginger moved to the door followed by his wife's eyes. Obviously he had come for his lunch and now he was leaving!

Maureen fell to clearing up the crumbs, the toys, the beakers, the ironing—those signs of life that Ceci envied for their unashamedness. Though embarrassed at being visited by a "lady" she asked well meaning questions to put at her ease. *Who* was she? Mrs. Laird? But Mrs. Laird had gone back to England? The *other* Mrs. Laird! *Ah!*

"You the one that boy took a shine to?" asked Old Nolan, motioning the door through which Ginger had departed. Maureen went crimson. Her mouth tightened and it was as if part of her rose, crossed the room, took

Old Nolan by the throat and tried to strangle him. Squeeze, squeeze _TWIST_. Instantly Ceci got to her feet.

"I—I must be getting back," she apologized, moving towards the door horrified at the pitch of frustration Old Nolan was knowingly driving Maureen to. "Supposed to call your husband Ronald Calvin." Nolan joked. "Ronald for Knox and Calvin for the good times," but when the Minister saw the initials RC...

Trapped in the room Ceci felt the tension between them mounting. Suddenly Maureen turned to her.

"Why did you stay around? On Bowen's land?" she demanded, all pretence of civility gone.

"Jock," said Ceci innocently.

Old Nolan pulled a flask from the side of his chair and took a swig.

"Mind you don't get shot at!" he muttered. Ceci clicked her tongue at him. "You're beginning to sound like one of 'em." Nolan burped.

At the sound of a fight erupting outside Maureen fled the room.

"Give it to me!"

"Mine!"

There was kicking, punching—a silence as prelude to a great scream of righteous anger. Then the arrival of Maureen identified by loud smackings and her voice rising as if she were tempted to pick up a child by its feet and swing it against a wall. Smash. Quickly Ceci eased herself through the door, past Maureen and the children and out of the house.

Riding back down their driveway convincing herself she should not have visited, Ceci was troubled by Old Nolan's phrase "one of 'em." Who had accused her of being like "one of 'em" before? Wasn't it Miss Robertson saying she resembled a Catholic? Well if Hell was full of Catholics swigging drink and spilling crumbs that was alright by her! But she _had_ frowned and clicked her tongue disapprovingly at the old man she remembered, biting her lip. Was it possible that in seven years Hexham had changed her that much?... Lifting her eyes she was shocked to find herself almost upon Ginger hanging about on the track on the pretence of some spilled bales. Hurriedly she got down, struggled to remove her gloves and help with the spilled

hay. Bending she got a good grip on a splayed bale but
pull as she might it would not move though she strained
and heaved, straw staining her skirt, dust falling into her
shoes. Intensely mortified she found Ginger laughing at
her, pointing out with delight that she was standing on
the end of the very bale she was attempting to lift.

"My wife's better at this for all you're a lady," he
joked, kneeling on the ground amongst the golden hay,
laughing. Ceci stepped back pulling her gloves from her
pocket, forced her hands into them and began brushing
the dirt from her skirt.

"Get your gloves dirty!" Ginger teased.

Her eyes fell; she looked almost as if she might cry. It
was his use of the word "gloves," her memory of how she
had felt when Mrs. Laird donned them to draw a map in
the dust of her kitchen table at the dwelling; Maureen's
earlier use of the word "Ma'am" to her, the way she had
not wanted to sit on any of their chairs and the feeling
that Ginger was somehow trying to punish her... all
these things made her sad and as she looked up he
crossed to her and tweaked her under the chin.

"Ceci—" he said, smiling 'til she was genuinely baffled by his friendly eyes, the moistness in them, the way
he shook his head as if she owed him an explanation or
there were something she had forgotten to finish telling
him. Frowning she scrambled back on to her horse and
looked down on him. He was peering up at her in an
injured way.

"Thank you for having me," she said quickly giving
an inclination of the head and riding hastily away. Behind
her for a considerable time Ginger remained staring.

If all mirrors were removed from the house, Miss Robertson
realized, people would be less inclined to compare their
own reflection with hers and her looks would improve
accordingly. That decision taken, she struggled out of the
house with one mirror after another, leaning them face
down against a wall while deciding what to do with them.

As the pile grew, Jock crossed over, turned a full
length mirror around and was impressed then utterly
delighted with his find. Apart from seeing his reflection in
puddles and windows, this was his first experience of a
genuine reflecting mirror. Fascinated, he posed and twisted,

turned and spun on himself, trying out expressions such
as Calvin thinking and Miss Robertson angry. Suddenly
Miss Robertson almost stumbled into him, her way blinded
by the mirror she was carrying. Jock did not move aside
for at the best of times he found Miss Robertson funny
and in any case was not afraid of women. Irritated, she
bent to set the mirror down thinking it was the *least* he
could do, even *given* his impairment, to have *moved*! She
glared at him as she bent but he was staring at a handkerchief sticking from her hip pocket thinking of giving it a
good tweak. *Tweak*! Out it came with, wrapped in it, her
secret hand mirror. Stooping eagerly he picked it up as,
freeing herself from her activity, Miss Robertson realized
in horror he'd got her mirror and soon everyone would
know!

"Give me that!" she said in a wobbly voice but Jock
held it above her head as if she were a small dog he were
inviting to jump for it. Miss Robertson tried and missed.
Jock took off wanting to be chased and waited on the
opposite side of the courtyard waving it, discovering in
awe he could catch the sun. As little diamonds of light
darted about Miss Robertson came slowly forward, eyes
hard as stones, heart pained to see him make awful
grimaces at her mirror and actually *touch* it with his
tongue! As she arrived he held it guilelessly to her face as
if he would surrender it but as she reached for it, jerked
his arm back and ran off again whooping and jumping,
then vanished into his hut. From within came loud triumphant blasts of his jew's harp shattering the still afternoon, making Miss Robertson flinch. She could not *stand*
that noise! After a quick look over her shoulder she decided on a desperate measure: getting down on all fours she
crawled in after him.

The discordant notes stopped as she forced her form
into Jock's tunnel, overcoming all fear and revulsion, and
pressed on towards the sparse circle of light in which she
could see her mirror lying. Wanting to be out of the place
as soon as possible she made a snatch for it but Jock,
ready with his pitcher of lemon honey and delighted to
have found a new playmate, tipped it gleefully on her
hand and all over the cuff of her sleeve, snorting with
laughter. Miss Robertson kept a good grip on the mirror,
ignored his giggling and mastering her nerves turned

around to crawl out. Sad that she was leaving Jock gave her behind a good pinch which sent her flying down the tunnel like a champagne cork, the mirror falling instantly from her hand and she scrambling over it in her haste to be gone.

Gasping she got to her feet, forcing herself to pant and look ravaged but no one was there. After a moment standing in the quietened yard she had a solution. Drawing her chest up she let out a short, sharp scream then ran to a shed where she knew a man would be working and trembled before him.

"Where's the Master?" she demanded, an edge of hysteria to her voice. The man looked up with dislike and shrugged. Miss Robertson gripped at a rake as if to steady herself, straightened her back and strode towards the house. Once inside she stood listening then moved towards the stairs and listened again, then with deliberation spiced by mounting excitement *ran* up the stairs and, without knocking, burst into the room where Calvin was writing. He turned in utter fury at the intrusion to see her panting against the door, lips pressed together, head forced back as if great weights hung from her hair— breathing in gasps. Deeply resenting involvement he spoke in a harsh tone:

"Control yourself."

"With the greatest goodwill in the world," she began, "I bethought myself to—to introduce that—unfortunate— to the word of God—" She glanced nervously at him to see what effect her words were having, then turned away as if unable to continue. Curious, Calvin pushed a chair towards her with one foot. Groping for it she sat and with difficulty and theatre, as if having to dig out the words from a very private place, carefully released the utterances she had decided on:

"He was—seated on the floor—when I—went in—" she paused for effect, "examining a—a vanity no doubt from your wife"—the words rushed out convincingly fast— "and then—then—Oh!" her fingers ploughed her hair, she appeared to go cold as, looking Calvin in the eye, she braced herself to assault him:

"He exposed himself to me!"

Before her Calvin's eyes opened defencelessly wide while Miss Robertson's gleamed with power and triumph.

Though it had cost all, she had had her moment of intimacy with him! As if realizing it Calvin got quickly to his feet and strode past Miss Robertson, determined to recover face. Hurrying from her presence he snatched up his whip, caught for his jacket, forced his feet into their boots and vanished from view. Marvelling at his swelling chest she ran behind him into the yard, past the station hand she had addressed and pointed at Jock's shack as if the very thought of going any closer were enough to cause her to collapse.

"You mustn't hurt him," she begged, clutching at Calvin's sleeve. Furiously he shook her off and beating his boot with his whip took the easier option, bent down and crawled into Jock's covey.

Miss Robertson stared fascinated at the shack, guilt, curiosity then anger stirring her as no sounds came out. Beyond she could sense the two hands watching and above a movement at Olwen's curtain suggested that instead of lying in bed under the sign "Bed Is The Place for Idling" she had dared to get out and peep from her window. Hastily Miss Robertson dissociated herself from anything that might happen.

Olwen peered down into the courtyard. She thought she had seen Miss Robertson vanishing behind a building but otherwise all was as usual, the labourers out working, her father no doubt in his room writing as he always did on a Thursday afternoon and she, with a hundred and one things she would like to be doing, forced to wear her nightdress and contemplate the sign Miss Robertson had written for Timewasters! Suddenly, there was Jock, dragging himself from his shack as if his foot were caught, a red mark across his face, screaming in small gasps. Horrified, she pressed her face to the window. Now he was standing dazed and her *own father* was coming out of the shack after him, getting to his feet while Jock ran in circles clutching an eye as if he could not see where he was going. She saw her father walk towards Jock as if he meant to grab his wrist but Jock backed away, turned and ran wildly on to the lawn—his torn breeches and bare feet strange against its ordered background. To her amazement she saw her father lead out his horse, jump on and ride straight at the lawn while Jock scrambled the fence behind the juniper trees, glanced back then ran fearfully on, Calvin's mount soaring over the obstacles in hot pursuit. Biting her lip she stared from the window at the spot where they had vanished.

Breaking yet another rule Olwen turned the big handle of the door Miss Robertson had not locked, ostensibly as proof that she trusted the child yet actually to make it easier to walk in on her, and stepped out into the still corridor. Still undecided she tiptoed towards Miss Robertson's room, and pressed one ear to her door.

"Oh I shouldn't have done it!" she heard the voice. "I'll be punished!"

Confident she would not be apprehended Olwen bent and peeped through the keyhole to see Miss Robertson on her knees by the bed arguing with God.

"You're already so cruel to me," she said, up at the ceiling. "What else is there?!"

Cautiously Olwen withdrew. Though there was no one in the house to observe her, she felt very uncomfortable hearing Miss Robertson naked with God.

Chapter 18

It seemed as if all roads led to Bowen's that afternoon as Jock, running for all the safety he knew, sped desperately over a crown of hill seeking to go to earth amongst his familiar spoor. As he ducked between broken shrubs, scrambled down clefts between hills, moving from one hand-hold to another, he left Calvin's horse turning in circles above but occasionally meeting him by cutting him off at gullies or ways he had seen out of narrow places. Jock knew the land better than Calvin and though he might be forced to turn and claw his way up sliding banks of earth again he stuck to the one thing on his mind: to get back to the dwelling, run in, and shut the door and be safe.

* * *

Meanwhile, Ceci was also heading towards the dwelling. She could feel the presence of Old Bowen, the isolation of the place. Up ahead loomed the old man's grave, the earthenware bottle as she had left it, planted on the mound, the bare twigs of some branches sticking from it, their leaves blown away. Getting down she left her horse and went to stand there. Who had he been, this old man whose family had so influenced her life? As she pondered she became aware that someone was watching her. Afraid to look she stood motionless, desperately conscious of eyes moving up and down and over her. There was not a sound to be heard yet the sense of being observed seemed to thunder in her ears. Becoming frightened she began to back towards her horse, meaning to suddenly leap on and ride away down the gulley, out the open end and back towards Moke. The feeling was coming from the dwelling itself, she sensed, and just as she turned to pull herself on to her horse she heard the sharp sound of the door cracking open. Spinning in horror she saw on the doorstep a man in dirty clothing, two silent dogs behind him, staring up the hill at her. Paralysed, she could not mount her horse but stood hanging on to the saddle as he walked slowly towards her, every burr stuck to his breeches indelibly printed on her mind, each thread of the sack he was dragging etched.

"Reg—" she gasped, seeing how changed the man was and realizing the reason his dogs had not barked was that they had been kicked too often and that times had been hard. Nonetheless Reg drew himself up and tried to look every bit as manly as he imagined he once had been.

"Made yer bed," he coughed at her, still on the attack and referring no doubt to the sadness permeating her features.

"And you," she tossed back untroubled by his manner and appreciating his open speech. Reg shifted slightly.

"A girl, eh?"

Ceci nodded. She had learnt, perhaps even from him she told herself, that words were a luxury and as he'd obviously been listening to local gossip, that certainly didn't need a reply.

"So it's you bin setting traps?" she asked.

Reg nodded.

"You mind he doesn't catch you," she advised a softness and caring coming into her voice which, as a longtime poacher and petty thief Reg had not expected to encounter.

Ceci found Reg looking at her with a certain amount of interest and solicitude and smiled back.

Reg frowned, gave his sack a pat, winked at Ceci and walked on past her as if to show times had not broken his spirit and he was off to empty another of his traps.

Watching him go she realized that had she not addressed him first, Reg would in all probability have said nothing. Had he deliberately come out of the dwelling as a boast of some kind? The place was in terrible order and he was certainly very welcome to it! Briefly she saw the hills around covered in sheep, as they had been that day she'd discovered a handful dead... Recalling them milling and thrusting against the old timbers of the paddocks and Old Bowen running out and shouting that it was his place she was overwhelmed with sadness and quickly looked in the direction Reg had gone, but he had vanished. Not far off she heard the sound of rocks falling; an echo, she presumed, for though it came from Bowen's land, without his horse Reg could not have gone that far...

Outwitted by Calvin, Jock found himself stumbling along a pinnacle of cliff turf, rocks falling as his feet touched them, raining to the river bed below. The hard breathing of his pursuers, man and beast, rose in his ears and though they were yards behind, he could feel their breath on his neck. Suddenly he turned to look back and for a moment stood balanced watching Calvin bear down on him, his horse shying away from the cliff, its feet sending turf flying. Slowly the land Jock was standing on began to slip. His mouth opened, his hands grasped at the air as Calvin rode forward and reached desperately for him. "Jock!" he cried. In the next minute he was gone.

Calvin got from his horse, crawled to the edge and looked over the cliff. He ran along some yards then scrambled with all hast down to the river bed. working his way over boulders and under branches. Up ahead he could see the form of Jock where he had landed in the cleft of a barkless windwashed white tree. Catching his shirt on branches Calvin forced himself forward. He could see no movement but for Jock's head swinging slightly as the fallen tree rocked with his weight. Breathless, he reached Jock and for the first time took his shoulders in his hands. The head hung back, the mouth open and the tongue, which had never in Calvin's hearing formed a word, lay still in his mouth. Distraught Calvin stepped back and poked at the head with his crop. Broken. Neck broke.

A new emotion came to Calvin: sadness and an incomplete feeling. Also feelings of injustice and frustration. With head dipped he walked back along the river bed, kicking stones. At the bend he paused and looked back at the body caught like a cat's cradle in the dead tree once more experienced a rush of emptiness that frightened him so badly he took out his handgun, lined up and shot at it once. Crack! The sound echoed up the gulley. It was too far away to see if he'd hit but the act had made him feel better. Putting his gun in the holster he turned and climbed back up the cliff path.

Sadly he headed back to Hexham not wanting to be seen. It had been a terrible afternoon which, in review, had begun when he was forced by a woman to show his innermost self; when she had wrung from him an unguarded reaction, had seen him as he *actually was*. From now on, he decided, Miss Robertson was going to see a change . . .

Returning to Hexham, Ceci struggled to prevent its atmosphere overwhelming her. She ambled with deliberate slowness across the lawn, threw her red shawl on a bench and pushed open the door with a foot. Inside, the house was quiet but she could sense Miss Robertson ticking away in the drawing room. Again using a foot she pushed the door open.

"Where's my daughter?" she asked briskly.

"She is being taught that Time Lost Returneth Never," snapped Miss Robertson.

"And my husband?" Ceci enquired casually, though it took courage to use that word knowing Miss Robertson did not credit their relationship any more than did some of the hired hands.

"Did you manage to 'pass the time' pleasantly?"

enquired Miss Robertson, refusing to respond to the word "husband."

Ceci looked at her then leant on the sideboard:

"Uncommonly smug tonight!" she mused, aware that somehow Miss Robertson *was* different and she could afford to speak to her like that.

"All mirrors have been removed from this house to discourage vanity," Miss Robertson announced seeking— it seemed to Ceci—to keep a grip on her authority by proclaiming it.

"That won't stop Calvin remembering how good looking he is," she said calmly, watching the older woman flinch.

Yes, she was quite sure of it now: Miss Robertson was either looking forward to seeing Calvin again or afraid of him!

At that moment the door opened and desire flashed on Miss Robertson's face as, pale and shaken, Calvin appeared there. He did not acknowledge Miss Robertson or Ceci but stalked straight past them to the decanter, his hand reaching for its neck. Was what she was seeing *real*, Ceci asked herself? Was Calvin actually going to *drink* in front of Miss Robertson? At the last minute she saw his eyes fall and his courage apparently fail as his hand returned to its side. Crossing the room she quickly poured a drink and held it out to him. Without looking at Miss Robertson, Calvin took it and, turning, Ceci saw Miss Robertson staring at her as if she were the original Eve who had given Adam the apple and invited him to sin with her.

Beyond her, Calvin dropped in his chair. Without saying "Excuse me" Ceci crossed in front of Miss Robertson and sat on the arm of Calvin's chair—a reckless gesture she was sure Calvin would not this time repulse. Livid, Miss Robertson gripped the edge of her chair and leaned forward as if to speak but in that moment Calvin said,

"Get rid of her."

Even as his words ended Ceci could see Miss Robertson's mouth opening wider and wider in the background.

If Ceci thought Calvin had experienced a change of heart which would embrace her she was not immediately proved right. Far from being tempted to experience joy at the

misfortune of another, she had felt for Miss Robertson—
ejected from their house with so little ceremony, for though
the woman had made her life a misery, in her own way
she had *tried* to contribute something. No had Olwen
taken her departure lightly. Never an easy household,
Hexham now found in the place of regimentation by an
outsider, spaces and lacunae opening up in corridors and
rooms where they encountered each other.

Since Miss Robertson's departure Calvin had taken to
allowing her to sit in the same room as him of an evening
provided she busied herself so it had become her habit to
stitch, unpick and resew the same pillowcase nightly till
she might wean him of the stupidity. Watching Calvin as
she stitched she was aware there was something very
wrong with him. Although Miss Robertson had gone and
Jock had not been seen since the day before her departure, the short time in-between had dragged like centuries
with every tick of the clock an accusation in the still
house.

"About Jock," Ceci began.

"He *exposed* himself to her," Calvin snapped. Ceci
stitched on, unable to imagine the scenario. That Jock
should have run off for a week was not surprising but that
Calvin should bother discussing it was.

"He *has* to go!" said Calvin, bringing the subject up
again.

"So where is he?" she asked quietly, looking up at his
worried face.

Calvin rose and began to move about the room,
keeping his back to her. Watching him, she had a strong
sense of something very wrong that she could not put her
finger on. To get a look at his face she gave a great rip at
the thread she was using which came out of the pillowcase with a noisy skkreach.

"*What* are you doing?" he said, whirling, accidentally
letting her catch the intense guilt on his face.

"Unpicking and resewing this again to make you
happy," she replied.

"You can *sit* there if you want," Calvin said dropping
in a chair as if he were about to give in and say what was
on his mind. Ceci let the pillowcase lie on her lap, deeply
aware that this was the first time in their marriage he had
been willing, perhaps even *wanting* her to be in the same

room with him; perhaps he was even ready to confide a problem to her.

As Calvin stared at the fire she waited, then decided to take the first step by confiding in him.

"I've been thinking," she began gently. "We've got a *terrible* life here Calvin. It's not fit for children to—to grow up with—" she said, feeling ashamed for criticizing their marriage before him. "I can't have the—the child of my body learning this kind of example," she faltered. "Women with me—that is—married couples—" What was the word she needed? "I know you don't agree—" she went on in a great rush, "should show *love*!"

Calvin did not even bother looking at her.

"You knew what I was when you married me."

"I can only thank God we haven't more children to mislead," she persisted.

"And if you were a good woman, we *would* have!" Calvin snapped, to Ceci's mind inexplicably. Did he really expect children to suddenly appear as part of her silent work? The remark was positively extraordinary! But though it was a definite achievement to be holding a conversation, she could not let Calvin blame their childlessness on her.

"The distaste on your face, it's no wonder we don't!" she flared, remembering the incident of her nightdress.

"Why should I pander to you?" he retorted, the expression on his face revealing they were getting closer to the kind of man he actually *was*.

"You feel you lose honour, Calvin, to appear naked before your wife?" she asked gently. "You feel it a weakness to consort with me . . . ?" Her voice rose appealingly. There was a certain relief on Calvin's face at hearing these words: clearly he was not about to deny them. Yet equally clearly he did not intend to change.

"What kind of a man will Olwen be drawn to when she's older?" Ceci asked. "What attitudes if she learning about warmth between people—*in marriage*?"

"I got a governess," Calvin said in a tone remarkable for its indignation.

"You don't *accept* love Calvin," Ceci sighed. "It's totally wasted on you."

"No reason to *trust* it," Calvin grunted.

Ceci leant on the mantelpiece, braced herself and said what she had decided to say:

"I'm sending Olwen to live with my sister's family."

"*Olwen stays*," said Calvin, his jaw utterly set.

"I know you're fond of her," Ceci apologized, preparing to understand him, "but for our pleasure we haven't the right to cripple her."

"After the favour I did you in getting rid of Miss Robertson!" Calvin exploded as if Ceci had betrayed him in a heinous way, cruelly timed.

"I've made up my mind," she continued in a normal voice. "Olwen goes to my sisters."

"All this *resolve*," said Calvin getting to his feet, "is very impressive. How do you intend to pay her fare?"

"I'll sell my parcel of land," said Ceci stoutly.

"Married women own nothing," Calvin informed her and though she controlled her face, it came as a terrible blow. "And she'll hate you for it. I'll go upstairs now shall I, and tell her? Wake her up and tell her you want to send her away like you did Miss Robertson but that I won't give you the money?"

"I want her to have some kind of a *life* Calvin!" Ceci pleaded. "Calvin, if you *love* Olwen—"

"Olwen stays," he repeated from the door.

"Can't we do *anything* together?" she begged.

He looked at her sternly as if the matter were closed.

"I'm sending her," she said.

Dragging his sack Reg moved up the river bed hoping for the odd hare, noting the stones had been disturbed as if a large animal or deer had gone that way... More likely a man, he realized, seeing on a fallen tree a thread of good velvet showing the man had scrambled under it instead of taking the easier course of rising a few feet up the bank and returning to the river bed past the obstacle. Pulling himself up easily Reg moved along from hand-hold to hand-hold, tempted to whistle but afraid of drawing attention. The sky above was a clear pale blue. It was a good time to be about and the best time for clearing traps for the prey was fresh, often needing finishing off with a stone. Swinging back towards the river bed his hand brushed against something on a branch; something that cut like wire, that glinted. Quickly he turned, straightening for balance and was touched gently in the face by Jock's jew's harp swinging to and fro, to and fro as the branch moved.

He fingered the harp and, as fond memories came, he unwound and tossed it in his pocket. A crow hopped blackly towards him on the pebbles. He pushed back his hat, picked twigs from his hair and pulled them from his jacket, wondering in which precise spot he had set his trap at dusk. For some reason the trees did not look familiar. It only took a couple to come down, strewing the place with branch bits, to disguise the most regular of places. Now he was quite sure of it: he was in the wrong place altogether! Looking around, focusing, he made out a shape strung in a tree, spreadeagled against the background, crabwise and stiff. It was Jock! Reg ran forward incredulous, tears splashing from his eyes on to the pebbles, his dirty fingers caressing the neat hole in the chest where the shot had hit. Carefully Reg lifted Jock from the tree, laid him on his shoulders and began to move back up the river bed, bowed both by the weight of the man he was carrying and his memory of how he had treated him.

Awakening in the early morning there were three things on Ceci's mind. She must win back Olwen's friendship and, though the thought of saying goodbye to her hurt deeply, prepare her to go to England leaving the finding of the means till later. Thirdly, of course, she must find Jock. If he wished her to revert to leaving food at the dwelling, well and good; she should really, she told herself, be marvelling that he had never run free before.

Strengthened by these resolves she hurried from bed and passed through the silent kitchen into the yard, still misty with beginning day. As she crossed to Jock's shack, labourers paused in their morning ablutions, looking at her as if they knew something. No longer afraid of them, she bent and crawled into the shanty to search for any signs which might indicate Jock's reason for departure, but all was as usual, she told herself. Never house proud, Jock's place was just a little more dishevelled than usual.

Congratulating herself that she had begun the day in a positive fashion she hurried to Olwen's room to make good her intention of winning back the child's friendship by helping her dress, shaking out perhaps a few of the

brighter forgotten clothes and getting the look of disapproval off the child's face.

"Wear something *cheerful*," she urged.

"I like my grey," said Olwen grimly.

"What about this one?" Ceci offered, ignoring the
sullen look on the child's face.

"Where's Miss Robertson?" Olwen demanded.

"Never mind Miss Robertson," said Ceci firmly, pushing in a drawer. "It's Jock we've to worry about."

She did not see the look on Olwen's face or catch her
averting her eyes at the mention of Jock.

"Come and have breakfast."

"I haven't washed! Cleanliness is—"

Ceci nodded, joining in: "Next to Godliness," she
said.

Moving along together on the horse Ceci kept up the
effort of sweetening the child's resolve, yet every time she
glanced back at her hair, pulled so severely from her face,
and the dark dress she had insisted on wearing, she was
conscious how aged the child looked and how childish
she, with her undressed hair tangling and her skirt billowing
around her.

"Jock! Where *are* you?" She sent the call ricocheting
around the hills but no reply came.

Suddenly she thought how to kill two birds with one
stone. While circling the hills for Jock, she could tell
Olwen about London: fire her imagination with the sights
and sounds that had so thrilled *her* at that age: the crowds
and bustle, the noise, the grand buildings, parks and
palaces, the monuments ... why, the child had never even
see a train, let alone a tram or horse bus!

Beginning with enthusiasm she laid London at Olwen's
feet, but the child would not be impressed, except for a
moment by the revelation that there were shops quite
unlike Sweetwater's specializing in children's toys.

"Jock!" called Ceci, giving the child time to change
faces. "We're here Jock!"

"Do people waste things in London?" piped Olwen,
reproducing exactly Miss Robertson's disapproving tone
at the idea of waste and frivolity.

"Yes," said Ceci. "And they have parties and carnivals and dress up and go to Punch and Judy Shows." She found Olwen looking at her thoughtully.

"I might like the Punch and Judy," she conceded.

Wanting to hug her, Ceci turned but the child was looking away, attempting indifference while one by one pulling the pins from her hair and letting her pale ash tresses tumble on her shoulders. Happily Ceci pointed the horse and galloped down the slope on the old dwelling and the weak smoke curling from its chimneys. *Of course*, she told herself joyfully, Jock had found Reg and, as in the old days, was living there together with him!

"I think we've found him," she said gaily, leaping from the horse, but Olwen gave her a look she could not fathom and remained seated.

Pushing the door to the dwelling Ceci came on Reg, dirty and withdrawn, staring into the fire.

"Get outta here," he said without looking at her.

"Have you seen Jock?" she asked, casually walking past him meaning to look for signs in the rooms beyond. Instantly Reg was on his feet blocking her way, hatred and disillusion on his face, and every inch, it seemed to Ceci, his familiar rude self.

"I'd sell this place if I could and where'd you be then?" she asked, giving up the idea of searching.

"Wouldn't make no difference to no one if you did!" Reg growled.

"I could send the child to my sister's in England for one thing!" returned Ceci. "Hexham is no place to raise a child any more than this was but at least you were straight."

Reg looked at her, his face softening, then crossed to the window keeping his back to her.

"So what's up there?" he asked guardedly. Beyond him Ceci could see Olwen on the horse, her fair hair catching the sun.

"Look Reg. There she is. That's her," she said, crossing to him almost touching his arm. "I've talked to her about London but I haven't said she might go. *He* won't pay the fare and he says this place is his so I can't sell it anyway."

"He cut up bad—if she went?" asked Reg, so filled with ill will towards Calvin he could not think of enough ways to hurt him. Ceci smiled.

"Come and meet her," she said smiling.

"No!" Reg protested but Ceci called from the window: "Olwen!"

"Oh Ceci don't, don't," begged Reg, his hand on her shoulder as the child ran across the yard looking golden and newborn, her hair flashing in the sun. Hypnotized by her purity Reg tried to get a smile on his face. The thought that she had come partly from *his* body made him feel thoroughly unworthy.

"This is our Jocky's brother!" Ceci said cheerfully, yet embarrassed to see a look of utter distaste spread on the child's face. She bit her lip as Reg straightened his hat, rolled his eyes in relief at the ceiling.

"Is he helping look for Jock?" whispered Olwen, disliking the man and frightened.

Ceci nodded.

"Daddy chased him off."

Dropping to her knees Ceci grasped Olwen's shoulders. "What?"

"He made him run out of the yard and jump over the fence. Then he chased him away on a horse."

"Why didn't you *tell* me?"

"Because Miss Robertson locked me in my room for being idle and I wasn't supposed to be looking out of the window. But I did."

Beyond them Reg trembled with anger. So great was his desire to smash Calvin's face he doubted he could hold himself until the two of them had gone.

"We'll just have to keep on looking," he heard Ceci say getting to her feet but Olwen, now that it was out, rushed on:

"One of the men said that Miss Robertson came out of Jock's hut shouting because he—"

"He *frightened her*—" Ceci interrupted quickly, not wanting Olwen to say anything more personal in front of Reg.

"Yes and then she ran into the house and told Daddy. And Daddy was angry and made him go away."

Reg clenched and unclenched his bruised hands, eyes brimming with unspilt tears. Suddenly Olwen looked up at him.

"Why is he so dirty?" she asked.

"That's enough Olwen."

"Daddy had his whip," she confided.

"Go outside please," Ceci said.

"The last Bowen," Reg mumbled as she left, a mixture of anger and grief in his voice.

"I'm sorry she spoke to you like that," apologized Ceci. "That's why I want to send her away. Before we do any more damage."

"She'll go," said Reg loudly. "I promise you!"

Ceci stared at him.

"I'll up there and talk to that bastard."

"I don't see that you can help."

"I don't *mean* to," he returned, reaching for his shotgun and beginning to shine it.

"Are you doing this for Olwen?" Ceci queried, a little confused as Reg blew into the barrel.

"I don't want *her* knowing who I am!"

"You're every bit as good as her 'papa'," Ceci said looking at him. "Listen Reg—I don't want him knowing about *me*—"

"Can't have it both ways."

Ceci began to fidget with a bit of straw. To have Calvin know Olwen was illegitimate and that she had married in that condition could do her nothing but harm.

"Only got to blow on a man like that and he runs," Reg reassured her as she rose, beginning to wish she hadn't mentioned the matter.

"I'll be up there," Reg repeated, following her to her horse, putting a hand on its rump and looking up into her face.

"*Thank you* for looking after Jock," he said, *the expression of thanks* taking her so by surprise she failed to ponder its meaning.

"So I get to keep him?" she smiled.

"He goes with the land," Reg said sagely, looking away. "He goes with the land."

Leaving him Ceci felt sad at the ring she had heard in his voice. Somehow, she told herself, he had become a better man. Something had touched him making him reflect and suffer. It was almost as if they were both of them travelling a parallel path with Olwen between them. Yet the price Reg now so nobly wanted to pay was none other than her peace of mind for to give Calvin any weapon to use against her was a bad idea. In the struggles that lay ahead, possessed of that piece of information he would be harder to handle. On second thoughts, she consoled herself, although she had been impressed and very surprised by Reg's resolve, it was most unlikely he would come. Indeed the farther she got from the dwelling the more convinced she became of its impossibility. The idea that Reg would tidy his appearance, turn up at Hexham and knock on their big front door was the least likely thing in the whole world.

Wrapping a spade in a piece of canvas, Calvin set off to bury Jock. In the emptiness of the house he found himself unable to live with his mounting feelings of discomfort. At first he had coped by forcing all frightening thoughts from his mind and reminding himself when confronted by them that his men did not use Bowen's Gully nor would the death of an idiot in a tree strike anyone as peculiar. After some days had passed, however, nagged by Ceci's questions he had visions of a constable arriving at the door, questioning him, saying he had forced the man over the cliff and refusing to believe he had in fact reached out to save him. Word of his arrest would then spread far beyond Moke and in this community, remarkable for its provinciality and humbug, none would believe he had not knowingly driven the idiot he had not liked to his death. For a moment he paused.

"Had not liked," he repeated to himself.

A certain sadness came over him thinking of the body he alone knew about, lying there unburied in a tree, refused the dignity of interment by his cowardice! Perhaps Jock was even now being picked at by birds, his eyes already gone.

Glancing carefully around he squeezed his horse through the gap in the wire and pointed it in the direction of the cliff, confident if there were any place he would encounter no one, it was here! He had always felt uncomfortable on Bowen's land, he reminded himself, and therefore this feeling of extreme nervousness was not to be wondered at.

Arriving at the cliff edge he looked down, turned in his saddle, moved along a bit and looked again. He was not familiar with the river bed and he told himself it was possible that two places looked alike. However, the way that tree leant out over the pebbles *was* exactly as he saw it in his dreams . . . Leaving his horse, he descended to the river bed, the spade in his hand impeding his progress, the trees before and around him blocking his view. Recognizing the way he had originally come down by the small landslide he had created, he turned to head towards the tree, heart beating at the thought of a week-old body, readying to smell it and eyeing the stones around thinking they would be difficult to dig. Stepping around a large rock he saw the tree: no body in it!

Returning to the big house Ceci gave Olwen her freedom and paused to listen. The house had a strange feel. She went to the mirror-stand to check her appearance and with a feeling something momentous was about to happen attempted to calm her nerves by reading. At a sound at the door she looked up.

"Calvin—what—?" she gasped, for the man looked truly awful. He quickly averted his eyes afraid she would see in them his fear and sense of guilt about the missing body. For the first time in his life he was frightened to a degree he knew he could not hide. Yet he did not want to run from the room. Ceci's earlier resolution to present an impenetrable front to him immediately weakened on seeing how distressed he was. However she knew better than to go close or to touch him.

"I'm sorry if I've upset you talking about Olwen going to London," she began, unable to imagine what else could have upset him so badly. To her surprise he walked straight past her out of the room and hurried to the hallstand to examine his face in the mirror.

"Calvin, there's someone wants a word with you down at the old place."

He turned on her, eyes blazing.

"Why?!"

"I—I'll leave that to him," she stammered awkwardly, managing to confirm Calvin's worst fears. Quickly he ran at her and grasped her wrists:

"Do you *know*?" he said urgently, frightening her with his intensity.

"Know what?" she said, backing away from him afraid he had finally gone mad. Calvin dropped her wrists and leant on the wall to steady himself. Someone had taken the body because the body was no longer there! Somebody would inform on him! From now until the knock on the door no place would be safe and it was too late to seek help, too late to make a confession.

Chapter 19

On a bright crisp hopeful morning Calvin opened the front door on Reg standing tall in his boots and old black hat, his shotgun held like a staff. Conviction burned in his eyes, fear in Calvin's. Quickly Calvin recovered himself. There was something vaguely familiar about the man, though he was not the sort Calvin generally noticed and certainly no threat. To his surprise Reg pushed past him into the hallway, threw open the door to the drawing room and then walked in. For a moment Calvin stood, utterly amazed at the man's intransigence, the extent of his rudeness. Unaccustomed to physical fighting or to ejecting tramps on his own behalf Calvin nonetheless stepped into the room.

"Shut that door!" Reg ordered, now wandering around in his muddy boots picking things up, his very appearance an affront, a danger in the room. He bent, opened a cabinet, took out a little snuff box and pocketed it, daring Calvin to assert himself. Yet Calvin said nothing. Tall with power Reg leaned on the mantelpiece and glared at the man he could now see was beginning to be a little frightened.

"I've been all over this place, settin' traps," he said, still daring Calvin to say something. He then lifted a small picture from the mantelpiece.

"Return that to its place," Calvin snapped.

"First things first," said Reg. "I'm sure my 'girl' would want me to have something nice."

He crossed to the decanter, ripped out the top and

took a good swig from the bottle, looking steadily at Calvin.

"I do things *one* at a time!" he assured him, then let out a long rumbling belch. Though he did not know why, Calvin began to sweat.

"I knew your Missus," Reg informed him, "before she was—Mrs. Bowen. *Knew* her," he elaborated.

At that moment the door swung open and Olwen entered, distaste instantly on her face at the sight of the dirty man from the dwelling.

"That's Jocky's brother," she whispered with repugnance.

The force of her words hit Calvin like stones.

"And according to him—your father!" he cried as a surge of fear rushed through him like anger.

"Make him go away! Make him go!" screamed Olwen, associating Reg with the atmosphere and pain.

Reg looked at her, picking a tooth. "*It*'s *you* that's going, little girl," he said meaning tenderness but sounding surly. Olwen pressed to Calvin who put his arm protectively around her.

"They're trying to send you away," he whispered, drawing her close.

Olwen began to shriek.

"Papa! Papa!"

Ceci opened the door at the tumult.

"Are you happy now?" Calvin demanded, pushing Olwen away and standing.

"Papa!" screamed Olwen.

"Out," said Reg to Ceci. "And her." He tossed his head at Olwen but as Ceci ran in she clung to her "Papa."

"It's all going wrong!" Ceci moaned.

"She goes," said Reg firmly.

"Slut," Calvin growled at Ceci, pacing before the window. Though his voice was trembling he was aware no one had mentioned Jock—unless this was a blackmail attempt.

"All over the shire, what I have to say," informed Reg, "you bin raising my bastard."

"Leave this room!" shouted Olwen, a phrase she'd heard Miss Robertson use to good effect.

"Your vermin crawl up the hill after you!" accused

Calvin, thinking his way ahead but no longer frightened. This reference to Reg did not bother him.

"I should have known you for what you were!" Calvin went on. "Miss Robertson'll make a *fine* witness! Once we've run this hooligan off my land—" Now that his shock was over the familiar sense of being in control and lambasting an adversary took over. "How could you give your purity to this scum!" Certain he had lost the battle for Olwen he was determined to deliver some hurt. "Take your illegitimate child!" he said pushing Olwen from him.

"I *hate* you!" screamed Olwen at Ceci whom she took to be to blame for the unhappiness around.

"You'll find out who loves you," Reg said gruffly to her. Head spinning, Ceci watched Olwen thrusting herself again and again at Calvin and being rejected. The sight of her screaming and thrashing at his turned back was so terrible she could scarce bear to look! How had she not realized what Reg would do? That Calvin could not live with this scandal was obvious! Even if it meant he would now pay her fare, how bitterly she regretted ever having raised the matter! As she stared at his back, slowly Calvin turned to her, detachment and—could it be—*relief* lingering on his face?! Had the body been washed away in a rush of water, he was asking himself, or had he still to wait for that knock on his door?

As time passed without the knock coming, gradually a sense of relief came and with it a gratitude which cleansed. Each day that the knock did not come seemed to Calvin a miracle. Now he did not count with dread the days *towards* Olwen's departure but with a growing sense of deliverance, the days away from Jock until very early one bright morning he was convinced all danger was passed. It was the day the coach arrived on the forecourt to take Olwen away.

Looking down from an upper window he saw her climb in, eight years old, in new travelling clothes, her cases on top. He saw Ceci leaning towards the window, trying to get her attention.

"Now be polite to the Agency Lady," her voice came up to him. "Remember to say 'Thank You'." He didn't doubt Olwen was staring straight ahead and ignoring her mother.

As the coach drew away he realized with a shock he felt sad, not for himself but for Ceci. Never could he recall having felt an emotion, other than anger, on behalf of another person. People had irritated, bored and at times amused but never had he felt in him the same sort of hurt as if the thing he was seeing had been done to *him*. There she was below, biting her lip, looking after the coach, squeezing a handkerchief in one hand, blinking. For a moment he almost considered going downstairs to join her on the step where she had sat down but realizing he would have to say something to her he thought better of it.

Together, alone in the empty house, they sat at opposite sides of the large table.

"Make the best of it, I suppose," said Ceci, after a pause.

"No sign of—Jock," Calvin said quietly.

"That's the first time you've ever used his name!" Ceci said looking up. His relief that the waiting was over was almost too much to bear: *no one* would come now, he was certain of it. To be able even to say the name "Jock" out loud filled him with a sense of well-being approaching affection for the dead man. He could almost believe he had had a fondness for him.

"Must've—wandered off—" he murmured softly, examining his hand. "You're free of them all."

"I feel a hundred," said Ceci.

"You're twenty-three," she heard him say in a voice so warm she could not believe it was he who had spoken. Looking up she saw something approaching awareness on his face which made her feel shy. It was as if with nothing left to fight for, after *all* they had been through, Calvin had arrived! Broken by suffering and by Ceci's persistent love, after seven years he was finally ready to embark on their marriage . . .

Tomorrow night he would go to her room, Calvin told himself, surprised to find the idea suddenly exciting and aware this would be his last night as a man who had not touched woman. With difficulty he glanced at her but she was looking at the table, colour in her cheeks as if she had read his thoughts. He felt a rush of warmth, the things he

would do and say in the years to come to this girl who
had been so patient with him, who had believed against
all the evidence and his own understanding of himself
that he was a good man. Wiping his mouth he excused
himself from the table, finding it too difficult to say
goodnight. He hastened to his chamber knowing that if
he slept he would sleep well and strengthened by resolution and a sudden sense of purpose would awaken early
for his last bachelor day.

Rising, his sense of self-respect intact, Calvin moved away
in the half light of dawn, a day's work ahead. He felt like
whistling as his hack moved comfortably along, its hooves
picking at the familiar trail. Resting his eyes on the hills
beyond, even now becoming light, an old nursery rhyme
was turning in his head when suddenly his horse stumbled violently forward, throwing him to the ground. From
behind a tree a man came running, a large rock in his
hand, knocked him to the ground as he tried to rise and
sat on his chest. Gasping and winded, Calvin looked up
into the face of Reg.

Reg raised the rock and gave Calvin good time to
recognize him.

"For Jock," he said, then hesitated, surprised at the
look of mystification and a longing to explain that came
on to the man's face, along with the assurance time would
not be allowed him. Quickly Reg brought the rock down.
Crack! He had waited a long time for Olwen to depart and
this little extra wait had been no trouble at all. The man
had been easier to brain than a pig, he told himself, and a
trifle less noisy. Stretching, Reg looked about. He hadn't
liked the look on Calvin's face at the last minute. Something wrong there. He frowned over the already pink sky
lighting the rocks on the ground, two of which he pushed
carefully under Calvin's head, turning him so he seemed
to have struck them in his fall from the horse. Slowly he
re-wound the length of rope he had used to trip Calvin,
crossed to the tree on the far side and untied the knot.
Taking his time now he sat and rolled a smoke, the light
of it barely visible in the widening sky.

"Giddup!" he shouted at Calvin's horse, hitting its
rump with a pebble, sending it in circles. But the beast
returned and stood by Calvin, forcing Reg to rise and give

it a sound smack on the rump before it would leave. He looked at the motionless body on the ground, the dark hair on the back of the head curling towards the color of his well-starched white shirt. With a low whistle he called his dogs who came cautiously forward from the shadows. Whatever the man had or hadn't been, he told himself, he was all over now. Whistling, he set off for the dwelling where his pack horse awaited, remembering there was one more thing he had to do before clearing out good and proper.

Reaching Jock's grave he slipped his hand into his pocket and drew out the jew's harp and hung it by its neck string to the branch he had planted there. Then he knelt in silence thinking of Old Bowen and Jock, the sight of their two hummocks together strangely sad. As the sun reached for his neck he walked down to the old dwelling and taking the last brand from the smouldering fire carefully went around spreading flames. There went his bedroom; there his father's room, there the girl's . . . He crossed to the barn. There went Jock's barn . . .

Riding away from the smoke, Reg left Bowen's Gulley.

Awakening late, for she had overslept, Ceci hurried down to the kitchen. Never had she overslept in Hexham before, Calvin's presence always being sufficient to ensure she woke early convinced there would not be time enough in the day to fulfil his demands or that she had already offended in some minor way. Hurrying to prepare the labourers' first meal, she hugged to her the warm sense of acceptance that had come over Hexham since yesterday. The air from the garden smelled good. Pushing the kitchen door open to get full benefit of the breeze, she saw a labourer galloping at her, his mount swinging in a circle before her, landing him on her step.

"What is it?" she asked surprised at the panic on his face.

"Quick Missus—" he gasped grabbing her wrist, pulling her towards the stables where she saw her own horse was already saddled and that of Calvin, standing loosely, trailing amongst its reins.

As she rode towards the hills in her apron she struggled to believe the man's words. Calvin who was so permanent and vital, Calvin around whom Hexham revolved, had fallen from his horse and injured himself to the extent his men had been thrown into utter panic? *This could not be true*! He could *not* be dead, she told herself, pointing out to the Fates the *unreasonableness* of it, the terrible mistake they would have been making if . . . Cresting the hill and coming to the named place of rocks her horse stumbled slightly on the loose stones as up ahead, by a solitary tree, she made out something on the ground which she knew beyond doubt to be Calvin. Four labourers stood close by, their backs to him, doing nothing. With dread she noticed their caps were off, their heads dipped, and when they glanced at her it was with disassociation, not compassion: they did not want to be the ones to "deal" with her. Slipping from her horse she ran at Calvin.

"Oh my dear!" she gasped, clasping his hands, trying to roll his body over, conscious of the men watching her with one eye.

"Calvin!" Could these blood-caked staring eyes, this mouth with earth in it be the man she had loved as an act of will? Horrified, she could not turn him back but shook his body as if to make him sit up or do something. "Say you hear me?" she shouted. "Help me!" she turned to the labourers who did not move.

"Calvin! Calvin!" she said, shaking him wildly. "Somebody *do* something! Help!"

Though news had reached Moke, people kept away from this twice unlucky widow as she passed in formal crinoline black, her black bonnet and Calvin's "best" mount, the one he used for journeying. Men came from the Grain and General Feed Store to watch her pass, a woman chatting with the new Minister who was trying to make an impression rudely dropped him to turn and stare after her as did a man coming from Sweetwater's, a thumb in his waistcoat. The greedy acquisitive eyes of Sweetwater followed her too as she passed along the road and took the fork to the little graveyard behind the church. Word went around Moke; the widow was visiting his grave again. Letting a suitable time lapse after hearing the remark, Ginger quietly left the grain store and hurried away.

*　　*　　*

Calvin Laird
Born July 1st 1846, Brampton,
Huntingdon, England...

That she could miss him so badly amazed Ceci, the ache
having replaced, even exceeded, the loss of Olwen. This
man who, if truth were told, she had at times even wished
dead was irrevocably gone and would never grace her sight
again. Time moved around her, backwards and forwards,
taking with it both appetite and sense of reality, leaving her
waiting always. Yet for what? Only the return of Calvin
would take away the waiting and he was never coming back.

She looked around the deserted graveyard, its silence
suddenly broken by fighting birds in the tree above.
Beyond the fence children played, life was going on. It
was a time, she recalled, when a person must take a grip,
dig deeper for their own resources and not let change
overwhelm them. Turning her back on the grave, she set
out for Hexham. Yet even as she jogged through Bowen's
Gulley and succeeded in shaking thoughts of Calvin from
her mind, Olwen returned to haunt her.

> *Ship Ship*
> *On the Sea—*
> *Taking my baby*
> *Away from me.*
> *Ship Ship*
> *On the Sea*
> *Taking my little one*
> *Further from me...*

Lost in her thoughts, she let the horse make its own way
until suddenly it came to an abrupt stop before two
hummocks. Looking down Ceci saw Old Bowen's grave
now with fresh sprigs in the broken earthenware bottle
she had left and next to it, to her total amazement, a *new*
grave with a large bunch of shimmering green lying on it.
Confused, she got down, kneeling to touch the broken
earth and suddenly saw a small metal object catching the
sun: Jock's jew's harp. Beyond all doubt he was buried
there, she realized, her grief already so thoroughly spent
on Calvin no tears could come. Jock was dead. And
buried. Was this something to do with Reg, she asked

herself, glancing quickly down to the dwelling and seeing to her horror a mere blackened smudge on the landscape!

In thought she brought her horse up the gravel drive towards Hexham, noting again the solemn splendour of the solitary house, the way it was hedged and framed by its fruit bushes and hanging arrangements, how perfectly the lawn lay at its feet like a servant. It was a fitting monument to Calvin. Putting behind her for the last time the sense of being alone in the world she recalled it had first possessed her on leaving the Immigrant Barracks and had not reappeared to frighten her again until this recent separation from Calvin. Now Olwen was gone too and she was truly alone. Handing her horse to Sam, she began walking to the kitchen door, bending to pick Olwen's parasol from a bush beneath her window where the child must have flung it, firmly winding its pink frills round the stem and securing them with the button. By the time the child came back she would have no use for this parasol, but nonetheless she would not throw it away. She sensed the foreman Sam looking after her as she walked towards the house and knew he respected her. Breathing out she turned the corner, recognizing that a new chapter in her life had begun.

As she bent to ease off her boots on the scraper, she became suddenly aware of scrutiny. Looking up she saw Ginger, formally dressed and fidgeting with his collar as though he had been waiting some time. To her surprise his eyes lit up at the sight of her. Was this a social call or had he come to offer condolences? As his feet found their way across the gravel to her, the concern and expectation on his face was unmistakable.

"If there is anything I can do—" he began.

Ceci shook her head slowly.

"You could come and stay with us," he said, reaching a hand for hers which she quickly put behind her back, shaking her head in a small arc.

"If—if you want anything," he began again cautiously.

"I'll know you're there," she replied.

Leaving, Ginger glanced back at the gabled house. How truly magnificent it looked, sitting there on the extremity of the gravel drive. How fitting that a girl like that should live there, he told himself. Imagine him inviting her to stay at Nolan's! Vaguely he saw a curtain move as if a room were being aired, heard a bird striking up in the rose arbour...It was unlikely that being Irish he would ever own a house like that...For a moment, though, he almost wished he lived there!

Alone in the great drawing room, Ceci stared at a potted plant. Nothing moved. Carefully lifting a finger to her mouth she made up her mind: where Calvin had succeeded she would succeed. What he had done she would do! Turning she picked up a hand bell and rang vigorously. Alone, *she* would run Hexham.

PART TWO

Chapter 20

Olwen would be arriving in London at exactly the same age she had, she told herself, after her family's brief spell at The Cat. "The Cat," she repeated, slowly trying to recall the pub in the Cheshire Dales Lord K had secured for them when her father had showed no signs of mending.

For eight months after the kick of the horse, Lord K had resisted his wife's urgings to get rid of their family. Ceci could remember gathering celandine leaves for compresses while her mother scoured hedgebank and copse for ground ivy. She remembered pressing the flowers and leaves in poultices to her father's painful shin while above her her parents talked in worried whispers. Lord Knevitt had kindly fetched a doctor from some distance who had arrived with implements and an air of great knowledge, giving the opinion there was a clot of blood involved though he couldn't say where. Clots could disperse, he informed them, or make their way up to the heart or lungs. He'd used words like "thrombosis" and thoroughly worried them. Though compresses of garlic and yarrow had been applied, tonics and restoratives and everything both his pharmacopoeia and Lord K's medicinal herb garden had to offer, no improvement had come about. Ceci's father had remained seated with the damaged leg up. To walk or stand for more than a few minutes made him angry with pain and as time passed with no sign of him mending, the undergrooms had got restless and the sight of him, for some reason, had upset Immelda which inflamed her mother to the point she insisted he not only be replaced, but removed at once. Though Lord K didn't want to do it, for his groom had been with him a long time and in ways they had much in common, his wife had her way. His successor, as she put it, would need the house by the stables and this was no time for sentimentality. True the man had been working with one of their children at the time of injury but the leg was not broken or even fractured and indeed he should look to himself for allowing Immelda's horse to strike him! The animal must have been overworked to say the least and to allow Immelda to dismount from an irritable beast . . .

A man of three daughters like her father, Lord K had quietly bought them the pub. It had not been much of a place, she recalled. In the days when routes were described by dwellings and "standing stones" The Cheshire Cat had been used by folk criss-crossing the moors seeking sustenance and shelter. From an ordinary dwelling, gradually it had become an occasional inn, then a pub, its fortunes swelling and waning as travellers' tracks rose and disintegrated with rains and the changing fortunes of distant towns straddling the moors. Its sole tree—long dead—had stood as a landmark to journeymen visible even when the house was not, until its last occupant had cut it down. Since then the place had become unlucky and had stood empty for eighteen months, its tree lying in a pile in the windswept yard until Lord K had sent out enquiries for a "suitable place," was informed and had purchased . . .

They had set out for it quietly in the grey of an early morning, their cart wheels turning wet leaves, picking them up, rain dripping on their covered heads, their chickens stuffed in crates, pig sold . . . Bump bump into the future . . . One small family, birds rising from the hedge around them.

The day her father's death took them by surprise Ceci had been hiding in the wood pile: that whole tree piled in lumps. In places the bark had fallen or been picked off to leave a smooth grey surface where knobbles stuck up. Her hands could reach through gaps in the wood to wet places beneath, touching sawdust turned damp by the rain, rotten bark pieces and hidden lips of clammy fungus. A few paces beyond, her mother was scrubbing the flagstones before the entry to The Cat, steam rising from her bucket, the plaintive scrape-scrape of her brush coming to Ceci across the small space between woodpile and door. Not knowing she was being watched she hobbled about on her knees on bits of rag, backing into puddles of her own making as the wind roared up the hill and over the low stone wall to hit the step. She paused to wipe her nose on the back of her hand, cold water running from the brush down to her elbow and dripping off, her hands puce and hairpins dropping in the puddles.

About to stand up, Ceci heard the gate squeak and quickly sank back into her hollow to watch. Her mother had emptied the bucket and gone inside. Up the path came a man who turned to look over his shoulder, then stared at their door. He had taken his hands out of his greatcoat pockets. Suddenly he pushed the door and went in.

Their taproom was spotless. Floorboards shone in the yellow light, a small bowl of primroses attracting it to them. Everything spoke of her mother's attention: the cleanliness of the bent willow chair backs and the square stools on the pale ash floor. Behind the bar with her back to the man stood a child of thirteen he recognized as "the middle one" polishing meticulously. There was a wafty faintness to her, a fading away like a poorly produced print.

"You be open today?" he asked.

"Yes," she said, turning.

Sneaking from the woodpile, Ceci came around the back of The Cat and climbed on to the block to reach into the water butt and scoop out some water. Smack! She hit the ice with the dipper, at the very instant her mother's ring started rattling loudly on the scullery window to tell her not to hit the dipper on the ice! Suddenly her mother had looked away, then vanished.

Curious, Ceci came in, passed through the scullery and went upstairs to find her mother staring strangely at her father in his window chair. Crossing the room, Ceci walked around the absolutely still figure, held on to the arm of the chair and peered up into the face. His eyes were unmoving and there was a trickle of something coming down his nose.

"Get the salt," said her mother, "The string's in the top drawer."

In a sense, thought Ceci, from that day it was as if some very basic part of her mother had been cut off; some part like a hand you knew wasn't there by the things it left undone. Already on her face was the carrying of coal, the scrubbing and dusting for strangers, those acts which would support them in the days to come when they moved to Aunt May's tiny flat in Clapham.

"We'll put four words on his stone," she said "'I Believe in God.'"

Though Ceci did not understand, she was afraid for her mother.

Exact to the last stone, the memory of that small House of God where they had left his body floated before Ceci. On top of a bald flatted hill the church had been visible for miles around. Hanging on to each other, clawing their way up in the wind, carting babies to be christened, their dead to be buried, the people of the Dales had scrambled up in full view of each other. Wedding couples gasped their way up and slithered down in the mud, while the wind banged the shutters so loudly it dislodged memorial tablets, broke glass and sent wreaths bowling after the bereaved. Nothing had stayed on the graves. Not even grass.

Two men from a nearby town had helped carry her father's body. Norah had stayed at home because climbing hills wasn't good for her and she, Ceci, had hidden in the woodpile biting her fingers and watching the small line etched against the sky, her mother leading, then the two men with the coffin, then her eldest sister Moll stumbling to keep up.

After her father, they had not lasted long. They had left a stone cross on a chalk hill and journeyed to London remembering The Cat as a cold stopping place. What different futures awaited her, her two sisters and Mother at Aunt May's! A household of women! No wonder she and Reg had had such a time of it! Reg growing up without a woman in the house and she without a man!

Forcing her mind back to the present, Ceci reopened the large maroon ledger with its spidery white weave and lined it up opposite the dark blue one so that the entries read across. She had had ample practice in keeping these books in Calvin's time, for from the day his mother had left she had assumed the duty with neither thought nor thanks and though it was more than her life was worth to ask questions, the system had not been difficult to fathom. Managing the station too was challenge she enjoyed, ever grateful to have been previously freed from the damaging influence of Harry. She was aware the men still fought but at least they did it out of her hearing. Sam, though he could not enforce work, knew what had to be done when, so taking his word for it she would ride out inspecting, as often as not finding the men asleep in the lucerne, sheltering from the midday sun under trees or enjoying smokos and card games. Although she had learned from Sam (who did it to excess) to look the other way, she usually pulled the men up and returned them to their work 'til in time they learned to watch for her coming. If trouble was brewing between the men, Sam would be off wandering the perimeters worrying about water or how to bring it up from Bowen's Gulley. A pathetic amusing figure, he could be seen stumbling from one piece of scrub to another asking himself where the water that supported it came from. At times he was shot at by strangers for a bit of sport. That they were strangers was clear because Ceci did not allow her men guns. On entering her employ all such firearms had to be surrendered and locked in a cupboard in her study—a measure the men actually appreciated as it made the keeping of honour safer in the heated moments when they called each other's pedigree into question. As to the strangers, they criss-crossed the land continually, sometimes asking in the kitchen for food. It was by approaching work parties and asking what was to do at the big house that they found work for in the High Country there were few secrets amongst men and fences, it was commonly held, were for sheep.

Ceci left the house more and more often, checking up on Sam, helping him assert himself. She had long since taken on a cook to release her from the kitchen—a quite unnecessary chore given their circumstances—and also welcome female company from the Old Country. As often as not the girls were terrible cooks which meant Ceci had to maintain a discreet presence in the kitchen also. Yet the presence of a cook provided a firm line between herself and the men. To have them coming into the kitchen, shouting at her for food, would have made it very difficult for her to command them or to give even the simplest instructions about when certain tasks must be completed by. The ordering of others, she found, was not easy. It called for a new form of self-discipline, a new way of holding oneself back.

She fingered the small brooch she had worn since her mother's death; a butterfly on a silver pin. How sad that she had never see her mother again; that now that she *had* some money it was too late! Especially sad that her mother had never seen Olwen!

For four years the shadowy existence had gone on. More often than not she sent Sam into Moke, for she did not want to be the subject of pity or curiosity. Her life was punctuated by letters from Home; from Molls talking about London and the children and how Olwen had settled in, the things she said and did, her surprise at the constant throng. Olwen seemed to Ceci to be becoming alarmingly sophisticated for a little girl! There were letters from her too, rushed with a breathless enthusiasm but moving from describing things disparagingly to referring to them as if any fool would know what they were and that they were quite essential. At times, alone in Hexham, Ceci wondered what she was doing there and what grand purpose had ever brought her to New Zealand. Soon, however, her peace was disrupted by an act which started a whole new chain of events.

Ill-will had been growing amongst the men with the result that they would only work grudgingly. Returning irritated to the stable yard Ceci heard a shrill scream from the kitchen as if even there things were not in order. Briskly she walked over the deserted yard.

"Ooh! Burnt me finger Miss," gasped the new girl, Madeleine, at the stove. "I want to go back down!" she piped awkwardly. "The men keep comin' in the kitchen!" Calmly Ceci showed her how to slide the bolt on the door and crossed to examine the pots.

"What about the—?" Ceci began, wondering why there was no gravy. She stooped to open the range door. "The meat Madeleine! You forgot the meat!"

Pulling a large side of ham from the larder she began to slice it with mighty whacks into exact even servings, Madeleine meanwhile frowning as the cleaver crashed loudly on the bench. Suddenly a commotion accompanied by the filthiest language they had ever heard broke out in the courtyard outside. Ceci caught Madeleine's eyes opening at words from the anatomy mixed in with various animal names, followed immediately by the sound of someone going down. Wallop! The door shuddered as the men fell against it.

"Oh Miss you should get help!" Madeleine gasped.

"I've managed four years now and I'm not troubling neighbours on account of I'm a widow," replied Ceci firmly as the door buckled behind her, one of the men evidently having pinned another there and now treating them in low terms to a litany of obscene images. Slamming the bolt back Ceci stepped out and strode towards the men now rolling away on the ground.

"How *dare* you swear like that!" she began, realizing by the ugly look she received she had better modify it. "Near the house!" she added quickly.

"Dog's crotch—" the pinned man whispered weakly.

"Be *quiet!*" Ceci ordered. At that the aggressor got to his feet and began to stagger towards her. Quickly she backed into the kitchen slamming the door.

It was not long before little Madeleine had vanished. Counting the missing sheets and wondering which worker she had left with, it came to Ceci that instead of sending polite letters to the agencies in Christchurch she should actually return there herself. Return? She had never set foot in the place for Reg had hurried through so fast that day twelve years ago she had seen less of it than of Lyttelton! Once fixed the idea made her realize she had been clinging to a ridiculous solitude, avoiding Moke and hiding out in the hills as if accepting at face value Calvin's assurance that no one would want to see her.

The idea of the impending journey filled her with excitement. It would be like re-entering the world again! There would be new people, fashions and ideas from Home, two-storeyed buildings, avenues, shops and best of all crowds! The thought of people who did not know each other milling and passing in the street with no urge to gossip or turn and stare thrilled her. But how would the journey be? Last time the hills had frightened her in an animal way. Would they still stare? The closer the departure day came the more she marvelled that she had spent four years in Hexham without so much as thinking of putting a toe beyond its boundaries other than to visit Moke.

When the day came a local trap took her some hours down the road to link with the main Christchurch route. Poor Calvin, she thought, as she swept away from the hills of Hexham. The time she had spent assigning complicated motives for his disapproval of her every act, his verbal destruction of her ideas and thoughts! All he had meant was: "Leave me alone!" Those criticisms carelessly flung at her, which she had taken to heart and worried about! How could she have considered seriously his assertions that she was ignorant, vain, a person of weak mind who could not remember, one who was constantly seeking attention for its own sake? She *knew* these things to be untrue. Why had she not known it then? If she could have *laughed* at the time, given him the freedom to be alone, it would all have passed. Her eyes moved over the horizon. Looking back, his words, particularly when he swore, had been flung at her with such force and hatred she had mistaken the depth of passion firing them for an impulse for truth. But the big Truth had not been about her at all but about him being invaded by a woman who accepted him with the good will and the affection he did not feel he deserved. How heavy her burden of trust must have seemed for him; he, who wanted no human entanglements, constantly turning to see her like a shell on his back. Poor Calvin. Thank God they had worked it out in time—discovered each other and left things well between them. It was not time that had healed the pain in her heart but the certainty Calvin had intended to come to her room, had almost lain with her in spirit that night she had felt his presence and slept in in the morning... And had that change in Calvin not been caused by the most defenceless of figures? Olwen, the child who without fear of invasion he had dared to love but lost, and by Jock. For she was certain that at the time of Reg's visit there was something that both men knew about Jock but neither had told her. Calvin had definitely been thinking of Jock towards the end and not with revulsion either... Had he actually *missed* Jock as much as she, or repented not being nicer to him when he was around? Though he had chased him off, she knew in her heart Calvin would certainly not have killed him.

The journey continued with two other travellers for Ceci to look at, each alighting in lonely places known to the driver where faint tracks led away to the hills. They were left waiting in the wind perhaps for someone to ride down and fetch them. They had not spoken to each other for up here privacy still meant something. Doubtless it would be different in Christchurch but this was still the High Country with none of the warmth and dust of the plains she remembered so well.

As the carriage swept through the hills by a more gentle and elongated route than she had taken those years ago, she was once again impressed by the barren emptiness of the New World, its utter desolation. She hadn't needed Lord K to tell her the age of England: she knew it in her bones. Walking on the earth she could feel it creaking, every place sacred with past. It was impossible to find even a glade where the very trees did not breathe their memories; where the earth did not throb with the feel that generations of feet had hunted, cultivated there and moved on...

The gardens too and the plants, thought Cèci as the coach jogged past mile upon mile of plain grass, could be read like a folklore or history book. Behind The House at dawn, dark fields of cabbage like purple heads undulated with the land and as the sun rose it sent needles of gold through spidery raspberry canes reaching to frosty shadowed slopes rising to bare crests, once lookouts, cut against the sky... Trees where archers had hidden guarded ridges, the grass around them wet and silver... Rising higher the sun picked out gnarled Autumn apples trained against Tudor walls, bricks crumbling to suckers of ivy... As the sun crossed walkways, bushes trimmed in peacock and lady shapes, it spoke of the last hundred years; as it crossed the French herb and ornamental gardens—a time before that. Flowered walks, arcades where wisteria and laburnum hung and filled the air with pepper smells, spoke of ancient lovers... Memories were entwined in grassed-over walks and between yew hedges used once for royal courting in the days when a niece of the Lord of the Manor had (secretly) attracted a King. Walks leading to sundials and little fountains, fish ponds and a rose garden all whispered their pasts. It could be heard in summer sighs, felt in the warm stones... The kitchen garden and water garden reflected the minds who had laid them out but the glasshouses, hidden compost heaps, and potting places in triangles of hedge where cuttings waited to be taken into The House spoke with warmth of today's living. Yet past or present, every person and plant seemed in the deepest sense to *belong*.

Looking about her as the coach ground down a hill Ceci could sense the land was still without memories, its settlers as strange to it as its plants to them. The birds with their peculiar, at times wretched, cries and the grass which cut their feet—to whom did it belong? At that moment she longed for the journey to be over; for the sound of human voices! She felt the *emptiness* a trespasser must always feel; the guilt and long shadows of knowing it was not her place and she did not belong . . . She tried to shake the sensation but it would not go away. This was not even a place where Man had always lived! It was not a place where he had offered sacrifice to the land or made the earth rich with his labour. It was a grasscovered rock in a lonely ocean roamed by white and brown trespassers; a childless land they had yet to make their own. Yet, she thought, as she rocked to the coach's rhythm, more than anywhere else this was her country now, and could she deny that for all its hardness she was beginning to love it?

They were down in the plain now pointing towards Christchurch, the wheels of their carriage making a different sound as they ground up dust and the flattened wads of dried earth. Cries came to her from nearby hovels. There were villages, settlements, two people here, six there. A dog ran across the track. Children stared. A man called out. They had left the High Country behind! Ceci swung her head from window to window as people climbed in, smiling more. They were fatter and had an easy-going contentedness as if used to living within easy reach of the things they needed. She felt herself dour, she told herself, *reserved* by comparison. People were looking at her, seated grimly in her corner of the coach, hands joined on the velvet dress she had stitched from ordered cloth. A lady from the High Country, they nodded to each other obviously thinking she was a large runholder or the spoiled wife of a wealthy immigrant to both wear velvet and survive in the High Country.

Chapter 21

Ceci paused outside the single-storey wooden building with its shingle roof and looked at the sign: SERVANTS REGISTRY OFFICE, and the arrow to the door. It would be best to settle the staffing matter at once.

Inside she waited on a hard wooden chair watching a disorganized middle-aged woman behind a desk sort cards into little piles. Ceci's shoulders shifted; she carefully moved a foot. The woman was so slow it was unbelievable, squinting at cards as if she had become shortsighted, then holding them at a great distance from her nose.

"A couple now you say?"

"That's right."

The woman frowned, moved her head as if the card she was holding had suddenly proved unsavoury to the touch, put it on a different part of the table and took another.

"That'll be two people?"

"Exactly."

She cocked her head as if to say "you can't always tell," and put that card face down somewhere else as in a game of pelmanism. Ceci's foot began to tap.

"Aha!" The woman grasped up a card in each hand, looking from one to the other as if she were suddenly seeing the thing work out before her eyes!

"A man *and* a woman?"

"Yes."

She frowned, disappointed, put the cards down somewhere else.

"Ah!"

She snatched a new card with a paper clipped to the back of it which slowly let itself down. Almost forgetting Ceci, she turned it round, settled back into her chair to read it, murmuring "Mmm" and "Aha." Ceci sighed out slowly. The woman looked up.

"It's the reference. I'm reading the reference."

Meticulously she refolded it as had been behind the card.

"Married, was it?" she looked up again.

"Yes," said Ceci patiently. "I want a married couple, that is one man and one woman who are currently married to each other. The woman capable of cooking for up to twelve. Twelve *men*."

"And the man to do what?"

"To—be around," she said awkwardly. "As the woman's husband and as a—a—married man—who is—part of the household."

The woman gave Ceci an odd look.

"You'd do better at Addington," she observed, referring to the location of the nearest Immigrant Barracks.

"You have helped before," Ceci began.

"Get them straight off the ship they don't *know* any better than to go out there! *These* ones—" her hand moved across the table in illustration, creating a draught which blew several cards away. Ceci reached down to pick them from around her feet and the woman rose to peer over her desk and see what was happening.

"The ones *here*," she continued. "If the girls aren't put to service afore they're grown—you *can't* teach them. They're—" her hands danced about seeking the word, "*gawkish*—" and knocked the card tin off her desk.

"I need a cook. Who is married. A good cook." Ceci restated.

"What happened to the last one?"

"Ran off with half the linen cupboard."

"Well *this* couple I'm *not* recommending," she hastened to add, "on account they wrote their own reference—"

She waved the card between them to clarify her integrity before sticking it behind her back. How would a woman like this *manage* in the High Country Ceci asked herself having forgotten that towns fostered situations like this. The woman was now staring euphorically, as if at a memory stirring.

"They would be in about now..."

"In?"

"Due."

She folded her hands together on the desk before her. "No cards?"

"Pat Hallam and his wife Bridget."

"Can she cook?"

"Oh! Hot meals, a clean kitchen—"

"But no reference," Ceci nodded, appreciating exactly the meaning of it.

The woman leaned forward as at a great intimacy: "I'll be honest with you," she began.

"I should hope so."

"She's a good cook," she said in an almost sinister voice. "And she doesn't waste or drink."

"What about him?"

"You wanted him to 'be around'? He'll do that handsomely."

"Is he a thief?"

The woman shook her head.

"A womanizer?"

She shook her head.

"And they *are* married?"

"Mortally."

"Then send them out."

Ceci rose, her impatience communicating itself to the woman along with her desire to be elsewhere. She did not see as she closed the door behind her a smirk being suppressed in the eyes of the agency woman.

After visiting the shops, wrestling with her purchases Ceci struggled along the corridor to the upper room of the hotel where she was lodging. Momentarily she peered from the window to the street below. Though Christchurch had its own life, it was still clearly a supply town and a place of new arrivals. Looking down on the bustle she sensed the hurry and greed; the idea that once they got beyond Christchurch things lay for the taking. They did not realize it took hard work to wring things from the land.

Part of her wanted to stay longer but already she felt how different she had become; how the High Country had changed her and the thought of Hexham unattended was not one she relished. After a brief disagreement with the proprietress concerning the theft from her room of the small butterfly brooch, she prepared herself to leave.

"You cannot imagine," the proprietress had said, "the difficulties a single woman faces in running a hotel. It makes one coarse before one's time. How lucky you are with your privileges!..."

Nodding at her Ceci was checking out of the hotel when she could not believe her eyes to see Miss Robertson helping a man alight from a coach. Clearly they were together. Her clothes were quite bright and as she turned, her face had a softening to it, a warmth. As she moved out of the man's way to guide him towards the hotel, Ceci saw he was good looking, well made, certainly younger than Miss Robertson—and blind. Clutching a Bible under his arm as if they were surrounded by thieves, he snatched at Miss Robertson's sleeve, an unmistakable radiance and pride glowing on her face. Ceci stepped forward.

"My *dear*!" Miss Robertson gasped and squeezed the man's elbow. "Oh Jack! It's someone I used to know!"

Making to let go of him she reached towards Ceci.

"Let me inside!" he growled roughly.

"Oh of course. Yes..." said Miss Robertson, hurrying him past Ceci to the doorway but returning promptly.

"God realized," she whispered letting Ceci in on God's Big Secret, "that had I been beautiful, I might have married someone of *quite* the wrong type... Someone I could not *help*..."

"Calvin died, you know," Ceci told her. "Soon after you left—"

"Oh I *am* sorry—" said Miss Robertson sincerely, seeking Ceci's eyes for pain but finding acceptance. For a moment they looked at each other feeling the strangeness of a life that had made them enemies and now, by the merest shifting of external events, almost friends.

Ceci returned to Hexham with a sense of coming home. Dusty and windswept she closed the front door and leaned on it, her travelling bag and packages at her feet. She let out a great breath of relief as the wagon scrunched away on the gravel drive outside.

How good it was to be home! So quiet and empty after the bustle of Christchurch! Suddenly she sensed something wrong. A loud crash came from the dining room and running there, she viewed with alarm the aftermath of a banquet which had taken place while she was away! Her main table, spread with the best linen cloth, was now covered in gravy blobs and meat chewings, the silverware lay every which way and knives stuck in crusts and heels of bread lay on the floor. In the centre of the table a large glass bowl with the remains of some preserved fruit in it furnished further evidence that nothing had been spared. Smoke lingered and wine dripped gently from a fallen bottle on to the white Afghan rug. Chairs lay legs up—mute witness to the hasty departure of the party who had knocked the wine over on hearing her at the front door. Horrified she looked around at the drawers standing open, the books on the floor, the kicked off muddy boots and fruit peel and pips in the grate. But the room looked more as if it had been *used* than ransacked...

Running to the kitchen she surveyed the disorder. Obviously this was where the banquet had been prepared. All the best china was out. Serving dishes were stuck with rinds and piled high beside dirty pots and foodstained measures. Corks rolled from under the table towards the larder door which stood open. As she crossed to shut it, a hen ran out clucking loudly. Standing in the outer doorway she looked across the deserted yard, took down a pan and banged "Cookhouse" on it. No one came. Indeed there was no sign of life anywhere. The place was utterly silent. Cautiously she re-entered, locking the door behind her.

Upstairs she unpacked her clothes and purchases thoughtfully. Whatever had happened she would have to deal with carefully. Her eye moved to the mallet which always lay by her bed as, frowning, she picked up a clothes hanger and crossed to the wardrobe. She paused to think. It certainly would not have been visitors from Moke who'd created the confusion. The wardrobe, she found, was locked and turning the key and looking up to move the coat hangers along she did not see a pair of male feet protruding beneath the clothing. Pushing the door to, she took a nightdress from a drawer and shook it out, pulled the pins from her hair and sat on the bed to think. There were no sounds from anywhere. Never had Hexham been quite so still. Crossing to the window she searched carefully for signs of life but found none.

As she got into her nightdress her mind worked on

what could have happened during her absence. That it *had* happened was no surprise for, although unthinkable in Christchurch or London, in the High Country where people got by with actions and not words, it obviously meant something. Somebody had addressed this direct personal statement at her. Who? Trying to read it, she got into bed. The doors were locked and if a person tried to enter she had her mallet. The moon would rise soon and shine through her open curtains illuminating all and there was no point in worrying prematurely about things that might not happen. In the morning she would most certainly get hold of the ringleader and, alone or not, he would be given his marching orders.

As she slept the wardrobe door shuddered free and the form of a naked man issued cautiously forth, glanced towards her on the bed and began to tiptoe to the door. Instantly she was awake, leaping up, grabbing the wooden mallet and running between the man and the door, mallet raised. To her surprise he shrank from her trying to cover his nakedness and on lowering the mallet she recognized the man.

"Sam!" she gasped.

Sitting downstairs wrapped in a blanket Sam looked up, down, anywhere but at her. Behind him the moon picked out the remains of the banquet.

"They don't fear me," he whispered. "That Harry that was got rid of. Well, he happened up here—said it was three years on and he'd married a wife and changed like. I told 'im to move on! Best as I could." Sam paused.

Ceci pulled her cloak around her knowing exactly what that would have amounted to. Sam shrugged helplessly.

"They was wax in 'is 'ands."

"Is he still here?" she asked.

"I *told* 'im." Sam frowned. "You don't go in there I said. He was always, you know, if he got any watchers around." His hand moved indicating his meaning. "But they'd took their rations and cleared off. Til they heard Cookhouse banged and down they come running. His missus in the kitchen. Told 'em to go in and enjoy their-selves for once."

"She said she was my new cook?" Ceci was incredulous.

"First they wouldn't," Sam went on. "He was passin'

drink around. They was wax in his hands. So drunk and filled with liquor they'd do anything—"

Ceci did not want to ask Sam how he had come to be in her wardrobe. In a low voice his words fell one by one on to the carpet:

"They made me wear women's clothes."

Ceci looked down.

"Said I wasn't a man to let a woman run me around," he breathed out. "Meaning you." He raised his face to look at her. "Wasn't fit to wear men's clothing. Took 'em off me and—took me upstairs—"

"That animal went in my bedroom!" Ceci gasped.

"Flouncing bits and things out of the drawers and wavin' them in me face!"

His hands made helpless gestures at the awful memory of what had happened to him. He pulled the blankets closer to him.

"They could hardly stand they was so drunk. One of 'em—he locked me in your closet so's I'd—So's you'd open the door—Said I belonged in a woman's closet." Sam bit off angrily.

"I'll deal with this," said Ceci.

"I want to leave."

"No."

"He made me wear women's clothes," Sam explained. "The men won't respect me."

Alone, Ceci sank deep in the chair working out strategy. So Harry had been back! How clearly she remembered him referring to her as "a bit of a girl" when she'd ordered him to take off his boots in the kitchen that first time when she had come as a neighbour to help Mrs. Laird! She had not mistaken his hostility then, nor his vulgar personal intentions when he had bumped into her in the kitchen, forced her against the hot stove and breathed his foul breath in her face in full view of her child. And now he had dared to come back in the full knowledge, for he would certainly have been told, that Calvin had gone and only poor weak poached egg Sam was there to defend the honour of the house!

Suddenly, she heard footsteps behind her.

"Sam—," she said without turning. There was no reply.

"Sam?" she repeated, craning to peer around the wing of the chair.

There to her horror was Harry—one hand on the neck of the full bottle he had come to retrieve. In an instant she was on her feet—his confidence increasing at the sight of her discomfort. Quickly she controlled herself.

"Put that down and get out."

He stared at her licking his lips.

"In the morning your wife can clear up this mess."

"She's not ma wife."

"Then you will both leave."

"She's gone."

"In that case you can leave right now."

"Clear up your own mess," said Harry, and crossing to her, blew on her face. "I can do what I like now," he menaced.

"Get out," she repeated, standing her ground.

"Bit of you first," he murmured reaching for her neck.

She stood perfectly still, knowing instinctively she would never be raped in Hexham.

"*Out!*"

He stepped forward to draw her to him, expecting her to back off, but she remained standing.

"Please begin," she invited.

He scratched his neck.

"You clearly find me attractive!"

Harry paused.

"I look forward to telling the men how badly you do it," Ceci informed him.

Harry frowned. Should he punch her in the face and teach her a lesson or would he be better off taking the wine and going?

"Outside!" she barked as he decided for the wine and reached for the bottle's neck.

"Wouldn't want to mess with you anyway," he said sullenly from the door.

Harry had gone by first light when she'd come looking for him with her shotgun but the problem of Sam was harder to resolve. Realizing she needed advice, Ceci went to the only person she could trust to give it: Ginger. Thus a week to that day found four riders on horseback—herself and Ginger up front and, some way behind, Sam and another man, Flinders, who stopped periodically for Sam to point things out.

"Sam *has* to leave," Ginger explained.

"People forget."

"Men don't!"

"It was—something of nothing," Ceci shrugged, unable to understand Sam's insistence on going. "Bad blood—and Harry coming back to show off! Sam's been here longer than me."

"Cromwell'll cope."

"Cromwell?"

"To his face mind it's 'Flinders'."

"You know if I'd come back a day later the place would have been cleaned up?" Ceci sighed. "None of this—"

"Cromwell's the man for you," Ginger assured.

"So how can you spare him?"

"Needs more scope, Cromwell. Not enough to occupy him at my place."

"And you could use Sam?"

"He's very silent, mind," Ginger went on. "You're lucky to get two words out of him at a time to rub together!"

Ceci glanced back at Flinders. He was tall and lean. It was easy to understand his nickname for he looked almost a figure leftover from the Roundhead days. From his sedentary horse he was surveying her domain and looking down on the clumsy, rounded, balding Sam who was explaining things without a word or wink of confirmation from Flinders; just his stern unwavering gaze.

"I 'ope you took all that in," Ceci heard Sam say. "That's 50 acres of green feed—black barley or oats—a paddock of swedes"—Flinders stared away as Sam frowned up, wondering if there was something wrong with him—"the 6-8,000 bales of hay is a third ryegrass and clover, the rest lucerne," came Sam's voice.

"What was he doing working for you?" Ceci asked.

"You mean for Catholics?" Ginger queried.

"I *mean*—if he's so good—a place your size didn't need him."

"He's got a 'past'."

"And he never laughs?"

Ginger nodded.

"Is he a 'lawn' man?" Ceci probed grinning wryly, yet unwilling to share the joke with Ginger.

"He'll up your yield ten times," Ginger guaranteed, turning back towards the stables. "How"re the Hallams working out?"

"Supposed to be something wrong with them but I can't find it," she confessed. "She's a good cook and won't let anyone in the kitchen. Even *me*."

"I can remember when you cooked," Ginger said giving her a sideways glance. She flushed and looked down awkwardly.

"I can't have that—link with the men—without Calvin—" she explained honestly.

"Be cheaper."

"There has to be—a—a—'presence' in the house," she stammered, wondering why he could not grasp that it was nigh impossible to be the only female on the ranch and feed the men without becoming subservient to them! Surely it was obvious that if the cook were a married woman her husband would protect *her* and as an employee the cook would side with her mistress, thus extending her husband's protection to Ceci by adding a man to their side, a situation respected by the other men and vastly superior to that of two unaccompanied women!

"With your Hallams and your Flinders you're set to go!" Ginger nodded goodnaturedly.

Ceci grinned. Yes, she thought, but where?

At that moment a great scream of female anger reached them from the kitchen. Almost holding hands they tiptoed towards the door from which a stream of abuse was issuing. Amused and incredulous they listened, open mouthed, giggling shamelessly at the expense of the Hallams.

"Ef she wanth me to shtay Oi'd lave and ef she wanth me to lave Oi'd shtay!"

"Oh Oi'm the one's soft with the wimmin!"

"Oi'll take the opporchewnity av sayin' to her ugly face phawts in me moind since we come 'ere!"

"Aisy now—"

"Aisy, aisy!!! Ye'll lave me kitchen wid a dipper o' scaldin wahther aroun your back and me feet assistin' ye out!" came the voice of Mrs. Hallam.

"You keep yer thrap shut towards the Mistress."

"An I tell ye to kape yer tongue still in yer head and not chip in when yer betters has the flure or I'll mop it wid ye!" she returned. "Oi'd not be servantin' for pigs at home."

At that Ceci decided to put her head in.

"Good afternoon Madam," said Mrs. Hallam in a very different voice.

"Do you have all you need?" Ceci enquired.

"Yes thank you Madam," she said politely.

"Two extra for dinner tonight please. One in the house—one with the men."

The well-fleshed pink-faced woman nodded quickly.

"Very good Madam. Thank you Madam."

As Ceci turned to leave she saw out of the corner of her eyes Mr. Hallam smirking at Mrs. Hallam who was grimacing and waving the rolling pin in his direction. Outside, she collapsed on the wall, laughing.

Pulling away from the wall an unaccountable shyness came over her and as she continued walking with Ginger she found herself unable to discuss even the simplest things without feeling acutely self-conscious. He asked and she answered that Olwen was with her sister; that her sister had four children; that Olwen liked being part of a big family, was strong headed and something of a ringleader. She heard that Michael and Kevin were at the fighting age, that Faith, next after them, followed them around slavishly, that Myra, the youngest, was a slow starter.

"What about Lizabeth?" Ceci asked, wondering why she blushed so self-consciously as if they were her children she was talking about.

"Ah, she still remembers borrowing your shawl when you visited," Ginger grinned. Ceci went as red as she remembered her shawl being. The intimate way Ginger talked to her of his children and looked at her as he did so made her feel threatened yet reassured at the same time as if he were willingly offering her fruits she had no right to share because he wanted her to have them. She felt a certain trembling in her hands, unnecessary swallowing and a wobble around her mouth when she wanted to give what should have been a sponaneous smile.

He never spoke of Maureen. In fact she almost sensed

him willing her away and making her a party to an agreement not to discuss Maureen. As time passed and her cheeks reddened she concluded it was altogether easier if they confined themselves to the matter in hand or talked about Sam and Flinders. Though she made a stern effort, the subject returned frequently to Family.

Ginger observed that Olwen would be getting a good education and Ceci shyly confirmed this, unaware that as she did so her hands twisted on the saddle giving away how much she missed the child. She expressed the hope that Olwen would wish to return to Hexham when school were finished and when Ginger politely asked, though he must have known, if education were now compulsory in Great Britain, she had replied Yes and told him as if her life depended on it that until the age of fourteen children must remain in school.

"Not long then," Ginger said, his eyes burning into her. Quickly Ceci looked away. In the corner Sam and Flinders were leaving one stable and entering a shed to inspect the equipment. She sincerely hoped they would catch up with them. Why was it that she who could march into the barn with her shotgun, confront Harry, drive labourers from under a shade of trees into the midday sun, could not be alone with the only person who had been genuinely kind to her in New Zealand without feeling intensely vulnerable? She must try and get a hold of herself!

Returning to the house she stood aside for him to enter. He hesitated on the doorstep as if he had forgotten something, then as Ceci waited for him in the hallway, hovered with his foot halfway over the lintel. His eyes, she saw, were taking in the shining floor, the mirrors, the rugs and ornamental hangings. *Of course*, she reminded herself! He had never been inside before.

Letting him stare, Ceci moved on into the dining room where two places had been set at the exquisitely prepared table, its cutlery glinting on the polished surface, a small dish of flowers slightly off centre and sparkling crystal ware and crisply rolled napkins highlighting the arrangement. At the opposite door leading to the kitchen she glimpsed Mrs. Hallam, a look of unmistakable pride on her features, the satisfaction of a job well done. Hands clasped before her, she stood checking the table and nodding at it. As Ginger stepped into the room she quickly withdrew.

Somehow the setting was romantic—intimate. Realizing it, Ceci's face took on a softness of nostalgia, not of intent. Slightly behind her Ginger''s face tautened, like a child about to trespass in a sweet shop, knowing he would do wrong.

Forcing herself to cross the room Ceci stood by the mantelpiece, lightly moving a statue as if its placing were suddenly of the utmost importance. By the door, Ginger struggled with his cravat as if it were throttling him. His stubby fingers dusted the back of his neck as he looked at Ceci by the mantelpiece, apparently having difficulty turning to face him.

"It—it's a nice room isn't it," she said shyly, forcing herself to turn.

"Oh yes. *Indeed*—" rushed Ginger, trying to break the silence hanging between them. She forced herself to the table, pulled back her chair and looked nervously across to invite him as, clearing his throat, he hurried quickly over and put both hands on the back of his chair to draw it back. Then he paused, making her notice the ginger hairs curling from under his cuffs and scrambling across the backs of his hands . . . the very shape of his fingers, their closeness to her. With difficulty their eyes brushed saying it was wrong, knowing it was already over.

"I—I have to—get back," Ginger said, his voice shaking and barely audible. Overcome with mortification, Ceci watched him leave. How could she have been so presumptious as to assume he would want to stop to dinner, she asked herself? What must he *think* of her? At least he had not been aware of the thoughts that had troubled her during his visit! Well, perhaps she may have flushed a couple of times but some men found blushing attractive in women and he was not to know it was not one of her habits. Excruciatingly embarrassed at what she could not but see as an exhibition of personal presumption she leaned on the front door which she had closed too quickly after him, almost as if seeing bad news out. Too embarrassed to even think, she propelled herself back into the dining room to sit at her place. It was because she did not get out often enough, she told herself, that she reacted to men in this ridiculous fashion! Why, even now he would be looking forward to entering his own home where there was Life and Love, taking his wife in his arms and telling her, probably with his mouth full, about the boring happenings on the hill! Oh, stupid a thousand times over she told herself!

The noise of Mrs. Hallam making an entrance disturbed her shame and motioning her forwards she indicated that the servings should be placed on the table. Having done that, Mrs. Hallam stood back for a moment.

"Will I uncover the lid off it for you?" she said.

Ceci lifted a hand in dismissal.

By now it was almost dark. Suddenly Mrs. Hallam appeared again with the sweet and the sight of the untouched food, now quite cold, enraged her.

"So where's yer foine friend Madam!" she quivered.

Ceci said nothing.

"Yez wantin' a couple as is married theirselves," she went on, "but when it comes to yezself yez not so perticeler is yez?"

That stung. Ceci pushed herself from the table.

"Just walkin' away from me cookin' loike de spoilt brat! Oi've a mind ter walk through that gate!"

At the door Ceci paused. "Mind I don't race you to it," she said quietly. Behind her Mrs. Hallam's face twitched with wrath as she began to clear the table then, thinking better of it, stomped to the door to give Ceci the benefit of her opinions. Standing under the chandelier, hands on her hips, she shouted upwards:

"Oh yes Madam. Very foine wid yer big house and yer lawn and yer 20,000 acres—yer servants and der werkers!" she said then waited, listening. Nothing.

"And havin' of yer choild educated away and yer husband borried!" She paused again to listen for it was very important to her that her rudeness always be heard and, were it to be overlooked, it would threaten the very fabric of her existence.

"Ye should have children in this house!" she shouted. "Scuffin'" the mats!"

Irritated, she peered up the stairs, at the ceiling and doors for some sign of life. Out of sight Ceci leaned against the wall, her tumult of feelings having subsided and the truth of Mrs. Hallam's words writ on her face.

"It takes Bridget to tell yer," she heard bawled up the stairs.

"When all's said and done yer a beggar fer love!"

Firmly putting the embarrassing memory aside Ceci flung herself into the running of Hexham though these days it had an uncanny way of running itself! Under Flinders's management the yield rose continually, and the workers, unable to get a word out of him, confined their affairs to themselves establishing a de facto distance between them and him. Their work was cut out. They couldn't fault the planning. The food was the best they'd known and the cook not attractive enough to need their attention nor refined enough for any curbing of their tongues. There was not one of them who did not prefer a good sting across the face with a dishrag to a request to remove his boots. The trouble, Ceci found, lay in the area where these two demigods—Flinders and Hallam—crossed. Each was so territorially alert that the slightest boundary dispute was readily—and in Mrs. Hallam's case *willingly*—escalated.

Tap tap the sound would go softly on Ceci's door. Seated at Calvin's desk doing the accounts she would know exactly who it was. The door would open without her answering and Flinders would be standing there waiting to be invited in.

"Come in Flinders and sit down," she would say without looking up.

He would enter like a ramrod, sit on the edge of the easy chair looking away out of the window. He always left his boots in the yard, his stockinged feet making no sound as he approached. Ceci would finish her column of figures and put her pencil down. When she turned to face him, he would begin:

"Hallam. Name calling."

"You're doing an *excellent* job here Flinders and I have twice raised your salary in recognition of that fact," Ceci would begin, not a little tired of their continual feuding. "The men are gaining in self-respect, we are more productive."

Such speeches always made Flinders frown hard at his stockinged feet and she knew that they pleased him.

"As to Mrs. Hallam—whom you will in fairness agree

is *most* competent at her *job*," Ceci would continue reasonably, "I think we have to—give her room to—completely loose her temper once a month and clear her chest. It's part of her—disposition—as sobriety is yours."

These conversations were predictable.

"Not good for the men. That going on."

"Their first concern is what Mrs. Hallam puts in their stomachs."

About that stage in the conversation the door would burst open:

"So uts here yez hiding yerself ye spotty dick!"

"Mrs. Hallam!" Ceci would show the expected degree of shock.

"Smelt his stockinged feet in me hallway Madam."

"Boil a potato!" Flinders would fling at her, his impoverished imagination being no match for her vernacular.

"Bile a pertater yerself!" Mrs. Hallam would toss back. "He's quare in his mind," she informed Ceci. "Makin' a hen huzzy of himself comin' inter the House."

His bile rising Flinders would get to the point: "I left a work shirt on that line—"

"Will yer look at dat dirty rag, sez Hallam," she would say, referring to her husband whom she called "Hallam."

"See?" Flinders turned to Ceci.

"Scorn it for a dishcloth I sez! Wouldn't touch it wid a poker for fear of blackin' it up!"

How Mrs. Hallam loved duelling! Though her husband had long since proved inferior at the art and Flinders was difficult to needle from his shell she never gave up.

"Getting on me wrong side Hallam—" Flinders would point out.

"Go swape under yer bed . . ." she'd advise him.

"Stoppit! Stoppit stoppit," Ceci got to her feet. "I've a mind to put this house—this station up for sale!"

They stared at her mutually aghast.

"I—I—" she spluttered on into the silence. "What am I *doing* here? I could live with my *own* folk at home, where people are civilized! *Normal*!"

"You do very well here Madam," said Mrs. Hallam, delighted at the chance for impertinence.

"Where would you be if I sold?" Ceci demanded. "You have a free hand here! Both of you! No one puts on airs!" For a moment they hung their heads. "So you put *up* with each other—you hear? Or I'll get rid of this place! I'm tired. I'm *tired tired*," she banged her fist on the desk, "of trying!" They stared.

"So shake hands and get downstairs," she said. Mrs. Hallam unwillingly extended a hand towards Flinders averting her eyes and saying: "As not I'll catch a desaise!"

With puritan resolve Flinders grasped her hand and cracked the knuckles loudly. Mrs. Hallam's mouth popped soundlessly open as the instant of forgiveness passed and fresh ways of persecuting Flinders came to her mind. Opening the door she made him leave the room first giving Ceci an "I'll take care of him" look as she closed the door behind them.

As she crossed the hallway through a shaft of morning sun, a jangle at the door surprised Ceci who went to open it. There stood a very proper English couple who instantly put her in mind of Immelda. The gentleman handed his card.

"Give this to the mistress would you?" he said.

Ceci stepped back into the hall, and opened the door to the sitting room glancing casually at their card as if it were a rare stamp. Entering the room after them, she perceived the woman giving the man a look of affront and realizing the silly creature had mistaken her for the maid, quickly set them to rights. What a futile arrangement, she told herself, when people could not open their own front doors land greet people without having a maid! They were scarce older than her, either of them.

"Mr. Prendergast had heard at the Club," the woman informed her, referring to her husband as Mr Prendergast though it was clearly written on their card that that was his name.

"What Club?" Ceci interrupted.

"Christchurch Club don't you know," he put in, slightly afraid the two women might scrap in public. "Ran into an old school chum."

"Harrow," Mrs. Prendergast inserted, keeping the exchange on a decent keel.

"We were put up for membership," bleated Prendergast. Totally taken aback by their strangeness Ceci could only stare. "How long have you been out here?" she asked.

"Two months!" said Mrs. Prendergast sighing at the ordeal and for some reason expecting sympathy.

"See a lot of runs," put in Prendergast.

"A friend of Mr. Prendergast's," said Mrs. Prendergast, matching him word for word, "is *helping* us—you understand—'*acquire*'."

"Certainly get down to it. Chaps out here," went on Prendergast, apparently believing it necessary to show enthusiasm, "dont mind rolling their sleeves up."

"But a *tenny* bit brusque one must say," advised Mrs. Prendergast as if remembering a close encounter with familiarity.

"Woman at the hotel shook her hand!" joked Prendergast.

"What *for*? And so unnecessary!"

"Bit of a liberty."

Frowning, Ceci left them to prepare refreshments.

Apparently they had ridden all the way to her station simply on the hearsay that she was a single woman with a large property; the idea of an unaccompanied woman managing or wanting to manage a station had struck them at once as lunacy. They had been advised to "get out there and put in a bid" . . . Or, as Mr. Prendergast put it:

"Bull by the horns and all that. Doing her a favour!"

As they rattled on, sipping at tea, Ceci began to feel disoriented. Was this really the country she had left? Had she once inhabited the same universe? Why were they staring at her? Probably her turn to speak.

"So how do you like the place?" she asked. "This country?"

"One is—er—*forced* to comment," observed Mrs. Prendergast as if under duress, "on the plainness of the *views*—" Views? Ceci stared wondering what she was talking about. "Are you English?" Mrs. Prendergast enquired.

Suddenly with blinding clarity Ceci knew the answer: "Not any more," and she said it with deep personal conviction, shocking the Prendergasts and making herself aware exactly where it left her.

"So have you been around my place yet?" she asked.

"Certainly not without a consent!" chirped Prendergast.

"Have a look," Ceci shrugged. "You've come this far—"

They leaned forward eagerly, half afraid to believe her.

"Look at the house too—" she went on, crossing to the window and knocking loudly on it to get the attention of Flinders who was crossing the lawn. "The foreman'll show you round. *Flinders!*" Mrs. Prendergast flinched. "You'll stop to tea?" she continued, moving to the door and stepping out in to the corridor to call: "Hallam!"

Mrs. Prendergast winced at the shouting. 'Do you think she means 'dinner'?" she whispered to Prendergast.

"Oh we couldn't put you to the trouble," he said turning in his chair as Ceci re-entered.

"We're proud of our hospitality out here. To all comers," she admitted with a smile. "Two more for dinner please Mrs. Hallam—"

"Who're they?" Hallam asked entering.

"That'll be all thank you," Ceci nodded and Mrs Hallam withdrew, making a great show of squeezing around Flinders as if to avoid touching him.

"Did you feed their horses Flinders?"

"Yes Marm."

"Then take the Prendergasts around would you? Show them the full extent of the place. Point up its limits—"

"I expect we'd be making alterations anyway—" said Mrs. Prendergast unwisely, a good indication of her natural lack of tact. Behind her, Flinders's and Ceci's eyes met in mutual derision at these strangers...

Given Flinders's thoroughness it was a considerable time before they returned, flushed and excited, Mrs. Prendergast forgetting herself to the extent of bursting into childish speech the moment they re-entered. Prendergast kept a better grip on himself.

"Have to bow to your management Mrs. Laird," he said. "Very likely run!" Behind him happiness fleeted on Flinders's face.

"What a garden! For tea parties...!" the lady trilled. "Is there a piano? We could play bridge on the lawn! It would be *just like England*! And how are the neighbours?"

"Come and wash your hands," Ceci said as if addressing children.

"Now don't go on Amelia," Prendergast chided.

"But Maurice *dear*!" she burbled. "Your friends could come up here and *stay*."

"Stations take *work*," he said in a voice suggesting the responsibility for the entire High Country momentarily rested on his shoulders.

"If *she* can run it—" said Mrs. Prendergast blithely.

During "tea" she showed no signs of cooling, the tongue darting greedily from her mouth as the courses arrived.

"You've been—generous with us—" Prendergast said, his eye firmly on the dessert.

"I would *definitely* remove that summer house," his wife muttered reaching for fresh utensils.

"I'm not selling," said Ceci, the hardness in her voice surprising even her. How dare they even *think* of removing Calvin's summer house! Mrs. Prendergast's face tightened and Prendergast's dropped.

"But wait till you hear his offer my dear..." urged Mrs. Prendergast, as if the sum of money at her husband's disposal plus the goodwill of the Christchurch Club could see them through any eventuality. Ceci who did not like being referred to as "dear" looked at her coldly.

"That's enough Amelia," snapped Prendergast, first name time obviously having come.

"But it's so *ridiculous* Maurice!" she protested. "A place this size for a—" Had he kicked her under the table? She had just stopped in time. "The house should be—*filled* with people!" she corrected. Ceci did not think so. It never had been, except that evening at Calvin's soirée.

"Are you sure we can't interest you?" Prendergast asked deciding good manner were the best course after all.

"I'm afraid I've got 'settler's mind.'" Ceci grinned remembering Old Bowen.

They exchanged baffled looks.

"If you—*change* it," Mr Prendergast said dabbing at his mouth reproachfully and hoping there was still a chance, "would you send word to The Club...?" Ceci stretched past them to refill their glasses and saw Mrs. Prendergast cutting into smaller and smaller pieces a tiny piece of meat on her plate.

After they had gone Ceci wandered the immaculate house thinking. The objects in it were better suited to the Prendergasts than her but not the "atmosphere." Here was suspended an exquisite Eastern hanging: there lay fine weaving from the heart of Central Asia; this was an example of English porcelain at its best and that of one of the better pieces of French furniture. She tapped her foot; she could be the curator of a museum! *She could be keeping a mausoleum for a foreign king or locked in a tomb*! The only sound was the ticking of the clock below. With an effort she pushed herself towards her bedroom and entered. Very softly she closed the great door behind her.

Chapter 22

All it had taken was a little self-discipline to rid her mind of Ginger, Ceci told herself, rising from Calvin's grave and turning to look back at the fresh blooms she had left. Had she done right in burying him in Moke's cemetery? It was the only grave of substance there yet Calvin did not seem to belong in Moke. For that matter when she had considered burying him at Hexham she had felt strongly that was not right either. Passing out through the gates she wondered if she too would end her days in Moke's graveyard. Would some stranger decide to put her in the same tomb as Calvin? Shaking the thoughts from her head she crossed to Sweetwater's store reminding herself it hardly seemed fair to visit Ginger's family without taking something for the children. She was glad of the excuse of a letter for Sam. It was his and he should have it. Otherwise, she told herself, she would certainly not have gone . . .

Holding the box of sweets, Ceci tapped politely at the door and stared around. The house seemed uncommonly quiet. After a long pause a woman who looked a bit like Maureen but redder and more severe appeared and frowned rudely at her neatness.

"And who are you?" she demanded.

"Hallo Auntie," said Lizabeth, putting her head round the woman's back. "This is Mummy's sister Aunt Edna."

As the woman stepped back to let Ceci in, she felt immediately the strangeness in the place. Something was wrong. Shown into the room where she had sat before she noticed it was tidier than last time but funereal somehow. And the child Lizabeth seemed different.

"Sit down," said Edna abruptly.

Ceci sat, the box of sweets on her knees, conscious of Edna opposite her, staring.

"Have I done something?" Ceci asked.

One by one the children trickled into the room and stood, solemn as death.

"Is Maureen here?"

"Yes."

"How is—Sam getting on?" she said producing the letter.

"Gone."

She let her eyes fall sideways. That would mean there was no forwarding address. Men just vanished in the High Country. Unless that Woman in the Tent . . .

"Ginger?"

"*Vincent* is out," corrected Edna as if Ceci had taken an unforgivable liberty in using her sister's husband's personal appellative or was even responsible for all that had befallen them.

A terrible scream from the room above made the children cringe.

"'Scuse me," said Edna standing.

"Mummy's not well," explained Lizabeth as Edna left the room.

How Ceci longed to comfort the children! There was Lizabeth—surely Olwen's age, yet looking so raggedy . . . She handed her the box of sweets. Lizabeth sat at her feet motioning the others to do the same and slowly twins Michael and Kevin, little Faith and even littler Myra sat in a circle, staring at the ground, unwrapping the sweets with concentration, while above them the screaming continued, accompanied by running feet, a door slamming, banging on the door, more screaming, the sound of a jug of water being thrown. As Ceci looked up Michael snatched Kevin's sweet and Kevin pushed him.

"I'll put the sweets away!" Lizabeth warned.

"You're not in charge!" said Faith.

All sticky around the mouth Faith turned to Myra, unwrapped her sweet for her and put it in her own mouth. Myra at once began to cry. Lizabeth spun to look and Michael leaned forward and wrenched the box from her hand, sweets flying all over the floor. Horrified Ceci watched Lizabeth kneel forward and grapple for the box, giving Kevin the chance to catch one of her swinging plaits and give it a good tug. At that moment the door burst open and there stood Ginger, clearly home for his lunch and ready to give someone a good swot. Biting her lip Ceci struggled to her feet. Here she was, an adult, supposedly in charge and they were squabbling around her like puppies. Ginger drew himself up then abandoned the pretence, let his shoulders sag and flopped in the chair opposite Ceci, his head sinking slowly into his hands.

"The constant *noise*," he groaned.

Ceci looked at the poor man. Clearly he was exhausted. And something was terribly wrong with Maureen. He ignored the fighting, the cries of "Pig!" and "Leave me alone!," the hair coming out in handfuls and the cloth of a skirt giving with a loud rip.

"I envy you, Ceci," he said quietly.

Suddenly Edna burst into the room, sleeves rolled up, and dealing about with a big hand.

"She'll not get better with this racket!" she advised the children who fell quietly to the walls of the room.

"He kicked me."

"Did not."

"Did."

"Let her stay with me for a while," Ceci offered.

Ginger frowned. Possibly it was a good idea. Behind him Edna folded her arms and glowered. She was beginning to have a feeling this was the woman who had started her sister's mental problems by making her uncertain of Vincent's affection. Who was this woman who had walked into their house bold as a pin asking for "Ginger"?

"It—it's *quiet* at my place," Ceci added. "The rest'll do her good."

For a while Ginger stared at the floor then nodded.

"Thank you," he said. "Thank you very much."

Riding back Ceci was glad to have been of use. Nor

had it escaped her notice that having something other than Ginger to think about in his presence removed all her self-consciousness. Indeed, was it not an indication that the whole thing had been her imagination all along?

She was glad to have control of her emotions again and felt herself viewing the world with an equanimity that embraced even the Prendergasts. They were after all a product of a particular background and had not been malicious. She may have been a bit silly and he lacking in—there was not even an English word for it! Not courage, or power... a certain "force" that the rough men of her new world enjoyed. It was true the Prendergasts had money but that was no crime. Their marriage was happy to the extent they gratified each other's needs and found pleasure where they could: in short, they were harmless. Which was no reason to look down on them. If being a New Zealander meant she would develop an inverted snobbery then better go home at once!

For a while after Maureen had arrived Ceci entertained the idea that once she recovered, they might become good friends. She had a strange vision of Ginger's children not fighting over a box of sweets but playing on her lawn. Hexham would be like a holiday for them, she told herself, not in terms of land because they had plenty but because the house itself was a wonderland for games like Hide-and-Seek. When Maureen recovered, when the time was right, she insisted, she would put it to them.

At that moment she looked up to find Maureen wide-eyed before her in her nightie, panting, fists clenched, a pair of scissors in one hand. The slightest move on her part, she suspected, would precipitate some desperate action. She sat not even daring to turn a page of the book she was holding. Prior to her illness she had only met Maureen the once, that first time she had gone visiting. She could not believe that Maureen, who had not yet become lucid, would recognize her, still less approach her with scissors! Yet she could sense the woman's anger directed at her, ballooning up inside and filling her with such a force she had become dangerous.

Softly in stockinged feet, Mrs. Hallam padded into the room bearing a cup of warm milk. Instantly she took account of the danger, came up quietly behind Maureen and whisked the scissors from her hand and as Maureen whirled, confronted her with the cup of milk: "Yer milk dear," she said. Maureen held the cup looking confused. For a moment Ceci feared she would toss the lot in Mrs. Hallam's face but Mrs. Hallam frowned hard at her, giving Ceci a chance to get to her feet and manoeuvre herself to a safer position where she could run to the door if necessary. Eyeing them malevolently, Maureen stood sipping the milk.

As time passed, between them Mrs. Hallam and Ceci made progress. Maureen was bathed regularly, always proving disruptive, deliberately sliding under the water so they had to lean right over and bodily wrench at her. Sometimes she would spout water in their faces or look past them as if she could "see" someone in the corner of the room. The first time she did this, they were so taken by surprise they loosened their grip and turned to look and in an instant she was out of the bath and rushing naked along the corridor and down the stairs. Cramped from kneeling they struggled to their feet. Out the front door went Maureen, straight across the lawn and into the summer house. Bang! Mrs. Hallam and Ceci issued from the front door just in time to see the summer house door click into place and deck chairs begin to go up against the windows. They tore across the lawn, skirts flying, Hallam out of breath but in the lead. She could not wait to get her hands on the summer house door and—and what? Despite her puffing and strength, she would be as gentle as a lamb when the time came and would break nothing. Leaning against the door, both women listened.

"Give ut a good push!" muttered Hallam.

"It's locked. Sssh!"

On their knees they listened. From within came the voice of Maureen as if anticipating pleasure:

"You mustn't," they heard her say. "You're not allowed—"

Mrs. Hallam leaned back on her heels:

"There's a body in there!" she gasped.

Inside the summer house they could hear Maureen running around the small space as if chased, bumping into things, knocking them down.

"No! No! No! No!" she shrieked.

If there had been a man in the summer house they would have heard him by now! Maureen was certainly

alone and reliving some incident from her past . . . By the
time Mrs. Hallam managed to force a window the poor
woman was slumped on the floor, her flabby body covered in the bruises she had received fleeing her fears. On
her body also were the marks of her life, the child bearing
and hard work for all to read. Wrapping her in a cloak,
Ceci and Mrs. Hallam led her carefully back across the
lawn to the house.

It had been a simple Christian act to bring Maureen to
Hexham Ceci told herself and the least she could do in the
circumstances. Ginger had been ready to buckle under the
strain, Edna finding the going rough and the children
suffering in all directions. Ceci noticed when Ginger visited
his manner was calming down, his clothes were generally
well washed and ironed and most important of all he was
under no illusion as to her reason for bringing Maureen to
the big house. Yet it seemed, Ceci mused, she always
found herself in the role of helping other people to achieve
their ends; almost as if her life were borne away on the
tides of *their* desires and needs. Thus while she was
deeply pleased to see an improvement in Maureen she
was conscious at the same time of spending herself like air
and it mystified her that where other people's lives seemed
to grow and thicken, hers remained a single fragile thread.

One particular evening, having spent time with
Maureen, Ginger came down and sat by Ceci:

"Mostly she just cries," Ceci explained when asked
about the daytimes.

"But she's coming round, getting more lucid," she
encouraged.

The word "lucid" seemed to worry Ginger.

"Has she said anything?"

What on earth could he worry about, Ceci wondered
Did they have secrets?

"Well she's—generally worn out."

"She's a fine girl," he said, covering his face with his
hands.

Ceci looked at him.

"You're just about my best friend out here Ginger—
Chin up!"

He brought his head out of his hands.

"Got to—make a way through this."

"You've got a lovely family." She looked at his bowed

head, remembering him saying he'd envied her. "*I envy you*," she added. With difficulty Ginger began to cry deep within himself. He rocked and cried and cried and rocked. Slowly he stopped and looked up but not at her.

"No man of iron!" he admitted.

As he blew his nose Ceci went to the window and looked out. She heard him strike a match and turning saw he had put it to the fire. She looked away again. Silently Maureen padded to the doorway, looked from one to the other, picked up a heavy glass paperweight and flung it with all her force at Ceci's back. Crash! It missed. Instantly Ginger ran to take her arms but she swung past him towards Ceci.

"You've had your lot!" she shouted at Ginger, adding, "and aren't *you* the clever one!" to Ceci.

For a brief second Ceci stood transfixed as Ginger grabbed Maureen from behind and Mrs. Hallam appeared in the doorway. She could not understand the terrible look on Maureen's face: a look of accusation, hatred and vulnerability. Apologizing to her Ginger grappled with Maureen and hurried her from the room.

When he returned later he found Ceci sitting on the floor by the fire staring into the flames. The room was lit by them for she had not yet illuminated the lamps. Scratching an ear, Ginger dropped down and peered at her in the soft amber light.

"Maureen's had a lot of trouble," he explained, not noticing the bleak look on Ceci's face. "She'll come right."

Ceci shrugged with a leaden heaviness.

"Shall I take her back?"

"It's just—sometimes I wonder what I've done *wrong*!" she said turning to him. "Other girls marry and have families! Maureen didn''t have to—to—" she paused, seeking an acceptable phrase to mean "go out seeking."

"The land was hers," Ginger observed, making Ceci think that was the reason he'd married her.

"With *your* nameboard up!?" she gasped disillusioned.

"My name's O'Sullivan," he said. "Her father's Nolan . . ." *Of course*, Ceci realized. Why hadn't she thought of that before? Ginger added another jolt.

"She was—'that way'."

"For *years* I've told myself you were the *one man* I'd

most—" Ceci expostulated, but stopped, afraid to finish the sentence.

"Wasn't mine," he shrugged.

"*What?*"

"Her father approached me."

Suddenly the ground trembled.

"Then *why* did you marry her?" she whispered.

"Thought she was a fine girl," Ginger shrugged. "Still do. Who'd want to marry me I thought!" he said picking at an ear.

Ceci sat quite still staring into the flames, scarce able to cope with the tumult of feelings that were rising.

"You *show* such love," she ventured.

Ginger shrugged. "Livin' together it comes."

"She's lucky."

"And children tie you."

"Poor me, eh?"

He turned to look at her: "And I thought *you* didn't care," he said.

At that she began to ache with feelings and longings, things desired and needed, things she had not admitted to wanting for a long time. As if being friendly, she felt Ginger put a hand on the back of her neck and braced herself as he moved aside wisps of hair with his thumb making a deep shudder come from within her. Half consciously he pulled her back to lean on his shoulder idly stroking her head with his free hand and staring into the fire. He's sorry for me, she told herself shutting her eyes, her lids hovering with the tranquillity of a death mask, face resting in bliss and her voice, when it came, disembodied:

"Did you ever find out whose it was?" she breathed carefully.

"Didn't ask."

With an effort she pulled herself away, conscious something was "wrong" and bothered by it. There had been the slightest tension in the tips of his fingers or had she been imagining it?

Deliberately she knelt a few feet closer to the fire and turned to flash him an apologetic grin. To put her at ease he smiled back as if they were still just friends.

"Didn't think it was the Angel Gabriel's!" he grinned, making a fist of his hand and pounding it in the grate.

"Ow!" he gasped. Spinning, Ceci saw a log bounce away leaving a long black splinter in the palm of his thumb. Quickly she reached for her pin cushion which hung in the chimney breast, pulled out a needle and held its tip in the flames. She took his hand and began to work the splinter loose, tongue touching her lips, energy concentrated, deeply conscious that splinters were painful and she must not cause hurt as she prodded and probed. She was unaware of the effect of her hands as she sought to dislodge the splinter. See his hand in the hands of the woman he loved, her fingers darting gently over it, feeling that sweet sweet pain as the needle pried, Ginger's tired endurance was pierced and the heaviness of his existence slipped away with a great sigh of abandon making Ceci suddenly aware of something peculiar in the relaxation of the hand she was stabbing at. Quickly she glanced up and saw the shut eyes, the mouth hanging slightly open. Instantly she dropped his hand. As it hit the fender Ginger came to, surprised by the startled look on her face. She was leaning away from him, covering her chest with her arms. With difficulty he controlled himself, looked into the fire and spoke his heavy truth:

"I do love Maureen."

Ashamed of having embarrassed him by imagining some familiarity Ceci murmured:

"I—I'm not important," but to her amazement, moved by some strong emotion, tears in his eyes, Ginger spoke into the flames words that seemed to choke him:

"I forbid you to ever say that!"

With difficulty, casting her eyes down, Ceci said in a quiet voice: "Go and say goodnight to Maureen."

Ginger rose, looked down on the top of her head as if believing that one day, sooner or later, he would be with her. Perhaps in another life, another time . . . But some day it *would* happen . . .

"I'll look in on Maureen again tomorrow," he said from the door. Ceci didn't look up. She stayed staring anxiously into the fire, conscious of him observing her, waiting for him to be gone. Minutes passed, she sighed and turned to find him still standing there. At once he stepped back into the room seeing her chest swell as she hurriedly got to her feet and reached out a hand to steady herself.

"Good night," he said, then quickly left.

As she heard the front door close, happiness played briefly on her face as if for a few moments she had been cherished. It was a wonderful warm feeling, the sort of closeness she sometimes awoke with which belonged to her alone. Who it was that held her before she woke up she could not tell, any more than she knew who was the invisible soul who had danced with her that night so inflaming Calvin . . .

On day, she told herself, she would find out.

Propped on lace pillows the following morning Ceci sat up in bed running the previous night's memories through her mind. Frightened to be thinking these thoughts, yet enjoying them, she now knew that behind that door lay things she had not imagined, things to which she had no right, things which should not see the light of day. . . She did not see Mrs. Hallam observing her, a tray of tea to hand and the look of the cat that got the cream on her face. Hallam cleared her throat loudly as if, every inch the lady, she needed to be invited in. The loudness with which she had cleared her throat however and her obvious intention of entering whether wanted or not somewhat belied the impression.

"To what do I owe tea in bed?" Ceci asked sharply.

"Sure you'll be too weak to come downstairs this morning after the time as you got up them last night!" Mrs. Hallam smiled, putting the tray on the dresser, folding her arms and smirking. Ceci's face flashed anger:

"One moment you're telling me this house needs kids scuffing the mats," she burst out.

"Yes," interrupted Mrs. Hallam. "And it's the *house* I was talking about."

"You *constantly* allude to my loneliness."

"Out of the frying pan into the fire!" Hallam sang gaily.

"I've no intention of—of—"

The infernal cheek of the woman! Thinking of what it was she had no intention of doing made Ceci realize its imminent likelihood and swallow hard as Mrs. Hallam's eyes narrowed for the kill.

"Be that as it may—Madame," she continued, managing to convey a wide range of implications in the word

"Madame," "*next* time the gentleman's here I'd appreciate bein' told—before I go to me *husband's* bed, (she put special emphasis on the word "husband") "whether it'll be one for breakfast or *two*—and downstairs or *up*stairs next time!"

"There'll *be* no next time!" Ceci blazed at her flinging back the sheets. But too late! Mrs. Hallam had already left nodding quite ecstatically at the door.

Furious at having allowed herself to be provoked by the woman Ceci leaped from bed and ran to slam the door after her, accidentally knocking over the elegant china tea pot and sending its tea streaming to the floor. She snatched up a towel, threw it to absorb the tea, then stooped mopping at it. Slowly, she arose and went to sit on the edge of the bed, a look of misery coming to her eyes. She twisted her hair in her fingers . . . It was no good. The time had come to act.

Leaving the room she went to her bureau, pulled out the Prendergasts' card and turned it over slowly in her hands, in her mind composing the letter she feared would change her life:

> *Dear Mr. and Mrs. Prendergast—If you are not yet settled, perhaps you would like to take the station on a rent-lease trial, as I have to get* away *from here!*

No, she could not mention the personal reason underlying this sudden change of heart. Nor could she stay longer now that she and Ginger had discovered how they felt! She must leave the place and the sooner the better! Never had such intense feelings of panic and the need to flee hounded her before! So great was her haste to escape these dangerous new feelings she could scarce spare time to pack . . . Mrs. Hallam could continue to help with Maureen but *she* must be gone at once! She must go to Christchurch and without fear or preparation face whatever future should lie ahead.

Chapter 23

From the step Mrs. Hallam watched the Prendergasts supervising the unloading of their wagon. It would not take long to get rid of *them*, she told herself. She watched their Wheeler and Wilson sewing machine being taken down and wondered who would do the sewing? Prendergast looked tired and sweaty, his wife fretful, thoroughly vexed.

"*No* Flinders! Get *Feast*! The *Groom*!" Mrs. Prendergast snapped.

No emotion showed on Flinders's face as he plodded around to the back of the house. If Flinders had had any sense at all, Mrs. Hallam told herself, he would have just shown the Prendergasts the pigs in the first place instead of being so thorough! She watched Feast appear, a well attired man who, it seemed to Mrs. Hallam, had had his balls bitten off. The sort who would do instantly whatever he was bid! She was of two minds to give a loud whistle and see if he came! Instead she wiped her hands on her stomach and went back into the kitchen.

"Soon roust the pair o'them!" she told herself.

The first Ginger heard of Ceci's departure was a chance remark by the boy of Moke's only For Hire trap, boasting that his father had gone up to Hexham to take a lady as far as the Christchurch Road. Carefully extricating himself from the Grain and Feed accounts books which he still did once a month he managed to leave without attracting attention and with deliberate slowness mounted and moved off down the street. Once outside Moke however he turned his horse to the hills, whipping the poor beast into a frenzy. Cresting Lookout Ridge Ginger paused. There below, Moke's small For Hire was heading from Hexham, had already passed the junction with the Moke road and was sliding gently downhill to the last outpost, the forge which marked the approach to the main Christchurch Road. His first impulse was to make diagonally for the coach and haul up alongside but realizing that was exactly the sort of scandal he was seeking to avoid he held still. It would be better to wait a couple of days, perhaps "drop by" Hexham, get 'Hallam in a cleft twig and make her talk... Risking a scene would serve nothing beyond embarrassing the girl who had remained innocent, no— *ignorant* of his feelings 'til the moment she had seen his face. That, of course, had frightened her, possibly causing her to stampede. On the other hand, this could be a routine trip to acquire more staff... What she could not have known, he told himself as the coach got smaller in the distance, was the turmoil in his *own* mind at that time. If anyone had been overtaken by surges of feelings, it was he! Still, the fact that the moment she had known what was going on she had stopped, was something he should always bear in mind...

Below, Ceci looked out as the trail wound its way through uneventful hills, down towards a dip where a small bridge crossing a creek was the last dot on the landscape to show humans existed. They came up on it: bump bump, crossed over and it was gone! Quickly she turned to look back at the hills then stared ahead. She knew she was doing the right thing.

Already her dark dress, the portmanteau and small business case at her feet were combining to make her feel separate from Hexham, reminding her that her trip had a purpose. She did not see from a hilltop Ginger watching the trap rocketing from view and suddenly taking account of the large trunk strapped to its back...

Gradually she relaxed on the familiar road, glad of the newcomers joining the coach, sensing their different lives and interests. The closer she got to Christchurch, the more determined she was to take herself in hand and as the hills fell away and the plain came and went without incident, she decided she would not return to the hotel with its temporary people and bustle but rent a small house in a quiet street. There she would come and go as she pleased, put her affairs in order without attracting attention. Why, she might even be better off in Lyttelton!

In Christchurch she would doubtless though she were to meet people and be seen as a rich widow—it was only to be expected . . . Yet her heart would remain her own. It belonged in the High Country and while she would be open to change she would not send it out on a piece of string. Her first visit would in any case be to the Bank Manager.

The Bank Manager nodded to his clerk to show Ceci in. Because she was the bank's biggest customer he did not wish to be found wanting. Everything on his desk shone and he intended to appear engrossed in the *Lyttelton Times* when she entered so that he could lay it aside as if her presence were that much more interesting than its contents. A little gesture like that, he felt, would set the relationship up. Then of course he would rise and extend a hand towards her! From her outgoings he could tell she had taken a small house in Chisholm Street, a strange move but no doubt she had a motive. Instinct told him money in large sums was to start moving about shortly and he fully intended to be as close to the sweet smell as possible! This would, in fact, be Mrs. Laird's third visit to him this week. On the first occasion he felt she was assessing him, yet even while thinking of it he'd got wind of a possible sale of Hexham and was leaning heavily on the idea in the hopes it would come to fruition. At that moment the door opened.

"It's been good of you to introduce me around," said Ceci approaching, her hand extended, the speed of her action cutting the ground from under his feet and making him curse for not having been quick enough in getting the *Lyttleton Times* down.

"Ah!" he said, struggling upwards. "Impressive sale for the Bank! When it goes through!" Would she have noticed, he wondered, his substitution of the word "when" for her previous word "if"? She sat without being asked.

"I've been thinking of apples," she began in a soft voice.

The Manager looked blank.

"Growing them you know?" Ceci continued. "I've had enough of sheep! Somewhere away from the wind."

Ah, she wanted to *grow* apples!

"The Marlborough Nelson area—apples—" said the Manager, showing he had grasped the point and could move nimbly when occasion demanded.

"Again, seasonal help," she went on, envisaging a different type of man from the swaggers and sundowners she'd been forced to employ. "I want a completely fresh start."

"You can do what you like, within physical limits," the Manager offered, thinking that she could not *dig* a canal across the plains though she could doubtless pay to have one dug!

"I thought I'd travel around first. To be quite *sure* this time."

"Good idea," he put in. Clearly it was the best course to agree.

"If you would continue with the accounts, I'll be putting things through, but—"

"Your special account. Yes."

"Well for contingencies yes, but aside from that, should you need to take any decisions—" she rose.

"I shall abide by the incomings and outgoings set!" said the Manager also rising. "Now! There's a *concert* tonight. My wife thought—"

Freed from it all Ceci moved along the beach, her body surging with the speed of her ideas which she saw rise and fall, which she held at then let go. So much to decide! The sea ran at her and retreated as the wind pulled at her skirt till she felt like skipping or cupping her hands and shouting at the sea. What? A message for England or people coming towards her in boats? She let the wind push and blow her along the beach arms flailing before it. Retreating to sheltered dunes she became momentarily sad at the memory of those she had decided for ever to leave behind: Reg and Ginger, Mrs. Hallam . . . Reg *might* have come back looking for her and explained something about Jock . . . Her hand pulled at the dune weeds as she scuffed sand from her skirt and rose. She must allow the past to fall from her mind as the sand from her skirt! She must see it as *The Past* and each day take one step towards her glorious and shining future. Bravely she began to walk.

This time the future would not begin with a broken-down homestead where she must struggle alone through winters . . . She was almost like a First Class passenger getting off a ship except that she already had a love and understanding of the land that was hers and did not want to take, but to give to it. How good it felt wanting to *give* and being free to do it! The wind rushed at her, stung her eyes with tears of exhilaration. Tomorrow the tour of the orchard areas would begin. Tomorrow she would take the next brave step to her personal future.

Pontney was on a level bit of land in the north not far from a yellow sand beach. Unlike the east coast where the sea was wild and dangerous here it was calm and the air was lazy. The few orchards lay blessed by sun and protected from the winds by gentle hills and though the area had taken some getting to, there was no doubt that with its ideal climate one day it would develop. She had been struck at once by the relaxed mien of the people. Whether walking or sitting they always seemed to be turning, smiling at each other—having time for being together, bending to lift up kittens or talk to children. It was a place where people yawned and stretched and where dogs lazed in the sun, uninformed as to the nature of sheep . . .

With a sense of ever-increasing wonder Ceci moved amongst the apples telling herself it *was* possible to choose a life! The first time she had tried this—by emigrating—it had failed miserably. But now? Olwen would like this place. The further she got from Hexham the less she found herself thinking about it other than to wonder *why* she had hung on there so long when all the World awaited. But then, wouldn't she have gone on hanging around Bowen's Gulley if Mrs. Laird hadn't intervened?

Reaching the second orchard in Pontney she began to feel certainty closing in on her. A *For Sale* sign was up but before making her presence known she decided to wander unaccompanied a little. How big and round the apples were, streaked red, yellow with the sun's rays! Though the occasional tree had blight, its branches black against the blue sky and its few crumpled brown leaves crackling in the breeze, it seemed somehow "right." From healthy trees the smell of the leaves was heavy, a *clean* smell which rustled and whispered through them till she could imagine their boughs weighted down with the pink and white blossoms; groaning, heavy. Like a bride in spring she would walk under these trees letting them snow petals on her. There was nothing like the *newness* of apple leaves: their clean greenness when they broke out after winter.

A large brown-skinned friendly soul in an apron came out to show her around, pointing things out, nodding, laughing her explanations. Yes, Ceci could make cider if she knew how. Purees and pastes too for that matter! She herself let the apples rot on the ground there being so many but Ceci could please herself! Together they moved on through avenues of trees.

Returning to the hotel after, the sun golding her face, Ceci saw a man on a bench raise his hat and smile at her. She waved back. The woman's price had been very fair and the friendly atmosphere of the place was so tangible the very trees breathed it. She thought of the good natured woman who had got bored with apples and was going to live with her children... Her life had been free from trouble. Tanned and beaming her decision was made. She would return to Christchurch tomorrow and instruct the Bank Manager. Though she had stayed away for a considerable time, every moment of it had been worthwhile!

Hardly able to contain her excitement she burst into the bank and saw instantly a letter for her in the Client rack. Eagerly she reached forward, pointing. Though it was upside down she could tell it was from England and had been forwarded from Hexham! Smiling the clerk handed it to her and breathlessly she sat to read it forgetting for a moment she had come to see the Manager. After a few minutes the clerk interrupted her.

"Excuse me," he whispered. "The Manager will be available in a minute."

Hastily she sped through the remainder of the letter. How *could* she suddenly be deluged with good luck upon good luck! It was unbelievable! It was perfect! Time had gone so fast she had scarcely sensed it and now Olwen had not only finished school but was on her way back to New Zealand! Quickly she counted on her fingers: this long for the letter to reach New Zealand, this long for it to get to Hexham, this long for it to get back down to the bank... Good Lord! The sea journey only took two months! She would be arriving next week! Looking up, she saw the clerk nodding again, evidently waiting to show her through to the Manager. She slipped the letter into her pocket and arose, flashing him a broad smile and tempted to tell him her daughter was coming home! She would love to have asked Olwen to bring some forget-me-nots to plant at Pontney! She and Olwen together as grown ups! What times they would have! What would they name the orchard? After somewhere Olwen liked in London? Thoughts clamouring in her mind she hurried along the corridor after the clerk.

The Manager did not seem to notice her come in but stayed staring at some papers on his desk.

"I've found it! It's perfect!" she bubbled over, unable to contain her excitement. "You can sell Hexham today as far as I'm—" What was the matter with the man? He was behaving as if she hadn't knocked, looking up with a cold, almost hostile stare.

"Sit down please."

Ceci began to feel uncomfortable. The Manager touched a bell on his desk and a boy appeared.

"Go round and ask Bull Warren if now's convenient," he said solemnly. The boy nodded and withdrew and the Manager bowed his head and continued marking an account sheet. Ceci looked at the strand of hair unsticking itself from his crown and tried again.

"It's difficult to be serious minded with my daughter arriving on the next ship. It's been such a long *time*!"

The Manager still didn't look up. What could she have done?

"I'm sorry I haven't been in touch," she began gently. "I took time to be sure." Her words faded into ominous silence. "Especially with Olwen arriving—" she trailed off telling herself the man was really subject to moods! And they talked about women! "Mind you, Olwen'll want to have a look at Hexham before it goes," she said, probing his silence and beginning to get worried.

Suddenly he looked up. "Will your daughter be staying on out here or returning?" he asked briskly, as at a sound from the door a bulldog of a man entered and the Manager rose.

"Bull Warren of Seymour, Jacobs, Preston," he said, the men exchanging glances which made Ceci nervous.

"Acting on behalf of Jacobs, Jacobs, London and Bath, in the matter of the will of the late Moira Laird—" he went on indicating a chair for Bull Warren to sit.

"Is she dead?" Ceci gasped in surprise.

"You didn't know?"

"Since my husband died she hasn't—she hadn't written. I went on sending the same percentage to her...In fact I increased it twice after Flinders..."

Poor Mrs. Laird, thought Ceci, biting her lip. No wonder there had been an atmosphere! The way she had bounced into the bank when she should have been wearing mourning.

"When did she die?"

"August."

Ceci nodded.

"What of?"

"Get to it, Bull," said the Manager irritably, but Bull chose to linger.

"She needed a great deal of care towards the end," he said, leaning forward pressing his hands together.

Knowing none of this, yet ready to believe Mrs. Laird had become quite unhinged Ceci looked awkwardly from one man to the other.

"She had left her estate—in its entirety—to her son. Your late husband. And if he should predecease her, then to his living offspring, male or female arising. As you know there were no offspring, and in a codicil added at his death—to avoid—er—misunderstandings—"

"She cut me out!"

"You were at no time in it to *be* cut out," Bull Warren informed.

"The estate was hers—from her husband—and would have passed to her son at her death. Had he not predeceased her."

"Well, I've still got my block," Ceci said stoutly.

"Unfortunately no," put in the Manager.

"That went to your husband's estate," Bull Warren elaborated, "which reverted to—"

"My land became *his*. But his doesn't become mine!?"

"Now unfortunately here, I understand you've made certain—forward commitments—" the Manager frowned at her, "which will have to be withdrawn. It is hoped you haven't sold off any parcels—"

"Didn't think of it."

"She had wished her son's body brought home to England for burial."

"I'll be buried with my husband!" Ceci snapped.

"You may marry again. How old are you?"

How dare they discuss her like a side of beef, she thought, pressing her lips together.

"Twenty-nine," said the Manager making Ceci feel she was being cut into smaller and smaller pieces.

"We'll need the account books to audit," he went on.

"Over my dead body," Ceci said slowly.

"—for the years of your—er—stewardship," he continued.

"So how much've I got?"

Bull Warren looked across at the Manager as if himself briefly interested in the answer to this question.

"Enough for a—" the Manager said, his hands suggesting vague uncommitment to the answer "—a passage back?"

Full of grief, she retraced her steps, trying to gather energy to deal with the problems which lay ahead. She could not return to live at Hexham. Olwen was coming. The rent on her small house expired in three weeks' time and the future looked very grim. In fact rather than a benefactress, she now felt like a prisoner of the country. First though she must visit Hexham, take what was hers and in fairness to the Prendergasts and Mrs. Hallam advise them to leave. She did not look forward to the encounter.

When it came, even stepping into the hall she sensed Hexham to be different and no longer hers for in many small ways the Prendergasts' presence was reflected in the house. Mrs. Hallam, she discovered, was long gone.

Believing she had come to advise them a sale was imminent they greeted her warmly but when she told them their precise situation their wrath knew no reserve.

"You mean you never 'took advice'!" shouted Prendergast, ashen before her.

"This is *most* outrageous!" his wife trembled. "We've been *horridly* misled!"

"I never got you up here."

"But you set yourself up as the owner!"

Well, that was true. Ceci looked at them in abstraction and suggested it could happen to anyone.

"Ridiculous!"

"Impertinent!"

She spread her hands. "If there'd been a child I could have stayed on—at its pleasure."

"This is *none* of our business and we are *not* interested!" snapped the woman, stalking about. "We've been sending this woman a percentage!" she continued as if personally ravaged though the money had gone to the estate. "*Why* have we been sending her money?" she persisted.

"We did live here," said Prendergast blandly.

"But we *worked*!" Mrs. Prendergast blurted.

Ceci wanted to be away.

"Put in the best bid—you can have it!" she said, looking around to decide what to take.

"Being auctioned?" asked Prendergast.

Quickly Mrs. Prendergast slipped her arm through his.

"You ought to have a word at The Club. Ask the others to stand down."

As Ceci gave details, Mrs. Prendergast pointedly observed it was all probably a pack of lies. Prendergast however knew Jacobs, Preston from home and was inclined to believe.

"I shall take what I like while I'm here—" Ceci added peeling an antimacassar she had stitched from the back of a chair. Quickly, Mrs. Prendergast snatched a handbell and rang viciously.

As the trap moved along the line scratched on the bald hills, Ceci told herself this was the last time she would leave Hexham: the last time she would leave Home. The big blue account book lay on the seat beside her—a pile of greying turquoise account books at her feet. On her knee the red account book was open. With difficulty she wrenched out the pages, tearing at them but finding them too well bound and the thread too firm at the middle. Getting a good grip and pulling this way and that she finally managed to shred and tear the pages and, sliding the window down, extended her hand out with a pile of pieces on it. The shreds danced and fluttered away to lie where they would in tussock and hummock, scrubland and bog, the snow of her hard work falling, caught in scab grass, floating on brackish water, fluttering from its window as the trap moved away.

Returning to Lyttelton, Ceci entered the small house in Chisholm Street, for the first time noticing how the front gate squeaked as she pushed it in, how its paint was peeling. She noticed now the unattended front garden and across the street curtains lifting and settling into place as she paused. Sitting in the kitchen, she peered through spaced fingers at the few simple things of her life, the pots and two chairs she had decided were all she would need while staying away. The place was temporary looking in the extreme and beyond the window the overgrown back garden, just large enough for a washing line, cried out the one word: neglect.

Chapter 24

Already on the last leg of her journey to New Zealand the *Perora* tacked into the wind, grateful to have enjoyed fair weather and a speedy voyage. Gradually the travellers turned their thoughts to what lay ahead letting what lay behind pale away in the exchange of addresses, the agreements to meet again and the hopes they would "do well" in the New Land.

Leaning against a rail, fourteen-year-old Olwen let her hair fly in the wind and thought a multitude of thoughts. Would her mother like her? Would *she* like her mother? Would there be anyone interesting in Moke for her to associate with? Would they stay in a hotel in Christchurch while she "recovered" from the voyage? Did she *really* want this young man she had collected to tag along once they got there? She turned to glance at William. Three years her senior, a shy boy who had naturally inclined towards her and whom she had been careful to impress with the refinement of her background and hints that she was in a position to help him once they landed ... That had been a particularly delicious feeling.

Never before had she entertained a young man either singly or in company, cousins and neighbours of course being different. But the fact she had been alone when the first class passengers had been couples older, often much older than she and with young children, furniture and plans, had made her feel both superior and lonely. They didn't know where they were going, whereas she had actually been *born* there and was the only one on the entire ship to be making her second crossing of the ocean!

Having some grip on the country they were going to made the relationship with William seem safer. In some ways he was like a big dog she enjoyed walking publicly. She felt comfortable with him standing, as he was now, quietly behind her, his face still, looking across the water. He was probably making up a poem. A lot of the time William did not talk. He was given to thinking. Sometimes when she spoke, she felt she had interrupted a deep train of thought. Yet the boy was undeniably frail though this she could forgive, for his manners were gentle and it was good to have a companion. Though he talked little about himself she sensed his family had tried to "get rid of him" by sending him to New Zealand; and that he had not been ready and felt unhappy about it.

Apparently there were people in the bowels of the ship called "Steerage People," though she had not seen them. It would seem their fares had been paid and they were of the more destitute classes, possibly bordering on criminal. Vaguely the thought excited her as she peered over the rail but there was nothing to be seen of them. Apparently they only came out at night for air and then had to sit underneath a grating at the top of some stairs and breathe it in.

"William, let's go and look at the airing space," she called.

Taking her hand, he led her to a thick rope which barred their way and pointed beyond it to the grille. How exciting! So that was where the people were kept! A pity she had not realized this before leaving London because her friends would have been most impressed to hear about it.

On that first trip six years ago—a lifetime away—she had been aware of people watching her, brave and alone in her red cape, grasping up at the ship's rail in the wind.

Other children's mothers had given her sweets until their own children were annoyed. *Why* had she been sent, she found herself beginning to wonder? For the schooling? It hadn't been compulsory in New Zealand and for that matter half the English children did not bother with the newly introduced law either. Had it been that her father was seriously ill and she was sent to avoid the sadness of an impending death? Yet surely he had died in an accident with his horse her mother had said. Oh Hexham! She remembered it as a large park... the lawn particularly, running across it in the early morning; the feel of the wet grass... bursting into the summer house; the smell of roses, sounds from the stables... She turned radiantly towards William. She was *longing* to show him Hexham!

Today it would all happen. Today Hexham would go, Ceci told herself, hurrying towards the auction and reminding herself she'd do better to think about her daughter, soon to arrive, and start appreciating the fact she'd be a *young woman* and not a child. As she turned corners she kept repeating this to herself as if fearful she might jeopardize the relationship they must build anew. Would she still have that amazing blonde hair? Her own hair had been a russet brown and Reg's, as far as she could remember when his hat was off, a dirty blackish brown stuck with mud! That was what came from marrying strangers, she told herself. You never knew, for example, where the blonde hair came from!

The auction was to take place in a large tent outside which men were already massing. They took no account of Ceci who slipped through a flap and entered to see beyond the rows of benches Bull Warren using his pencil to stab at points of detail floating apparently mid-air between his belly and that of the Auctioneer. The hammer lay on the table. Beyond it a clerk was scurrying from one display board to another, moving behind screens, checking the sketches and drawings of Hexham, the lists—CONTENTS OF HOUSE, STOCK AND EQUIPMENT... such preparations for the sale of *her* house! She glanced outside at the men who would bid and saw them reaching into pockets, scratching ears, turning away from each other as if it was alright to be friendly before or even *after* the event but for now it was each man for himself...

Inside, Ceci moved unseen from one display board to another, looking keenly at the etchings of what were once her possessions: the desk she had sat at, her bed . . . Hearing the tent flap open and the men pressing into the enclosure, she withdrew further behind the boards and watched them nodding to each other as they squeezed along the benches. Obviously all were acquainted: probably rich farmers or members of the Christchurch Club she told herself. Which of them would be Hexham's new owner? And what would Hexham fetch? Suddenly the hammer went and the Auctioneer moved forward to begin his spiel:

"You know it's big," he said looking around, "20,000 acres mixed. But nothing missin' here. Cos *this* place 'as been *looked after*."

At that Ceci felt like approaching the rostrum and bowing!

"In the same family since—" he went on, stopping abruptly as Prendergast blundered in late. Quickly he signed a "no more" to the man at the door and sought to re-establish his ascendancy. He could not *stand* to be interrupted when he had everyone's attention and was building to a peak!

"Shall we start at five an acre?" he growled in a deep voice. "To include," he picked up a sheet of paper, "rugs various, Turkestan, Afghan, Bukhara . . ."

Ceci's eyes filled with tears as the man glared at the sheet finding some of the names beyond his pronunciation. "The hell with fancy names!" he joked. "Enough antiques and valuables here t'stock a market!"

A man tapped Ceci on the shoulder.

"Have you a programme?" he said in hushed tones.

She looked up at him questioningly.

"Are you *bidding*?" he whispered.

She shook her head. Quickly he put his hand in the small of her back and propelled her behind the hoardings to an exit flap and out into the air. She leant against the tent, listening:

"One oh five. Give me Do I have—One six it is. Seven Eight. And a half nine—So One eleven in the back—One 12, 15. Round numbers. And up to—to—*One Twenty*!—" Ceci gasped amazed. It was thousands they were talking in. Suddenly she became aware of Mrs. Prendergast bearing down on her. Quickly she braced herself for the onslaught, preparing a look of polite enquiry and a pleasant smile to go with it. Mrs. Prendergast, however, stepped around her and rushed on into the tent just in time to see Prendergast made an utter fool of. Wanting to bid he had leapt to his feet and raised a hand.

"Nod's as good as a wink here!" said the Auctioneer, ready to sacrifice the newcomer for the good of the crowd.

Prendergast looked around, confusion on his face. The price was still rising but he could see none bidding. Nervously he settled for flicking at the air continually with one finger, the edge of panic on his face as the price took off again rapidly.

"Beggar doesn't know what's up!" one man nudged another. "Watch this!"

By now seven or eight men in the room were playing with Prendergast who was going white with rage. Eventually, he grabbed his wife's wrist and stormed out of the tent leaving the auction to resume at a slower pace as if the room had suddenly breathed out. They knew how to deal with newcomers, the Old Hands told themselves. It took more than having money or joining The Club to be accepted out here! As the climb upwards became serious and more intense, the atmosphere thinned and the price separated the men from the boys. Standing outside Ceci saw Prendergast run from the tent and felt sorry for him.

"It's the most huge and perfect house you ever saw!" Olwen told William. "She may even take you on hire." William frowned hopefully. "But she has no telephone," Olwen continued, "which must be awful." She turned away. Suddenly she no longer wanted to smile. The closer they got to Home, the more uncomfortable she began to feel.

"You may find country life dull after London," William offered, thinking that from what he had seen the sight of a field of sheep would do little to inspire Olwen.

"I *know* my mother," Olwen said screwing up her face, "but I can't *remember* her." Trying to translate the impression of a mother as seen by a child of eight into an adult image was proving very difficult. "When she sent me away," Olwen began, memory clouding her eyes, "oh never mind. I'll be pleased to see her." She sensed William observing her as she tried to shake the feeling off. "It's just that I'm a little frightened..."

On the shore Ceci too was worrying. What would they find to say to each other? Suppose Olwen didn't like her! The fact that she had hurried back as soon as she could meant little for Molls had always promised to remind Olwen constantly of *Home* and that when school finished, back she would go...

"I'm getting nervous now," Olwen said, her fingers drumming the rail. Around her people were fussing with their belongings, staring across the water at the Port Hills of Lyttelton, picked out crisply in the early morning light.

"About meeting your mother?" asked William. "She'll be nervous too."

"Do you think she'll like me?"

"I'm wondering if she'll like *me*," William returned, making Olwen want to hit him for he was supposed to be understanding *her* problems, not fussing about those he didn't yet have!

On the quay Ceci was pacing. Suppose Olwen wasn't on the ship! She bit a thumb. People around her waited in twos and threes, families with children, business men... Going behind a crate she took out her hand mirror, propped it up and looked at her hair. It was alright but nonetheless she poked at it till it was quite unsettled, then in exasperation pulled out all the pins, letting her hair fall and beginning hastily to put it back up again.

"How much longer?" she asked a bystander. The man shrugged.

As people began to flow down the gangplank, getting greeted, congregating, moving away, Ceci's eyes furrowed the crowd desperately. For a moment she thought she saw the fair head of a girl hanging back at the top of the gangplank, a young man of seventeen or so encouraging her to step forward.

"I don't see her down there!" complained Olwen.

"Come on!" William reached for her hand, starting to trip down the plank. Suddenly Olwen saw a woman ducking under the ropes, running full tilt at her and instantly sensed it was her mother. She tightened her grip on William's arm, the emotion too much to bear, and stood stock still. The years of separation driving her on, Ceci thrust through the alighting passengers and drew up just short of Olwen, breathless. Olwen extended a hand. To be shaken. Slowly Ceci took Olwen's hand and drew her inwards, putting her other arm around her and holding her, deep emotion on her face. Vaguely she noticed William watching Olwen from behind. Becoming conscious of Olwen's stiffness, that she was embarrassed and wanted to be let go of, Ceci released her. Olwen stepped back and drew herself up awkwardly.

"William I want you to meet my mother," she said in a detached voice. Ceci instantly grasping it was she who was being introduced to William, not William who had been introduced to her. Quickly she extended her hand in a friendly way to take William's. She had, she told herself, already made a complete fool of herself in the child's eyes by running at her in that way, crying and pushing, and had she actually shouted?

Taking a carriage to Chisholm Street, she took care to be quiet and behave in a more motherly manner. Apart from everything else she would have to plan very carefully the breaking of the various changes to Olwen.

As their carriage stopped before the rickety dwelling Ceci caught Olwen perusing it. Getting down she paid for the ride and began to unload the trunks while Olwen wandered about and the boy William stood by, arms hanging limply and not offering to help. This, she decided, was not rudeness but the simple fact he had never had to unload his own trunks before.

"William!" she called.

"It's good of you to—adopt me Mrs. Laird," he said, turning to her with a winning smile.

"Lift the other end of this trunk."

"Thing is, I was in a bit of a spot," he went on, taking out a large silk handkerchief, shaking it free and beginning to fondle his nose with it.

"Pick up the trunk William."

"What are you doing in this peculiar place?" called Olwen. "Are all the hotels full?" Seeing William dropping the trunk on his foot, she crossed over. "Aunty moved us to a nice house," she went on.

When I sent her the cheque, thought Ceci. William straightened up and gave Olwen a look that suggested he thought she had been insensitive.

The relationship between these two, Ceci told herself,

was not strictly her business but on the face of it, it did not look like a relationship which would weather well in a place like a new country...

Once inside, rather than break the news to Olwen, Ceci couldn't resist asking, "Aren't you a tiny bit glad you came?"

Olwen twisted a cloth in her hands, wrinkled her mouth. "I knew I had to come back when school finished," she said honestly. "But it doesn't seem *Home*!"

Ceci saw sudden fear in the girl's eyes. "It—it's just such a let down *being* here!"

"We'll learn to talk again."

"I try but everything comes out *wrong*!" Olwen exclaimed.

This could not be denied; nor that Ceci too was finding it very difficult.

"I don't think I can *stand* it here!" Olwen declared, screwing up the cloth, flinging it in a corner and walking out into the yard. Everything was so *different* from what she had expected or remembered she could scarcely bear it. Clearly now was *not* the time to tell her about Hexham Ceci thought. Suddenly Olwen came in from the yard, ran up to her and grasped her hands:

"*Mother*," she pleaded, "*when can we go to Hexham?*"

Chapter 25

Hating herself for not having admitted the entire truth about their circumstances earlier, Ceci watched Olwen fidgeting at the gate while William carried out the picnic goods, umbrella and rugs they were taking up to Hexham, dropping and tripping over them. Clearly the girl was on the verge of tears.

"We don't have to go if you don't want to," Ceci pointed out.

Olwen gave her a childish glare as if to say: "Well now we've made the sandwiches and gone to all this trouble we'll *have* to!"

"I *liked* that place," she began, "you should have asked *me*!" Ceci shifted uncomfortably.

"I feel half a person without it," Olwen complained.

Ceci believed her. She didn't feel so grand herself! But at least she had told them before travelling all the way up to the High Country that Hexham wasn't theirs.

"Are you buying somewhere equally good?" Olwen demanded.

"Let's take it a day at a time," Ceci sighed.

There was so much the child didn't know. It would be totally self-defeating to pour out all her own woes at one time. Olwen looked at her sideways. What was her mother thinking? It seemed there was trouble brewing somewhere.

As they changed to the big coach which would speed across the plains, Ceci wondered if perhaps they should break their journey at Turton's Accommodation House for neither William nor Olwen were very fit. As for the leg up to Moke, William said he had *never* ridden and Olwen that she had forgotten how! Looking at the twenty or so people mounting the coach, exchanging last words, getting on and off again for things they had forgotten, Ceci was aware she could not share their excitement. Around her men were hurrying in and out of the office, looking up at the rack, checking. There was a definite sense of a beginning adventure as the coach prepared to take off and cross the Great Plain. William helped Olwen in then turned to her and just as she was half way between coach and ground he suddenly let go of her elbow. She gripped at the coach's side and spun to see William burying his face in a hankie.

"He has nosebleeds," Olwen explained, leaning forward and grabbing her wrist. Above them the men on the coach top peered down with amazement on William.

Beyond the plain, tired by now, Olwen fell asleep and let her head fall against Ceci. As the coach swayed and lurched, her mouth dropped open and her hand slid away. Ceci reached forward, took it up and placed it back on her lap and spoke in a half whisper to William.

"Do you have any letters of introduction?"

William shook his head. "Your father just *sent* you out here?"

He nodded.

"To 'make a man out of me'," he grinned.

Ceci frowned at the cruel and ridiculous idea his father had had in divesting himself of a son like that!

"Did he give you any money?" she enquired.

"Just this," William said producing an expensive pocketwatch.

It wouldn't take long for him to pawn that Ceci thought!

"William," she said gently, "out here you have to be able to '*do*' something. '*Being*' isn't enough."

"I write poetry."

Ceci turned quickly to the window, fearful he might catch the expression on her face as the horrors of her own initial experience in New Zealand returned. The *irrelevance* of sensitivity, of *words* even, of the *simplest* forms of beauty in this harsh sheep docking culture!

William proffered his watch:

"Do you want it?"

The poor boy hadn't even guessed what she was thinking!

"Put it away at once!" she shook her head.

William was visibly moved by the journey. Having left the vast plain and gone some way into the hills he made out in the bleakness three thatched sod type buildings, no more than dots. Getting closer in he saw it to be a T-junction, a smaller track leading off towards lumbering brooding hills on which heavy clouds seemed actually to sit. A coach the size of their own was facing away outside, waiting no doubt to collect those bound further on the trunk route while their coach turned around and headed back to Christchurch. A smaller dray could be seen around the side of the building, pointing towards the hill track and as they came to a stop, jolly travellers came out of the low building, wiping their mouths, getting ready to nab the best seat while the horses were changed.

As Ceci transferred Olwen and their belongings to the local dray she looked around for William. There he was, in the middle of the open space, peering around as if thrilled by the utter emptiness. Suddenly a man shouted and she saw William run forward and leap into the onbound coach! Quickly she hastened over and called him out. Grinning sheepishly he came with her and climbed up next to Olwen who gave him a very cool look. As Ceci got up front, the driver called words to the hostelry, cracked the ribbons, waved his whip and off they went flying towards the hills in a rattle of wheels.

Tiny in the landscape the little trap made its way over the hill road, the driver, a Moke man, not needing much telling but clearly surprised when Ceci asked him to rein in some distance before Hexham. The cart shuddered to a stop as he turned his bland face questioningly at her but she merely nodded, smiled, got down and told the others to alight.

"We're here," she announced cheerfully.

They fell out, amazed at the dry brown nothing of the place, biting at the air which bit back at them; the silence which made their ears ring. They were absolutely Nowhere.

"Just a couple of hours," Ceci said to the driver.

"I'm back this road three-ish," he replied. "You see me coming—you shout."

The cart took off in a churn of cracked mud.

"There," said Ceci, indicating to William and Olwen what she believed was the cut in the wire originally made by Calvin to allow her passage over the hill to the old dwelling.

"Leave the rug and umbrella here."

The gap had, she noticed, been replaced by a gate. Despite everything, she still felt herself to be the owner of Hexham and she did not like others putting gates where she had not decreed.

"Come along." She began to walk away up the road. Best, she thought, to peer at Hexham unannounced. It would hardly have done to let Moke's trap hurtle through Hexham's gates, churning gravel and flicking it all over the lawn of the new owners.

As they neared the entrance, Olwen's heart began to pound. In addition her mother was behaving in a most peculiar fashion, almost skulking. But when she saw again the house, her breath was taken away. How right, thought William, to have approached it in silence! This magnificent sight—gracious, uplifting—so *unexpected* in the countryside! Moved, he gazed at the warm purples and oranges of its climbers spilling over on to the verandah; its hanging baskets disgorging the brightest of colour in this otherwise wilderness of brown. Already his mind was humming with poetry. He saw the white summer house, like a marble egg lying in rose bushes...

"Why can't we go in?" Olwen demanded.

"Somebody else lives there now," said Ceci.

Inside in the drawing room a middle-aged woman stood by the window, focusing hard beyond their gate. She hurriedly touched a bell.

"There are some people by the gate," she murmured. "See what they want." She signed to the maid with her hand but kept her eyes firmly beyond the window.

As the maid appeared on her lawn the woman saw to her intense frustration that the people at the gate were walking hurriedly back towards wherever they had come from. Thwarted, her lonely fingers curled uselessly at the velvet curtains.

Talking together, moving over the hill, Olwen and Ceci looked back to see where William had got to.

"If you buy somewhere *else* I can marry William and you can retire," Olwen suggested, waiting for him to catch up.

"Oh—and what's William going to do?" Ceci asked.

"He can be your foreman!"

"He's had four nosebleeds coming up *here*," Ceci pointed out, not wishing to sound unkind but readying herself to be brutally frank with Olwen.

"I don't know why we've come to this stupid place!" Olwen observed, "*I* wanted to show William the *house*!"

"Don't you remember this place?"

"You shouldn't have sold it," Olwen informed her.

Ceci summoned her nerves. At least now they were alone.

"Well, now you've seen it," she began, "I'll tell you."

"You're going to say something I don't like," Olwen said warily. "Where am I to live if we haven't got Hexham?"

"Olwen," Ceci began.

"Oh, you're being *hate*ful!" she interrupted, scared by the tone, "because you don't want me to marry William!"

"Hexham belonged to Granny Bath," Ceci explained. How ridiculous the name sounded! "We're on our own now...and we have no money."

"*You've* got money—"

Ceci shook her head. "Out here you either *bring* money—a lot of it—or you belong to someone else's."

"People don't talk like that at *Home*!" snapped Olwen.

"I expect they used to," Ceci sighed. "Apart from money, whether you're a Catholic or a Presbyterian here, or Irish, or Scottish in the wrong place, or *English without money*, these are the things that matter. We are without money and we have to decide what to do."

"How can I do *anything*," screamed Olwen. "I've been in *school*!"

"Well, maybe you'll have to marry," Ceci said, adding, "someone who can support you."

Olwen looked at her, livid with insult.

"*You* did alright when *you* came!"

"Did I?"

"I hate all this! William won't believe I was born at Hexham!" Olwen shouted. "Anyone can peer through the gates!"

"You were born *here*," Ceci said pointing at the ground.

"I wasn't! I was not!"

Ceci observed William getting closer.

"My life seems to happen in this one spot," she said, feeling the place pulse through her and acquire one more association: that her daughter thought she was being wilfully mean.

"William likes me!" Olwen retorted.

"William—can you leave us a minute?" Ceci called. "Don't you remember this place Olwen?" she asked gently, bending to touch two slight hummocks on the ground, the shards of a broken earthenware pot on one, a dead twig on the other. Olwen frowned.

"No."

"Look," she said, pointing down at the fallen gate, the remains of the broken wall, the few rain bleached stones of the old dwelling lying around like teeth.

"Calvin wasn't your father," she began. "I never—"

"He was! He was! He was!"

"You assumed—"

"How can you *do* this to me?" screeched Olwen, dropping to the ground, seemingly crying. Ceci knelt to comfort her.

"I've looked forward to your coming more than anything," she began.

"I *had* my life over *there*!" Olwen screamed.

"I want you to know the truth," Ceci pleaded again. "You must *listen*!"

"Leave me alone!" Olwen shouted.

At that moment William arrived.

"I've made up a poem!" he announced.

"Oh, don't bother reciting it!" Olwen snapped getting to her feet. "They've no time for poetry out here."

"Under a lowering sky," began William, trying to remember it. "Under a lowering sky," he repeated. Ceci and Olwen breathed out politely. "*Under* a lowering sky," he suddenly remembered, "The empty land Frowns with concern Its brown grief waiting For men to come . . ." His voice trailed off as if uncertain about the last line.

Ceci regarded him with a deep sadness. The poor boy could "feel" the place. Much good, she was sure, it would do him!

As they waited by the trail for the cart Ceci looked at Olwen fretting. She had grown up with one idea of herself, poor child, and suddenly it had been whisked away. No wonder she felt lost! It had been shock upon shock upon shock since she had come into the world! Even those eight years Olwen now idolized as "blissful" had been filled with so many atmospheres it was amazing that she had not turned out a great deal worse! Calvin had not loved her as a real father. She, her mother, had been prevented from expressing deep emotions towards her for fear of angering Calvin. The child had been in an intolerable position with Miss Robertson, not knowing whom to obey. She had seen her mother's slender authority totally eradicated—for that must have been the impression she had carried away with her—so was it any wonder Olwen now spoke to her rudely, as if to a sister? Even in England Olwen had been merely a "cousin" who spoke differently from the other children. No wonder she felt insecure! Whose fault was it? And how could she make amends with so little to offer?

Standing a few feet off, Olwen cast reproachful glances at her mother, at the clouds lowering and the wind blowing over the brown grass, bending and flattening it. William moved from foot to foot 'til finally the ominous rattle of the trap relieved them all. Pulling up, even the driver could sense these were not the same people he'd set down some hours ago.

Frowning, the man put up the cover of the trap, expecting rain. Even the woman had got inside this time. He looked up at the clouds. There was no point in talking to disgruntled people. Hoping to be done with his day's work before the sky broke, he urged the horse forward reckoning the clouds' odds against the full run down to the Christchurch route, the turn around, and the ride back to Moke—unless, of course, there were folk waiting to be ferried to some local outpost. Also he had to drop off a bundle at the blacksmith's, he told himself, leaning forward in the seat, crooning encouragement at his back.

Finally the blacksmith's shanty, a fence with some tarpaulin stretched from it, loomed up ahead, the tarp clapping loudly in the wind. It was a poor place but the man was able to catch some passing trade for three tracks converged here. Slowing, the driver called out, jumped down, then taking from beside him the box to deliver he hurried towards the blacksmith whom he could see keeping a good hold of a horse's foreleg inside. The man whose horse he was shoeing turned casually to look at the familiar old trap pattering the local byways, making a penny where it could. He saw a woman sideways on in the trap looking so sad, so lost in thought . . . she did not even turn her head to look at this last sign of human habitation before the road dropped down to the Christchurch route. Slowly he blanched, recognizing Ceci. Unable to believe what he was seeing, he rushed at the trap.

"How could you not tell us where you were!" he flung up at her, grasping the sides of the trap, vaguely taking in the two travellers beside her. Olwen flipped her head round sharply and saw her mother bending away from a man.

"Not now, *please* Ginger," Ceci whispered.

"*Where* are you living?" he demanded.

Ceci's chest heaved. She breathed out as if she would like to shout something but must restrain herself. Olwen frowned at William who leaned forward and saw the driver coming up behind Ginger. He saw Ceci pleading with her eyes, begging the driver to get up quickly and take them away. As the driver leapt to his seat Olwen gasped as the man's hand reached into the trap and seized Ceci's wrist fiercely. Horrified—and a little disgusted—she saw him holding her mother's wrist as if he would never let go. Discomfort fleeted on Ceci's face. Almost in tears, she took her other hand and carefully unpeeled his fingers and drew her hand away, shaking her head. Crack! came the driver's whip. The trap shot forward. William saw the man step back then run into the tent to expostulate with the blacksmith, apparently demanding his horse back at once! Ceci remained staring straight ahead. As Olwen turned she saw Ginger wrenching the horseshoe from the smith's hand, flinging it aside and trying to drag his mount away. Her mother's face was crimson.

"I will not discuss this incident with anyone!" Ceci told herself.

They could see what had happened and there was nothing more to be said. Beside her, Olwen moved a little closer to William.

Back in Chisholm Street Ceci kept her eyes down peeling potatoes. The rent expired in three days' time and she had received a note asking her to call on the Bank Manager. Opposite her at the table, Olwen's red eyes showed she had been crying. She did not know, for she had not been told, that as far as her mother knew apart from the change in her pocket they had between the three of them enough for one passage back to England.

"I *hate* the way everything has turned out!" she informed Ceci.

"*All* that horrible journey—what for?"

"If you really hate it over here—" Ceci began, without looking up.

"I do! I hate everything!" Olwen assured her, glaring at her mother. It had occurred to her to run away but obviously in the circumstances that wouldn't work.

"All those years thinking—"

"Didn't you wonder why Granny Bath would never 'receive you'?" Ceci asked softly.

Olwen looked up. Her mother's face, bent over the potatoes, looked so sad. She ran around to her, flung her arms round her neck.

"Mama! Ma*ma*."

Ceci's mind was too full for words. That Olwen had finally "broken" meant more to her than anything that might come from the interview with the Bank Manager tomorrow. At least they had had this moment before knowing which, if either, of them would be going back with the "one passage" the Bank Manager had hinted remained.

It was a sombre Ceci who entered the Manager's office and admitted truthfully she was beginning to wonder how they were going to survive. He indicated a chair and as she sat, his first words genuinely surprised her:

"Before you rush into anything I have a property you can afford—"

"I can afford nothing."

"A small hotel towards Taylorville."

"Taylorville?" Ceci repeated, knowing by "hotel" he meant a drinking house.

"Taylorville? Wallsend? Brunnerton?" he continued, as if expecting her to recognize at least one of the names. "No? Grey River? Greymouth?"

Ceci nodded vaguely for Greymouth sounded familiar.

"A colleague on the Railway Management Board," the Manager ploughed on.

"Is that the Greymouth on the West Coast?" Ceci interrupted.

"Yes," he nodded, "the Newcastle of New Zealand as they say. For reasons best known to himself—possibly a decline in the sale of beer—" said the Manager, presenting his thoughts in such a muddled manner Ceci was left to make the best of them. "As you know this almost *decade* long depression," he sighed, "despite which demand for coal has increased—"

"Then why's he selling?" said Ceci, following him closely. "Why's your friend selling his hotel?"

The Manager would not be lured by a direct question. "Difficulty in *marketing* coal has meant, should I say *led to* cut backs in employment," he continued.

"And less money for the men to spend on a Saturday night!" Ceci thought to herself.

"I am in a position to see," he continued, "that an opportunity exists at a price, how*ever* disagreeable the weather."

Was he actually proposing she buy a pub on the West Coast while clearly listing all its worst faults?

"Cold fog winds. Mist. Rain," he went on as if

admitting some drawbacks would exonerate him from concealing others.

"Where did you say it was?" Ceci asked, putting his overeagerness to point up the problems of the place down to pity for her because she had recently taken a fall.

"Grevillton."

"And why would *I* buy it?" she asked, a really excellent question the Manager had difficulty in answering.

"Well it—it's *somewhere*," he stammered.

Ceci nodded, knowing what he meant.

"And I can afford it."

"Just."

"So it's take it or leave it."

The Manager nodded. "The community there I understand are very—close," he continued. "From the Northumberland and Durham area, many of them."

"And how will they take to a woman running a pub?" Ceci asked.

"Well, there *are* women there," the Manager conceded. "I believe they are active in the Temperance Movement to be honest. The—er—Wesleyan Methodist 'Band of Hope.'"

Surely the Manger didn't think this was a recommendation? It was a good job he did not depend on selling for a living!

"But the pub is for men only. Right?" Ceci demanded. "Cards on a Saturday night?"

The Manager nodded as if his stock of honesty were exhausted.

"I'll take it," she said rising.

The Manager rose.

"In the event your daughter is not—er—attracted by the prospect," he now said, "the Murchisons need an escort for their son who is returning home for treatment. Passage, of course, to be paid. The boy is four," said the Manager, following her to the door but unable to keep the touch of irony from his voice. "I believe your daughter had such an escort once?"

"You haven't an opening for a young male immigrant clerk, have you?" Ceci said, turning to him.

The Manager shook his head.

"I'm afraid we are producing too many of our own already," he said, giving his honeyed smile, opening the

door for her to pass through, glad to be rid of her. And
very glad to have killed two birds with the one stone.

By the time Ceci returned to Chisholm Street her
spirits had lifted. The solution had come just in time.
William and Olwen looked up at her as she pushed open
the door. Instantly she could tell they had been arguing.

"Have you heard of Grevillton?" she began.

"Organizing strike activity," William said. "It's in this
paper."

He pushed the *Lyttelton Times* across the table at her.

"Horrible picture of dirty wooden shacks and railway
wagons," added Olwen.

"Would you like to live there?" Ceci asked.

"A *lot* of people I'd meet *there!*" Olwen retorted.

"You might... I'm hoping to."

Olwen turned away.

"Does it sound romantic William? Bleak rainsoaked
hills?"

"Damp sacking!" scoffed Olwen.

"The whine of saws, the smell of burning sawdust,"
Ceci read.

"You should read what the editor says about the
trouble there!" snapped Olwen. "Not the hyperbole!"

For a moment Ceci gaped. Had Reg felt like this
when, quite without thought, she had used words commonplace in London that he had never heard of?

"Well I've bought a pub," she said stoutly. "Come
rain, cloud, miner's dust and the Temperance League, I'm
away over there to put my shoulder to the wheel!"

"I think it's a ridiculous idea and terribly vulgar!"
Olwen observed.

"Where else can she go?" asked William.

"I have nothing to offer but my work," Ceci said,
"but in *my place* I'll starve. I'm buying this pub with the
money *I earned* by my own work. I'm just thankful it was
aside in the 'small needs' account."

"It wasn't *enough!*" said Olwen coldly.

"I'll make that pub work!" Ceci went on. "People over
there like as not'll be more *kindly* than some we've met."

Olwen shook her head at her.

Ceci put her open hands on the table and looked
from one of them to the other.

"Well," she said, "there's the invitation."

PART THREE

Chapter 26

Now she was counting the pennies though William didn't know it. Apart from the £4 to cross the mountains to the West Coast it would be 3s 9d each second class for the train from Christchurch to Springfield where the rough road began. As they chugged inward across the plains in a direction she had never gone before there was not much to be seen. A tramp was walking beside the track. He might once have been a shepherd Ceci thought, looking at his last remaining dog, his swag in its mouth. The sight put her in mind of Reg. Was he wandering like this now? As they crossed great expanses of land owned by different farmers she noted the boundary dogs they had left to guard their perimeters and stop the sheep crossing over. How lonely those dogs must be, she thought, seeing their owners only every few days when they brought them food. Throughout the plains there was little sign of human habitation and as the train rose slowly above the level to make its rendezvous with the mountains, her mind settled on the fact that Olwen had gone and that she would miss her and the question of what lay at the other end of their journey.

She was not inclined as they ascended into the mountains to listen to talk around her or preoccupy herself with thoughts of the dangers they anticipated lay ahead. Their talk was of runaway horses, of coaches turning like pebbles as they fell thousands of feet to smash below, roads severing themselves from the rock to plunge after them, trees and rocks blocking the road on blind bends and passengers being obliged to walk back because rivers could not be forded.

She did not see beyond the windows, or hear above the sound of the horses' hooves the cry of the driver urging them to "Come up my beauties!" Instead her mind heard the hiss of the iron, the crinkle of a newspaper being turned as she slipped into memories of a damp Sunday afternoon in London with the room full of wet washing, nowhere to go and no money to spend. It was after Norah had died and the sheen was rapidly going off a city which talked endlessly about the Suez Canal and other things which had nothing to do with them. She had been reading aloud to her mother and Aunt May from a stack of newspapers May had brought home. They liked the wordy editorial bits best and would intersperse acerbic comments and remarks.

"This is about settlement in New Zealand," she'd begun.

"Can't you find anything better than that?"

May had poked some hot coals out of the grate and lifted them into the iron. It was an afternoon to induce sleep.

"The Association is granting assisted passage to Port Lyttelton—"

"Nice of them," said May.

"—to a limited number of the working classes, being gardeners, farm servants, labourers, who must be of the highest character—"

"Very likely," scoffed her mother.

"—*as certified by the Clergymen of the parish,*" Ceci went on.

"Who wouldn't know," May said flatly.

"They're looking for single women," Ceci announced. She recalled there had been a marked silence into which May had poured the opinion that the editor was implying that now the colony was established it was cheaper to get a lot of young women out there to breed than to keep paying grown workers' passages.

"I think that's enough of that claptrap," had said her mother. "What about the ironing?"

"It's completely free for single girls!" read Ceci.

"I should put that paper down if I were you."

May advised. "Not that it isn't funny," she added, "settlers rushing out there, stocking their kingdoms with animals and labour and forgetting to order women! Labourers without wives and the 'gentry' with no one to 'do' for them! I reckon we three all could go! If women are scarcer than gold!"

"Place is probably covered with lizards!" her mother scowled.

Ceci tossed the paper aside and yawned.

"And the only reason they're giving away free passages," her mother assured her, "is because they've no other way of getting people out there!"

"There was a Notice in earlier," murmured Ceci. "I cut it out."

The women frowned as she went to get it.

UNMARRIED WOMEN AND WIDOWS OF GOOD
CHARACTER AGED 15 TO 23 REQUIRED FOR
DOMESTIC WORK IN SELECT SITUATIONS.
SATISFACTORY PLACEMENT TO BE FOUND
WITHIN 3
DAYS OF STEPPING ASHORE.

As she finished reading she'd looked up. Her mother had started to iron, May was staring at the grate. Quietly she slipped the Notice back into her pocket.

"Is everything alright?" she'd asked. On an instant they'd smiled at her in a puzzling way. She remembered her mother, even before she had taken the decision, watch the child she had reared perch fledgling-like on the edge of the nest, then launch into the blue, singing. Her mother had known she would go, that she would never see her again; that she would worry and hope she'd taught her enough. She would know her child would see things and hear things she had not been prepared for and would experience the personal ugliness of others. Her mother, Ceci told herself, must have worried for her like a limb lost. But all she had understood when she finally announced her decision was that they were happy for her. That moment on that afternoon before the washing, those two sisters must have known they would grow old together in each other's company, their differences still between them, sharing only the memory of one dead child and a child they'd loved. Daughters floated away like sticks! Molly had long since gone off with her young man and very private they were too! Sighing, Ceci looked out of the window. If she worked very hard, would Olwen come back? Or would she already have attached herself to some young man? Next time, *if* she came back, would she *stay*? Ceci's thoughts were as heavy as the coach as it shuddered up the wild track, its occupants jolted and juddered inside, their speech broken by the ruts.

Coasting an incline it ground down a pocked hill and swung out over a gorge. A fine exhibition she'd made of herself with Ginger outside that blacksmith's shanty! A fine way to be caught behaving in front of one's child! The incident was too embarrassing to bear thinking of! She would cross the mountains and never think of Ginger again! Yet surely there could be no harm in the privacy of this coach amongst strangers to recall some of their moments together? Had there not been something immeasurably tender, poignant, vibrant, palpable in every moment they had spent together? Like creatures born of the heart, they had been sacrificed on the altar of Reality. Surely there was something powerful there, something precious aching for resolution? Quickly she turned her mind away. The passengers were gritting their teeth, nodding stubbornly at each other as the coach levelled out, the land temporarily smoothing around them. She had better start not thinking about Ginger right now! With a terrible plunge, the coach began its descent on the other side of a climb. For a moment panic gripped her. Had the horses run away? She could hear the driver chatting merrily to those on top, yet unless he had his foot pressed to the brake they would all be done for! Surely the man must have wrists of steel to control them as they thundered downwards, one minute catching the rock, the next swinging out over the gorge. Ceci blanched. The road was now cut from a vertical rock: no more than a chiselled mark already wearing away. In places the overhang was about to fall and the sides were merely held up by wedges of tree. Maybe tomorrow the scratch would have vanished from the rockface and another coach would come, finding the rock bare, all signs of road gone! Ah, but they were going up again! If this was the way they were to take hills, God help them all!

William hung onto the top of the coach. This was certainly an adventure his father would approve of! The clouds spun by below him. If his nose were to start up here it would be impossible to loosen a hand grip; he'd just have to sit there and let it stream. Olwen had gone back! That was not very adventurous of her. Indeed Mrs.

Laird, or "Ceci" as he was invited to address her, had the more kick. She could scarce be ten years older than he! Off to the west coast of New Zealand already! If his father could see him now!

Inside the coach Ceci began to look at the other travellers. Four were obviously "gentlemen" and from the way they talked, one would seem to be a contractor, another something to do with a Railway Board, the third clearly dabbled in "finance" and the fourth she could not tell. Squeezed in a corner was an Old Timer listening to them with one ear and occasionally letting loose a great wad of tobacco juice which flew through the window. She guessed he found the "gentlemen" amusing and the way he punctuated their speaking with throat clearings and spittings indicated *what* he found amusing.

As they continued their climb upwards into awful grandeur and silence, desolate bare standing rocks appeared glaring back into the wind, back towards Christchurch. As they scuttled between them, William's lips moved, making poetry, gazing at the land so long lonely, land pressed under the sky knowing only the elements which had torn and gouged at it.

"I made up a poem," he remarked to the four labouring men squashed on the top rack with him. They looked over, not unkindly.

"About the precariousness of life," he added.

They could not understand a word he said.

Soon the coach slowed and stopped in mist by an unnamed lake, its clear cold water vanishing at the edges in a white cloud, as if, despite the height, the land here met and merged with the sea. Apparently it was a rest stop for the horses.

William stood, his feet sinking in the rounded grey stones bordering the lake, observing their terrible consistency and staring at the cloud becoming mist becoming rain.

"Come on!" called the coachman to him.

And they were away again, rushing down a narrow track, waterfalls thudding steeply on to it, crossing and plunging hundreds of feet to a river below. As the coach barrelled over branches brought down by a previous storm, the men on top ducked as it leant and swayed, touched trees and swung away again, its outer wheels flirting with the edge, grinding the air, the river's roar growing louder and receding.

"Hey ho me beauties!" called the driver bringing them up sharply by the now raging torrent. He got down from the coach and briskly slapped its side. "Down ye get." Amazed, Ceci watched the empty coach slip down the muddy bank into the water and begin to traverse the hungry stone-eating river, the brave horses struggling through the current, their hooves grasping between rocks, water belting through boulders and half-way up the wheels. Alone at the front she saw the driver strain and the tarp wrapped luggage at the back dip into the surging water, the wheels buckling in at strange angles. She was informed the road had been washed out and they were to continue some distance on foot, crossing by a makeshift arrangement of tree trunks conveniently left by a previous storm. Standing on one of them, Ceci looked up the bushclad hills almost meeting the sky above her.

"Goodbye Ginger," she whispered softly. "Goodbye."

Again they were climbing and this was truly a high and magnificent pass, surely 3,000 feet above the sea! Behind them lay continuous mountain ranges. Ahead—the deep drop to the Otira Gorge, hung with rich bush. Shimmering iridescent waterfalls plunged from view to become silver streaks vanishing far below. At this, the irrevocable final pass, there was a sense of a Beginning. There would be no more bald mountains or Plains of Christchurch, no more High Country! Even now she could turn and run back if she wanted for from now on they would drop down steadily to the West Coast and the sea beyond. Yet standing on the summit she had the feeling that she was not travelling away but *towards* something intended specifically for her. It was as real as the figure had seemed who had danced with her that night enraging Calvin; as real as the Presence she felt holding her when she woke up in the morning; it was almost like a memory that had not yet taken place.

Rapidly they descended, the tight lipped passengers hanging on unwilling to talk. At a sudden grating thumping on the roof the driver shouted to his team and the coach stopped on a blind bend.

"One sick. Open the door," came a voice from above.

Ceci quickly leant to open the outside door, the Old Timer grabbing her wrist as the door swung out over nothing. Blanching, she pulled it in in time to see the inside door open and William, a handkerchief to his mouth, being handed down and rearranged on the floor.

As they came level with the Otira River the feeling was of utter loneliness. High bushclad hills met above them, cast them in permanent shadow. Dwarfed by precipitous mountain walls an Accommodation House crouched, giving off the sense that human life was far far behind. Here they would take their breakfast and welcome too!

Though they had been gone only some hours the physical fact of the mountains gave a tremendous sense of having left. Suddenly the air was different. The conversation rang with new names as passengers pointed at the slashes of the red *rata* tree colouring the Gorge, the *punghas* and *toi toi* growing by the track, the trees clad so heavily in moss their trunks were indistinguishable. Above hung giant spiders' nests. *Keas* and *kakas* hopped on to the path and greeted them noisily as talk turned to The Maori . . . The Kaiapoi Maoris, the Old Timer told Ceci, had used this pass in fine weather up until the time the white men came. They'd used to cross that way to the West Coast, he said, to get loads of greenstone jade for their workings. They'd come down by the Otira Gorge, he explained, swimming the three deep pools. But they couldn't come back that way carrying 70 pounds of jade apiece, so they'd had to go another route called the Whitcombe and it was there they'd met up with the Northern Island Maoris and slaughtered the lot of 'em.

Looking from the window Ceci saw that the land had become humid and mossier, the undergrowth being impenetrable with ferns sprouting from the highest branches of ghost trees and sucking the life from them. Their new team of horses splashed through frequent standing puddles dripped into by the trees and flung mud off the track into the wild and magnificent bush.

As she stood before the Taipo River watching the trembling passengers cross one at a time on a narrow wire bridge which swung dangerously at tread, Ceci saw the Railway Board Man on the far bank being quietly sick in his handkerchief.

"Now Dimwitty was a town," the Old Timer rattled

on. "Two banks, telegraph communications. I had me a good time there! Yes, Sir!" he assured her. "Four papers, a coach service, three religious denominations ter keep the interest up, livery stable, *sixteen hotels* my dear and two double buggies. Plus eight wagonettes, two expresses, three drags," he went on. "Granity, Rough River—those dance floor saloons! . . . Oh the drinking and the gambling— Keep It Dark, Wealth of Nations—I done 'em all."

"Those pubs where you had such a good time"—were they on the goldfields?" Ceci asked.

The old boy nodded.

"But I'm going to coal," she said. "Grevillton. What's there?"

He scratched his chin.

"A butcher. As I remember. An' a pub. Two pubs."

Riding along the side of the great Teremakau River they came upon occasional patches of cleared bush, signs beginning of humans, sawmills and worn out water traces attesting to earlier goldworks. In a rush Ceci was filled with a tremendous feeling that everything was going to be alright! They were coming to a place where ordinary people lived and loved! It would not be like the East Coast with its plentiful land and prim money tightness, its Canterbury Association and landowners relying on their cleverness and other people's work to get by! . . . She could feel the West Coast would be a place where people worked, took their chances together; where men pitted themselves against the land, burrowed in it, sweated, and were not ashamed to get dirty. How good to be respected as much for their failures as for their successes, she sighed, peering beyond the window through the feathery rain and seeing a settlement cut from the luxuriant vegetation ahead. As they passed she saw small gardens bright with flowers, poor wet washing on a line getting wetter and warmer, children in hand-me-downs running at the coach waving and shouting. Behind them smoke rose from the settlers' homesteads and a solitary man appeared— looking very real after the loneliness of the crossing. A cock crowed. On an impulse Ceci leaned forward and whispered radiantly to William:

"I *know* everything's going to be alright!"

The Old Timer winked at her, his mind still on pubs and drinking saloons.

"The lights goin' and a beautiful woman with petticoats flyin'—" he said dreamily at Ceci. "Get that young boy on the hand piano and you're away!"

Chapter 27

The man Billy walked down the street of Grevillton. But for his height his solid frame under its coating of coal dust looked like that of any other miner. The touch of grey in his hair was concealed and his grey eyes peered from a well blackened face. He saw a coach swerve to a halt outside and across from the abandoned pub. He saw the door open and a delicate youth climb out and extend his hand to a very young woman who hovered on the running board as the boy's feet sunk past his ankles in mud. He saw the girl peer amazed from one end of the short mud-riven street to the other, from which coal dust obligingly blew in great clouds, engriming everything. He stepped back to watch.

Ceci crossed to the pub, looked at William and inserted the key in the door. It gave with a loud creak. She pushed the door back. Billy saw them step in.

Ceci stared around her in amazement.

"I can't *believe* people would drink in a place like this!" she gasped.

It was utterly filthy. On the boards, trodden with earth, lay a scrap of paper with "Romans 10.9—Galations 1.4" written on it and apparently pushed under the door. Above were cobwebs and in the corner a broken bottle. It looked almost as if it had been vandalized. Hurrying through to the back Ceci found with relief chairs and tables which had been stacked and were ready to be put out. Through a dirty window in what must have been intended as the kitchen, she glimpsed some barrels in a small storage yard. At least that was good for she'd paid for that beer! Turning her back on the window, she rolled up her sleeves.

"Right William! To work!"

William nodded briskly and began rolling up his sleeves too. As they worked, he looked across at her kneeling by her bucket, scrubbing and humming. Her face was dirty but half of the floor was clean. The stacked chairs waited on the edges of the room and climbing on a bench William began to flick at the ceiling with a cloth. Achoo! he sneezed as the dust came down and the bench wobbled to the point where he might fall off. Ceci crossed and opened the door to let fingers of sun reach in and inspect their work. Standing in the doorway she stretched and breathed in the street, then leaving it open she returned to her scrubbing.

Billy was amused to see Ceci come to the door, her face streaked with dirt. He was on the point of coming over to say hallo when the sight of horseboned Marie, the Town Conscience, hurrying down the street made him change his mind. He watched as Marie paused outside the pub, then stepped in through the open door.

As her shadow spread across the floor Ceci looked up. Quickly she got to her feet to offer her hand but the woman put the cracked tips of her red fingers in her mouth, stepped around her and stood surveying the room.

"Well I don't know," she began in a concerned voice, suggesting she wasn't sure if what was going on ought to be. She walked forward and peered through the door to where the tables had been stacked and shook her head.

"You don't need to be here," she told Ceci.

"The place is opening," Ceci informed her, William coming to stand beside her.

Marie moved to the centre of the room and folded her arms, breathing heavily, then turned and headed out into the street. In a minute she was back.

"I thought it out," she said. "We can't be doing with a pub here. I can't be fairer than that."

"I spent my last money buying this place," Ceci said coolly.

"Well you won't make none here because I'll see no one comes," Marie returned taking a step towards her.

"I'll leave when I'm good and ready and not before,"

Ceci replied feeling the lines were already drawn up. Marie shot her a look and left, the threat of organization in her eye.

Ceci glanced nervously at William.

"Welcome to Grevillton!" he grinned.

As Marie stepped off the duckboards she sensed Billy intended a word with her and did her best to avoid him.

"Marie," he said sadly as to a pupil who always disappoints. "Is that the way we treat newcomers?"

"Quick and clean Billy!" she said. "The best way!" and hurried on past him, a touch of guilt on her red face.

Waiting, Billy saw Ceci march out stoutly with a sign she had made and direct William to mount a chair and hang it. "Hexham," he read wonderingly. The girl stood back and looked up at it, seemingly pleased, then re-entered the pub. Moving slightly, Billy could see through the open door that the floor was shining and the chairs set out. Now the girl and the young man were backing out with a bench which they set on the duckboards beneath the sign. As they went back in again Billy worried for them.

"Go and buy us some potatoes William," Ceci said picking a small coin from her change purse.

"Just potatoes?"

"Potatoes are good for you," she insisted, unable to meet his eyes. "And as *many* as you can get for that. *Try*."

Billy watched the boy come from the pub with a string bag and hurry down the street to Grevillton's only store. He decided he'd give the women a chance to see how they behaved towards the boy before getting involved. He saw William get in line, pause and await his turn while the women around nudged each other and looked at him. Then he saw the storekeeper Mrs. Evans lean over, grab the boy's bag, take it behind the counter, stuff something in it and return it in a very peremptory manner to the boy. The boy looked bothered. Going pale, he reached out a large potato and handed it back to Mrs. Evans who snatched it and shoved another in its place. The boy scrambled in his bag and handed that one back too. So Mrs. Evans was giving rotten potatoes!

By now William was quite pink. Not only had he never been obliged to shop before, never had he been treated with anything but the utmost consideration and courtesy.

"How much is that?" he asked politely.

"Thruppence," snapped the woman.

He gave her the money, thanked her pleasantly and left the shop.

Suddenly an awful thought occurred. Kneeling down he tipped all the potatoes on to the ground, rolling them gently over, desperately hoping he would not need to assert himself. There they were: more bad potatoes. Getting to his feet he braced himself and re-entered the shop. He must do it for Ceci. She had, after all, paid his fare over. The women looked at him silently as he came in and emptied his bag on the counter, handing back two potatoes touched with mould. With a tightening of the mouth Mrs. Evans replaced them with two much smaller ones.

"*Weigh* them," William shouted at her. "Without the bag!" Never had he behaved like this in any cause. Mrs. Evans looked at him sullenly and pushed his threepence back at him.

"I want two pounds of potatoes and I want them now!" he said white with anger and fear, his heart thudding. With bad grace Mrs. Evans obliged.

He would not repeat any of this to Ceci, William told himself. There was no need for her to know how unpleasant the people around here were. Hurrying from the shop he brushed the clothes of a large miner in the entrance.

"Excuse me," he murmured to the man.

"Marie, Jeannie, Agg." Billy shook his head at them. "And you Mrs. Evans."

"They can get out!" said Jeannie.

But she bit her lips and certainly looked ashamed.

Continuing on down the street to allow himself time to regain his composure William saw the other pub the Old Timer had mentioned: The Central. Men were entering and through the open doors came the sound of shouting, dominoes clacking, coins jingling and glass breaking. They were dirty men, working men. With a thrill William told himself he would soon be one of them! He would join those men who clapped each other on the back and were looked up to by women! He would get a job and pay Ceci back for his ticket! Also they would have to try and get some of that custom over to their own pub now...

To William's amazement the street simply ended in an iron bridge across a turbulent river, below which clung broken trees which had washed down from the mountains. The river's banks were matted with coal dust and dropped bitumen. Behind him on the level ledge of land, the draughty shacks and shanties of Grevillton piled up in perpetual shade while on the opposite bank felled pines like scattered pencils lay every which way, ascending up a darkened hill to a crooked edge of grey sky. At the foot of the hill he could make out a row of coke ovens and behind them a tall brickworks chimney slewing smoke to defoliate the pines. Could this be a coal mine, he asked himself, advancing on the bridge towards the maze of rails which crossed the flat area beyond, losing themselves at what were obviously entrances to the hill itself? Now he could see the pines were without leaves or greenery: they stuck like simple poles from the blackened earth in a scenery of blight and man-made desolation. It was now twenty minutes to midday, he realized consulting his pocket-watch, yet the sun had not been able to rise above the immensity of the hills in which the mine was set.

As he stood amongst the rails, his limp blond hair shining, his pink fragile skin delicately exotic against the background of the mine and the darkened hills beyond, he sensed miners looking at him and began to stumble towards a small group by the coke ovens. Halfheartedly they directed him to a wooden Administration Hut in the centre of the area then watched him, replete with string bag of potatoes hitting his knees, trip over a rail, ill at ease in the industrial environment. All around were strange sudden noises: the air compressor letting off; abandoned wagons clanking into each other; a hooter blast.

With determination William mounted the steps and knocked on the Administration Hut, deeply conscious of the working men watching him. As there was no reply he pushed the door open and saw a room lined with maps headed MAIN SITE—PLAN OF SUMP PORTION OF DIP WORKINGS. In one corner were stacked spare lamps, the odd pick axe and items he had not seen before and a quite filthy man standing on one side of a desk disagreeing vigorously with what was obviously the mine Manager standing on the other side. William hovered in the shade of the miner's back. The situation did not seem very sanguine.

"I inspected," began the Manager, knocking on his own desk to reinforce his point.

"Yon brattice were torn," interrupted the blackened man.

The Manager took a breath.

"Unless brattice screens are efficiently—" he began again.

"—foul air were right through," accused the miner. "Choking 'n' coughing."

The Manager's tone suggested he was about to terminate the exchange.

"If you can't control the men under you—" he threatened.

That did it. The miner stepped back.

"If tha cómes down, tha'll bloody well see!!" he shouted. He turned abruptly and slammed into William then stepped out. The Manager now saw William.

"I want work," William said firmly.

"Just done layin' off sixty."

"I'll do *anything*," William offered.

A look of cynicism crossed the man's face. "You will?"

"Yes."

"Then clear off and close the bloody door after you."

Nursing his potatoes, William climbed back down the steps and passed through the working men sensing as he did so their discontent. Glancing back he caught them looking at him as if he were a rare form of plant life. He consulted his watch. Almost noon. By ten past without any doubt the sun would have vanished behind the next hill! That gave them only thirty minutes of sunshine a day! Still, perhaps they wouldn't notice it being underground.

Wandering disconsolately back through the shanty town, he noticed people had planted holly trees by their shacks, perhaps to try and keep something washable and green close by. Their berries were the only bit of colour to be seen . . . He had to admire these men with their impossibly hard lives. Ahead of him a group were even now turning into The Central, cleaned up, arms linked, singing as if they were the happiest Jacks in the worlds! As he stared he sensed rather than saw someone observing him and turning saw coming from a shanty a well-dressed man whom he took, by reason of his case, to be a doctor. The doctor paused as if he felt he had something to communicate to William then thought better of it and hurried on.

Up ahead a group of women were gathering outside The Central, a look of intent on their faces. Keeping well to the other side of the street, William slowed, recognizing the woman who had come into their pub and also those from the store. He had the strong impression they were going to make trouble for The Central and was glad they didn't notice him sneaking by with his potatoes, pretending he hadn't seen them.

As she waited for William, Ceci too was watching the miners going in and out of The Central and keeping one eye on the gaggle of women heading that way with placards. "Down with The Devil's Dominion," she read, and "War on Debauchery." So *these* were the Temperance Women, she told herself! The poor things hardly corresponded with the image she had had! Why not one of them could not have done with a square meal and even that woman who had confronted them in her pub, hostile as she had been, had had far too much life in her to object to drink on moral scruples! Turning from the window she surveyed her empty room and in a matter of seconds was day dreaming. There she was in her posh gloves falling back, dropping the hay—and Ginger was saying: "My wife's better at this for all you're a lady!"

By Sunday morning Ceci was beginning to feel a little irritated with Grevillton, and to wonder if there was more to the woman's remark about seeing she had no customers than she had imagined. As people from outlying shanties passed her pub in the mended clothes that passed for Church Going she felt the men casting nervous half glances towards her while their wives tried to pretend she wasn't there and to prevent their children looking. There was something going on here which she didn't understand.

"William?" she called, going into The Hexham. "We're going fishing."

What was the point of sitting around all Sunday when they had been open three days and no one had been near them? William looked at her. He knew she was trying to show them she didn't care.

Although the river bank was beautiful William did not feel moved to write a poem. He found himself looking at Ceci. Who had loved her and why was she alone now? Trespassing on her with these thoughts thrilled him in a new way and when she turned to look at him dangling his sapling at the water, he almost lost balance. It didn't look as if either of them would catch anything, he concluded. Fishing was definitely an art. It was easier to look at Ceci, or think deeply or enjoy the reflections on the water. She looked so pretty leaning forward, her chin tilted, strands of hair blowing across her face. He wanted to go over and put his arm around her. Suddenly she turned to him:

"I'm thirty years old William and I have two pounds left!" she said, her eyes heavy with the responsibility of it. Now seriously he wanted to hug her. But she caught the way he was looking at her and clouded her eyes.

"Do you still think of him?" he asked quickly. Ceci flushed. Had she been that obvious with Ginger? And William had no business giving her those peculiar looks when he was supposed to be missing Olwen. As she fumbled for a reply, suddenly the stillness of the afternoon was broken by a loud commotion in the undergrowth.

"Waidda minnit!" came an aggrieved male voice. *"Hey!"*

He sounded very frustrated. There was a beating through the undergrowth, then from a small distance a female voice clearly striving to reach a wider audience.

"Why—you—*dirty—beast!*"

Ceci and William's eyes bulged. They spun expectantly. There was more crashing in the undergrowth then a resounding slap!

"You said," the angry male voice accused. Crack! There went another slap followed by the sound of the man's indrawn breath, a squeal from the woman as if she had been pinched good and hard and another rasping crack of a slap followed by the man fetching his breath up from a deep place. Suddenly a woman appeared before them.

"Hello," she said innocently as if nothing had happened.

"What's going on?" Ceci asked, nodding in the direction of the bushes. As she stared the sound of a departing horse came.

"Oh that," the woman said. "Lucky your husband's with you!" she said. "Getting so you can't get about these days!"

William grinned. But Ceci noticed the woman was carrying a swag...

Heading back to town they could not shake her off. She said she was "Annie," tried loosely to link arms with Ceci, soon discovered she had a pub and suggested with considerable enthusiasm that she could work for her. Ceci shook her head resolutely. She didn't want to hurt the woman's feelings—obviously she was "on the road"—yet she certainly couldn't employ her. Nearing Grevillton their attention was taken by shouting and beating noises, the sound of people striking pots and animals squealing. Amazed to hear this on a Sunday afternoon they turned the corner on an even more extraordinary sight. A herd of pigs, apparently drunk, were tearing through people's yards, trampling fences and vegetable plots, slamming into each other, falling down groaning. People were rushing to drive them off with sticks but they kept falling over. As Ceci squeezed between two women she caught the words:

"Fix your own fence!"

"Your pigs!"

"She shouldn't be allowed!—" said the first woman, looking up towards Ceci's pub, where a group of pigs were sloughing something up from a pool in the gutter and belching. As Ceci hurried to reach the spot, she heard the sound of an axe striking wood and splintering, then rushing liquid. Aghast, she perceived a stream of ale running under her side gate to join the pond in the gutter! Flinging open the gate she rushed in. There was the woman Marie with her axe poised over the last intact barrel which a smaller woman was manoeuvring into a better position for her to hit at.

"Marie!" said the smaller woman in warning.

"Take no notice Jeannie," Marie replied. "Look at the trouble you've put me to coming here," she told Ceci, straightening up, her red face streaming with sweat. "Could you not have found a poorer hole to inflict yourself on?"

Ceci felt William behind her.

"Put the axe down," she said.

"Oh my dear!" gasped Annie throwing her swag into the kitchen. "Let me help you clean up! Get out of here you!" she said to Marie who had already laid the axe down and was walking from the yard, head high. Marie paused to glance at Annie as if she wouldn't touch her with a clothes prop. Behind her Jeannie told Ceci:

"You're a traitor to your sex!"

As the gate swung to, Ceci had to shake herself to realize what had happened was true. The beer, running away before her eyes, was her last asset! She looked at Annie, sleeves rolled, the hem of her skirt hitched into her knickers, waggling her feet in the beer and joking:

"Hope it does me verouka a power!"

Suddenly she felt like bursting into tears. From inside the kitchen Ceci could hear Annie talking to William. She had a great way of being cheerful even describing the most awful things:

"Oh you don't ever want to go up the Incline dear!" she said. "It's 2,000 feet up in the clouds and as desolate as a place in the Bible. Unlined draughty cottages. Filthy!" Her enthusiasm made it sound like a recommendation. "And no proper water or drains and the grade up is so steep it's like going over the roof of a house. Talk about cold!"

Ceci heard William ask in his polite English way what she was talking about and guessed he didn't like Annie being there.

At that moment Ceci made her entrance with the dish of potatoes.

"My Lord is that all you got potatoes?" Annie burst out. The tiniest frown revealed Ceci's awareness of her bad manners.

"Where do you live?" she asked politely.

Annie paused. "Fact is, I was lookin' about."

William frowned but Ceci could certainly understand a woman being unaccounted for.

"Don't you have any family?" she asked, wondering if perhaps she was being too direct. Annie replied in a highly conversational way.

"I had three kids, yes. One was poisoned. One was killed by a falling tree and the other," she crammed a potato in her mouth, "drowned."

Ceci's face showed barely concealed incredulity.

"And then me husband went to Greymouth—with our savings—and vanished," she went on gaily. By now William too was staring.

"They found his hat by the wharf. Floating," she nodded as if unable to stop herself.

"You said earlier he was ki—" William interrupted.

"Ah," Annie was too quick for him. "*That* time his hat had just blowed over the wharf! He came lookin' for me when he'd spent our money," she smiled winningly. "By that time mind I'd got a job in a laundry at Westport. Oh it was a grand big laundry. You shoulda seen—"

"And what happened there?" William could almost smell it coming.

"I wasn't very happy," said Annie, giving the table a very level look. Then she turned to William and told him straight in the eye: "It burned down."

As they got ready for bed that night Ceci handed Annie a nightdress.

"You could wear this." Annie sat on the bed in her vest examining it.

"I didn't expect you got such nice stuff."

Ceci got into bed. "What was your husband's name?"

"Er—Cyril. You ever bin in love?"

Ceci wanted to say no but her eyes gave her away. Annie grinned, pulled her feet up and began to examine them.

"It was no good for Cyril up Denniston," she confided. "He could hardly breathe even *without* the damp and coal . . . bronchial."

"And he died up Denniston," Ceci said, meaning it not as a question but a statement of assumed fact.

"There was only the wagon track going up and down," Annie nodded. "Everythin' went in those wagons. His coffin was goin' down in one when t'wire rope snapt. The truck went hurtling on and smashed at the foot and his coffin went bouncin' off and split and his head went one way—" she looked across at Ceci to find her gasping at the ceiling.

"Where did you say that laundry you worked in was?" Ceci queried.

"Waimara. I mean Westport."

No sooner had Annie's head hit the pillow than she

was snoring, and eventually Ceci too fell into a dream-
ridden sleep.

Chapter 28

She awoke with a start. Those grand ideas about not
giving in to pressure must go if they were not all to starve!
In Marie, she was dealing with an antagonist who knew
only one way to confront opposition. Thank God they had
moved in two of the barrels before she'd struck. Quickly
Ceci dressed.

"Where are you going?" William called from his cubicle as she stepped on to the corridor.

"To come to grips with that—Marie person. We can't
go on like this."

"Shall I come?"

She shook her head firmly and hastened downstairs.

As she hurried through the shanty town it was stirring to life. Evidence of the hardships its people endured
were very obvious. Finally enquiries led her to a broken
corrugated iron dwelling halfway up a hill outside which
children squatted on the ground playing jax—a kind of
five stones. She knocked nervously at the door which fell
open on a small boy, bare from the thin shirt down, his
face showing signs of early infant starvation. Bending, she
was asking where Mummy was when Marie appeared,
the child's breeches in one hand, needle and thread in the
other and two children running out behind her.

"Marie—" Ceci began.

"*Mrs. O'Shea*," the woman corrected.

"Let us *try* to be friends." She extended a hand.

Marie folded her arms and leant in the doorway
blocking it.

"I just wanted to say I'm not here to take food off

your table," Ceci explained. "I want to earn an honest penny by the work of my hands."

"Is that why you've taken on the biggest whore on the West Coast?" Marie shouted loud enough for the neighbours to hear.

Back at The Hexham William watched Annie stumbling down the stairs in her nightgown, obviously just awakened.

"Where is everyone?" she asked, swilling water around in her mouth and spitting loudly. William hastened to disappear.

"See about getting you custom this morning!" said Annie tightening her sash.

Five minutes later, she was to be seen in a low cut blouse, leaning in their front doorway calling to passers by: "Hey you! Come on! You over there! You won't know if you don't try!"

William drew back as people hurried past scandalized. Two doors down Jeannie came out on her step to give her a smouldering look, but Annie continued looking up and down the street. Finally she made out a horse and traveller entering town for the first time, hesitating, looking about. Swinging her arms she ran and all but pulled the man off the horse. He seemed not unpleased, William noticed. With lips pressed together, Jeannie watched the greenhorn pulled into the pub on the arm of Annie.

"William!" Annie shouted, but he had vanished. "Never mind, dear, you sit there," she said, returning to the doorstep again.

From across the street Billy suddenly glimpsed her. He let out a whistle then drew back. Annie bent this way and that. Where did that whistle come from? Suddenly she saw an arm beckoning enticingly from behind the opposite building and quick as a light, gathered her skirt in her arms and ran. As she peeped around the corner Billy grabbed her wrist, yanking her straight up in the air, and off the ground.

"Don't be being up to any of your tricks in there," he warned.

"Aw *get back* to Denniston!"

"I've enough tales of you to stuff a pillow."

Annie wrenched her wrist free and marched bravely back across the street.

She wasn't afraid of Billy! Billy called softly after her, "That's a good woman in there."

Just to annoy Billy she shouted at the back of a passing man: "Don't be shy now!" and laughed as he scuttled away.

Returning, Ceci hurried up the street towards her pub from which, even now she could hear noise coming. Pushing open the door she found the Bar Room full of men and looking around for Annie saw her bending low over a man, her chest swinging in and out of her blouse at him. Annie glanced up at the door to check the prospects.

"Be taking you upstairs next time dear!" she promised, rising, pulling up her blouse and hurrying towards Ceci.

"There you are dear. Doin' better already! Fact some of 'em've paid fer their drinks twice! Passin' trade but—"

"Annie you mustn't *do* that!"

"You're too stiff," Annie winked. "Watch!" and she vanished into the crowd, hips swinging. An angry William sidled up. "She's giving out it's her pub," he complained.

Quickly Ceci hurried behind the bar, opened the till drawer and decided to take a more liberal view of who did or didn't own the pub! Carefully she stepped over the dirty mugs Annie was half way through wiping out *with a sock*.

"William, get a *towel*," Ceci grimaced, pulling the sock from a glass and getting on her knees to peer further under the shelf.

Even now people were arriving, attracted by the noise. Entering the town on a deadbeat horse, a man who looked equally worn himself listened with one ear. To the casual eye he was a classic fossicker, boots cracked and hat battered, just a gold-panner, yet there was a touch of bitterness around his mouth. As if he had nothing to lose he slid from his horse, tied it and went up the creaky step on to the squeaky duckboards and pushed open the door.

Annie saw him sit. Well, you never knew! She thrust through the small crowd to stand above him.

"Nice place you got here," he said looking at her.

"Play your cards right I might let you stop!"

Oh she was quick this one. But it struck a nice note and he felt she meant it. Maybe the woman would even be prepared to take him under her wing and put an end to his wandering days...A nice bosom on her too...

"Let's see the colour of yer beer!"

She nodded. She'd heard it all before. Slowly he pulled a gold nugget from his pocket and turned it in his thumbs till her eyes lit up. Then he put it back in his pocket.

"Can ride into Greymouth with me tomorrow if ye like! I'm cashin' up!"

"How many ounces you reckon you got?"

The man took her in with his eyes and nodded as if to say "fair few." He felt she was interested in him now but she was thinking it was always the difficult fellows found gold!

"Buy yerself somethin' pretty. If 'n' yer husband'll allow," he went on. There would be no husband, of that he was sure. But just as well to find out before spending more breath on her.

"Heavens I've no man here!" said Annie. "Can you imagine runnin' a place like this on yer own!" She loved the drama of it and threw her arms up in exasperation feeling the man was looking at her in an evaluating way. He stood, stretched himself and seemed to grow taller as his eyes roamed the room taking in what it had and had not got.

"You sit there dear and I'll get you one on tick," said Annie. Was someone about to take responsibility for her? The thought was truly entrancing. She would follow any man to the ends of the earth if he would only promise to put food in her mouth and keep her accusers at bay.

Quickly she hurried to the bar, leaned over and said to Ceci, "There's a man over there might be doin' me a favour!" She winked. "Give me time dear!" Ceci grinned. Annie didn't seem to need much of that! She passed up a beer. It looked as if their acquaintance would be short after all. But at least Annie had helped her to get the pub established.

Annie placed the beer on the table. Where had the man gone? She looked around. Aha. He was having a good nosey. She saw him cross to the bar, lean on it, and look down and she sincerely hoped he wouldn't take a shine to Ceci who was after all much better looking and the real owner! Standing, she bit her lip.

"Got any grub?"

The phrase wrenched at a pain in Ceci's stomach she had long forgotten. Slowly she turned to look up. The face above was changed—roughened by seven years wandering West Coast ravines, sleeping out. The beard was now wild and there were patches of grey in the hair, broken nails and maybe a bit of rheumatism in the wrist...but it was definitely Reg. He was holding his eyes quite still, determined not to be recognized by her. She had seen the anger fleet across his face, no doubt because he was penniless, when she'd looked up. It could not have been more than a second. But by the time she was on her feet he had gone.

"Is that the man who's—expressed an interest in you?" she stammered weakly to Annie as she returned to the bar with the empty glasses.

"Can't afford to be particular." Annie grimaced.

"Ask what he done with his dogs," Ceci said, seeking a way to be certain. She gripped the bar as Annie walked trustingly towards Reg, trying to lose himself in a corner between two grizzled old men showing each other stones.

Ceci watched Reg's face go very hard as he said two words she could read on his lips:

"Ate 'em."

Annie's mouth dropped. Reg spun to glare at Ceci. Almost kicking the chairs from his way he strode with his old anger towards her, making her afraid as if it were her first day back at the Bowens' homestead. Even now, though, the defiance he had taught her rekindled itself.

"That woman would have taken me on!" Reg accused. "It's not her pub!" Ceci threw at him. This hit Reg hard. He softened, turned away scratching at his ear and when he spoke it was as if he were a small boy complaining: "Seems like since you arrived, I don't own nothin'."

Barely had Reg done leaving when Annie was upon Ceci.

"How could you play such a trick on me!" she burst. "All my life I've striven to—" she fumbled for a word "—be *decent* and people have got in the way! *Nobody* tries like I do!" At that, Ceci felt bad. Beyond her the room was hushed listening and men by the door were draining their glasses and going away.

"What're you staring at?" Annie shouted whirling on them. "You're none of you worthy to look at me!"

Uncomfortably, they began to edge behind her to get out of the room. As the last man left, Ceci saw Marie, Jeannie and three other women outside trailing their placards, quite fascinated by the affair. Annie closed the door and leaned on it. "Sorry," she said and began to gather the glasses. Ceci remembered Marie's words.

"Annie," she said. "I heard a remark today I'd rather not believe."

Annie glanced out of the window at the Temperance Women then walked quickly into the kitchen.

"Annie," Ceci repeated moving after her, her tone suggesting she had something serious to communicate. Annie spun shouting:

'I swear to God I've never been with a man!'

"So who was *that* man?" William enquired, meaning the man whose departure had triggered the exodus. Annie snorted at him from the kitchen.

"Olwen's fa—" began Ceci. "What am I saying! Who are any of us, William!"

Quickly, she hurried after Annie.

"You finished with this dear?" Annie asked, lifting the bowl of dirty slops, potato peelings, tea leaves and spoiled beer from the sink and turning to her. "Let me do it for you!"

Instead of going out into the yard with the bowl Annie turned and went up the stairs. Quietly Ceci followed and saw her enter their bedroom, cross to the window, set the bowl down on the dresser, tiptoe forward and raise the window. She then lifted the basin and deliberately sent its contents flying down into the street. Below, Reg, turning to watch a woman pass with a "Save Your Soul Now" placard, was just in time to see the contents of the basin give a group of women below a good drenching. From the window above he saw Ceci peer out.

"You don't want to take any notice of people like that dear," Annie assured her.

Reg shrugged. A peculiar pair of women they were and no mistake. He looked at The Central. Maybe he would do better in there. Mounting the steps he pushed open the door.

Chapter 29

The Central was obviously a miner's pub. Not a man there that wasn't a miner! Still dirty from work and all knowing each other, they were ranged in two groups in the thick of a working man's row. He heard the door clang as one of the men was thrown out and cast a wary eye at the returning barman. Now *there* was a big bruiser: not the sort a man should get in a fight with he told himself, watching the barman squeeze behind the bar and give him a straight look.

"Won't find yourself bought a drink in 'ere!" he told Reg. Reg turned his back on him, took out the gold nugget and began to flick it up and down slowly. He'd had a lot of luck with that nugget which actually he'd found in the pocket of a prospector's corpse. The barman took it in. Though they'd never had prospectors in The Central before, times were changing, he admitted, giving Reg a beer and receiving in exchange a look to suggest he was just about making the grade. Shifting his feet, Reg stared across the brawling men as the barman leaned forward on the counter.

"Big happy family. Miners."

"I want yer names on this piece of paper," shouted one of them, by now standing on a chair.

"The hell with it!" said another from the wall. "We're all for the chop."

Cries of "Sign!" and "*I* ain't singing," and "Out out *out!*" filled the room, quickly followed by the forcible ejection of the man who had disagreed. Reg scratched the back of his neck. Usually him in the odd man's shoes, he told himself.

The barman started boasting. The women outside

had tried singing Another Soul Perdition Bound at *his* men leaving the pub, he said, but he'd gone for them with a broom handle. It was that big cuss Marie you had to watch out for.

"Her husband's in here now," he said, proudly pointing at Jonas. "That there Frank, his wife Jeannie—right little caterwauler! Terrible thing, a wife with no respec' for her husband's habit." Reg nodded. "Catch 'em fiddlin' with *my* barrels they'll get a thrashing!" he advised. "And they know it!" Some of them, he added, weren't past setting their brats on the men.

"That one there—" he pointed at a fellow. "Eleven kids." Under the leadership of the woman Marie they'd even been known to set on their men as they left the mine on payday and wrestle their pay off them! But he'd like to see anyone to try wrestle anything off *him*, he said. His was a *real pub*: a *man's* place. The other one up the street had never amounted to much. Well, he said generously, it'd had a bit of a go when coal was something . . . but *now*. It had a bad history and the miners were through with it. Mind you, stuck there on the end of the street it caught the odd throat passing along the West Coast track.

A glass was banged down before him. "Fill 'er up. It's for Jonas."

"Who's paying?" he demanded.

The fellow shrugged and Reg saw the glass remain empty on the bar.

"Me drink!" came the voice of the man Jonas, now seated on the floor.

The landlord smiled wryly.

"I'd throw 'im out if it weren't I'm sorry for 'im on accounta his wife!"

"Church-goer, is she?" said Reg, feeling it time he said something.

The barman shook his head, one eye on the fight now reaching the stage where he must intervene. The two groups were going at each other hammer and tongs.

"Now here's a man for you!" a lean fellow was shouting. "Stand up! Stand up now!"

He dragged to his feet a poor weakling and began publicly to shake him. "Say it out loud so we all can hear!"

"They put food in our stomachs!" the little man almost screamed.

Reg turned away. He didn't understand these people or what they were talking about. To a man they all came from what was called the Old Country—a place he'd never visited. They'd been brought in to work the coal the lot of them. To cries of "Over the road for softies," he saw the frightened man bundled from the door amidst cheering and shouting. Suddenly the room became quiet. Reg peered as a well-built man with greying hair and a touch of grey in his eyes got to his feet, all heads turning to face him.

"Seems to me," the big fellow began, "if the mine has problems—"

"Now hold on Bill—" said the man with the paper now standing by his chair.

Reg looked at the nugget in his hand thinking the place was like a foreign country!

"No one here has the right—" the big man was saying above the hubbub.

The small fellow climbed on his chair again.

"When there's *no more coal being turned* in this town," he shouted looking around, confident he had the miners' attention. "*Organization!*" he cried.

It was typical, Reg thought, that they should all be here fighting about how to run *his* country. *He'd* been born at Ikaraki; he knew from his birth certificate, not that he could remember anything other than Moke. 1840! And where were this lot then? He reckoned they should ship the lot of them back again! Like the girl. They were too clever by half! All of 'em. He turned his back on the room.

"I defy the man to stop me forming a Union!" squeaked the small man from the chair.

Turning again Reg saw the man Billy step into the space before him, awkward yet with a certain grace. Looks passed around the room. It became quiet. Gradually another man rose and limped out, his discomfort obvious. Yet a third disentangled himself and a fourth broke away to the surprise of those sitting around him. Embarrassed the small group began to move towards the door. This time cries of "Over the road!" and "Out!" did not follow them. Instead from the door Billy paused and passed his eyes over the room. Some men looked away and some looked down. A young man hurriedly rose and ran to him and Reg saw the door close, leaving some sixteen frowning miners, not a few of whom clearly weren't entranced at being there. A sour look came over the barman's face. He'd been happy to have his pub known as a Union pub but he hadn't expected it to go this far. Reg watched him angrily sinking his fingers into the empty glasses, counting the empty chairs.

Ceci was on the point of giving up. Annie who was obviously more experienced in such matters had assured her it was impossible to get miners to change pubs and had in fact gone to bed. Suddenly before her very eyes the door opened and in strode some nine mining men as if in the habit of coming there every night! Glancing around, they began to push the tables together as for a meeting. One of them came to the bar. How angry those women would be with her *now,* she told herself, when they'd finished drying their clothes . . . Heart pounding with hope she started filling the glasses.

The men, it seemed, were discussing the joining of some union though half of them did not know what a union was. They believed it meant sitting at home and were afraid both for and of their wives. Many it seemed had had the experience of being fired or laid off in different mines throughout the West Coast coalfields. "Which of us would get took back?" was the general fear as the men got up and drifted from the table, moving to stand about the room fingering things, peering from the window.

"Troublemakers'll go first," observed one, carefully shredding a place mat Ceci had made. "Not that I'm *agin* unions."

"Nor me," said another.

Clearly none entertained any idea of being reinstated after a strike. The consensus of opinion was that if many were inevitably to be laid off, what good would it do to put *all* out of work by taking a strike now? In addition, very few mines were left for them to wander to.

Gradually their glasses came back to the bar, Ceci slipping an arm around the keg and tilting it to get the last drop. So engrossed had she been in their conversation, in the humble way these big men worried at things they could not quite grasp the significance of, she had barely noticed the keg emptying. Now she observed them in a silence they shared well.

Taking the glasses she had filled to the table she

returned to the bar, tilting the keg again to fill the two remaining glasses, a panic beginning in the pit of her stomach on realizing the keg was empty. As she paused, the two men whose glasses had not been refilled crossed to her and leant on the bar. How short had been her victory over the Temperance Women!

"Nother one m'dear," said the first, indicating his glass.

Ceci drew herself up.

"There isn't any left," she murmured.

The man turned and shouted to the room: "She has no beer!"

"In the back is it?" asked the second, meaning to fetch it for her.

Ceci shook her head, tears gathering as the men rose to their feet. "Those damn women!" said Billy, barely loud enough for Ceci to catch.

Stricken, she watched them whispering, giving her polite nods then leaving the bar. She sank her head in her hands. Suddenly at an alarming thought she pulled open the till draw and began desperately to count the money. There was not enough! There was not enough to buy in more beer!

At that moment William chose to enter towelling his hair.

"Where's everyone gone?" he demanded. "I was just coming to help." Seeing the dismal look on Ceci's face he added, "Cheer up!"

Suddenly she exploded.

"Don't tell me to cheer up William! The profit on two barrels of beer is not enough to buy in one and I need at least six to get ahead enough to buy two!"

She slammed in the till drawer. Crash!

"We're *finished*!"

"We took more than that," William began, flicking water from his ear and starting to count the money on the bar.

"I spent my *last* money buying that beer! Damn this place to hell!" Ceci shouted. "And *you* haven't exactly distinguished yourself!"

William looked at her in amazement.

"And I don't owe you any form of behaviour so you can stop staring!"

His face showed he considered this outburst quite unfair and apart from anything else thought he'd cut rather a fine figure collecting and shining those glasses. Ceci ran up the stairs wanting to run and run. She burst into the room where Annie was lying half clad on the bed and began to ransack the drawers wildly. Annie crinkled her face.

"What are you doing?"

"*Leaving*!! No I'm not!" she cried.

What was the point? If she were to rush out into the street with her bundle of belongings she would get to the open bush and then what? She flung herself on the bed.

"I *slaved* and *slaved* and I finally got some custom and the beer ran out." She began to sniff. "I can't *buy* more."

Guilt played on Annie's face.

"Took me wages from the till—"

Ceci shook her head. "Oh, there wouldn't have been enough anyway!"

For once she gave in to grief and allowed herself to cry shamelessly. William hovered in the corridor listening. He heard Annie make cooing noises.

"Not gonna let a little thing like *that* upset us girl!" he heard her say. "*We're* not finished! Lend ya one a me special blouses! We'll bofe go over The Central get jobs as barmaids!"

Despite herself Ceci burst out laughing so loud she nearly choked.

"Stand that place on its head," went on Annie. "Annie and Ceci's French dance routine—wiv *garters*."

Tears glistening on her cheeks, Annie hugged her, mopped at her nose with a finger, pinched her shoulder. Though she was younger than Ceci it seemed at times Ceci didn't know anything. Outside, William heard the lull and crept quietly down the stairs.

Hearing rumblings in his back yard the barman of The Central grabbed a large cosh and opened the door to see Billy and eight men standing amongst his casks.

"Think it was the women did ye?" one of them called.

"I've teached *them* their lesson!" he replied from the step.

"A couple at cost," said Billy, "and we'll part friends. If we'd stayed there'd've been a fight."

"Why don't you ask me to split profits with her? Bloody woman."

"Come on man," they cajoled.

"Whole town's persecutin' the girl," Billy pointed out. Grudgingly the barman gave in. There was no sense in being difficult about it. He'd win the custom back.

"Good as gold," he said nodding.

"Here we go then gal!" called Bain, marching into The Hexham, a barrel on his shoulder. The men looked around. Lawson strode into the back and because there was no one there took the liberty of flicking open the larder doors.

"Bare as a dormouse's behind," he said, surprised.

Upstairs on the bed, Annie and Ceci turned their heads like squirrels to listen. Was that men below?

"Splash yer face," Annie urged Ceci.

As the voices grew louder Ceci crept nervously downstairs and insinuated herself into the room. Carefully she squeezed behind the bar. Looking up, Billy saw at once she had been crying. Why had they come back Ceci asked herself. Had the world gone mad? Suddenly she saw the two new casks propped there—open and running—a pile of change for the first few drinks standing beside the small amount she had left on the counter. Frowning, she looked across at the men, quaffing and talking as if they'd never been gone. She passed her hand over her face. Suddenly she felt faint. They had so nearly been finished! What with the women refusing to serve her in the shop, thinking she had just come there to peddle herself . . . Even now, with the potatoes finished, they'd have to think carefully before deciding whether to buy food or more beer! Billy saw her go pale, sway and lean back holding her head. He saw the young lad William come in, cross to her quickly and help her from the room then return frowning. That young woman had a lot of responsibility, Billy told himself, what with the boy and Annie whom, he knew full well, would be very demanding. His heart went out to her. Things would surely get worse.

It would take courage for the men to run the women's gauntlet but unless they did, this woman would surely starve! He remembered the circumstances in which the previous owner had hastily departed. This poor girl probably wouldn't last long either.

"Here," he beckoned to William. William came over.

"Want a job lad?" he said softly.

The boy stood staring, unable to believe it.

"7:00 a.m. tomorrow back of the brick kiln. Three and six a day."

William saw the big man turn away and sink his face into his beer. Not a soul at the table had heard! But peeping around the door at the custom, Annie had seen Billy whispering to William and instantly felt insecure. Pulling back she hurried into the kitchen where Ceci was sitting, head in hands, a glass of water before her and quickly said:

"You want to watch some of those fellows in there," indicating the bar room.

"Why?" Ceci looked up questioningly.

"That Billy, the big feller, well he's a liar to start with!" Annie nodded vigorously. Ceci blinked, trying to clear her head.

"Well, you just remember for the future," Annie finished. "If ever he says something you think is a bit— *different* from what you thought—remember I told you."

As dawn broke over the silent pub William looked at his pocket watch, put his feet on the cold floor and struggled into his inadequate clothing. Carefully he tiptoed past Ceci and Annie's door, let himself out downstairs and closed the door behind him. As he neared the iron bridge he found himself joining a stream of hardened miners—all facing the same way—their rough clothes coated in the coal dust of previous days and a heavy inevitability in their walk. One or two nodded at each other without speaking or glanced at William as if he'd suddenly "come right" and become a man. He looked timidly about him.

"Forgot yer lunch lad," said an old miner.

As William flowed off the bridge with the men to begin his first day of Real Work, he glanced at the mine works, mean somehow against the massive hills. In the gloom of early morning he felt frighteningly alone.

Dirty and exhausted as the day went on, William picked up and carried load after load of bricks in the company of two other brick boys who boasted that the seams of clay in the coal mine made the best bricks in the whole world! Hardened by the work they talked cheerfully,

whistling, unbothered by the terrible heat of the kiln floor.
Every Friday, they informed him, he should spend one
day's pay buying a new pair of boots for it took only a
week for them to wear out on the hot floors. When he
collapsed, they carried him outside, propped him in a cool
place and got on with his work. It was well known Billy
had got the boy the job, a gesture of solidarity with
newcomers which those who did not appreciate kept
quiet about for Billy was well liked as a fair man and could
readily be forgiven the odd quirk.

Back at the pub, Ceci opened doors, calling, seeking
William everywhere while Annie used the occasion to
point out he'd probably taken up with some of the bad
company they'd had in the previous night. His bed had
been slept in but he was well and truly gone. Already she
had counted the money and decided they could not afford
food and that it would have to go on more beer. It was to
this end she was making arrangements when a letter fell
through the door. "Miss Olwen P. Laird, 28 Chestnut
Crescent, Finsbury Circus, London, Great Britain . . ." She
read with excitement, turning the envelope over and
hurrying to sit.

How far away that world! With its broughams and
hansoms surging across the bridge, its iron coal hole
covers on pavements, its letterboxes with "V R" on the
front, its iron lamp posts, gates and railings; those park
benches with iron feet in the shapes of lions and eagles!
Great iron bunches of fruit and iron flowers clustering on
public water fountains on the Embankment! Here there
was only wood and tin! Oh those hundreds and hundreds
of people passing in brightly coloured clothes, the noise!
The World of London! Of *Laughter*! And of *Life*!

Lovingly she opened Olwen's letter, the news from
Home, the familiar scenes and place names floating before
her. Olwen was well. She had a young man of established
background who talked of going to India and while she
was not sure if New Zealand was as interesting as India,
at least it was *somewhere* she could refer to which gave the
impression her situation was "toward" . . .

"Toward" Ceci repeated to herself knowing Olwen
meant "prosperous" and finding herself remembering
Hexham. What a world away *that* was! And Ginger. What

would he think to see her sinking in the mud like this, the larder bare and Annie out "on the scrounge"! She'd swept past him so grandly in the local trap—staring ahead—refusing to look back or explain things. He'd never find her now! In the safety of Grevillton she took out the scene which had proved so embarrassing and examined it carefully. Ginger must have thought she'd been up at Hexham visiting the new owners. He probably thought the bank had auctioned Hexham on her behalf and thus she had simply taken her money and cleared out! How he must hate her! Dear Ginger. What was he doing now?

Chapter 30

In a dry wind Lizabeth watched her father chopping wood, raising his axe to a great height, then bringing it thundering down, his body vibrating with the emotion he was spending on the wood. Crash! There went his frustration! Crash! There went his pain! Crash! There went his anger. Laying the axe to one side, he lifted his hand to his eyes as if feeling faint then sat on his chopping block. Slowly, Lizabeth came forward, recognizing the way her father's body was shaking as sobs. She saw the silver of tears flash between his bent head and the ground and when she reached a hand to his shoulder, he began to cry in earnest. After a minute he shook his head, the tears flying away like drops of light and wiping his nose on the back of his hand, tried to laugh up at her.

In Grevillton the day drew on without sign of William or Annie. Ceci wandered from kitchen to bar room to kitchen, up the stairs, down again, into the yard and back upstairs to look in William's cubicle. The street was empty. Nobody came. Finally she threw herself into a chair and let the spectre that they would all starve to death in

Grevillton fleet before her eyes as she passed into a hunger-induced trance.

"Tell me about your House Dream," she saw herself say to Norah, the vision of the two of them cuddled together on a sofa in Clapham before her eyes.

"I had it again last night," said Norah, propping herself up on one arm.

"Did you get in?"

"I got in," she affirmed. "There was an old staircase in the *middle* of the house and it was narrow and dark with a door at the top and one at the bottom. You had to open that door to get on to the staircase. There were no lights and the stairs were steep and covered with boxes and rolls of carpet... broken chairs—it was hard to get up. I went on hands and knees. At the top I was afraid of being caught."

"By her?"

"She's just in the garden."

"And nobody lives there?"

"I don't think so. But I always feel they shouldn't catch me—I'm not allowed there..."

"Then what happened?"

"Then inside the house became like a much smaller house in a narrow street in a—a *town*... And I *found my room*!"

"Did you get in?"

"I went round the back of the room to get in and it was very secret. There was nothing at all inside! Just this room that was *light*—It was one room inside another room—"

In the half light Norah drew with her hand the image of a room inside a room.

"But the room was empty?"

"Yes."

Norah was very still.

"People don't know about it once I'm there... So it's safe."

Norah had always been dreaming that dream. She would be walking along in her dream then *suddenly* over a briar hedge, there was the House, stark against a white sky. It was always autumn because the briar was bare so she could peer through it to the ploughed space she had to cross, the dangerous part of the dream because she was

fully exposed. She'd hide in the hedge then make a run
for it. The house varied in shape but was never flat
fronted like Lord K's but complicated with recesses and
abutments—barred windows with broken shutters nailed
over them, strands of ivy across paths leading to broken
doors, shaded lintels, cracked stones. There was an Old
Woman there who knew about Norah and tried to keep
her out with a stick so she'd wait before making a run for
it. Once inside she always tried to get upstairs and find
this secret room. On the mornings when she'd "made it"
she'd be radiant.

"Now you tell me about Heaven."

Heaven, Ceci said, was a big allotment with vegetable
patches separated by grassy paths with narrow tufts hanging over them. The paths weren't trimmed and in the
corners grew poppies, like field poppies but very much
bigger and their petals didn't drop in a day. They waved
in a noisy breeze from a wind which drowsed through
heavy elms on hot summer days. There was water everywhere in barrels that were always full so no one went to
the well but crossed to a barrel instead to fill their buckets.
You never saw anyone. There were no men tending the
garden. No shady corners with compost heaps, dark
hedges . . . Just she—alone in Heaven—she could stay as
long as she liked without having to keep an eye on the
palings and be ready to duck and crawl out on her
stomach . . .

"What about the flowers?"

Well there were patches of pinks in the dry brown
earth, sweet-williams, antirrhinums, sometimes peonies,
very, very fat and heavy, faded, nodding in the heat, the
sort they used for May Queens. No hollyhocks because
none of the plants were taller than her and there were no
woods or hills in Heaven. Just this allotment and you
walked along the path. There were spiders and ants as
usual. Norah thought it sounded very dull but didn't say
so. "What would you do when you got tired of it?" she'd
asked.

She would *very* soon get tired of Heaven . . .

Ceci opened her eyes at the sound of the door. There
stood an engrimed William, arms laden with groceries.
Pushing herself from her chair she ran forward, scarce

believing he was real while for his part William forced the groceries into her arms, holding both her and them to him as if the food were a child between them. His burnt and blistered fingers clasped at her sleeves and his mind recently exercised by choosing between a tin of jam for sixpence or a tin of salmon at the same price tiredly groped for the words he had forgotten. Though he could not remember his speech, never had he felt so proud and happy in his life! The woman was shaking in his arms, verily trembling.

"Oh William! *How*?"

He shrugged, savouring the glory and unprepared to admit someone got the job for him from pity. Why should he when Ceci seemed about to lay her heart at his feet!

Winter settled over Grevillton with heavy certainty and evil weather. The Central stood abandoned, slipping into decay, its "CLOSED," "FOR SALE," "GONE AWAY," signs hanging outside, faded by the rain. A piece of broken guttering dripped on to the ground. Passing The Central, Marie and Jeannie gave it a glance as if to say "That's a step in the right direction."

They looked thinner, the worse for wear and knew well they could not flatter themselves it was *their* action which had brought about the closure of The Central. No, it had been the Strike which had gone on to split their community. All the men who had joined the union and stayed out had been fired in a time where name calling and animosity had reached heights unknown in living memory. Sadly they hurried past. The non-union men left had the one or two days' work a week and many said were it not for Ceci's pub existing as an alternative meeting place, those men too would have joined the strike... Marie's Jonas had long since "gone over the road" to Ceci.

Now was a time of funerals and quiet starvation, of bread hidden and bread shared. Even sitting quietly in the bar room, Ceci could hear the women outside whispering about a neighbour who had bought two eggs and asking where the money had come from. Looking out on the lean faces of this small cluster who wanted to protest against her Ceci felt desperately sorry for them. Countless times she had asked them to come in out of the wind and keep warm but they'd shaken their heads. It was more than they could bear, she knew, to see their husbands drinking money which might be going to their tables.

Yet Ceci did not ask the men to drink. Her pub had become the meeting place for the surviving miners—a place which was warm and quiet, away from their pathetic children and hungry wives whose eyes they could not meet. Here they planned strategy, the three glasses of beer they occasionally bought being passed slowly from man to man, each taking a sip. Were it not for William buying the groceries, she too would starve.

Leaning on the bar chewing a finger, Ceci passed her eyes over the meeting in progress before her. There were no raised voices or shouting. Yet she knew it was more than her life was worth to drop a spoon. "Bein' as all the things we want've bin tried nor 'ave we thought nor owt more as 'ud be safe, I dreckon we should think on an' pray God for guidance," came a voice, greeted by general nodding and grunts. Ceci changed elbows and started to chew a different finger. She was in a strange position, she told herself, depending on William for groceries. Of course he had the lion's share of the food, she and Annie eating very little. She hated the way the women of Grevillton saw her. Though their protest was nothing more than a tired habit their funerals were as real as the *No Credit* sign which appeared with the regularity of a barometer in Mrs. Evans's store. William had told her that one morning, late for work, he had passed a house outside which a group of women were congregating as if something were wrong within. Going in he had found an older man hanging from the main beam—his wife sitting on an upright chair her limp fingers clasped around a piece of bread in dirty newspaper she had just brought home from a neighbour's. William had climbed on the table and cut the man down. He said he knew him by sight as one of the strikers. He'd pushed the tongue back into the mouth and pulled at the eyelids which snapped open again.

Indeed it was not unusual these days in the early morning mist to pass a shabby cortege following a plain coffin on a hand hearse. Working miners going to and from work would pause, caps in hand, with a look of shame to let it pass while small groups of unemployed men stood about, watching. Behind the coffin would come the woman followed by her six perhaps seven children, her walk numbed. The awful desolation of these funerals deeply grieved Ceci who remembered funerals at Home, despite their sadness, as being joyous occasions where families got together and assured each other their cluster of human souls could shore itself up against death and eternity, against *any* eventuality, and *survive*! There would even be singing and remarks about who needed a corset to hold that stomach in!

Dragging her mind back to the meeting, Ceci saw that it was breaking up and the men beginning to leave. Realizing Billy was staring straight at her, she went scarlet. This was not the first time this had happened. Often when their meetings fell into a lull she would look up and find him gazing intently at her. Quickly he would look down and as the noise of the meeting rose, the incident, if such it was, would be forgotten. She tried as usual to give him a little smile but it wouldn't come. Nodding at her he closed the door behind the last of the men and as she turned, she found William observing her as if he were disapproving.

Returning along the West Coast trail Reg decided to take another look at Ceci. Nothing to lose he told himself and after that last narrow escape he'd like to repeat the yarn to someone. Never good with words he slowly rehearsed how the tale should come out. First establish the fact that the runholder whose sheep he'd been poaching had come up on him, caught him with the sheep in one hand, its throat neatly cut and him stood there with the knife still dripping in his other hand. He'd sort of drive the listener into the paddocks, slam the gate, then deliver his punch line.

"Whadda you think you're doin' with my sheep?" he'd repeat the runholder saying.

"Do the same to any sheep that bit me!" he'd have himself reply stoutly. Reg shook his head. It still came out wrong. Whatever voice he tried that line in it didn't come out as funny as it should have. Still, he'd enjoyed going back to the High Country and however hungry a man got, despite having to cross the mountains, there was always meat there to be had. It was a good coincidence the trail he used passed through Grevillton . . .

Seemed to be a bunch of women outside Ceci's pub again he told himself, thinking they looked more like scrag ends than women. Why they would stand there gossiping on a cold day when they doubtless had shacks to go to mystified him. Sidling over he sensed them looking at him as if he gave them the creeps.

"I know what'd get her out," one of them was saying.

Reg leaned on the wall.

"Marry 'er."

"Still be a pub."

Was this Ceci they were talking about he wondered?

"Not in the hands of the right man," a wiry woman added. Reg heard laughter and the name "Simon" mentioned.

"Got the devil's own tongue on him when he thinks he's doin' Right."

Reg's stomach rumbled loudly. Obviously these were foreign women married to those miner men. Means it'd be the first time they'd clapped eyes on a proper New Zealander so they'd no business looking at him as if he were dirt. With concentration he let off a fart.

"Now you put it to him, Marie—" said the small woman ignoring him. "He likes you. You'll have to be a bit clever mind."

"Have 'im *propose*," said another woman.

My my my Reg nodded. He could certainly earn himself a drink this time! Somebody wanted to get Ceci married off to deprive Grevillton of a pub! Donning a look of entrenched vacancy he listened on. Were they seriously considering using the place as a Sunday School? It was always difficult to know what women meant especially when they were laughing.

"Well, if she don't act right after they marry he'll put her away! You know Simon! Sweet as two peas 'til you speak up!" Suddenly the women shushed as the door of Ceci's pub opened and their husbands began to trickle out. Pleased with himself, Reg waited until they'd gone, then sidled in.

So the young whippersnapper who'd been staring at Ceci as if he was in love with her last time was still there, Reg told himself, watching William collecting glasses and going into the kitchen with them like a girl. Crossing to the counter he cleared his throat and banged a golden guinea down. Ceci spun.

"You wanna watch yourself girl," he began briskly. "Your friends out there cooking up a husband for you."

Ceci threw back her head laughing.

"They must think I'm pretty stupid! I'd *never* marry again!"

Reg banged his guinea again to make his point. Quickly Ceci began to pull.

"You'll say Yes when the time comes," he said, expecting her to push the guinea back at him.

"As a married woman I'd lose all I own!" she shrugged lightly. "Can't do that to me twice!"

"Ah, but you got a singular talent for losin' property girl!" Reg jibed. "Got any grub?"

Sighing Ceci walked into the kitchen just in time to see William óbviously sulking leave by the back door. What was the point of staying in the pub all day she asked herself? The men had gone on the afternoon shift and wouldn't be back. She knew each of them; she could count the hairs on their heads and they would not return for two days at which time they would order three pints precisely between the nine of them. If William wanted to sulk instead of enjoying his day off that was William's affair, she decided, gathering what little food they could spare into a hamper, throwing in Olwen's letters for good measure and returning to the bar.

"I've no reputation to lose," she said lightly to Reg. "Have you a horse?"

Reg slipped his guinea back in his pocket and downed the beer. All things considered, he told himself the day wasn't going so badly after all.

"The coast," said Ceci. "I'd love to see the sea."

As they rode along, Reg noticed women looking at Ceci and looking away again but he sensed she didn't care. On this glorious winter's day he could feel she was overjoyed to be getting out of Grevillton.

When they reached the coast, Reg stood holding the hamper and watching Ceci watch the waves roll in and in.

"Ain't you bin here before?" he asked.

"Don't get around much."

"Coach."

"Who's got money to fling on coaches?"

Leaving the horse on the beach below, they climbed the steep cliff, Reg with the hamper slung on his back occasionally turning to help Ceci. She couldn't draw him on the subject of Jock and his opinion on Olwen varied between her needing "sortin' out" and "a good thrashing." When Ceci read her letters to him and tried to share Olwen's enthusiasm about "immunization" explaining it was "very modern and to do with germs" Reg responded by picking at his scalp and examining things between his fingers.

"I have told Edmund," Ceci read out, adding "that's her young man—" "that my parents own a large Canterbury sheep station and I defy you to say different! I wish you had not told Molly"—she used to call her Aunty Molly!—"the circumstances surrounding your failure to continue my allowance." Looking up Ceci saw that Reg was picking his nose. "To be a hindrance," she continued, "is one thing but if you must write sordid details—" Reg's face flashed anger.

"Please use another name because I'd die rather than admit—"

"That she's a bastard," he said flatly.

"She only wants to be respectable," reasoned Ceci, folding the letter. "What did you ever know about young girls?"

Reg looked at Ceci sideways.

"Knew a thing about you once!" he remarked.

Ceci was taken aback. The remark was positively flirtatious! It was as if Reg had crammed his entire adolescent experience into that moment!

"She gonna marry that fellow?" he asked.

"It looks like it," Ceci shrugged.

"You tell 'er to watch out!" Reg warned.

He could not be more specific and Ceci wondered exactly how she should word his request. Edmund was clearly from what they called a well-to-do family though it would not be established wealth and the glamour of that sort of thing would be bound to have an appeal for a girl like Olwen. In any case there was no telling daughters.

"So where are you bound for?" she asked Reg.

"Rimu past Hokitika."

"Eight men and a packhorse sunk in the mud down there!" Ceci grinned. "Good luck."

"Rubies," Reg explained, referring to the recent strike which was luring him.

"I'll tell Olwen not to be taken in by appearances then shall I?" she asked as they scrambled back down the cliff.

"Just you watch out for your*self!*" advised Reg. "That suitor'll be along and get ye and there'll be *another* town wi'out a pub!"

Dropped at the entrance to Grevillton Ceci couldn't help laughing at the memory of his words. He understood so little about women and had such a quaint way of expressing himself. She'd been sad to see him go even though he'd assured her he'd be passing through again, adding *if* gold or rubies were found north. Swinging the hamper she walked the short distance to her pub. Annie was leaning from an upstairs window.

"Was that Reg I saw you with?" she shouted, ready for a scrap.

"He just dropped in to tell me some ne'er-do-wells been set up to propose to me." Ceci grinned. Annie's manner changed at once from indignant to afraid.

"Will I have to leave?" she asked, hurrying into the bar room.

"*Stay!*" Ceci assured her, amazed she could even give *credence* to such rubbish. "The pickings are getting sparse, but—"

"Well you never know," Annie said. "If you got married your husband might want me out."

"Well I shall be on my guard from now on and see it doesn't happen!" Ceci assured her good naturedly.

Annie remained looking. Maybe it was a joke but if there was one thing she couldn't stand it was jokes about where she lived! "Alright Ceci," she grinned with relief.

In the days that followed, Ceci began to wonder if her expedition on the horse had totally outraged the local citizenry for her pub remained ominously deserted. William had taken to skulking about resentfully as if afraid for his job. Annie's joking had stopped and the atmosphere had become so depressed Ceci could not even remember the cause of her recent elation.

Rain began to fall in earnest. It rained and rained 'til not a living soul was to be seen. From the window her eyes moved out over the muddy street, over rain bouncing in trenches churned by carts which had passed, bouncing in pocks in the deep mud. Grevillton in continuous rain! All doors and windows were closed. Rain, rain. Beyond the town, drip drip from the trees, the heavy vegetation. Rain over Grevillton and the mine accentuating its heavy grey hopelessness. Rain running in rivulets down the despoiled hill behind the mine, the felled trees shifting in mud slides, and up above—rain.

She turned away. In the bar room the flowers were gone. The clock ticked. She sprawled in the rocking chair, her body stiff and only her head touching the backrest. Rain beat on the window. The vision of total emptiness, stillness, browness before her faded in and out, replaced by the elaborate grandeur of Hexham as she first saw it. How clearly she remembered how it had looked as she stood there with the baby on her hip, breath indrawn. Again there arose the graceful antique furniture, the grand fireplace and before it the highly polished floor graced by white embroidered Kashmiri mats; the sun pouring through the fine windows again and again, piercing the curtains, scattering light on the pale wood floor and beyond it the green of the lawn; the sound of summer insects. She pushed herself from the chair and went to the window.

Grevillton in the rain!

As she turned from the window the hallway of Hexham rose before her; its fine staircase with the Japanese wallhanging; the spot where Mrs. Hallam had shouted there should be children in the house scuffing the mats! Children! Ginger's children—all five of them! She allowed herself to imagine them tearing up and down the hall of Hexham, sliding on the mats, arms out, having a whale of a time. Suddenly Ginger appeared and said good naturedly:

"Now stop that you lot!" Ceci felt him cross to her and kiss the back of her neck. Guiltily she spun.

There was William at the open door—wet through. He looked as if he might collapse. Quickly she ran forward but as if knowing her thoughts he moved past her into the kitchen.

Coming down the stairway, Annie saw the boy was wet through again. Of course there was nowhere to dry his clothes. They must be the only family in Grevillton she told herself who did not pinch coal from the mine! Mind you, the others had small boys to do it for them, brats who ducked between the wagons and ran off before they were recognized. There was nothing for it she decided. She would have to get some herself!

Quetly she stepped from the pub, a pillowcase stuffed in her bodice and, head down, she ran through the rain. There was no one in sight. A faint light came from the Mine Manager's office, glinting on the sodden rails. Annie crossed the tracks, bending to pick up bits of coal, put them in her pillowcase then straightened up again. She ran and stooped, ran and stooped, hair stuck to her head, rain drizzling down into her bodice. Every contour of her body was clearly marked as the wind slashed her thin clothes about her and coal dust ran in filthy rivulets into her shoes and collected at her waist. Struggling to get a better grip on the now full sack she tried getting it across her back like a sausage, bending double, not wanting to spill coal or damage the delicate sack. Then the fright came. There, in her field of vision, two well-shod male feet were pointing directly at her. Slowly she raised her head to the knees, the waist and finally the umbrella handle and the face of the man she knew to be the Mine Manager: Mr. Jephcott. She was certain he didn't know her. A man in his position wouldn't. Yet it would be best to say nothing for even her accent would reveal she was not a miner's wife and the field would narrow accordingly. Ready to outstare him and still clutching her sack of ill-gotten coal she followed Jephcott to the Administration Hut. He looked hardly a man who enjoyed life. It was a known fact he kept the town butcher in business being the only person who ever bought a roast and talk had it he and his wife got through two of them a week. Yet there was not *that* much fat on him. Looking at the back of his dry collar as she followed him through the rain she could well believe the number of women who reputedly wished to pull the sides of roast from his shoulder as he left the butcher's shop and brain him with them...Why, were the seams stronger, she would have been tempted to do the same with her pillow-slip of coal!

Inside the hut Jephcott looked at Annie. As an adult female trespassing on the mine, she must be viewed as the thin end of the wedge. Filthy as she was he had been obliged to offer her a chair and as he waited, standing behind his desk with thumbs in pockets, it occurred to him that she was not going to speak. The sack of coal was clenched between her thighs, her arms were folded and her mouth tightly sealed. Jephcott took out his pocket watch and laid it on the table. The long night had begun.

Unaware of Annie's predicament, Ceci hoped William would not have caught cold. He worked far too hard for a boy of his constitution and she felt bad about him supporting her.

"I don't pay rent," he replied quietly as if grudging her the solicitation. It was *awkward* when Annie was out. Frequently Ceci sensed William preparing himself to say something she would find unacceptable. She peered from the window at the rain sloshing down, churning the mud, and as evening became night, worried for Annie. William's opinion that she could look after herself was small comfort for she had often sensed he wished Annie were away and as she heard him pacing the corridor and pausing outside her room before going to his cubicle, she could almost believe he was *glad* Annie was not there. Falling asleep she dreamt of someone who loved her getting nearer and nearer so that by the time she awoke she was really missing him. Who it had been was a mystery, but opening her eyes she lay for a long time thinking before realizing in the grey light she could not see clothes on Annie's chair. By now, she realized, there was certainly cause to worry.

Stepping from the Administration Hut Jephcott reminded himself it had been a thoroughly uncomfortable night. He had reasoned with the woman, made several very fine points indicating the wiseness of revealing one's identity in good time—meaning before the arrival of the constable—yet she had sat there like a wet lump, lips pressed together, leaving him only the one alternative. Reminding himself again that to start the day unshaven and without a hot breakfast in one's stomach was not an experience to be undergone even in the interests of catching a thief, Jephcott stepped from the hut and turned the key on Annie. She gave him a few minutes then hurried to the window. Beyond the rails the first men were beginning to arrive, grey and hungry, ready to burn away their worries in work. Furiously she scrabbled at the window to attract attention but they walked past, seemingly unseeing. Turning to Jephcott's desk she picked up a blotter and as Billy passed, began to rap loudly on the window with its handle. He saw her at once and with a quick glance round crossed to the door, whipped a knife from his pocket and went to work on the lock. Behind her on the floor he saw the bag of coal.

"Well it's been hard up there since your mates stopped coming," Annie said as an excuse.

"Go on Annie," Billy said. "You better be quick."

Feeling ashamed of having lied about him she slipped through the door and ran. Poor thing, thought Billy, watching her in her filthy clothing flee the site.

Crossing to join Jonas he saw William by the brick kiln and noticed how tiredly the boy moved. All jobs were exhausting but brick boys were poorly paid too. It occurred to him as William fell against a stack of bricks, knocking them on to his foot, that the boy was not getting enough to eat. Apart from being thin he was dizzy and as like as not feeling the pinch Annie had mentioned since their three pints a week drinking money had been withdrawn. Annoyed with himself for not having thought of it sooner, Billy went over.

William glared at him.

"Job goin' below lad. Full week."

"I haven't the strength," he admitted.

"Take it boy! I'll cover for you," Billy advised.

Still the boy looked aggrieved: "Why'd you all drop our pub?" he asked.

"Edgecumbe went under a wagon," explained Billy, surprised the news hadn't filtered up. "The three pints a week money goes to his wife."

Back at The Hexham, apart from worrying on Annie's behalf Ceci was berating herself for ever agreeing to run a pub in a place where none could afford to drink. In fact now that the miners had stopped coming, she was without even the sight of their wives and the loneliness was unbearable. If no one came no one protested! As to the other women of Grevillton, was her position any different from theirs? Yes, because they had a *right* to depend on the men who brought home the money whereas William was not even a relation. Just as she was feeling demoralized Annie burst in, filthy, covered in grime and totally dispelling William's assertion that she had finally found a bigger fool than Ceci.

"There'll be a man coming to look for me," she gasped, tearing through the bar room and up the stairs.

"A nice one?" Ceci couldn't help calling after her.

"Not for me dear," shouted Annie from the top of the stairs. "I bin there before!"

That meant the Police, Ceci realized. So Annie *had* been in prison.

The next minute she was hurtling down the stairs, swag in hand.

"Oh *Annie!*" Ceci hugged her.

"I'll wash in the stream," Annie gasped, wriggling from her grip.

They embraced again.

"I bin happy here," she said, her voice breaking. Ceci felt bands tighten round her heart. Biting her lips she saw Annie run to the door and turn for a last firm glance of friendship before vanishing into the street.

It was not long before the knock came on her door.

"Do you have a woman here?" asked an out-of-town constable. Ceci shook her head.

"We haven't had a customer in two weeks," she told him.

"*Living* here," he repeated.

"Nobody lives here but me," she said sadly. "And William," she added, remembering the fact.

Annie had gone. She could hardly grasp it. The pub which she had once imagined could never be emptier seemed emptier than ever! The thought of Annie out there in the rain which had begun again pained her. Worrying about her she hardly heard William stamping his feet on the boards, pushing open the door.

Looking up, she realized he was different. Wet through, yes, but standing as if he'd suddenly received a knighthood.

"I got promoted," he announced.

"William!" she replied, trying to sound pleased yet aware that what she would really like would be for him to take his salary and start a decent life on his own away from Grevillton!

"Aren't you pleased?" he demanded, wiping his dripping nose on his sleeve. "From twenty-one shillings a week to two pounds ten! *And* a full week."

"It's not right that you should go on supporting me,"
Ceci said, rising, wishing he would stop turning into a
Grevillton miner on her behalf.

He crossed to her, took her wrists almost roughly.

"I want to," he said, tightening his grip on them and
drawing her towards him.

"William—!" she began in panic. Best to make a joke
of it. "At the rate you're going you'll be Mine Manager
yet!" she said. William grinned, pleased, relaxing his grip.

"How did you do it?" she asked, suddenly possessed
by curiosity. At that William let go her wrist. Though it
was a shame about Edgecumbe and he felt guilty about
concealing the way he'd got the job, it was well worth it if
it meant earning Ceci's admiration!

Chapter 31

For a few glorious weeks they had enough to eat and
William had the pleasure of seeing roses return to Ceci's
cheeks. Though she would rather have been an ordinary
friend it was clear he wanted more. She was not unaware
of his pride in feeding her, nor ungrateful, nor did she
find it unjustified—given his background—that he should
feel this way. One by one he had said goodbye to clean
hair, clean fingernails and a thousand other things he had
once regarded as prerequisites of decent living, all on her
behalf. Every morning when she saw him struggling into
wet clothes and cracked boots, she would feel almost
ashamed of being a woman, ashamed that she could not
go to the mine. As he stood in the doorway saying
goodbye she would feel guilty. Ultimately it was the
element of the boyish crush in his treatment of her that
saved them embarrassment. At the end of the day he was
satisfied to come home and simply find her there, smiling,
interested in him, wanting to hear about his day.

Gradually the names Bain, Woods, Morewell, Tom—who was Aggie's husband—and Frank—Jeannie's husband—the young one Spiller, Lawson who was friends with the man Billy, Lewis who argued with Mine Manager Jephcott and many others became well known to her. The conditions in which they worked sounded horrifying and most unsafe but it was good to get an idea of their bravery, to be able to put faces to the men who had married the women she had seen outside her pub. The doings of Jonas with his enthusiasm and unfortunate turn of phrase, young Talbot or Neill who seemed to be William's age, came to sound familiar to the point she could almost guess what a particular man would have said or done. What a community it was to be a part of! Certainly William admired the men and sought to be like them.

After a few weeks however, things changed. Work became scarce and even the Full Week men found themselves on one or two days, congregating in the rain at the mine mouth and hoping. Some of the younger men without families, Talbot and Neill amongst them, stayed in the Single Men's Quarters playing cards and gambling, despondency preventing them facing up to the situation and getting out. Despite their urging William would not join in but hung about with the older men, at the mine mouth, hoping for more days, rubbing his hands in the rain. Grevillton it was said was used to hard times.

By now William owed at the store and was deeply conscious of both that and the little he brought home for Ceci. Oftentimes in the evenings she would catch him frowning at the wall with the concern of a man far beyond his years and though she constantly assured him she was not hungry, his sacrifices were not lost on her, nor hers on him . . . Nightly the same piece of bread would be pushed from one side of the table to the other, each in varying degrees of faintness insisting they did not want it. Yet Hunger had come to stay. It roamed like a beast, taking with it children and the elderly. It walked through the pub and rattled the empty larder doors. It scoured Grevillton 'til there was no longer anything to be scavenged and even the greens which had sprouted in drippings from The Central's broken gutter had been torn up and eaten, dropped in a stew pot to pad out the roots its owner had collected . . .

Soon Ceci succumbed to weakness and, to William's worry, lay on her bed passing in and out of consciousness. What was going on behind those closed lids he did not know. At times she looked peaceful—in her mind wandering the Estate's valley, gazing at the slack grey river which lazied through, cutting a low bank here—throwing up a ridge of stones there . . . From the river bed, she saw distant beechwoods, a wet rustling green in spring: rich gold in autumn. She saw the woods, full of life with squirrels scampering in deep ditches filled with generations of leaves. Under exposed roots they ran into hollows, lingering to stare at her from sandy ridges and mossy banks. With armfuls of sloppy bluebells she found herself coming home; or by the edge of the river wandering where the earth was boggy and giant kingcups sprouted. Her feet roamed hedgerows; wood anemones, sorrel and celandines blinked up at her, giving way in summer to cow parsley, hemlock and stitchwort and in autumn the cuckoo pint as time flashed by in a dream. Then came the deadly nightshade and bittersweet. Winter. The face of William hovered above her with a glass of water.

"I shall simply get rid of your mother!" came the voice of Immelda. "If you tell. And your stupid oaf of a father! Now spin her. Push her about! You may all join in! You bring your slate and chalk *here* in future. After school every day. Do you understand?"

"But Miss—"

"*Don't speak!* You may collect it in the morning. *If* I let you have it. *If* I'm here!"

"Are you feeling better?" William pleaded, his desperately worried voice smothered by a loud thumping which also dispelled Immelda. He looked at the tossing head, her eyes' sharp movements as she heard the crack of sails falling and booming out, straining sounds, the squeaks of pullies clanking, ropes scudding and the gasp of wind hitting canvas. Immelda and England were gone! Gone was everything!

"Gone," gasped Ceci.

"No—" William assured her, holding a wet cloth to her face. Gone Mewly who'd trained her in the hotel!

As gradually her memories caught up with her and the kitchen girls faded into dismal early betrothals like hooks into raw fish, the call for Women of Good Character rallied her and she emerged to a weak consciousness sensing she would never return so completely to her Homeland again. It was Gone. Irrevocably and for ever. Summoning the last of her energies, she came Home to Grevillton. At last the fever had passed. As she lay weakly in bed looking around her room one thing stuck in her mind: Annie's remark about Billy. What, she asked herself, could Annie have meant? "You just remember for the future. If ever he says something you think is a bit—*different* from what you thought—remember I told you." Hearing it again even in her weakened state it sounded as if Annie didn't want to be explicit, perhaps to protect Billy. Was she suggesting Billy's behaviour could not be taken at face value? The idea of him being a liar was patently ridiculous yet the sincerity with which Annie had said it—at least the amount of *energy*—made her words difficult to dismiss. Seeing things in a new light now and worrying about Billy's intentions she got unsteadily to her feet and came downstairs for the first time in days.

As she came right again, she noticed a new strength in William. He was undeniably thinner—doubtless from having force fed her the little he could afford during her illness, but had become wiry and seemed to survive on sheer willpower alone. The store had been paid off he informed her, not as a matter of priority but because Mrs. Evans had refused to furnish further food until such times as her bill was met. During the first week of Ceci's illness when she would not eat this had been done and since then Ceci had enjoyed the milk and eggs she needed and the small amount of bread she would take. For his part William had clung to his determination to see her well. Now, on two days' work regular and no bills, no Annie to feed, they were back on their feet. If the two days lasted they believed there was a remote chance they might begin to get *really* well again.

Ceci smiled at William. He guessed she had a surprise. Since recovering she had taken to searching for food far from the outskirts of Grevillton and that day, backtracking this way and that, had heard a sound in the bush she thought was a wild boar. Hands tightening on her stick she had crept towards the snuffling noises which turned out to be only a bird whirring its wings, the sound

magnified in the stillness of the bush to resemble grunting.
Motionless she stood watching it flap about on the ground.
It was bigger than a good sized pigeon: a native bird of
some sort like a partridge or pheasant. She watched it
flutter on to a branch and sit and, biting her lip, bent
carefully to pick up a stone. Part of her whispered that
what she was doing was unthinkable but the other part
told her to draw back her arm and fling the stone before
the bird took off. Carefully she threw, the bird cocking its
head to watch the stone sail by. Boldly it hopped to the
ground again and began to move about on the floor of the
bush in little darting runs. Slowly she undid her apron,
she told William, letting the greens she had gathered slip
away. She crept forward. The bird paused, its head on one
side, listening to insects in the earth. Raising her apron, in
a sudden dive she was on top of it! William was amazed.
Although she could feel it fluttering beneath her, she said,
she had forced herself to the act and found, then snapped
its neck!

William looked at her with admiration. She was trying
hard not to boast and obviously felt a little guilty about
killing the bird, yet she wanted his approval! Though he
would not mention it, the scratches on her arms suggested
she had dived into more than one bush to catch it. He
congratulated her.

He too had good news. He had obtained an addition-
al full day for the morrow in a tunnel which had just lost
two of its three men to sickness!

Once the meal was served they ate quietly, the decision of the best way to devour the bird's tiny legs to get
the most enjoyment from them having been preceded by
considerable discussion. Afraid of losing the tiniest whiff
of steam or aroma, they kept their mouths firmly closed
and their eyes on their plates and with willing stomachs
and full of hope ate the last of the bird and drank the
broth.

Awakening the next morning Ceci let the glorious
feeling of having had enough to eat the previous night
spread through her limbs. Though she was sorry for
William outside in the rain, she afforded herself the comfort of lying for a few moments savouring the well-being.

The wet day brought a letter from Olwen with the
news, not that she was *thinking* of getting married but had

already done so! From her tone she would seem to have been under no duress and was *pleased* with herself rather than happy about it. The hurry, Ceci assumed, had been occasioned by Edmund's posting to India and Olwen's fear that once he had gone, he might not bother with her again. Hardly the best basis for a marriage, Ceci told herself folding the letter and looking from the window.

William, who had walked to work in the rain, came home bowed by it. It pulled coal dust from his hair, sending it in rivulets into his shirt. Uncaringly he stepped in puddles, his feet needing no guide, his entire body knowing the way and making for home in the straightest line possible. A tree plunged into the river: he did not look up. Arriving, he stepped on to the porch, pushed the door open and collapsed.

Ceci ran forward struggling to pull his limp body in and shut the door on the rain which was beating on them. William was groaning. His head was hot. Could *this* have happened when they were just getting back on their feet? In utter panic, she tore the clothes from him, wrapped him in blankets and struggled to warm a brick to put in his bed. Clearly he was delirious. As she fumbled for his pocket watch to take his pulse his heavy breathing filled the room and his eyes rolled. It was as if having finally let go, he could not come back.

Days passed with William sunk in fever. Ceci paced desperately. "I didn't care about Olwen," he confessed weakly. "It's you I've let down."

Pained he should feel guilty on her behalf, Ceci assured him: "We may have privations here, William— but I have never regretted any of my decisions. Especially you."

"I must go back to work," he moaned, struggling to get from bed.

"William!" she wrestled with him. "In the name of *God*, William, will you get *well*?"

He collapsed on the floor.

"It'll be spring soon!" she pleaded. "Just rest a little."

To William's annoyance his eyes rolled and he passed out.

Downstairs Ceci opened one cupboard after another, biting her nails. There was nothing there, not even a rat dropping. For four days William had been ill and she could scarce feed him. Kneeling by the rocking chair she tried to pray, her face vibrating with a deep sincerity, the intense and desperate belief of one who had run out of options. When it came she did not hear the tap on the door 'til finally it became a knock. Getting to her feet she hurried to open it and there, dirty from the mine, cap in hand, stood Billy.

"I—I'm afraid I'm not open these days," she stammered.

"I come to enquire about the lad."

"I—I'm afraid he's not very well!"

She took him upstairs where William had passed out again.

His eyes were flickering open and closed as he fought to come back.

"Doctor?" Billy asked.

Ceci shook her head.

"I brought his wage," he said putting a hand in his pocket and drawing out some money which Ceci took knowing it to be charity.

"I'll get the doctor at first light," she said humbly.

As she was showing him out downstairs she remembered Annie's remark.

"It may be hard to keep his job open," Billy said. Ceci nodded.

"I'm sorry," he murmured.

When he had gone Ceci returned to the empty grate, one arm supporting the cupped elbow of the other, face half hidden in her hand. Despite what Annie had said, that man was like a father to William. Why was it when she'd asked William who Billy was he'd just replied "One of the men," and seemed not to want to discuss him? Once when she had spoken to Billy downstairs she had even caught William looking at her as if her behaviour rankled. Could he be *jealous* of the man or was there something that didn't fit which everyone knew but her because no one had told her? She had never claimed to know a lot about men but there was something odd here . . . Gradually his words sank in: If William was not back at work soon he would lose his job!

Rising early the next morning she changed William's water, then tiptoed from the pub knowing what she must do. She hurried down the street past the provisions store, hardly seeing the small group of women clustered there, following her with their eyes. When she reached the mine entrance she turned into it, crossed to the first group of men and asked for the Mine Manager's office.

Once inside, although she found Jephcott difficult to look in the eye she came straight to the point and asked for William's job.

"I'm as *strong* as the boy," she pointed out.

"Happen you are Marm," Jephcott said, rudely pushing back on his chair and viewing her as if she were a lost dog.

"If you'd *allow* me to keep his job open," she said humbly.

"God made you a *woman* madam," said Jephcott, thumbs in his jacket, "and therein lies your vocation."

Furious to the point of tears at the disdain he had managed to get into his voice, she ran from the hut and stumbled across the rails in a blind haste to be gone.

"I'd take her down the pit any day!" a man remarked, nodding after her. Billy turned to see who he was talking about and with one swipe levelled the man.

Crossing to the Administration Hut he waited for Jephcott to look up then tried to put in a word for William.

"In fairness—we pulled together. You bin saved a wage," he reasoned.

"The job justifies the *man* Billy." Jephcott yawned tiredly. "Get it right."

"That lad's sole breadwinner!"

Jephcott stood, a sure sign talk was over: "Ten days is ten days. And keep that woman off the site."

Billy paused the merest fraction weighing things up but a look at Jephcott's face decided it for him. He turned and left.

As soon as his day's work was finished, Billy summoned his courage, walked to The Hexham and knocked on the door. Though acutely uncomfortable about what he was doing sincerity strengthened him and standing before Ceci with arms at his side, he spoke:

"It pains me to see you struggle."

Ceci waited.

"I'd like to—make things easier for you."

She looked up into his eyes ready to distrust him, yet curious for his meaning.

"You're a independent, not to say, proud woman. You could share me wage."

What was he saying?

"I'm proposin' to you," he said, clarifying the issue. At that, Annie's words suddenly slipped into place! So this was the man the women had set up to propose to her and then swindle her out of her pub! No wonder he'd been so nice! She felt so let down, so shocked, so angry she could hardly speak and had to struggle for breath. That *this man*, whom she had, she must admit, actually *liked*, had been stringing her along and that she'd fallen for it was totally unacceptable!

"How *dare* you!" she cried out.

Surprise on his honest face, Billy moved his head uncertainly.

"If there was *one person* I would not have looked to for a trick like that!"

He frowned. This was getting out of hand.

"I thought you were *sincere!*" she burst out, stunned by his reversal and even more livid at herself for fulfilling Reg's words.

"I never *never* would have thought it was you!"

Billy picked at his ear:

"What?"

"Even when *nobody* comes here," she pleaded, "the boy upstairs sick and me scratching up roots to feed us—Even *now*—they'd do this to me?"

By now Billy was badly lost. She seemed to be a hysterical, unreasoned woman, which he hadn't suspected.

"What do *you* want with this place?"

Did she think he was marrying her for this pile of tin and timber?

"Get out! *Out!*"

Quickly he turned and left. Her heart thundering, Ceci became aware of William behind her in pyjamas.

"Somebody set him up to propose to me!" she defended herself. "He's never to come here again! Do you hear?"

Instead of looking glad, William looked angry.

"He got me the brick boy job," he said softly. "And the one below."

Ceci began to look uncomfortable.

"He covers for me. Shifts things I can't lift."

She began to bite her thumb.

"He gave me the advance to buy groceries that first day," William continued softly.

"People who owe him favours keep quiet about me; that's why the mine kept me on."

Ceci began to feel the bottom sinking out of her stomach.

"Everyone trusts him!" William shouted. "Management! The men!"

"So why didn't you tell me before?" she shouted back, injured.

A flash of shame crossed William's face but he converted it to anger.

"What am I to say when I see him tomorrow?" he demanded. "Raving like a lunatic! I heard you!"

"Well you're not entirely blameless yourself are you?" Ceci snapped.

"*I* have to work with him!"

"Really? Have you still got a job?"

They paused, unable to believe they were fighting.

"I'm sorry William," Ceci felt ashamed.

"You've made things very difficult for me," William assured her leaving the room, frowning.

Still feeling ashamed she saw William set out for work insisting he was well enough and that with all the sickness around he'd get someone's job. Hardly had he left when the postman arrived at the door:

"How are you this morning?"

"Terrible."

"Good. Sign here."

Taking the letter in her hands she saw it was from the bank in Christchurch though what *they* could have to say to her she had *no* idea. It was unlikely they'd written to apologize for their previous good advice! She tore open the envelope to find a smaller one inside addressed to her in care of the Bank. "Mrs. C. Laird, care of the Bank of New Zealand, Hereford and Colombo Streets, Christchurch. Please forward," she read. Her fingers trembling, as she slit the envelope, removed and unfolded the single sheet of paper.

Chapter 32

Dearest Ceci,

The letter began. Her heart missed a beat. Quickly she turned to the signature:

"Your loving Vincent (Ginger).

She turned hastily back to the beginning.

> *I am not much for letter writing. Now that I am without Maureen,*

She stopped as if slapped. *"Without* Maureen!" she repeated to herself. Urgently she read on in silence.

> *If you are reading these words as another man's wife, if there are fine things you cannot bear to leave,*

What was he saying?

> *I beg of you to come . . ."*

Reading on, his words spun in her mind:

> *If the bank had given me your address, it would be me, not this letter before you! I sought you for months before thinking of the bank! I never forgot you, my dearest Ceci, my dear, my very dear.*

At that tears began to stream down her face.
From the window, even the view of Grevillton seemed

enchanted. Suddenly the sun broke through the clouds and picked out colours on the stained roof of the corrugated iron shack opposite. She would *leave Grevillton*! It had *all been a mistake*! Just a testing point in her life to see if she'd dared when times were bad! Ginger said he had done well but was prepared to sell up and join her or do anything, do *whatever she wanted*!

The Nolans, Hexham, Moke . . . names which had not been near her mind in many months! Such a great surge of joy rose within her she felt it would bear her away like a wave. *Soon.* That Love she had always felt waiting was rising to meet her!

Arriving home from work, William heard an unaccustomed sound upstairs. *Singing*!?! He looked around the bare room to see what had changed, then, irritated that she could be happy when he was tired, deliberately kicked a chair, making it crash over. Ceci came running down smiling like a young girl. Never had William seen such a smile on her before. It unsettled him.

"What's the matter William?" she said, sounding almost cheeky.

Their poorest of meals passed for her in a state of enchantment. The fact that William had managed to return to work and weather the whole day failed to preoccupy her for more than a few seconds and though she was vaguely conscious of him waving his spoon to illustrate which bord he went up to get to which incline and where it turned left then right, it was only Ginger's voice she could hear.

> *. . . should have known how I felt about you even before . . .*

"Told him to be careful but he said it wasn't dangerous . . ." went on William

> *". . . rattling by on your backside in that cart—"* recalled Ginger making Ceci laugh.

"Point was," William reasoned, "with the coal dust he couldn't *see*."

> *". . . love you as you ought to be loved," said Ginger.*

* * *

Suddenly William looked up to see a delirious smiling Ceci.

"You weren't listening to a word I said!" he exclaimed bitterly.

"William, if I give you this pub," she chirped brightly, "can you manage?"

Riven with jealousy he picked up his bowl and walked from the room.

What happened while he was out? It *had* to be a letter and not from Olwen! There was a *man* in this! Angrily he strode into Ceci's room and began rummaging in the top drawer of her dresser.

Aha! Here it was—crisp and crinkly in his hand! Quickly he slipped it in his pocket and went on to his cubicle with his soup. Downstairs Ceci took her dish to the pump to wash. So William didn't want the pub. It would be a good chance for them both to leave. Of course if he *wanted* to stay on and be a miner... She returned to sit in the rocking chair, convinced that the setting sun was reaching to touch her window sill, that in some ways she would be sad to leave Grevillton and that life had never looked better before when suddenly William appeared in the doorway, judgement on his face.

"Without Maureen," he quoted coldly.

"I beg your pardon!" Ceci gasped.

Between finger and thumb he was holding her letter from Ginger!

"Give that to me!" she jumped up.

"I'm only thinking of your own good," he said, for all the world like a Victorian papa, walking past her with the letter, hanging on to it.

How *dare* he read her letter! Running across she tweaked it from his hands.

"That. Doesn't. Mean. She's. Dead." William said unkindly. "You'd do better apologizing to Billy."

"Don't interfere!" Ceci spat at him.

"I never thought I'd see you running after a married man," William returned.

"I can't wait to go!" Ceci burst out.

William nodded at her and went upstairs. Of course he was *right* she realized in fear! Ginger had not said *anything* about being widowed. And she had *shouted* at

William—been ready to rush off and leave him barely recovered from his illness. But William *had* to be wrong!

After a bad night she sat down to write the letter.

Dear Ginger—Dear Ginger—

she began.

I'm very sorry to hear Maureen—

She stopped and started again.

Where is Maureen?

Looking at the ceiling she managed to express the thought right.

What do you mean—*without Maureen?*

Gradually she became aware of William watching her. "Who is this man?" he demanded.

"Go to work!"

"You're alright here! You've got a place!"

"Do you think I'm just a machine who sleeps and eats?" she asked. "I want a *life!*"

"I do my best," William stammered.

Ceci jumped up.

"Oh William I'm sorry. I didn't mean that. I meant—somebody to want *me*—for *me*."

William's face suggested *he* did, but he said:

"You don't know that this man does!"

Ceci bit her lip and looked down.

"It was that man at the forge, wasn't it?" William asked solemnly. "The one who came running."

Ceci had no answer for that.

"I'm going to work," William said, his words for some reason covering Ceci with shame. Looking at William she realized he wanted to be away from the house and in male company. She sensed he no longer felt jealous towards Billy or guilty about having concealed the help Billy had given them, or even uncomfortable about his duplicity in being friendly with Billy at work but cooler in The Hexham. To William it seemed the more he thought about

Billy, the more he liked him and at that moment having allowed his possessiveness full rein, he was ready to draw it back in again. He was through with wanting Ceci. She could choose whom she desired.

Billy and William passed in a tunnel.

"Mornin' Bill."

"Bill."

There was no denying the atmosphere had cooled since Ceci's outburst. William could feel Billy's hurt. Should he say the woman had gone a little mad lately? Was that what men said he wondered, resenting the upbringing which had made almost a woman of him. Feeling short tempered he began to shovel the loose coal into a wagon but however hard he shovelled the pile got higher and he could not keep up.

"Bloody poetry!" he shouted, kicking the coal face.

Billy glanced up. Looking about he crossed over, took William's shovel off him and in four quick flings made the pile vanish. Wordlessly he leant the shovel on the face, picked up his pick and walked back. William did not reach for his shovel. He kicked the coal face again and wanted to punch it.

"Damn women!" he muttered.

"You be good to them," Billy said sagely.

As the days passed Ceci paced and peered from the window waiting nervously for Ginger's reply. When it finally came she sat in the most private place she could find and opened it.

Returning home that night William found her slumped in a chair—one arm extended, the letter on the floor where she had let it slip. Instantly moved, he knelt to take it. Ceci did not object. Standing by her chair he read that Ginger was "deeply hurt" that she had not trusted him with her address; even *more* deeply hurt that she had felt the need to ask what had become of Maureen. Glancing over at Ceci, William imagined her reading that, being doubly convinced of the man's innocence and bitterly regretting having been so untrusting as to ask. Possibly even resenting his having suggested it. But her eyes were red and she'd been crying. So *obviously* the woman wasn't dead!

"... because you will keep asking until I tell you,"

William read. "Maureen is in an institute for the criminally insane . . ."

William's eyes fleeted quickly over the remainder of the letter.

She had strangled her father who had apparently been teasing her on an old score and had provoked her a word too far.

". . . make any difference to our lives together," William read.

Ceci looked up at him like a small child who had lost everything.

Kneeling he took her in his arms.

"Oh *William!*" she sobbed.

For a moment he held her. Maureen was criminally insane.

That meant they would hang her. If they didn't, they would never let her out.

"Go to him," he said in a gentle voice.

Ceci shook her head.

Not for one moment would she consider William's suggestion.

"How could I go to him without—without—" She could not even bring herself to say it. Had he wanted her merely as a cook or housekeeper, perhaps with her experience of not being touched by Calvin *she* could have managed. But him?

"I have no *right*," she explained. "He's married."

What kind of example would it be to his own children now growing up to see their father being unfaithful with his heart while their mother lay in an institute? The right thing was to write to him, Ceci insisted, and encourage him to be loyal to Maureen: to show his children he respected the woman who had brought them into the world and *was his wife*. Ceci got up and began to pace. She would urge Ginger to hold out to Maureen the hope that one day she could come home, she explained. He and Maureen must both work towards that end and . . . and . . . her voice trailed off.

William watched her cling to this resolution. Nodding to her he left the room.

Should she tell Ginger, Ceci wondered, it would inflame Maureen's pain further were she to come. Briefly she thought of Maureen in "hospital" knowing this fact.

"Though what you are asking I have wanted more than anything in the world," she found herself saying aloud, "this would not be right." She looked around the room. "We must pursue our duty as best we can and thank God the mountains are between us!..." How could they bring their bodies together without consequence, she sighed, once their hearts, that most dangerous part of them, had met? For that matter, how could Ginger have considered exposing his children to the local scandal of having her, in place of his wife, in the house! Was *that* why he had been prepared to move? Poor Maureen! Suddenly her heart went out to her. There must be a design in it, she insisted. The bitterness and the pain of realizing that she and Ginger were not intended for each other, that that was *not* the great Love she had felt creeping up on her was pushed aside in the belief that suffering had a purpose and Hope was merely the engine by which Life was driven. All life was Hope she reasoned, and Hope was a thing of its own, needing no fulfilment. Who would live life if they knew on setting out what lay ahead? Had not Ginger been a form of Hope to brighten Moke and lighten the darkness of Grevillton? That purpose had been served and she was grateful. If that light had gone out another would come in its place and while she would occasionally allow dreams of him like sparrows to flit through her mind in shafts of sun she would not let them settle. With resolution she took her writing tablet and with no thought for herself wrote her reply. From the doorway William observed. Her eyes had returned to normal. Her mouth had set. She had put him behind her.

Her letter finally reached Moke and journeyed up past the green creepers that climbed over the Nolans' battered gate. Sitting on that gate, legs apart and skirt crooked, Faith saw it pass.

"Letter!" she shouted.

Crouched in the bushes waiting to throw stones at passing travellers, twins Michael and Kevin saw it too but weren't interested.

"Geddown off that gate!" shouted Kevin. "You'll gev us away!"

Wise to their tricks, the returning mailman took a swing at the undergrowth with his whip.

"You're not suppose to sit with your legs wide," shouted Michael at Faith.

"And *you're* not suppose to fling stones at horses!" Faith yelled back.

By now Lizabeth was handing the letter to Ginger.

"Get down get down!" Michael shouted at the sound of an approaching horse.

Unfolding the letter at the crumb covered table, Lizabeth saw her father's head sink into his hands.

> . . . *In these circumstances—Much as I love you.*
> *All* . . .

"Will Ceci come?" she asked, knowing the answer. Ginger shook his head.

Rising he went out to his horse and began to fumble in the pannier. There was no good thinking about it. Part of him had known she would not come. It was just as if the axe he had been expecting to fall had finally fallen. All the same he wanted to go away and cry. "Daddy! Daddy!" called Myra, trundling towards the shape she loved, pulling at his jacket and wiping toffee over the hem. What a mess the child was!

"Wash her would you Lizabeth?" he asked dryly. "This is lunch."

Coming to take Myra—Lizabeth believed he would not cry for Ceci again.

Down at the gate Kevin reached his arm out of the undergrowth and pitched a stone at the approaching horse which was now close by. It gave a little hicuppy leap making Faith grin. The man fell forward, steadied his horse as they usually did and glanced backward to see what it had trod on. Then he rode right up to Faith and stopped before her, making her go quite purple. His head was actually on a level with hers and he was staring straight into her eyes. Was he going to blame her for making the horse jump?

"Nolans?" he asked.

She nodded. So now he was going to report them! As if to make her fear come true he turned into their entrance drive and continued on up towards the house while Kevin and Michael poked their heads above the bushes to stare after him like hares.

Inside, Lizabeth was just about to leave the room with Myra and the food roll when she heard the man knocking and entering the house. She stood by her father who had gone stiff. The instant the man appeared in their living room Ginger knew and before even being told, so did Lizabeth. Quickly she ushered Myra into the kitchen and stood holding her.

The stranger looked at Ginger.

"Wrists," he said. "Yesterday."

Ginger covered his face. The waiting was over.

Maureen was dead!

Maureen! Maureen! In a silent scream he saw her mouth working, the scream echoing all over her face! Maureen crossing to Old Nolan, who finally realized he'd gone too far but could now only hang on to the arms of his chair and try to outstare her. Maureen bringing both arms down from a great height and gripping him by the throat, her own face screwing in the effort, eyes on the ceiling, squeezing squeezing away and Old Nolan's arms picking uselessly at the air, his face pinkening, his eyes beginning to bulge...

Two men came with Ginger to the small room and there, spread-eagled on the bloodied floor was Maureen.

"Best to see yourself."

Thrown forward yet recoiling, Ginger grasped at Maureen's hips, her shoulders, lifted her to him. She was quite stiff. His tears fell on to her and with them his sense of guilt for having abandoned her in her neediest hour.

"You could've cleaned her up," he said bitterly, blaming the men.

"Waiting for the coroner," one grunted.

"Some folk think we do 'em in," murmured the other.

Into his guilt came the voice of Ceci whom, *even while Maureen was suffering*, he had told he wanted more than anyone in the world! "Not any woman Ceci but *you*," he had said. "Must have you by my side..." Even while Maureen was cutting her wrists he had been reading Ceci's words: "Don't throw Maureen from your mind like an old shoe! Ginger I thought better of you!" *Even while she lay dead* Ceci was forbidding him to say he had nothing to lose for he had the respect of his children for the woman who was, who *still* was his wife! "Respect, support and comfort her," she had said.

He became conscious of the two men trying to pull him to his feet:

"Poor woman," he murmured now feeling genuine grief. "Poor dear dear woman."

Chapter 33

In Grevillton the rain had stopped. Walking, shopping bag in hand, Ceci saw the only other person in the street coming her way. It was Billy, keeping to the far side of the street, looking equally uncomfortable. She felt ashamed. Looking up she thought to apologize but he was looking down as he passed her. Quickly she dropped her head. Too late he looked up and seeing her looking down, frowned and passed on leaving her humbled. Although she had already bought the few things she could afford she did not feel like going home for the pub was lifeless and William, who had recently been so kind to her, at work. She wandered the short muddy streets of Grevillton, slowly ascending the hill through shanties which led to the very poorest of shacks. Surely here the people were worse off than she, she reasoned. Like her they had no family to turn to. In Grevillton the entire generation of grandparents were missing for none had emigrated. Without realizing it she walked past Marie's house—indistinguishable from the others—and out of the corner of her eye saw a man, toes poking through his socks, standing in the slime of the street. She didn't turn to stare. "Give me me *boots!*" she heard him growl towards one of the shacks. As Ceci moved between two shacks, stepping on stones to avoid the running slime she heard Marie's raised voice:

"So where're you meeting?" Peeping back around the corner she saw Marie standing where their door let out on to the earth, a pair of battered boots in her hand, glaring at Jonas who was making ready to walk away without them. He pulled out both trouser pockets as if to prove having no money on him merited the return of the boots. Quickly Ceci hurried on. One thing was for sure: they weren't meeting at her pub!

Marie thought otherwise. Being without coin had never stopped Jonas before! As he walked off in his stockinged feet she hurried after him and wrenched his shoulder around.

"And cut that tongue of yourn out too!" she said, knowing its borrowing powers. "Yon pub woman—"

"You're unfair Marie," Jonas interrupted, a solemn look on his face. "When her boy was sick she put in for his job at the pit."

Amazed, Marie's arms fell to her side.

"I have to admire that," she admitted, then quickly added. "But don't tell her I said so!"

Jonas gave her a solid look. He'd known that remark would be worth a few pence and had been saving it for a better occasion! To use it to retrieve his boots seemed somewhat wasteful. He observed Marie standing nodding, the wind knocked from her sails. He began to walk on.

"Hey!" she shouted, pitching his boots after him so that they landed short of him in the mud.

"We're not meeting at her place," he said, no longer in the mood for baiting.

"Can if you like!" she shouted, reconciliation springing to her face. Jonas pushed his muddy feet into his boots. A lot of good meeting in a pub when they'd nowt between 'em to spend!

As the hooter started to blow, blackened men began to flow from the tunnel entrances, brick kilns, coke ovens, stepping over the rails and heading for the gate. On a bend in a gloomy mine tunnel, wagon trucks were shunted together, a tangle of wire coming from under them. Their couplings rubbed. The boots of the men treading past them on the incline echoed. As the last man vanished around the bend, Billy glared up the darkened tunnel. Was the boy *still* there? Yes. William was daydreaming or moping, standing lost in thought on the abandoned wagon track.

"Bill?" he called. There was no reply.

"Time!" he shouted. Still the boy ignored him. Leaning his pick on the coal face Billy began to walk up the track towards William, keeping to the left side of the rails. Around the bend the front wagon of three moved slightly, the two behind following and giving it a light thud. It jumped, slowed, then took off on the rails making a rocketing noise, gathering speed and heading for the bend. It tilted, didn't jump the rail but continued on, vanishing from view.

Almost up by William, Bill stopped to listen. What was that? Suddenly the truck careened into view.

"Mind!" he shouted. "Look out!" But William just stood—lost in his own world—the truck booming towards and almost on top of him. Billy flung himself at the boy, soaring in the face of the wagon, his head catching William in the back, sending him like a rocket to smash on the coal wall. Stumbling, half turned by a glancing blow from the truck Billy regained his feet, staggered backwards and struggled well out of its way. For a moment his body had seemed to bend over the truck as it hurtled past. How it had missed him, other than to turn him around, he did not know. As the truck raced on he fell again, and getting to his feet heard it come to a stop further down, where a line of wagons waited. He did not hear the soft cushioning sound as an object attached to the arriving wagon softened the impact. Nor did he miss his arm, snapped clean off at the shoulder joint and hanging, caught by the sleeve, to the wagon's front.

In shock, Billy got up, head spinning. William, he saw, was lying at the foot of the coal face, unmoving.

"William—" he called, shaking him. "William—" Struggling in the poor light he managed to pick the boy up, heave him over his shoulder and keeping a grip on his legs with his right arm follow the route he knew so well down the tunnel and out at the mouth, aware only of a pain in his head and the urgent need to get the unconscious boy home in the shortest time possible. Why he found the journey so difficult he could not understand for the boy, despite being unconscious, seemed to keep slipping off his shoulder.

Reaching The Hexham he struggled in, blood and dust clinging to him. He lowered William on to the table.

"Oh my god!" shouted Ceci, running forward, clinging to Billy's right side, thinking William was dead.

"What happened?" she begged.

"Argument with a truck," Billy murmured, swaying slightly and crossing to flop in a chair. Surprised at his casual manner Ceci glanced quickly at him then back to William on the table. Then suddenly she spun to face Billy. *What had she seen!?* Her mouth fell open. On his left side an arm was completely missing and he *didn't even know it*! She covered her face. Glancing up Billy saw she had almost fainted and got to his feet.

"No I'm alright," she stammered, holding an arm out to stop him approaching. "Stay there." She began to back away as Billy one arm extended but obviously thinking both were out, advanced.

"Don't worry," he said, assuming her concern was for William, "I wouldn't let your son die!"

Gripping her face she stood, ready to speak about anything but his arm. "He—he's not my son!" she stammered. Had she really been so awful to the poor man when he'd even thought she was an unmarried mother?

"You're the finest woman I know," Billy returned quietly. As he looked at her he became aware of something strange in the way she was looking at him. "Can I pass you something?" he asked, looking at the grate, for her wobbling head gave the impression she wanted something from there.

"Oh," he said leaning towards the small brush lying near his feet. In a dream Ceci watched him bend forward as if his arm were there, his shoulder joint pointing, grasping towards the brush. She could not take her eyes off him.

"Where's the damn thing," he muttered, still fumbling—but the brush didn't come any closer and no arm appeared in his field of vision. In horror he looked at Ceci and saw on her face the truth of his situation. Slowly, without taking his eyes off her, he let his right hand come up and around and find the space. His fingers closed over it. Breathing in, he rose and walked past Ceci to the door and out of it into the street.

"Billy!" she shouted, running after him. "Oh my

God! Billy, Billy." In the dark there was no sign of him. Apart from the lights of a visitor two doors down in Jeannie's house, the street was bare. Becoming accustomed to the gloom she made out a shape on the ground a few feet away and running to it found Billy had collapsed.

"Billy!" she gasped, bending over him, struggling to get him on his feet, smearing her dress with blood and coal. She looked desperately about and realizing the pointlessness of her activity ran quickly to the house with lights and hammered on the door. Within, Jeannie and Marie sorting through charity clothes heard the anguished knocking and rushed quickly to the door.

"For God's sake get a doctor!" Ceci screamed, pointing behind her at Billy.

"Move!" Marie pushed Ceci aside.

"My fault! All my fault!" Ceci moaned, sliding down the wall of the house.

"Get inside you!" she heard Jeannie shout at some children. "You. Run for Doctor Murdoch!" Through a daze she saw two men carrying Billy into Jeannie's house and felt Marie pulling her to her feet, a tenderness in her voice, though her words were brutal:

"Have I t'be slapping you for hysteria?" she demanded.

"William got in an accident and Billy—" Ceci prattled uncontrollably.

"So you're sitting in the street?" Marie asked, shaking her.

Quickly Ceci came to her senses as the women's eyes met.

"Thank you," she said humbly, a hand brushing her face.

"Get in and look after William," Marie nodded pushing her towards The Hexham.

Entering the pub Ceci found William in a chair, confused, and doubly so to see her with blood and coal on her skirt, her voice sounding so strange.

"What was I doing on the table?" he asked weakly.

"Billy brought you."

William thought about this for a moment then said he would see Billy and sort it out tomorrow. But Ceci shook her head, eyes moist:

"I think, I think—" she stammered. "He won't *be* there tomorrow."

In the half light of early morning Ceci made her way towards the mine as the first few men were trickling in, beginning to arrive. Quickly she hurried forward:

"Excuse me, where does Billy live?" she asked.

"What for?" they grinned, rudely.

"Where does he *live*," she insisted. "I *must* see him *now*."

"Single men's. Unit J." They shrugged, motioning with their heads in the direction of a wooden barracks-style building.

Ceci ran quickly across, tapped on door J and waited but there was no reply. Stepping sideways she took the liberty of peering through the window into the small spartan room. There, on an upright chair, sitting exactly the way Old Bowen used to sit was Billy, facing away from her and towards the wall. His shoulder was swathed in bandages.

"Billy!" she called, tapping on the window and seeing him ignore it. She rattled the door. "Open the door!"

Gradually her hand fell to her side as she realized the hopelessness of the task. Sorrowfully she stepped off the wooden platform and began to walk back across the site, vaguely conscious of the door of the Administration Hut opening and Jephcott, followed by a hungry looking man in his thirties, swag in hand, coming down the steps and heading across the tangle of rails towards the Single Men's Quarters.

Out of the corner of her eye she saw Jonas and some of the other men bunched by the brick kiln, peering after Jephcott and turning noted that the swagman was waiting by the verandah while Jephcott rapped sharply on the door of Unit J.

"You in there! This isn't an old men's home!" she heard him shout.

Lingering for a moment she saw five of the six doors burst open and worried single men fastening braces, dragging lamps and shooting guilty glances at Jephcott, stream out to the sound of doors slamming. Then silence. Jephcott hammered on Billy's door again.

From the bridge Ceci paused to look back. The row of units was silent and Jephcott was turning angrily from Billy's closed door and leaving. Still waiting the swagman hesitated, then followed Jephcott back across the rails.

Unable to bear more Ceci quickly began to cross the bridge while behind her Jonas, still watching, saw Billy's door open quietly and Billy step out with a bundle. He closed the door and hurried, head bent, along the verandah to step off the end and run behind the building. Jonas covered his face with his hands.

Stepping off the bridge, Ceci headed up river—away from Grevillton. The muddy brown water crashed by below, the last few trees from a storm moving in it. Slowly, very slowly she moved along half aware of a movement on the other bank quickening and passing her. Glancing over she saw heading into the wind—Billy!

"Billy!" she shouted and began to run parallel but he did not hear. Quickly she doubled back, running for all she was worth for the bridge.

Bump! Bump! went the bridge as she ran over it. She turned away from the mine and towards the hill, breathlessly hurrying. Now she did not call. Billy was walking fast. Slowly she gained on him but the closer she got the more she slowed 'til suddenly, as if sensing her, he turned. Then she stopped completely. He waited.

"Is it because of my arm?" he said gravely. "You can do without a one arm man."

"Don't leave, Billy," Ceci began.

"Only know the mine," he said. "Coal mining. Coal's me life."

Suddenly Ceci felt terribly awkward and shy.

"When you asked me to marry you Billy," she began, wanting to tell him she had misunderstand but he interrupted.

"Don't need to lumber yourself with me now girl."

"I'd consider it a privilege."

"And the boy'd support us both?" He shook his head at her.

"*I'll* do something."

Filled with an energy she did not understand she reached for both his hands finding only one.

"I'll open a laundry. Water's free! Those miner's clothes . . ."

"Filthy as they are," Billy interrupted, "no miner's wife could afford the pittance. And the single men hang 'em out."

"Then I'll skivvy for management," she said earnestly.

A change came over Billy.

"No wife of mine'll set foot over that step!" he growled, surprising her with the depth of his emotion.

"We could do something *together* Billy," she said more quietly.

Billy put his hand on her shoulder.

"Who can afford anything here?" he asked gently. A strange feeling came over her. Something was happening. Billy looked at her hard.

"You are exactly as I imagined," he said truthfully.

Suddenly she felt as if she were trembling from the inside out. Who was this man? He was putting his hand on her shoulder and turning her back towards Grevillton, beginning to walk with her.

"I—I didn't mean to intrude," she began, desperate for something to say.

"You're right for me," he replied.

The sudden realization that this was *true* hit very hard. Ceci gasped. *This* was it. This was the *love* she had been waiting for. She had not seen it creeping up on her but it had *arrived*! The colour drained from her cheeks as she suddenly recognized in Billy the man she would marry.

Waiting to close the lych gate, Ginger saw his five children pass through. All were dressed in what passed for black; all had been crying. He took a last glance at the tiny corner of Moke's cemetery reserved for the Catholics, at the tall stones of the neighbouring graves beyond the hedge. His Maureen would be remembered by a white angle, waving what looked like a wet piece of tissue at the grander Protestant graves beyond. When all was said and done it was as well it wasn't properly consecrated land for had it been she could not have been buried there.

As they reached home, Edna came to the door, her face as flat as the sandwiches which awaited them. Though she had not attended the funeral she too had been crying. It had been a sad business about Maureen.

As Ginger and the children moved about the room they did it as strangers. Edna poured their tea. They didn't sit. Ginger nibbled at a sandwich. Edna had a feeling he was going to say something.

"I'll go and get her then, shall I?" he asked brightly,

as if clipping cheer from his voice. Or had she imagined it?

"Yes." Lizabeth nodded.

Gradually Edna became a deep angry red. She could not believe her ears and would have spoken out but for the children's faces, each saying this was what they too wanted. She saw Ginger put his cup down and move slowly towards the door. Although the children followed him outside, Edna didn't.

As they watched him fling his water canteen and blanket over the saddle, little Myra called out:

"How will Ceci ride back?"

Ginger reached down and chucked her under the chin.

"Like a lady!" he grinned, giving a broad loving smile. But as he rode past the windows he felt Edna's eyes, so similar to Maureen's, tearing him apart.

As her wedding day approached, Ceci began to have feelings she could not come to terms with. There was definitely a hesitance. Billy had said they were right for each other and she had believed, *did* believe him. Yet . . . Was it her fear of being a public spectacle at the wedding or the thought of walking down an aisle with everyone's eyes on her that made her tremble? All these things seemed "natural" when they happened to others but for them to happen to *her* was alarming.

The day which should have been longed for, when it came, seemed dreaded. As the miners' wives crowded into the small room she had so recently shared with Annie and sat on her bed, pinning and altering a crumpled silk dress which had yellowed, she stood frozen with self-consciousness before them.

"Heaps too big dear! Give me a pin," said Marie, pulling at the dress.

"That Marjory. Big as a pig!"

Apparently it was the dress's fifth turn. Pins in her mouth, Marie joked while Dot, threading a needle, told Peg to stop trying to find somewhere to use a faded silk rose she had brought out from England.

"Put it here?" Peg asked Ena.

"Oh throw it *away*!" shouted Marie. "T'was off yer mother's hat!" She snatched it and threw it on the bed, glancing at Ena who was quietly threading closed white cotton buds on to a tiny wreath to fix in Ceci's veil.

"Look sharp Ena!" she said.

William put his head in.

"Now William you sleep downstairs tonight," Marie said firmly.

Ceci went purple and William withdrew.

"Must get up off these knees," gasped Marie, dropping abruptly on the bed which creaked loudly. "Will you listen to that!" she grinned. Ceci flushed again.

"Now get along!" said Marie, putting an arm around her. "You're one of us now. Isn't that grand? A miner's wife!"

"You make it sound like I'm finally a member of the human race!" Ceci said, aware of their acceptance, pleased by this ultimate accolade, yet hearing her very voice and words distinguish her from them. Twisting the rose, Peg glanced from the window:

"Will you look at that mud!"

"Give her a bandy-chair!"

She rolled her eyes. To be dropped in the mud of Grevillton in borrowed finery when all she wanted was for the day to be over!

"William!" shouted Marie down the stairs. "Get over to Eakin's and borrow his hand-hearse."

A strange procession they made, Marie carrying William's shoes while he struggled through the mud in work boots pushing the small polished cart they had covered with a drape. On the platform struggling to keep balance, knees up under her chin and feeling like a pig being wheeled to market, Ceci glanced nervously at her guard of honour holding the cart upright and keeping level. As the small wooden church lurched into view, the last few miners and their families could be seen outside turning to watch.

Nervously Billy waited in the front row. Next to him stood Jonas, his best man, the two twists of wire which would serve as rings in his hand.

Entering the porch, Ceci clung to William's arm and glanced nervously at the organist who was kicking the pump organ viciously and pulling faces at it. Not a sound was coming out. Suddenly Marie marched at it and gave it such a slap it started terribly loud three bars into "Here

Comes the Bride." A sea of white faces turned to watch Ceci as she hung back petrified, an inexplicable feeling of racing against time possessing her. Though Marie nodded at her *she could not move forward.*

"You were man enough to put in for your boy's job!" Marie whispered. "Now get goin'!" She pushed her from behind.

Suspended in space Ceci moved up the aisle. She heard the words and said the right things in a high voice, Billy replying in his deep firm one, the depth of his commitment palpable in his voice. She felt her hand lifted, held between his thumb and warm palm as with two of his fingers he forced the little twist of wire over hers. The Minister then handed her the other wire and with both hands she slipped it over Billy's finger.

No sooner were the words over than benches were being pushed back as Grevillton prepared to welcome the newlyweds. Turning shyly from the altar Ceci found herself on Billy's right side and felt his arm move across her shoulder in full view of the congregation. At that she knew the man's pride. As the staring faces turned away to the scones and tea, a sense of relief came.

"Flash those about someone'll have them off you!" joked Marie.

People laughed.

"Terrible way to start," murmured Billy looking at the ring.

Ceci disagreed. "I think we've got everything," she said softly. He smiled at her.

"Here," Marie patted a chair, and pulled Ceci down beside her.

It was almost as if, now that she was seated, she had become invisible. She watched Billy cross to thank the Minister and saw people waiting to shake hands with him and deciding which hand to offer.

"Don't we sign some Register thing?" Billy asked.

"He'll be here!" the Minister assured him. "Had two weddings and you can expect him to stop for lunch."

"What if he gets drunk?" asked Billy, his words surprising the Minister.

"Borough Clerks don't get drunk!"

"Scones are running out," Billy observed.

"He'll bring it round to your place before bedtime,"

added the Minister, amused at the layman's reliance on detail.

Billy put his hand in his pocket.

"Well are we married or not?"

"In the eyes of the Church—Yes," he explained pedantically. "And, when you've signed the Register, in the eyes of the State also."

"Now I'd like to say," came the voice of Jonas, "as one of us is about to become Assistant Publican—"

Billy turned, grinning: "Can't open without any beer!" Red faced Marie leapt to her feet to defend herself but was greeted by loud boos. She waved a hanky to exonerate herself.

"We wish you all happy!" shouted Jonas above the uproar. "And welcome Ceci as one of us!"

"One of us!" rang out the voices as tea cups were raised and a still pink Marie shouted: "That's your cue!" at the organist. Quickly the woman gave the organ a kick which sent her tea cup plummetting to the floor and, slowly the waltz came, Billy and Ceci leading shyly into it. Gradually the floor filled up around them, the hard working people of Grevillton putting their bodies into the unaccustomed pose of dancing. Lost in the crowd, Ceci found herself thinking a most peculiar thing. Would Ginger, from the postmarks of her two letters, have gotten any idea of where she was living?

Glad it was over they stood on the porch.

"Will I carry you over?" Billy asked. Ceci quickly scuttled in, immediately aware that someone had been there in their absence for a white bed sheet lay over the table and under it were the obvious bumps of dishes.

"They've set the table!" she exclaimed, peeling back the sheet on eggs, buns and butter!

"Bacon!"

The door shut behind her. She turned. Billy was leaning on it as if it were his house. Suddenly she felt shy, totally trapped in the room.

"Come here wife."

Her voice sounded strange in her throat: "Not till we've signed the Register!" she said with genuine shyness, though it sounded coy. He walked firmly towards her. She took two leaps away from him. He took a step nearer. Suddenly she ran through the inner door. There was silence. Billy stood listening.

Standing behind the kitchen door Ceci was listening too. She heard Billy's steps come out of the bar room and begin to go ever so slowly up the stairs, getting quicker, then running. Biting her lip she stepped to the foot of the stairs and looked up. There was no sign of him. Quickly she jumped back into the bar room again. There, just inside the open door, was Ginger.

Ginger was white, drawn. He could not believe he was seeing her in bridal clothes. Nor that she was actually there, even though the door had not been locked. He looked at her face moving from side to side, the lips touching each other as if she felt she were bewitched or hallucinating. He stepped towards her, took her wrists. At that moment, were he to do anything, she could stop him not. Her emotions, already prepared for giving, overflowed. This was Real. Her breathing came fast, hard. His own mouth moving though words didn't come he touched the veil attached by one corner to her shoulder. His hand strayed to her neck, to the wisps of hair lying there. *This shouldn't be happening*, she told herself! *He wasn't there!* As if to contradict her he moved close, very close so she could feel the disturbed air brushing her face. With pain he whispered:

"Maureen. Is *dead*."

He saw behind her Billy, minus his shoes, collar and jacket, step into the room. His shirt was undone to the waist. Billy saw the younger man holding his wife's wrists. He felt her feeling herself his captive. He moved to stand by the side of them looking anxiously from face to face. Ceci was with difficulty getting her breath, trying to pull her eyes away from Ginger.

"Billy. This is Ginger," she said weakly.

Conscious of the tremendous passion each was restraining he spoke quietly:

"You're a free woman."

Ceci tried to turn to him but her whole body was difficult to move, as if she'd been punched or winded. She saw Billy had turned away. Carefully she disentangled herself from Ginger's grip as if his hands were the manacles she must slip her wrists from. Crossing to Billy she saw he was frightened.

Just as she lifted her hand to touch his shoulder there was a fierce jovial rattling on the door.

"'Allo 'allo!"

With that voice the atmosphere shattered and became something unemotional and mundane. There stood the Borough Clerk and with him the feeling that form-signing was normality and the emotions covered by the forms artificial.

"Right then. I've t'be getting home," he said, slamming the Register book on the table, the certificate already made out. Drained, Billy said to Ceci in a voice which was exhausted:

"We're not married yet."

"In the eyes of your friends we are," she said in an equally weak voice.

Ginger stared across at them, not hearing. Suddenly he became aware of the significance of the Borough Clerk who had brought the Register.

"Haven't they signed yet?" he asked, the Clerk mistaking the desperation in his voice for officiousness.

"You the witness, eh?" he asked.

Ceci saw Billy's face tremble. Facing the mantelpiece in a deep personal agony for the first time in his life he was frightened and afraid to find himself so. Pulling herself away she crossed to the table and reached for the pen, feeling Ginger's hand trying to stay hers. Unable to help herself she looked up, Ginger reading the look to mean "I will always love you." But before he was certain, she had bent her head and was signing the Register.

"Billy—?"

He heard her voice. With dread on his face he turned slowly and saw her, one hand on the book, holding out the pen to him.

How she hated to see the great man humbled as he crossed to the table. She could not look at Ginger. She straightened out, held her hands together in front of her. Suddenly Billy came right. He put his arm around her shoulders and gave them a mighty squeeze. Ginger saw Ceci hang her face and caught a tear flashing past her hair to fly into her bodice. In a trance he saw Billy sign then look up, a new baptism on his face. The pen lay on the table. The Borough Clerk picked it up and held it out to Ginger. Ginger heard him say:

"You may kiss your wife."

With fierce love in his eyes, Billy turned Ceci towards him so their bodies were facing on and held her to him. He could not tilt up her chin as she burrowed her face in his chest but he knew she was crying. Over her shoulder he saw Ginger hurry from the room. Feeling her sadness and the reason for it Billy spoke tenderly:

"We've a hard climb ahead," he began.

Ceci's voice, when it came was no more than a birdlike whisper.

"I'm ready."

Even as she spoke Ginger was riding his horse hard out of town, turning on to the trail. The further he got the slower he rode. He rode slowly and more slowly until he was hardly moving at all. One word kept repeating itself to him:

Away—away—*Away*!

Chapter 34

That Billy was a good man there was no doubt but what Ceci had not envisaged was the extent to which he would miss the mine. He could not shake the idea that a man belonged there in the daylight hours and that any other work was "woman's work." Even the total commitment he expected from a wife came as a surprise and as she became conscious of him expecting her to hold in abeyance certain abilities, even to present ideas in such a way that they seemed to emanate from him, she began to wonder. Was *this* the Great Love she had been waiting for? It seemed as a woman she was a different being from a man for Billy and William talked in a way forbidden to her and their comradeship which respected each other's boundaries did not include her. In this, though, there was some relief for she found herself unembarrassed living with Billy in front of William. It was a fact they dismissed almost as if its existence were unknown.

The problem of survival loomed large as ever and to the extent she was allowed to help. Ceci decided on fish. By trial and error she constructed a trap from two old wicker baskets, the one inside the other with its base holed. Sure enough, when placed in the current fish were forced through to the second basket and found themselves unable to return past the inward pointing spikes. Not a little pleased with herself, she would sell these fish, barter them for other supplies and, if there were enough, save some to eat.

As day began, Billy would loosen his arm from her, steal silently from the pub and creep to the river bank where as the light cleared he would kneel, sink his arm into the cold water and draw out the fish trap. The sound of the fish wriggling, breaking the water, was the first good sound of the day apart, of course, from Ceci's breathing as she stirred in his arms. To get back home before the rush of miners was his first aim. Should he oversleep and see them on the track above he would freeze instantly and they, in kindness, would not look down. Returning home through the backways, he would leave the fish in a tub of water in the yard for Ceci to deal with. Then, after a breakfast of bread if William was in work, Billy would wander the hills round the mine gathering wood for their own use and for sale. Being alone all day did not agree with him, his mind always swinging back to the mine and the men that worked there, calling, shouting to each other, winning the coal. To watch William hosing off at night was more than he could bear. With pain he would watch the boy come in, his very dirt proclaiming him a man, stride gainfully across the room and—leaving the door open—wash in the yard. Even as Billy turned from the yard other miners would be passing the door on their way home and as he turned back to the yard he would see William in singlet, lathering up with crude soap, the coal falling off him in rivers. Outside girls would blush when William passed and he could afford not to notice. This was a man; this was how a man should be! He studied the expression on William's face as he washed, knowing it showed the passing of the day's events below; the things that had happened; who had got into trouble with the foreman and what trouble was expected the next day. He neither grudged nor envied William his life but ached constantly for the world of man's work, of work talked about and work done.

As he wandered alone in the woods many thoughts troubled Billy. How much of this Manhood, the qualities people respected him for, had been to do with the fact of his work? Was the loss of his arm undermining his sense of self? In the silence of the woods as he moved amongst the trees looking for likely ones, he grew dejected. Hopelessness assailed him as he hoisted a fallen trunk on his shoulder, laid it by his pile and set off looking for more. Although sweat streamed from him it was with a heavy fatigue he knocked beetles from the dead wood, flicked them from his collar or out of his pants and told himself he was not a man. Wiping the dirt from his face he would rest, afraid to be seen by the occasional woman searching for berries. Some passed quite close to him without noticing and he would never call out. They moved on, bending, stooping, frowning earnestly in their never ending search for food . . . He should be down the mine, Billy told himself, not in a place women were sent berrying. Sitting, he would fix a stick to the end of his rope and when they had gone, send it flying into the air trying to lift his spirit with it as it soared, curled and descended over a branch. Quickly he would wrap the rope round on itself, give a hard tug and stand back. Crash! Down would come the branch, sundered from the tree, smashing into the undergrowth where so recently the woman had been berrying. Bending he would take it, lean it against the tree trunk and smash it to pieces with his foot. As the day wore on he would secure his wood pile with his rope, hoist it on his head and return home well before mine shifts changed. Hurrying back with one ear listening for the hooter, he kept the mine always in sight. The path only had to come out on to a bluff and he would be overlooking it, hearing its clanking and clanging sounds borne up to him on the still afternoon air.

Daily William grew stronger, feeding on energy he had previously spent on Ceci and the silent example of Billy. While Talbot and Neill told boys' jokes and made out they were real lads on the side, it was William who was respected amongst the men; William who showed the courage.

"Go on then, know-all!" Neill would heckle.

"Give us the shot then," William replied calmly.

Nobody liked placing shots. It was dangerous and the method they used was "up to them." Carefully William would poke out a hole, measure it with his finger and slip in the shot then start scuffing coal dust together with his boots.

"Get me some clay."

"In't none."

Though it was safer with clay, if there were none to be had, they made do with whatever was to hand.

"I'll do without!" replied William, packing dust previously dampened with urine around the shot.

"That's dangerous Bill."

"Said you could stand back!" Slowly William would light the fuse, then run.

Crack! Flash! Crumble!

"You can come out now," he would say into the cloud of dust as the coughing men got to their feet. "See!"

It did not take any longer for William to discover he could turn a dangerously placed shot into the price of a loaf than it took Talbot and Neill to discover they could win it back off him at cards! And the deeper William got into betting, the more dangerous shots he found himself placing.

He took to staying away from the pub more and more and while Ceci could not understand this she did not like to enquire whether he was on shift or passing time in the Single Men's Barracks. She was conscious that he owed nothing and occasionally put money on the table but his black moods, like those that came over Billy, puzzled her. Daily she watched Billy's resentment of the Mine Manager, Jephcott, grow and gradually learned it was not because he had been paid no compensation on the grounds the accident had taken place after the hooter had gone, but because Jephcott had come to his hut and banged on the door in front of all the men. At the time he had lost his manhood he had been publicly thrown out.

Alone in the street Ceci stared at her basket of fish. The store refused to trade. William had left no money on the table. The cupboard was virtually bare and the firewood lay unsold. She had spent the morning moving from one pathetic shanty to another, worried women coming out, bending anxiously over her basket sucking their fingers, their thin children pointing at the smallest fish as their mothers shook their heads. Ultimately she had started giving the small fish away, keeping the two large ones till last. Knocking on Doctor Murdoch's door she held out the second largest fish, smiling. "Go on with you!" said Mrs. Murdoch appearing. "Billy's arm's long done with and did he not amputate it himself? Five minutes stitchés and some cleaning?"

Ceci had repeatedly tried to give them fish as they wouldn't take money. Over her shoulder she saw a miner's wife pushing her four children ahead of her through the gate each one carrying a bucket of stolen coal.

"Very well. Thank you—" said Mrs. Murdoch sighing and taking the fish.

Left with one fish she looked up at the sky. It was noon. Soon the fish would go off. There was only one house she had never approached. It lay just beyond Grevillton and was the only permanent structure with a decent fence. It was a house nobody visited and if anyone saw her go there she would be in trouble. Walking a few paces towards it she looked over her shoulder. Even Mrs. Murdoch had gone inside. Quickly continuing on round the bend she hurried to the house, opened the gate and walked guiltily up the path and knocked on the door. Behind it a big dog started barking and suddenly the door opened and a woman looked out.

"Would you be interested in fresh fish?" Ceci asked seeing the woman was worried at being approached.

"I haven't seen you before," she said, the touch of fear in her voice plain. No wonder! As if Ceci would have dared to visit the Jephcotts' house!

"I—I usually don't get past the village," she stammered. Mrs. Jephcott prodded at the fish as if hoping to prove it was off.

"It'd do good roasted with a sprig of rosemary," Ceci began. Mrs. Jephcott sniffed, her tongue visiting the corners of her mouth.

"Or in cider with apple bits." Looking up, Ceci saw the woman falling.

"Now if you could get your hands on some root ginger—"

Suddenly Mrs. Jephcott looked at her with piercing eyes.

"Why don't you come in and cook it for me?" she asked. "George!"

To Ceci's utter horror, Mr. Jephcott, home from the mine for lunch, appeared behind her wiping his mouth and glaring at Ceci whom he found suddenly looking down.

"Whitebait season yet girl?" he demanded.

"Give me the money George!" snapped his wife.

Ceci stood, unwilling to lift her eyes from the ground. She heard change jingled in Jephcott's pocket and the voice of Mrs. Jephcott murmuring:

"Whitebait are the *tiniest* things George!"

The next minute the money was in her hand and she turned to the gate.

"Harder to tamper with," she heard Jephcott say as their door closed behind her.

So he was aware of the depth of animosity felt towards him she realized, thankful he hadn't recognized her. Had he thought she was the wife of some laid off miner who fished...? Or a casual tradesperson...?

In the dining room Jephcott was saying:

"I just can't—quite—place—If she comes here again get her name."

Mrs. Jephcott wiped her forehead. The man was utterly paranoid.

"They can't all be miner's wives," she said patiently.

"How do you know?" he snapped back.

Mrs. Jephcott began to gather up the dishes.

"Because that girl's seen other things," she assured him. "It's in her bearing. The way she carries herself."

Ceci looked at the money in her hand. A tidy sum. As the sole fish merchant in town, it seemed she could set her rates. Rinsing her basket in the river she crouched and looked across at the mine, thinking. The "Mending Taken" and "Firewood" signs had been in her window so long a casual visitor would never take the place for a pub! Let Billy afford the luxury of avoiding the Jephcotts if he liked she decided, rising. She could not! There had to be food on the table and she would put it there. If it was the last thing she did she would make fish eaters out of the Jephcotts! Why, with an income she could build up supplies in the kitchen cupboard and perhaps even on a fish diet Mr. Jephcott would be less choleric towards the workers. Furthermore, could it not be said she was the only one in Grevillton who was getting something out of the man? She looked at the coin in her hand. The woman had not asked for change and had paid a very generous price. Ceci felt vaguely guilty looking at the few women before her in the store counting their pennies but quickly reminded herself she was also the only adult in Grevillton who did not seethe with anger at the very sight of Jephcott. To her he was no more than a man, perhaps a silly one at that. Yet still she felt guilty pointing at things on the shelf and buying them.

Hurrying up the street the basket on her arm felt heavy and as the clink of Billy's axe grew louder, she became nervous. Pushing open the gate she found him expertly balancing and splicing kindling which she must later bind and add to the mounting pile of unsold bundles. She had thought to go in through the front door and pass straight into the kitchen but perhaps it was better not to depart from the normal procedure. Lightly she pushed open the yard gate, positioning the loaf and vegetables under her arm to partially cover the variety of goods in the basket but Billy did not look up. It was almost as if he knew.

"So who bought the big one?" he said.

"I gave it to the Doctor—" she lied, going red.

"So you gave the medium big and the big one to him?"

"Yes." Ceci held on to the lie. Suddenly Billy looked up:

"So you sold all the little 'uns?"

"The rest is on credit. Billy, if we *burned* that wood we could sell cooking charcoal," she said, desperate to change the subject.

"When coal's free?" he said directly at her.

She passed on into the kitchen before he should see into the basket. But the food looked so good in the larder, so *reassuring*.

During tea she casually led Billy out on the subject of whitebait. He said they were small fish like sprats which swarmed at the mouth of the Grey River for ten days to three weeks and were prepared in a simple batter as patties. Whitebait patties were common fare on the West Coast he added and anyone who'd been there could have told her. Considerably excited Ceci begged Billy to make an expedition there with her, the idea of a day at the coast in itself enchanting. Billy chewed on his finger thinking.

They would have to jump a coal barge going down river he said, clearly not averse to the idea though he frowned hard when William looked up at him. Withdrawing from the conversation Ceci paid scant attention to them till she became aware of a row developing. William it seemed was recounting an incident involving Jonas whose pony had apparently refused to enter a tunnel that morning. He was displeased when Billy interrupted to inform him that ponies knew when there was gas. He stopped talking abruptly. Billy filled the void by blaming worn out brattice screens for allowing gas to accumulate in tunnels and when he finished talking William flatly insisted it had nothing to do with brattice screens. This brought them to the awkward point that William worked in the mine and Billy didn't. Quickly Ceci intervened, swinging the account round to a more personal level and encouraging William to give what must have been a very good rendition of Jonas and Jephcott confronting each other for Billy soon forgot his humiliation and returned to the more familiar theme of Jephcott's villainy and corrupt practices in the mine.

"What bothered Jonas," William explained, "was the last thing he'd given her was a good thrashing to *make* her go in. He tied her and when he came back, she was dead."

As the pony had been "his" he'd asked permission to bury her but Jephcott, sensing he was being told his job, had directed Jonas to take the beast straight to the local butchers on "his" account at which, as Ceci could have forecast, Jonas began to walk out of the tunnel. Jephcott shouted him back, threatened to charge him for the loss of the beast, humiliated him before the men, refused to allow them to remove the pony and made Jonas personally cart it to the butchers. The tale left a bad atmosphere at the table. Billy immediately returned to sulking about Jephcott having no right to put the carcass "to his account" when the beast was mine property, Ceci aching for both Jonas and the pony and William feeling he should have asserted himself somehow more in the incident.

Clearing the table Ceci asked herself if she had done wrong in dealing with Jephcott for the more she heard about the man the less she liked him. Yet Billy and William had eaten the food and surely Annie would have even *slept* with Jephcott to feed *her* family . . . As she went upstairs to prepare their bed her conscience bothered her.

One the other side of town Jonas's family were still waiting to eat for Marie had a surprise. Coming in, she held dinner high above her head. "Meat!" she announced. A sigh went up as the children ran forward expectantly realizing the smell they had thought belonged to a lucky neighbour was indeed for them! Suddenly Jonas got to his feet, face white with anger.

"For God's sake I didn't steal it!" shouted Marie backing off frightened as Jonas snatched the scrawny leg of meat clean off the plate and held it before her.

"It was *cheap*!" she wailed.

Like a madman Jonas ran through Grevillton in his braces, passing Dr. Murdoch's house, his tidy children sitting at their table talking politely. On he ran around the bend till the Jephcott's house came into view.

"I remember where I saw that fish woman!" Jephcott was saying, picking a fishbone from his mouth. At that moment there was a terrible crash of glass breaking in their front room and leaping and stumbling from the table Jephcott and his wife ran in. There on the floor lay a cooked pony shin.

"You can see they're not starving," Jephcott said coldy.

When Jonas got home his hands were still greasy. There was no sign of the children but Marie was red eyed.

"Stupid bloody fool!" she shouted at him. "He'll know it was you! Isn't it enough to starve the children without taking on the man who feeds us?"

In bed Ceci lay with Billy, moving her thumb over the closed pocket of flesh the doctor had sewn.

"Seems to me that Ginger was sweet on you from the word go," Billy murmured. Looking back Ceci could not see what she had ever seen in Ginger beyond perhaps the ghost of an infatuation. It was just a sort of "romance" brought on by isolation...Not the mature feeling of a grown woman.

"I fancied him," she yawned. "But I never did anything."

He pulled her to him.

"Musta felt it—that woman—even though you both behaved proper."

What a good man Billy was, Ceci thought. Here he was worrying about Maureen.

"The fact is, it was probably *that* back of his poor wife's breakdown." Billy frowned squeezing her to him. "You and me," he said, "we ought to have a child."

Ceci smiled. What a beautiful idea and how basically sane! Yet here they were in the depths of poverty, virtually dependent on the river's whims and William's and daily there were rumours the mine was up for sale...The mine! The mine! Even in bed it came between them! Everything in Grevillton came back to the mine! Now she too had been drawn into its world of increasing danger and declining productivity...Into this world, did they both desperately want to bring new life?

Chapter 35

The day for the whitebait expedition came and armed with string, old cloth and buckets Ceci and Billy crept cautiously through the bushes towards a barge tied by the river bank. They could see the man at the front getting ready to loose her and crouching down, waited for a chance to run. Moving forward Billy beckoned to Ceci and slowly, being careful not to bang the buckets, she advanced. As the barge moved gently to and fro, the gap between it and the bank got smaller and larger, smaller and larger.

"Now!" said Billy grasping her wrist but she held back.

"*Now!*" he repeated urgently. Finally she got up the nerve, ran forward and made a jump for it while Billy lifted the tarp for her to scramble under.

Once they knew the barge was under way they took to peeping out at the abundant vegetation along the river bank: so beautiful, green and free. The man at the front whistled and Ceci felt like a runaway urchin as she carefully tucked cloths between the buckets to stop them clanking. So excited was she she could scarce wait for their arrival at the sea.

Finally from sounds on the bank they knew they had reached the terminal yard where, Billy said, coal was unloaded. Ceci listened anxiously as he warned her to expect wagons and a welter of rails and told her to be ready to run to the nearest cover when he gave the sign. Her pulse informed her this was the most exciting thing she'd done since scrumping on the Estate as a child but now an adult, she sincerely hoped she would not be caught!

Flinging the tarp back she ran and in a matter of minutes was leaving the yard on Billy's arm, chin high, as if they had actually had business there. Her pleasure at the sight of the sea was instantaneous and the thoughtful expressions which had occupied her so much of late had blown away. As her eyes tripped from capstan to cloud, from wave top to rock and back again he sensed they too were holidaying.

As she threaded the saplings through the pillow cases and clothes, dexterously fixed them on hoops and fastened twine and sticks to them, her mind turned to Billy. Why had he never married? A big solid man like that, kind and gentle, good with young and old alike. Why everybody had not wanted to marry him she could not imagine. Surely he must have *fought* them off when he was younger. Was there a "situation" there?

Billy watched her bend over the nets then straighten and fling them far out into the water, pulling fast on the string, steering them about with sticks. The girl was so quick and agile! She flashed him a grin. Yet despite the strength which came from her character there was a *slightness* to her, a fragility. He looked at her well-shaped intelligent hands, the sort his own mother had described as "praying hands." Sitting back on her heels she was now leaning away from the water, utterly content. After the Fair Sex of Grevillton, how extraordinary it was to see a woman so completely without the vulgar or the brutal toughness they needed to survive!

"Be nice to get away from the mine altogether," she began. "You're better away from the mine."

"Light hurts me eyes." Billy murmured, coming over to sit beside her. She leaned on him. Suddenly the waters before them were teeming with whitebait, a great white blur so thick it was hard to believe.

"At least we did this right," Billy said, grabbing Ceci round the waist as she nearly went into the river, hooking his foot round the capstan.

With all her might Ceci strove to haul in the catch. Whitebait flopped on to the quay. They were on her skirt, in her shoes, tiny fish, not two inches long. Quickly they shovelled them into buckets.

"How are we going to get them all home without spilling them?" she asked, pulling fish from her bodice.

Billy shaded his eyes as if the light hurt them. Where the sky met sea it was so bright after the shade of the mine hills and more particularly the mine. Suddenly Ceci realized he was sad; that the contrast had served to remind him of where he wanted to be or, more correctly, that she would have to carry *two* buckets home while he carried the one.

When it came time to return they tiptoed into the rail yard and looked about. Although the rail ran as far as the mine on the Grevillton side of the river, it was impossible to tell which wagons would be shunted on to the home rail first for the yardman merely had to switch a point.

"I can't figure it," Billy confessed.

Picking up their buckets they began to walk away from the coast and up the track till they became two small figures vanishing in the vegetation where the track rounded a bend. Just as Ceci was wondering if they would have to walk all the way, they heard an approaching train and backing off, clasping one bucket to her chest and setting the other down, Ceci watched Billy size up the situation and make ready to throw their cloths and sticks into the wagon. As the train came round the bend making slow progress on the gradient Ceci saw to her dismay there were no flat wagons they could simply jump on! All were high slag wagons.

"This or nothing!" Billy shouted to her, running at a wagon, hoisting himself up and over and signing her to quickly pass up the buckets. As the train gathered speed she ran alongside bending, slopping whitebait freely, gasping as they cascaded into her hair and Billy wrenched them off her. Running for the last bucket she caught up with the train and found Billy leaning over, reaching for her. Though afraid to be left behind, she was afraid to leap.

"Give me your wrist!" Billy shouted, lifting her from her feet, virtually hauling her as if winching a body from the sea. Panting, they sat on the floor of the wagon, picking fish, getting their breath back. Grinning, Ceci looked up at the walls of the wagon rising above them, the trees and sky passing overhead and as the chugg chugg of the train filled her ears she had the strangest feeling Billy wanted to make love to her.

Billy looked at her delicately shaped chin, the soft brown almost Irish curls, that vulnerable unhurried grace which had returned and with it the serenity and total lack of vanity he so much loved. As she turned to him, her face had the earnest trust of a child, a youthfulness of spirit that would never fade. He would not do it to her in the wagon. She was much too good for that.

Clank, clank, the train had come to a stop. Cautiously Billy and Ceci peered over the top to find themselves quite close to the bridge of Grevillton at the point where wagons waited to be shunted over in the morning. The lights of the shanty town blinked nearby and the voice of a child could be heard crying. Hoisting himself out Billy helped Ceci over and, filthy and numb from the wagon floor, they hoped they would meet no one while sneaking round the back of the houses and home. Still they could not wipe the grins from their faces for the day *had* been a great adventure and here they were, safe back at Grevillton! Rubbing their behinds they congratulated each other. As Ceci bent to take their buckets she noticed Billy peering earnestly between the wagons and across the river at the light in the mine yard, the hunted look of not wanting to be seen on his face again.

"Let's go home Billy," she urged.

"You go."

"Forget the mine. It makes you angry."

"Ssshh!"

Realizing it was no good she picked everything up and moved sadly off into the dark, the buckets hurting her knees. Turning for a last glance she saw Billy peering between the wagons, making his way silently towards the bridge.

It was a long time since Billy had crossed the bridge or the rails of the mine yard but he knew instinctively something was wrong. There was a light in the Administration Hut and the raised voices of Jephcott and the Foreman reached him clearly, arguing about whether or not to report a fatality.

"Not even put it down?" came the surprised voice of the Foreman.

"Figures have gone in. Don't draw attention." Billy heard a drawer slam and could imagine Jephcott making it plain the talk was over.

"We'll make extensive safety proposals to the *new* board, *after* the sale," came his voice from nearer the door this time.

"Cost nowt to put a man to supervise shots," the Foreman grumbled, obviously speaking from his same place and not willing to let the matter drop. There was a pause which Billy recognized as "dangerous."

"This is a safe mine," came the voice of Jephcott as the door opened. "Connors has his eye on your job."

"Don't think I don't know what's good for me," pleaded the Foreman, "but—"

"This is our first blow out. It has to be his fault," Jephcott insisted, the Foreman then appearing behind him at the door. As the two men stepped out Billy withdrew into the shadows.

So there had finally been an accident and the corrupt bastard was about to cover it up! Just as his had been covered up, wiped off the slate because it happened after the hooter had gone!

Billy was not surprised to find the men had gathered by the time he reached the pub. All his old mates, Bain, Woods, Morewell, Frank, Spiller, Tom, Lawson...He found Ceci keeping them in conversation, the room arranged for a meeting as in the old days. Even without having overheard it he'd have known from their faces a man lay dead, one of their number wiped out with the indifference of squashing a fly. Somewhere a woman would be weeping and children pulling at her skirts! From the pit of his stomach a great anger rose. That mine ought to be closed, yet if it were, how could any of them afford to live?

In the kitchen Ceci heard their deep voices passing speech from one side of the table to the other, their long silences. Why they had come she did not know, but clearly it was serious. The whitebait could wait till tomorrow; in their buckets in the yard they would stay fresh. Hurriedly she took down the tea she had brought with Jephcott's money and made a brew. From the look on Billy's face he could certainly use a cup! The man had been *black* with anger.

Picking up the tray, she pushed open the door to the bar room and saw Billy look up and was filled with the awareness she shouldn't have interrupted their meeting. Quickly she pulled back, leaning on the door, grasping the tray.

"How silly of me," she murmured, overcome with embarrassment yet at the same time hurt. Suddenly the yard door opened and there stood William.

"Are you going to the meeting?" she asked.

He shook his head, his eyes passing over the tray of tea.

"He tell you to stay out of it?" he said rudely.

Ceci began to shake her head to deny it.

"Got a chip on his shoulder," went on William, for the first time using unkind words about Billy.

"And you're the only one can't see it!" he added staggering past her to the stairs.

She sensed he had been drinking. Yes, she'd smelt it.

But there was no beer in Grevillton these days so it had to be illegal hooch. But where was he getting it and with whose money?

Unsure whether to await Billy or retire to bed, Ceci pondered the man's moods. By the time he came upstairs, so black was he she dared not ask what had happened. After such a wonderful day too! She could have physically strangled the mine for coming between them again! If only she could free him from it! Or was she asking too much? At times it was as if that mine were his manhood...

Chapter 36

Putting the affair of the previous night behind her, Ceci set off to sell the whitebait. It was the usual uphill climb. She began by trying for sixpence a scoop, Mrs. Evans at the shop offering to trade a tin of salmon for two scoops.

"Salmon's sixpence a tin!" exclaimed Ceci, waving her measuring cup. "These are fresh!"

"Won't be tomorrow!" Mrs. Evans replied sagely. "Leave a bucket here and I'll see what I can get. Split the profit with you."

Knowing she wouldn't see much change out of that one Ceci shook her head and went out into the street.

"A penny a handful," she told the children who surrounded her. "Go and get someone with bigger hands!"... As it was, after they'd done slopping and emptying she'd only ended up with two buckets.

Gradually women gathered, sinking their hands into the squirming bucket, running off with handfuls and not even paying for them. One was trying to wrench the cover off her other bucket.

"Leave that!" she said sharply.

One bucket gone—eight pennies... She stood wondering which way to go 'til finally the forbidden idea presented itself again and by a roundabout route she approached the Jephcotts' house.

"Whitebait! But you have to buy the entire bucket."

"Oh you clever person!" Mrs. Jephcott beamed, clasping her hands before her. "How do I cook them?"

"Well as patties, or frittered."

"I do wish you'd let me engage you as cook! They'll be rather awful boiled."

"You make batter—" Ceci began.

"I would absolutely *love* them but I couldn't *possibly* make batter!"

"I'll make it for you!" said Ceci, checking quickly over her shoulder. "Do you have eggs?"

"Of course!" exclaimed Mrs. Jephcott hurriedly closing the door.

In the kitchen Ceci stood dazed. How could she have come so far from this kind of civilized existence? On the table was a beige mixing bowl, eggs piled high in it . . . She moved her fingers towards them almost as if afraid she was about to steal.

"Why don't you have a few to take home," Mrs. Jephcott said. Ceci quickly cracked two eggs into a cup.

"You take two eggs, see—I'll just mix you the one batch—"

"There are left-overs in the larder too," Mrs. Jephcott went on, swinging the door open.

"I don't think I could," Ceci said, not even daring to look.

"Otherwise they'll go to the dog," Mrs. Jephcott explained, which made Ceci look up at the ends of roasts, hams, half pies . . .

"Go on dear," Mrs. Jephcott urged. "They'll never be missed."

"I appreciate your sincerity," Ceci began.

"But you don't want people knowing you've been in my house," her would-be benefactress sighed sadly.

Suddenly Ceci realized the woman was genuinely hurt.

"It's alright," Mrs. Jephcott assured her. "I'm used to it."

She slipped a coin into Ceci's pocket.

"Keep this against the hard times."

Ceci's mouth tightened. She was making the batter out of kindness, in the same spirit as she had once gone to help Mrs. Laird. Idly Mrs. Jephcott watched her mix the flour, baking powder, salt and pepper, whisk the eggs, add milk.

"You could make a nice terrine out of those left-overs," Ceci suggested. "Mince 'em up with a bit of fat, throw in some mace or nutmeg . . . You got nutmeg?"

"Where did you learn to cook like that?"

Keeping her back to Mrs. Jephcott Ceci rinsed the

whitebait. This was hardly the time to tell her it was a hotel kitchen she'd been sent down to because a room guest's advance had ended her days as a chambermaid!

"Did something happen at the mine yesterday?" she asked evenly, sensing the woman's hesitation.

"Are you—connected?"

Ceci thought for a moment.

"I came here as an independent trades person," she said honestly, "but business wasn't very good."

"Ah so you don't 'mix'!" She could feel the relief in Mrs. Jephcott's voice. "Well some idiot didn't check his shot properly and it back-fired on him," she said, her voice conveying the exasperation her husband must have brought home with him. So it had been a blown out shot. That was what had happened.

"There now," Ceci said turning. "When you're ready to go, fry a scoop at a time."

She reached up quickly, put the bowl in the larder, instinctively covering it with a muslin cloth and turning, servant like, closed the door.

"Shall we keep this arrangement of ours a secret," Mrs. Jephcott beamed, "you teaching me how to cook?"

Frowning, Ceci washed her hands.

"What do I owe you?" the good woman went on.

"A day's work catching them, three and six." She knew the price was a little steep.

"Will you come again?" Mrs. Jephcott said at the door. "As a friend?"

Ceci's eyes said "I'll try—"

"Wait a minute," said Mrs. Jephcott, pulling Ceci's basket off her and hurrying back into the kitchen with it. Stepping back into the house Ceci heard the larder door go. When Mrs. Jephcott returned, she found there were six eggs and a new packet of biscuits in her basket.

As she passed through the town she met Marie.

"I see you've been buyin' eggs at a shilling for six!"

"Take some," urged Ceci, thrusting forward her basket.

Marie shook her head.

"You and that man of yours earn every penny and I'll not be the one to take it off you!" she said.

They walked some way together.

"There's murder'll be done here one day!" she went

on. "That swine Jephcott said to Mrs. Twomey as lost her husband yesterday he's *sorry!*"

"Oh was it Mrs. *Twomey!*" interrupted Ceci.

"There he is now the big pig!"

Ceci followed Marie's glance and saw Jephcott on his way home for lunch. Marie spat after him. "It's the wake tonight. Are you coming?"

Sadly Ceci turned into The Hexham and reached up to place the eggs on a shelf.

"Where did you get them?" came the voice of Billy from behind her.

"Traded them at the store," she murmured.

"Stock up," Billy said, "but don't overcharge."

She heard his footsteps go up the stairs and was overwhelmed with an urge to confess. Running to him she clung to his back. But she said nothing. Finally Billy went on up the stairs.

Ceci stood feeling the money in her pocket. Three and six. It was far too much to spend at once. Where could she leave it?

Carefully she hid it under a cup in the cupboard.

Inwardly troubled she sought Marie at the wake that night.

"Do you always do as your husband says?" she asked.

"*Pardon?*"

"I mean—do you feel we—we are *supposed* to?"

"What is the matter with you?" said Marie, breaking off from filling the tea pot. "There's no law. When I first married I probably did."

Around them children and adults were milling quietly as Peg and Dot moved about with teacups, accepting groceries from other wives and putting them in the poverty striken cupboard. A miner was taking the hat round. "It's just I feel so terrible if—if I think for myself," Ceci stammered, finding it difficult to put into words.

"Well you're *used to* thinking for yourself, aren't you!" Marie soothed.

"Sometimes I feel quite *evil* to be disagreeing. I used t'be good at it!"

"*I* thought Jonas had some special sense denied me when we first married!" Marie recalled, laughing at the memory. "Now the poor dear's just some big clod I have to watch out for. Look at us laughing at a wake!"

They stooped at once. Marie saw the biscuits and three eggs in Ceci's basket. "Bit expensive," she said turning Mrs. Jephcott's biscuits in her hands. Biscuits were generally considered a useless luxury for people who didn't eat properly. "These biscuits been in that shop since we moved here," she added opening the packet. "Probably stale." She shot them on to a plate, put it in Ceci's hands and propelled her towards the gathering.

When she got home Ceci felt the need to check under the cup. The money had gone! For the next two days she was extremely uncomfortable. Had William taken it to pay off some gambling debt? There was no knowing what he got up to with Neill and Talbot! Nor could she discuss the matter without implicating herself. Whichever of them had taken it would not admit to the other therefore neither would not know it was *her* three and six.

Still worried, she found herself at the fish trap next morning, reaching an arm down into the cold water. There had better be fish today, she told herself for otherwise they could buy no groceries. To her dismay the trap was empty. After carefully examining it to check it was not broken she rose and re-set it further upstream, breaking a stick to mark the spot. Then she stood, biting a finger. No fish, therefore no money, therefore no shopping. She did not see Billy who had trailed her, parting a branch, watching.

Half an hour later found Ceci outside Mrs. Jephcott's house, knocking confidently. As the door opened the dog, who by now knew her, ran forward joyfully to lick her hand and from behind his tree Billy saw the look of pleasure on Mrs. Jephcott's face as she recognized Ceci; the pleasure of one woman seeing another. "I'll make that terrine and some cakes for you now if you like," came the voice of Ceci, clear across the gap to him.

In the kitchen Mrs. Jephcott opened the larder.

"I'll make us some tea!"

As Ceci rolled her sleeves up Mrs. Jephcott bustled happily with the kettle. "Do you have children?"

"A daughter in India," said Ceci, surprised to hear herself say so. It was the first time she had admitted this out loud apart of course from telling Billy and *he* had been more surprised to learn she had a *daughter* than that she was married and in India!

"India!" exclaimed Mrs. Jephcott impressed. "My! Aren't you the mystery woman!"

Ceci grinned. Mrs. Jephcott had certainly understated that!

"Isn't this the most terrible place?" she went on as Ceci worked. "These mining people are *impossible* to penetrate! You'd think with the situation here *someone* would skivvy for me!"

"They stick together—"

"But if it weren't for the mine, *none* of us would be here!" Mrs. Jephcott protested going on to explain that the belief which had been sustaining her throughout had suddenly been dashed to the ground. You would have thought, she explained, now that the mine was being sold, now *finally,* after *all* she had been put through living here, they would return Home. But none of it! Her husband was staying on as Mine Manager! "As if he were part of the equipment like a—a *piece of coal!*" she blurted. Ceci looked up at her. It was not difficult to understand what a blow this must have been for the woman: friendless, alone, shunned by all in a way worse than she had been when she came.

"I know my husband has a job to do," she went on. "And to my way of thinking George is as much a victim of circumstances as the miners! It's not as if he *owns* anything!" She turned to Ceci for support. "What may I call you?" Suddenly Ceci felt trapped and as she paused Mrs. Jephcott's face became unutterably sad.

"So you are connected," she said slowly. At that moment Ceci felt desperately sorry for the woman. What's worse she would have to refuse the gift of half the cakes for there was no way she could take them back to The Hexham without drawing Billy's attention.

Sadly she let herself in. No cakes but she had bought the wherewithal to make some. Billy was seated, watching her as she moved about the room as if she deserved a good thrashing. With a growing feeling of unease she turned to him.

"Why'd you move the fish trap?" he asked quietly.

"Well it was empty," she shrugged.

"So who gave the money to buy groceries?"

Trapped, Ceci flared back. "Alright I've been there!"

"I made it plain to you," he shouted, leaping to his feet.

"She's just an ordinary human being who likes fish!" Ceci roared.

"Who you cook for!"

There was a pause.

"You took his money at the mine! Grovelled for it!" she defended herself.

"Come in 'ere reeking of cakes!"

"Called him Sir you did! At least I don't call her Madam!"

For a moment she thought Billy might hit her. If not then he would upend the table or fling the food she had cooked on the floor! But he pushed the plate from him, looked at it in disgust:

"Blood money!" he said, leaving the room.

"I've done no wrong!" Ceci shouted up the stairs after him, hearing him slam their bedroom door.

Was what she had done wrong? Jephcott had not known she was Billy's wife and Jephcott was already complimenting his own wife on her baking prowess.

She hurried upstairs to find Billy sitting on the edge of the bed. Scrambling on it, she gripped his back. He grasped her tightly. "Don't go there any more," he said in a tremulous voice.

"Alright."

At that moment she became subject to him.

And the change was not hard for Billy's goodness and his ability to cherish more than compensated for depriving her of taking initiatives. Accepting the sacrifice she had made, Billy began to flourish and the mine ceased to dominate him.

Together they worked to repair their guttering with wood salvaged from The Central, Billy on the ladder manually forcing the tip of a nail in then whacking it with a hammer, Ceci on the ground pulling out nails from the old wood and straightening them.

"Did you empty the trap?" he asked.

"Yes."

"And?"

"One fish," Ceci said, handing him a nail.

"And?"

"I gave half to Mrs. Twomey. The other half's drying."

"So what about us?"

"We'll give us a miss today."

"Take sevenpence from the tin and get us a loaf." Billy said. "If we ration it out till William's paid—"

"It's time William left."

"I'm looking after you," he insisted. "And you don't have to be hiding money or worrying about William any more. If someone gives trouble—you tell me and it'll be sorted."

Billy gave the nail a whack.

"Alright."

Ceci looked up at him. Was this half state of being the condition she had almost envied Maureen for having? Was this the "happily ever after"? Above her Billy went on nailing. Compared with Billy, Ginger was really quite short and stocky she mused. Why *had* she found him *handsome*? Had his cheek bones been that much lower or more gentle, his brow higher, the effect would not have been there! Again, the depth at which his eyes had been set or rather buried in his face had given him a fiery quality when he smiled, making him look older. And of course the hair. Not a proper red or ginger; a brick brown really. He'd had the sort of curls—though she had never actually met a Maori—she imagined Maoris to have. The general effect of his build, she considered, had *made* him look virile and to this, she had added her own illusions! If you took them away, or put his personality in a different body what would remain? Really, he was a very ordinary man especially compared with Billy. Yet though she was Billy's wife and obeyed him, she was keenly aware of something indefinable missing and the question that bothered her was: did that something really exist? Peace of mind was what Billy had given her. In her quieter moments she was still given to worry about Olwen though. The girl no longer wrote. Unless, as she had done, she wrote letters in her head and omitted to post them..

Chapter 37

One morning Billy awoke possessed of the idea that they should *leave* Grevillton. More than an idea it was a conviction, yet Ceci could not explain her reluctance to go. She had the feeling that somehow part of her life was to happen there and it had not happened yet. Despite Billy's urgings, the vague unease persisted. While she wanted to please Billy and could see that Grevillton held no future for them, she could not lay these feelings to rest. Billy insisted he wanted better for her; she too wanted to be off William's back; all three were aware that in another place there would be work aplenty.

"This is the last place people know where I am," she stammered, adding: "I mean Annie and Reg and Olwen," in case Billy had thought she meant Ginger.

"Tied to a pile of boards," shrugged Billy.

He wanted to abandon the pub which would certainly prove impossible to sell and take off walking. Wherever they went, the other side of the Alps, the North Island, his haste suddenly struck Ceci as indecent. There was in it an element of panic he could not reason or explain. Ultimately, she decided, it would not be fair to hold out any longer, but just as she was about to give in something happened to change everything.

Standing in the mud riven street, clutching a hat box and valise, Olwen's eyes took in every detail of Grevillton's delapidation and dealt judgement accordingly. She saw the mine, lowering and clanking on the hill, smoking, threatening, and spitting dust and dirt at the settlement. Carefully she asked directions of an engrimed resident who turned and pointed towards The Hexham, then watched her gingerly pick her way to the ramshackle pub.

Who was this fair-haired girl tapping on the door, Jeannie wondered, coming out on her doorstep to look. The girl could not be more than eighteen. Her clothes were extremely smart and there was no reason why a person like that would possibly come to Grevillton. Why look at her standing there, turning and looking around! Then the door opened, Ceci appeared, a change sweeping over her as she stepped out, took the rigid girl in her arms and squeezed her. The girl didn't seem to respond. Odd, thought Jeannie, as Ceci pulled Olwen into the pub and closed the door.

At first it seemed to Ceci that Olwen's intention was to do nothing more than make trouble. She had acquired a large new vocabulary they didn't understand and when, in his clumsy way, Billy asked what her plans were she replied:

"I'm not in the habit of broadcasting my manoeuvres."

The word "broadcasting" apparently came from a thing called "the wireless" which they had in London. But when Ceci asked "Wireless what?" Olwen became irritated.

Apart from her strange and difficult way of speaking Ceci sensed that she must have been badly hurt. Partly she held herself responsible for the poor foundation she had given Olwen, but Billy was less forgiving. He could not stand to see her "cheek her mother" and it soon looked as if Olwen would wreck their relationship or even that such was her intention.

"That was a short marriage," Ceci said, sitting on Olwen's bed in William's cubicle; William had been banished downstairs.

"He was having fun, so I thought I would too," said Olwen, smoothing the hair from her face. "And *they* seemed to enjoy it." How Ceci could just imagine Olwen flirting around! "I just didn't think they'd tell him." She frowned. Oh the poor girl! In a way Ceci could see the fairness in what she'd done. Why should a husband after all be allowed public dalliances and laugh them off in his wife's face as "harmless flirtations"? No doubt he had felt quite justified in throwing Olwen out for doing the same thing. Presumably society would say she'd been "asking for it."

"My fare over here was to get me out of his family's way." Olwen admitted bitterly. "Do you think I should tell people here I was married?"

"You *are*," Ceci replied, shocked.

"Am I never to be forgiven one mistake?" Olwen begged bitterly.

"Being untrue?" Ceci queried.

"*Marrying* him!" Olwen snorted, amazed at her mother's naïvety. "I want a *new life*."

Sensing the element of panic in the child Ceci sought words. Now was no time to talk of duty and responsibility. Olwen would have to learn to live with them again first and her clothes would be unsuitable and her days hard to fill.

William, however, was impressed by Olwen. Even her haughtiness, so different from the red faced willingness of the mining women, attracted him. The only sight that came near to her in Grevillton was a picture on a biscuit tin in Mrs. Evans's store. Daily Ceci watched tongue in cheek as William's descriptive passages at meal times became more and more lyrical, usually figuring him as the hero of some drama in the day's events. Would he start writing poetry again she wondered? At the same time he tried to make his speech more manly, which was an interesting combination. She listened to him describing Jonas—whom he referred to as a "bit of an old lady" limping past with a dripping hand, looking for someone with a First Aid tin. He, William, of course, had torn his shirt into strips to bind the bleeding hand.

"Rotten handles," William explained. "Head had come flying off a shovel."

What a good audience Olwen was, cringing and twitching at command. Nor had William spared her the description of the man killed by the blown out shot. Another man had trodden right on him going up the tunnel, found he had his foot half way into the man's opened skull . . .

It looked to Billy as if each was equally struck by the other, William reminding Olwen with pain of the London she had left and she heightening a sense of indifference in William towards London. Clearly he was proud of the way he had changed since those days. Add to this Olwen's need to be comforted and William's burgeoning manhood battening on her adulation and the possibilities were endless.

During breakfast Olwen had been aware of William looking at her as she described the dancing, the numerous parties they had gone to. "I had so many clothes," she said with deliberate nostalgia, evoking a mood she now found impossible to shake.

"Don't you have *any* money?" she asked her mother as they sat in her cubicle that night.

Ceci shook her head.

"What about that 'father' creature?"

"Try him," Ceci shrugged. "Reg gets by."

"I don't know how I let my life come to such a terrible place," Olwen moaned, head in hands.

"Do you think we choose our lives?" Ceci asked. "Why—if I'd *planned* to marry a coal miner from the age of nine—I doubt I could have managed it"

"—in a more complicated fashion!" Olwen interrupted.

"I—I feel I'm where I'm meant to be," Ceci began, seeking the words which would heal. "I'm with my man, in my house, amongst people who—know me for what I am."

Olwen turned desperately to her and grasped her wrists: "Is there nothing more?"

How could she explain?

"I *feel* very rich," she said, becoming *aware* of it as she said it. "Looking back, stones become diamonds."

Olwen shrugged. Now her *mother* was getting lyrical. "Am I a diamond or a stone?" she asked bluntly.

"A diamond."

Something in the way Ceci had said that reassured the girl. She ran into her arms.

"Oh *mother*."

"You're a beautiful golden child with your life ahead of you," Ceci reassured her, squeezing her shoulders.

"But I've got *nothing*! *Nothing!*"

How *awful* the child should think that.

"You've got your*self*," Ceci said seeking better words.

"That didn't get you far!" Olwen interrupted.

"It—it's like an ocean to cross," Ceci went on. "It's ahead, behind, it's all around you."

"You could have slept with anyone in the world and I would have been different," Olwen complained through tear-stained eyes. "I'm half horse half mule!"

There was nothing Ceci could say to that.

"There is a wild part of me that all the living in London won't fix," Olwen admitted with some confusion.

What must it be like to be half Reg, Ceci asked herself. Or was it Old Bowen coming out in her? He'd had a "melancholic" streak and they did say children took more from their grandsires!

Olwen caught the thoughtful look on her mother's face and mistook it for regret.

"We've both done our share of whoring, I suppose," she said in that brittle way she had. Ceci glanced through the open curtain, hoping Billy had not heard.

"Life is a race Olwen. You must keep running," she urged. "You mustn't stop and expect to be a spectator."

Olwen shook her head:

"I won't win."

"*All who run*, win," Ceci insisted, even then hearing Billy's steps approaching.

"Did I hear you calling your mother a whore?" he demanded.

"How good is your hearing?" Olwen asked insolently. Billy took a step towards her as if tempted to deliver a slap but Olwen was not remotely afraid.

"This is *my* room," she said in a casual voice. "Get out."

Controlling his voice with difficulty, Billy spoke.

"And this is my house young lady. And as long as you are in it you'll speak with respect to your mother!"

After he had gone, Olwen lay crying on her bed. In their room, Ceci appealed to Billy:

"You were too hard on her."

"She'll have to straighten out."

Ceci rose and moved towards the door:

"I'll go and comfort her."

"You'll *stay here*," Billy commanded.

Slowly Olwen got up and went to the top of the stairs and stood listening. Quietly she tiptoed to where William lay on his makeshift bed, deeply conscious of being in the same house as Olwen. There she stood in her nightdress, looking unhappy but very beautiful. Scarce able to believe it was happening he propped himself on his elbow and saw her approach and sit on his bed.

"I'm not staying in this house another day with that man!" she said resolutely, smouldering with hurt which made her look even more attractive.

"Edmund said I had a common face," she went on,

an element of question in her voice. "He was a pig himself!" How William would have liked to sort Edmund out! "Nobody really cares about me," she informed William, turning to look at him. "Imagine you and me stepping off the coach in Christchurch! I'm wearing my best blue... People look at you and wonder where we come from!" She let out a long sigh and when she thought he was ready for it, added:

"Take me away from here William!"

William shifted uncomfortably.

"I can't take you anywhere," he said, "you're *married*."

At that Olwen started to rock and cry as if she had been struck with a hammer. Her body shook with the misery of a captured animal 'til he drew her to him.

"Just because I went through a ceremony I'll never be happy again. Oh I can't *stand* it! I can't bear to live like this—!"

William was at a complete loss to know how to deal with her.

"Take me *away* from here!" she pleaded, grasping his hands.

"We can't leave in the middle of the night!" he protested.

"O o o o o o nobody will *ever* do anything for me! I didn't even have the most *ordinary* things other girls have! I've had a *terrible* life! I was sent away—!"

Suddenly she stopped and looked at him:

"Do you think anyone'll ever like me again?" she asked seriously.

After a beat, William's hands and arms and body said "Yes."

Still feeling terrible about the preceding night Ceci padded along the corridor with a cup of tea for Olwen and paused before pushing back the curtains of Olwen's cubicle. Gone! Had William heard anything? She hurried downstairs and peered around the screen which had been placed before his camp bed: gone! In panic she ran to Billy.

By now William and Olwen were waking up in a damp field.

"Do you sleep with *anyone*?" he asked tactlessly.

She flicked the hair from her pale shoulders and glowered.

"I *like* you—"

His next words hardly pleased her.

"We have to go back."

"But we made up our minds!" she protested. "Let's stick to it!"

Confident she would have her way, she wandered down to the stream to wash but when she returned William's mind was firmly made up.

"They can't eat without me."

"I'm not going back and I want some breakfast," Olwen announced looking towards a house whose roof poked above the trees. "Go and break a window."

"I owe Grevillton's shop too," added William.

"Well you certainly don't have to worry about a *shop!*" Olwen snapped.

"You've a lot to learn out here Olwen," William said in a grown voice. She flicked her head and walked straight off. For a while William waited, staring at the clouds moving slowly towards the mountains. As time passed he began to frown.

"*Ol-wen!*" he shouted, his voice echoing round the hills.

Olwen marched determinedly on. She would not go back! She would go on! She would meet *some*one. *Some*thing would happen! It had to! But as she walked and felt the immense desolation of the place she became aware how unlikely it was that anything other than a wild bird would disturb the tranquillity. Stopping, she began to feel frightened and wonder if she were lost.

Back at The Hexham Ceci was arguing with Billy.

"You mustn't be cross with them when they get back," she pleaded, making Billy point out that she was prepared to tolerate a set of standards in her daughter completely different from her own. This, he implied, made her a bad mother—a remark which rankled for, since leaving Hexham and coming to see Calvin and Miss Robertson as "ordinary people," she had often wondered how it had been so easy for them to come between her and her child. She looked at Billy. His anger was already softening. It was almost as if he was thinking she might have been like that herself at Olwen's age.

"If you'd run off at that age you'd have managed alright," Billy conceded. "So don't worry."

William marched on after Olwen, feeling by now very angry. He had made a mistake in leaving but she had compounded it by behaving like a petulant child. Well he would certainly find her and when he did back they would go without a single word...

Crouching by a river, hungry and cold, Olwen did not know where she was. If people cared for her enough they would come looking for her! Already she could hear the voice of William calling in the distance. Well let him seek! She heard his feet crashing through the stones... getting closer and closer and almost passing her. She would not even call out! In an instant he saw her. He looked very angry.

"They'll laugh at me," she pleaded in a small voice.

Suddenly her grandness, her defiance, her posing and dissembling struck him for what it was: the pathetic façade of a frightened child. His heart went out to her. No longer was it her looks or speech which drew him but the need to protect this desperately frightened creature, who had beome a victim of circumstance. Crouching beside her he took her wrists in his hands, shook his head solemnly, beyond words. No one would laugh he told her. He would see to that. "We'll go back," he said, "till I pay the shop off. Then you and I will go. I can turn my hand to most work and I'll make it up to you Olwen. You'll be happy again. You'll see. We'll go somewhere people don't know!"

"You'll stay with me?" she asked incredulous. William nodded.

Slowly the girl got to her feet, for the first time in her adult life feeling utterly safe. William would sort things out with her mother; William would sort things with Billy.

She did not hang back as they entered Grevillton but prepared to take her medicine bravely. Entering The Hexham through the kitchen yard, they found Ceci who spun on them.

"Oh my *dears*!"

"I'm sorry," said William. "I take full responsibility."

Suddenly Billy appeared on the step and crossed quickly to Olwen, hand extended.

"I'm sorry Olwen."

Overwhelmed by acceptance on all sides, Olwen was possessed of the urge to cry. Ceci felt joy rising. William and Billy too sensed an elevation, a quickening amongst them as if they four were being lifted and placed on an altogether new plateau.

As they sat in the bar room that night, the decision was made. As soon as the store was paid off they would go.

"Just imagine, four people walking across New Zealand," Olwen marvelled, at last talking like a normal person.

So this was why, Ceci realized, she had not been able to leave Grevillton before! She had been waiting for Olwen.

"I always wanted things to be good between us," said the child, looking up at her. As she bent to kiss Olwen on the head, Ceci could not help but feel happy for her. For William too, not least because the day he had missed he had been off shift! That night as she lay in Billy's arms upstairs—she was aware that William was kissing Olwen in the room below with, no doubt, a shy confidence Olwen's accumulated experience would find flattering. Turning to kiss Billy she reminded herself that they had much to be thankful for. Although they would not be stopping long, she felt an air of happiness had descended on their small "family" to stay.

Chapter 38

Despite their impending departure and the uncertainties that lay ahead, the idea that they should have a child had taken a firm hold. Partly it was to do with the desire of each of them to see a tiny dependent version of the other on which to lavish affection, and partly the feeling, when they came together, that what they had, would grow to be if expressed in a child, sufficiently wholesome to withstand whatever Life might throw at it. It was not the *experience* they wanted when they performed the Act but *each other*. To that extent their driving desire could be fulfilled with a smile and it seemed more and more often they found themselves inhabiting each other. In every way, children would be such a natural expression of their relationship Ceci could not wait to conceive. The fact she had not already done so she put down, with no small reason, to the effect of their inadequate diet on her body's functioning.

As they lay long in bed, Billy reasoned that given the amount of walking ahead of them, they were lucky she *had not* conceived. Further as neither had eaten properly in many months nor could promise food to a child it would be best to wait until they were settled somewhere. Ceci was still a young woman he pointed out: thirty-four years old. There would be time aplenty to have four, even five children, if they wished. Yet because they did not know how to prevent them it meant self-control. Many of the miners' wives had times when they avoided their husbands, Ceci knew, but she could not ascertain when these were. Lying in bed they thus restrained themselves causing their passion to mount to even greater heights. On this particular morning they lay long. William had already gone to work and Olwen was wandering outside. As the sun through their window climbed the wall, telling them it was late, never had they felt so lazy and luxurious. In addition there were probably fish just waiting to be picked from the trap!

Down the mine Talbot nudged Neill to look at William who was working happily, his face preoccupied with his own future. Suddenly an almighty thundering explosion made the tunnel judder as if it were on rails. BHWOOOOOOM! In a rush of air William shot sideways like a ninepin; Talbot flew upwards and Neill smashed back against the wall as the cracking, wrenching sound of mighty beams tearing, props rendering, roofs caving in magnified around them and the gasps and shrieks of the terrified men were smothered by the sound of a giant ball of fire whooming towards them, getting bigger and fiercer 'til KKKRRRAAAKK! There was another explosion. Gathered gases sucked to the fire were going off all around them! William got to his feet.

"Talbot!" he screamed.

Neill lay on the ground. William shook him, grappled with him then dragged him into a cave in the coal wall where they crouched wondering which way to run. Three miners stumbled past panicking. Two were running back the other way as the light of flames flickered at each bend and the roar of the fire became deafening. "Jesus," Neill murmured.

With a crash the supporting beam gave and part of the ceiling caved in.

"Quick!" shouted William pointing to the hole to the upper level. "Up 'ere!"

Men ran to him, scrambled up the collapse of coal into the tunnel above and stood gasping in the smoke, confused.

"Which way?"

"Here!"

One ran to the left.

"No!" William screamed.

The second man took off to the right as to the left came the sickening sound of hundreds of tons of coal coming down like drizzle.

Trapped alone, hunched terrified in a cavern, Jonas shrieked: "Mother of God!" and the roof came down on him. He did not exist. Gone.

Up above men were running like insects ahead of smoke which belched from the entry tunnel. The cracking, banging from underground was clearly audible. They leapt over the ground as if it were on fire or they expected it to split beneath them. One had a bloody head, another's shirt was aflame. Cringing with dread, Jephcott watched.

"Cotterell!" he shouted.

As Ceci drew closer to Billy according herself the luxury of this special lie-in, she felt him stir. Voices darted up from the street below, cries:

"...afire..."

"...fire..."

There was running steps. The present suddenly returned. Billy's eyes focused. In a minute he was out of bed and by the window struggling into his pants, catching at the flies with the fingers of his one hand. As Ceci turned, half aware, he was already dressed and smoke was passing their window.

"She's smokin'," gasped Billy.

"William!"

As Billy ran down the street Ceci struggled into her clothes. Beyond the window she could see the black column rising, the people below running, banging on each other's doors.

Standing in the shop Olwen became aware of Mrs. Evans staring past her, horrified, at the people streaming by. In the next minute she had pushed her bulk from behind the counter and run out into the street to stand, hand over her mouth. Following her out, Olwen too saw the smoke and started to run.

As Billy arrived at the mine mouth he found rescuers armed with ropes, picks, shovels and lamps, backing out, unable to enter.

"We can't get in!" shouted Woods to him.

He ran at Jephcott:

"Quick man—give me a lamp!"

"If you're holding a lamp with one hand you can't carry a body with the other," Jephcott said cruelly. "You're a liability."

"Carried a body with one arm before," Billy growled.

"Carrying a lamp too?" Jephcott asked. "I can't waste lamps."

"I'll hold it in me mouth! Give me a damn lamp!" Billy shouted, but Jephcott had turned away. The scene was of unutterable confusion.

Quickly Jephcott crossed to Cotterell and the foreman who, with maps from the Administration Hut spread before them, were desperately trying to establish how many men were inside, where they were working and which was the best way of getting to them. He glanced at the barriers being erected to keep women from the mine mouth. Quickly he climbed on a box and, picking his words with care, asked for their "co-operation"; asked them to behave with "decorum" and, admitting that fire had occurred in some section of the mine, pointed out there was no reason to believe there would be any fatalities. The first rescue party were even now trying to gain entry he said, their names being recorded on a sheet of paper, under the clear understanding that they should come out at the first sign of gas and that none should stay in too long. Thus they should be able to see, he informed them, that all that could possibly be done was being done. Looking at the women ignoring him Jephcott told himself it was a scene which beggared description.

"Break through the venting holes," Billy ordered, snatching up a lamp from the mine entrance and followed by Lawson, Tom and Woods ran towards the tree-covered hill that the mine burrowed into. A short way up it they began desperately to smash at the hill with pick axes, tear at the stones, sweat streaming from them, reminded by the smoke coming from holes in the ground of the desperation of their search.

Inside William and Neill were running down an incline, smoke, flame and noise behind them. A slab of coal slowly disengaged itself from the ceiling and descended as they passed under it, catching Neill who went down. William shook him:

"For God's sake get *up!*"

Neil did not move. "*Run!*" William urged, then rolled Neill on to his shoulder and continued on into the dark, feeling his way forward with one hand. Soon he found himself on the edge of an enormous crater and just stopped himself going into it. Carefully he laid Neill down, pressed his back and hands to the wall, and tried to explore with his feet the rim of the basin, desperately anxious to find a way around it, for there was a hint of daylight at the end of the tunnel which continued on the far side of the dip. At a terrible sliding sound he spun to find the piece with Neill on had disappeared into the pit! William could not go backward or forward. Above him the roof began to rumble and slip and with the desperation of one without a choice he shut his eyes and leapt forward into the black. To his surprise he landed on a coal fall not far down up which he began to scramble. But it was not leading towards the light. That had gone now. Blocked. Blindly William crawled on.

Up above, Olwen arrived on a scene like a painting of a medieval lunatic asylum. Desperately she ran into the rushing, screaming people—seeking. People were tearing at their hair and each others' clothes. Ceci too ran, seeking, panic, fear on her face. Seeing Marie also running, she dashed to her. They stood together—bodies pressed close, too frightened to speak. Olwen saw them, their pain binding them, and ran up. Quickly they opened their arms to let her in and all three stood clutching at each other—eyes shut as the noise around them swirled in and out.

By this time Billy and his men had broken an opening into a ventilation shaft into which Woods lowered himself then reached up for Billy whom Lawson lowered. Carefully Woods guided Billy's legs while Tom, kneeling beside the hole, dropped down the picks...

"Listen!" Billy thumped the coal. The men put their ears to the wall then began to smash at it, opening up a way into a regular tunnel and climbing through.

"What part are we?"

Billy began to mark out in the dust a map of the mine as he remembered it.

"Won't be at work stations now," Woods advised.

"I'd move *upwards*."

"Were you workin' yesterday?" Billy asked.

Lawson nodded.

"Past bord three where Twomey got it."

"Our William was lower down," Billy frowned.

They all paused, thinking.

"I reckon we're here," Woods said, stabbing at a corner of the map.

At the first cross tunnel they came to they hesitated, knowing they were well away from the fire for it was quiet and the smoke did not reach them. It could be an area men were making for. Shaking hands Billy and Lawson went one way and Tom and Woods the other. When the tunnels divided again, Billy and Lawson shook hands, their eyes met and Billy chose the way sloping down...

Up above, the first official search party to have succeeded in entering the mine ducked under the smoke and continued moving cautiously inwards. As they passed cross tunnels dipping down, a faint flickering glow came up to them from the fire burning below. They pressed wet cloths to their mouths. Should they go back or on? To a man they were afraid of being trapped by the fire whose roar the could already hear throbbing and echoing.

On the ground above the turmoil was increasing. Though Jephcott was giving out that the trapped men were expected to be led to safety "as soon as conditions allowed" none gave him credence and some were heard saying the carpentry shed was already being cleared for the laying of bodies...Through the crowd Ceci thought she saw Mrs. Jephcott walking towards her. Quickly she turned away. By the mine mouth Ena was struggling with her husband, a casualty of the first rescue party.

"Yuh no more use to them!" she was shouting. "Yuh gassed! Yuh makin' it harder fuh the others!" but he was resisting her, wanting to go back in again. "Now cummon yuh dear brave creature," Ena gasped, dragging him off.

"Oh its burnin' like a piece of coal," Marie sobbed. "And we 'ad such a row last night!"

"Stop it!" Ceci begged.

"Rocks fallin' down on them! Cryin' out to God!"

"Be quiet! Get back!" the foreman shouted as the women pressed forward. "You're not going in again!" he told Ena's husband, now free of her and reeling back towards the gaping hole. "A couple of days in bed and he'll be fine—" he reassured Ena. "Just gas—"

"Outta me way!" shouted the gassed man, pushing towards the entry again. "Leave go of me!"

"Take him home!"

As the light faded the outside world began to arrive in the shape of Coal Board officials who were told: "Search parties have already reached the men." At the gates journalists were asking: "How many weeks back was this mine sold?" Volunteers from other mines and men from the hills who had seen the smoke and arrived with swags and blankets to help, thronged over the bridge while the Salvation Army prepared soup kitchens for the night and moved amongst the despairing wives trying to calm them. "You'll do no good staring," they say. "Come and sit down." But the women shook them off angrily. The Administration Hut had been turned into an emergency room and the carpentry area, as predicted, ominously cleared of all furnishings. The column of smoke had been seen rising two miles off.

Parched and dehydrated at the bottom of a sloping tunnel, William realized he was trapped. Not only was the tunnel blocked by a massive fall but beyond it he could clearly hear the flames raging, seeking a chance to

get through to him. He stood screaming. Not far away
Billy moved cautiously down his tunnel.

"'Allo? Bill?" he called.

Faintly he heard William's screaming. Was it screaming?
He listened again and started to run.

Standing well back Jephcott viewed the hillside. One
side of the mine had caved in entirely and from a brilliant
pit, red flames were throwing yellow flowers in to the air.
From numerous holes on the other side smoke was pouring.
The hill was like a cake on fire, but gradually, slowly, the
smoke *was* lessening and the spirals becoming shorter . . .

"Should be able to get some of them out now—" he
said lamely to Cotterell. He glanced over at the women,
still pressed round the mine mouth in utter silence. They
had been standing there for hours and he knew nothing
would shift them till their own particular dead came out.
The list man at the entrance was yawning. For the past
hour nothing had happened and were he not sick with
worry, sleep would have claimed him. Suddenly he cocked
his head, stood and moved towards the mine mouth
listening. By now the tension amongst the women had
built to an alarming pitch. Suddenly one of them broke
through the rope but another pulled her back. She broke
through again, and stood like a mule before the mine
mouth, turning on the spot, biting a finger. Nobody
bothered with her. Finally she came back under the rope
and joined the other women peering urgently at the mine
mouth which had ceased belching smoke. They heard a
cough; then the sound of footsteps, magnified and coming towards them. The rescuers were coming out! They'd
got the men!

Pressing forward they saw a lone man stumble out,
pulling the smoke rag from his mouth, rolling on his side.
Ceci bit down on her fingers. Other searchers came out,
leaning on each other, unable to walk straight, looking
ashamed. The women breathed in and continued waiting.

"Soup is ready now," the Minister announced at the
request of the Salvation Army, whom he had already told
were wasting their time. "If you would like to adjourn to
the refreshment tent. We have it on authority that the first
party of men will not be led out for at least forty minutes..."

They stared dumbly at him. With his hands he invited them to move away from the mine mouth and towards

the tent but they remained standing, their eyes following two of the men who had come out and were now reentering with piles of sacking...

They began to push forward again, their whispers becoming noise and spreading back in a great wave. Had they found where the men were sheltering? Were the men going to be brought out?

Suddenly the stretcher started to come out. Under sacking and by the dozen. The chaos was of a different sort now, the desperate women beseiging the stretcher bearers as they emerged with their burdens for identification, surging forward, trapping them, preventing them reaching the cleared carpentry area.

"That's Theresa's John, mercy help him!" went up a shriek as the sacking was pulled off a charred corpse.

"Go home!" shouted the foreman at hysterical women. Some whose husbands had already been identified to them as dead had kept forcing their way back into the throng.

"We're waiting for our husbands!" they begged, as if by waiting they could have another chance at the stretchers. Screams shook the hills as women fanned out amongst the dead. Suddenly Ceci realized she had not seen Billy and that his name had not been on the list of searchers! *Surely* he would have gone in! So where was he?

"I was looking—" she began, bursting into the Administration Hut.

"These are the rescue party," said Dr. Murdoch indicating the six blackened men lying gassed on the floor.

Quickly she moved on to the "dead" area, scanning the lengthening list of names at the door, then to be doubly sure check under the roof. What a terrible sight those thirty bodies arranged in aisles, bent women moving between them!

"He's moving! He's moving!" she saw a neighbour insisting.

Walking away she was passed by Peg struggling towards the carpentry shed behind stretcher bearers, grasping at the lifeless hand that swung beneath the sacking:

"He's *warm*! He's not dead! *Leave him*!"

No Billy. No William! She hurried back to the mine mouth.

"Excuse me, have you seen—"

"Jo Murtagh—haulage road," said the list man, ignoring her. "Lovelock—no. 3 incline. Withers—on his own—bord no. 3."

Dead. All dead!

Behind her Peg's voice rose even louder:

"He's *not dead* you fool! You're taking him to the wrong place!"

"He's dead Mrs. Collis," the bearer insisted. "His back's broke."

"Can you give me any news of William?" Ceci pleaded, grabbing the list man's sleeves.

"Check the other lists," he replied.

Standing in the middle of the field, Ceci began to shout:

"Billy! Billy! William?"

Now there was even no sign of Olwen!

"Mr. Jephcott! Mr. Jephcott!" she shouted, rushing at him, but he walked off telling Cotterell: "Watch what you say to the press."

Ceci sput on the spot. All around women were biting their knuckles, Salvation Army people were whispering "Courage!"

"Jonas!" went up a terrible cry, all the heartbreak in the world in Marie's voice. Ceci's heart wrenched for her. But crossing to comfort her she heard:

"Two on this one." Instantly she knew the phrase was for her.

"Bill 'n Bill."

"Bill'll make it," said the second voice.

"Where'd you find them?" the first voice asked.

"Clear over 11," the second answered.

"Anyone else there?"

"Just them."

Slowly Ceci moved to the spot to find Billy and William, face to face on the same stretcher.

"They was one on topper the other."

"Musta bin bringin' the lad out."

Ceci knelt, hands grasping, shaking them, their clothes dropping off them, their arms untangling as they fell apart. Which one was dead? In a dream she saw them transferred to separate stretchers and felt Olwen at her side as they were taken off in different directions.

"What's happening?" Olwen gasped.

Suddenly Ceci could not think and was unclear which stretcher to pursue. Stumbling blindly after the last she found herself in the carpentry area, Olwen beside her screaming like a wild cat. Before her lay William.

She took off chasing the other stretcher, desperate to catch at life's last minutes, her hands grappling with the blackened hand of Billy, while behind her Olwen's wail went up and up to the skies...

Ceci followed the stretcher into the Administration Hut.

"He's had far too much gas," Dr. Murdoch said, disentangling Billy from her hands. "Not now *please*."

Blackened from embracing Billy Ceci stumbled back to Olwen and found her clasping William to her and refusing to put him down.

"Get away! Leave him alone!" she shouted at the man who would pull her from him. "We're taking him home!"

In the fading light, Ceci and Olwen carried William back to the pub for the last time, his body slung like a hammock between them.

Inside, they laid him on the table and with buckets of water and soft cloths, faces streaming tears, they lovingly washed him and wiped the fair hair, now coming clean, from his wet face.

Sniffling unselfconsciously they prepared him for his final rest.

"I—I'll go back and see Billy," Ceci murmured.

Olwen nodded. Alone now, she could let out her grief. Kneeling by William, she laid her head on his chest as if all the heaviest weights and rocks in the world were in it.

"I would have made you happy," she whispered.

"I can't revive him," said Dr. Murdoch with resignation, conscious of Ceci's hands gripping and regripping each other, her chin wobbling and her already red eyes tensed and nervous. "Leave him with me a little longer." Quickly Ceci turned away, anger at the mine growing. The poverty and uncertainty it caused she could forgive, but not this terrible indifference towards the existence of the very humans who worked it!

Returning to The Hexham, she found Olwen, eyes red and swollen, standing quite spent next to William.

The girl was almost calm. Seeing her mother step trembling into the room, close the door and lean on it, Olwen realized that at any moment she would burst into tears. Moving to her, she took her in her arms. Her mother was trembling violently:

"They're going to pay for this!" she said in a deep voice.

"Sssh!" said Olwen holding her.

As the rage subsided, Ceci looked over Olwen's shoulder at William on the table. How new and fresh he looked: how pink and free from pain. What a man he had become, this boy who had supported her when the world was against her; whose father had sent him out to "make a man out of him." Never would he have the satisfaction of knowing what a grand man the boy had become.

"William," called Ceci, for one moment actually believing the boy might sit up and look at her. Olwen glanced with pity at her mother. On the table, the lifeless body of William refused to move.

Chapter 39

Ceci sat by the bed anxiously holding Billy's hand. Olwen stood behind her, her fingers fiddling with her mother's shoulder. Billy was conscious but looked very groggy. He was trying to smile; trying very hard to reassure them. The messsage in his eyes was clear:

"I'm here. I'm alright. Give it time." Understanding, Ceci bit her lip, blinking back the tears and nodded. She tried to smile cheerfully. The newspaper had described them as a town of widows. More than sixty men had been killed, the sons, fathers and husbands of Grevillton. Ministers had come from outside to preach moving eulogies; messages had come from all over the land, from the government, Lodge Groups, other mines and from private individuals. It had been described as New Zealand's worst mining disaster. Journalists had spoken of the funeral procession as stretching from view, the two hundred women and children left without breadwinners pressing closely behind the stream of coffins bought on credit. Bodies that could be identified had been allotted separate graves; the remainder had gone in a large pit, the digging of which, Ceci recalled with discomfort, had started before the bodies had finished being brought out.

Some credit had been extended by the store, the coffin builders and others for it was most likely that national feeling and the scale of the disaster would result in funds being set aside for such purposes. Mrs. Jephcott was no longer seen on the street. Ceci imagined it was too great an ordeal for her to face. Her husband, however, soldiered bravely on, filling out forms, making lists and planning the reconstruction to be done. It was his belief that those miners who found work as a result of the tragedy would very soon forget it as would their families. First though there was one matter to be got out of the way: the Royal Commission of Enquiry. Still, industry was industry and the mine did provide work. This was not to say of course that the Commission would be less than *impartial*, but a scattering of Expert Witnesses . . .

Two opposing thoughts disturbed Ceci. First, that at the moment she had paused not knowing which Bill was dead, the face of Ginger had flashed vividly into her mind. She could not understand this and moreover felt terrible about it. The second was that there would clearly be no child for Billy. He would be a man leaving no mark on the world. It seemed such an irrelevant thought it bothered her and the fact that the two thoughts had occurred as if they belonged together was a further cause of confusion.

When the day for the Royal Commission of Enquiry came, a curious hush pervaded the abandoned Central which was to be used for the hearing. It had been rearranged as a courtroom with a Judge's Bench, a Prosecution or Enquirer Bench as it really was, a witness area and a separate "gallery" for the public.

Pressed together there, the miners' wives looked across at Jephcott, Cotterell, the foreman and Coal Board officials in Sunday suits, whispering amongst themselves.

"... careful restructuring has maintained the mine as a viable economic prospect," came a voice none recognized, "to the extent that it has been recently re-acquired and when the economy recovers it is believed..."

What did that mean, people asked leaning forward. He certainly wasn't a local man. Did he mean that because they couldn't sell coal they were employing fewer and fewer people, jiggling the figures about till it seemed worth someone's while to buy the place?

"Will you be quiet over there?" asked a clerk, leaving the women to stare at the original speaker with his large sheaf of papers and his apparent object of filling the Judge in on the background of the place. The past ten years, he said, had seen a decline in the output of coal owing to difficulties in marketing it, the mine being on the receiving end of a general depression. The company who had recently acquired it, he pointed out, were listed on the London Stock Exchange and were throughly reputable. "It is believed the continued prospects for the mine are good," he concluded, "and that when the economy picks up—output will once again return to a high level and the community flourish."

Ceci found herself looking at Jephcott.

"To date, this has been an accident free mine."

"Thank you," said the Judge nodding to the reader, who sat down.

"This Commission has been convened to determine the cause of the disaster," the Judge explained, his eyes passing over the crowded room, "on the morning of..."

In the "gallery" the women watched like hawks as Jephcott and the foreman took the stand together.

"So what you are saying is that there is gas in the mine," the Prosecutor asked Jephcott.

"I am not saying that," Jephcott replied slowly. "Gas, as I am sure you are aware, is a natural product of coal, which is why coal is burned to—"

"Shall we say," the Prosecutor clarified, "there *could* be gas?"

"My duties as Mine Manager do not include speculation on vague geological possibilities," Jephcott said slowly, thumbs finding his waistcoat pocket.

Unable to restrain herself Marie stood up:

"Sssssssss!"

Ceci pulled her down.

"In the event that there *were* 'naturally occurring gas pockets'," the Prosecutor continued.

"Do not follow speculative lines," the Judge directed.

Ceci looked at Marie. Surely they weren't trying to establish whether or not there was gas in the mine? Any child in Grevillton could have answered that one!

"Under what circumstances, in your experience," the Prosecutor laboured patiently, "if it does arise, is gas likely to do so?"

There was silence. Suddenly Marie could stand it no longer. She got to her feet and shouted:

"After rain, in disused tunnels!"

"The next time you speak you go out!" shouted the clerk.

"We have no way of determining the—the—likelihood of—changes in the—ba-ro-met-er-ric," said the foreman stumbling over the word as if he had been reciting it, "pressure."

"Let us leave barometeric pressures!" the Prosecutor insisted. "Were there any actual instances which led you to believe there was a likelihood of gas being present?"

Jeannie, Ena, Peg and Dot shook their heads. How was it possible for anyone to be so stupid! Those men ought to go down a mine themselves! Ceci looked at Olwen and saw the girl had a peculiar look on her face as if she understood some fact which had escaped them. She sensed her mother looking at her and gave her a worried frown.

"We have screens called brattice screens which waft fresh air in and out," said the foreman lamely as cries of: "And they're most of them torn!" came from the back.

From then on proceedings became difficult to follow. Phrases such as "the figures which I believe to be correct," and "I am not in a position to give an opinion," and "It wasn't part of my job to ascertain," had a sedative effect on the gathering along with the growing certainty that they were not supposed to be understanding what was going on and that it was not intended for them.

On the stand Dr. Murdoch said that of the forty-two bodies he'd examined burning was only the direct cause of death in eighteen cases. In his marked Scottish accent, he said deaths had been occasioned by such other means as falling coal and flying sleepers.

"Slippers?" the Judge interrupted seriously.

"Wooden planks for securing rails," the clerk explained, the moment of humour passing in the niceties of establishing whether in the case of a man concussed by a sleeper as opposed to crushed by a fall of coal and *then* burned, the primary cause of death would be the actual sleepers, fragments of which had remained embedded in their scalps. Dr. Murdoch described men shafted by split rails, lungs which had exploded; death from smotheration, from smoke and the inhalation of "fumes." Ceci noted he avoided using the word "gas" possibly in the interests of objectivity. Rescuers were then called forward who spoke of coming on bodies crisp as pork . . . It had clearly been a fire of great intensity, the Judge concluded, if it had buckled the rails and twisted the ironwork beyond recognition.

When it became time to establish the cause of the fire, however, people leaned well forward. On the stand Jephcott led in with the confidence of a man on the home stretch. His stance, the inflexion in his voice, the way he turned to look about the room as he spoke, all suggested a man of the utmost reason.

"If a miner, through inattention," he began slowly, "causes a shot to be poorly placed, and sets the fuse, as is well known to himself, that shot will be ineffective for the purpose intended and will jeopardize general safety."

Drawn to look at Olwen, Ceci saw anger and certainty meet on her face. She began to shake her head slowly. Beyond her Jeannie and Aggie sat confused, still waiting for something they could understand to be said. Now the Judge was whispering to his clerk and it sounded as if the clerk were explaining what a "shot" was and then what the phrase "placing of a shot" meant. The Judge seemed to find the information both esoteric and fascinating and nodded with satisfaction and leant forward, his interest renewed as Cotterell came to the stand:

"The hole must be made in a proper location and the shot packed in firmly," he explained in answer to the question of how shots were placed.

"And how are miners to determine 'proper locations'," the Prosecutor asked.

"They've never had difficulty before!" Cotterell said, the edge of roughness to his voice. At a glance from Jephcott however he quickly corrected it. "That is to say, it's part of their work."

By now even Marie could see the position the Judge was being manoeuvred into. She pressed her lips together, folded her arms tightly on her chest. "A 'blown out shot,' Your Honour, is an improperly placed shot which backfires," Cotterell went on solidly.

"Could a—'blown out shot'—" the Judge asked, enjoying his usage of the phrase "—cause fire?"

"A flash anywhere can cause fire," Cotterell said smoothly, "even in this room."

Slowly the ugly farce wound down as people returned to their seats and there was scribbling and muttering at the tables. Dr. Murdoch then provided one brief moment of drama by getting to his feet without being invited and insisting it be recorded that the majority of deaths had been caused by such secondary results of the explosion as crushing and suffocation. Instantly Jephcott's lawyer was on his feet shouting: "May I request the word 'explosion' to be expunged as speculative and replaced by the word 'fire'."

To Murdoch's obvious fury the clerk erased the entry leaving the doctor to glare and shrug helplessly at the "gallery" where Marie slowly shook her head back at him.

How dared they! Fires could happen anywhere but explosions were caused by gas! Their men had risked their lives daily working with gas and now its existence had been denied, or "expunged" as they put it. Why, the explosion had been so immense it had been felt in nearby houses! Marie's head was thundering as the results were read:

"... The findings of this Commission are that the disaster was caused by a shot placed by a miner or miners unknown which lead to a devastating fire..."—the man's voice faded in and out—"... recommended that in future shots be placed only by men trained in their use..."

Looking, Ceci saw Jephcott nodding earnestly in an apple polishing way as if he were only too happy to comply with any directives the Court were kind enough to offer.

"And that Management, Board of Directors and Company at large," the voice went on, "are not guilty of negligence in the maintenance or operation of the mine . . . That Management was efficient and safety measures adequate . . ."

For a moment there was utter silence, then Marie stood:

"Rubbish!!" she cried out. "Liars!"

As slowly an understanding of what had been done to them filtered through, the fury of the miners' wives congealed. There would be no compensation, no relief. Because it had not been the mine's "fault" they were free to starve. Credit was withdrawn at the store as the long winter of their suffering began.

Where previously in the rush of imagined credit wives had bought as many unlikely and unnecessary things as they could lay their hands on they now found themselves being refused. The day before the Royal Commission hearing when Ena had said, "Four eggs and I'm finished," Mrs. Evans had replied: "May I remind you your husband's living?" as she smartly lifted the eggs from Ena's basket and handed them to a recent widow. This week, however, it was: "Cash only if you don't mind." In the previous weeks accounts had been opened for everyone from the common law wife of a dead miner to the eldest child of the large family of a widowed miner killed in the disaster. The eleven-year-old girl had used the account to buy everything from tinned sweets to biscuits and although Mrs. Evans had protested to her husband that people like that would never pay, his response had consistently been: "Keep your voice down." Now, of course, he had been found out!

The community, always polarized between those who had work and those who didn't, now knew the more precise distinction of those who had a man alive and those who hadn't. Jephcott had been right in thinking the plentitude of repair work arising would stand him in good stead with the diminished workforce. He even lowered the wage. In the name of survival, women whose men were working found themselves giving a wide berth to the widows and a scene repeated with appalling regularity outside the store was that of a widow waiting for a former friend to come out with some groceries. Seeing her she would call, greet her as if casually pleased to meet, then as a look of annoyance crossed the face of the woman with the groceries, would start tugging at her basket, eyes pleading. The woman would move her head and say angry words as the widow's voice rose in desperation, begging. Guilt on her face, the owner of the groceries would turn and walk briskly off. Gradually bringing her panic under control, the other would take a bitter swallow and await the next comer: anything rather than return to that one room shack where her children would run at her and she, sinking into her chair, would cover her face with empty hands.

In the bar room, Ceci, Olwen and Marie bit their lips and moved from one foot to another. They clasped their elbows and frowned. The air was nervous with extreme hunger, desperation even. Olwen moved to the window, her glance falling sideways into the street.

"Look," she said softly. The two women came over to stand behind her so they would not be seen from the street.

"Tt tt tt," said Marie

"Makes you sick," Ceci sighed.

Marie turned and walked back to her original spot but Ceci stayed by the window.

"And eggs," she said.

"She had a tin of salmon," mumbled Olwen profoundly.

Suddenly Marie burst out, almost in tears:

"We were that close, she even offered to help me smash your barrels! I went round there, her kids' mouths so full they couldn't open them! Crumbs all over the table! Told me she was just off to borrow a loaf herself! I only wanted two slices!"

Ceci began to pick bitterly at the tips of her fingers.

Marie exploded again:

"I shoulda crossed that room and found where she'd hid that bread when she heard me coming!"

Olwen looked at the two women. There was nothing to be done here. Besides, her mind was made up.

"I'm going to look for my father," she said. Curiosity fleeted on Marie's face. She gave Ceci a quick glance.

"He—he may have some money for us."

Ceci and Marie nodded. The girl was after all an adult and they had nothing to suggest. The way things were going they would all starve. Nothing more desperate than that could happen to her on the road. Hunger was the great leveller.

"I'll visit William's grave before I leave," Olwen said quietly.

Setting out for the hills she was certainly a different girl from the one who had run away so short a time ago! In an old dress of Ceci's, she looked almost humble, bending down to kiss Billy goodbye and moving to the porch with her mother.

"Callery Gorge—past Hokitika—?"

"Yes," said Ceci, "and if he isn't there, every other prospector will be! So be careful!"

Olwen stepped out, turned to look back at her mother. How deep the pockets in her cheeks had become. How thin her neck... Sadness and a caring reflected on Olwen's face. Ceci ran to her; they squeezed hands.

As Olwen walked out of Grevillton she feared for nothing. She was to look for a man called "Legs," who she could not remember but was supposed to have met as a child. "Legs," apparently, was a nickname relating to his having "legged it" at some time in his past. All the men had nicknames she had been told, and most of them pasts. This did not bother her. She would see what this man had to say.

Ceci stepped back into the room, closing the door.

"Come on—" she said to Billy taking his arm and beginning to move it around his head. "Doctor said a little will power—you'll be right as rain..."

Marie watched, arms folded.

"You've got to get those muscles working again Billy," she said, yet even as she moved his arm, part of her despaired. He was not improving. His speech was difficult to understand and he could do nothing for himself. Though she sensed he tried hard, even listening to conversations exhausted him. With considerable guilt she found herself torn between being grateful to him for staying in the mine long enough to be with William at the end and being angered that he had not made allowance for the gas and come out sooner. By all accounts William, certified dead from smoke inhalation, should have been beyond help by the time Billy arrived, yet Billy had insisted he'd been there at the end; that the boy had been conscious, breathing, knowing he had been found. In the quietness of the night Ceci often thought of William laying in Billy's arms hearing his name spoken, dying in the company of another.

Remarks that Billy had stayed in to "prove himself" on account of his arm found no favour in Grevillton. More than natural bravery or a love for William, Dr. Murdoch suggested the man would have wanted to bring the boy back safely for Ceci's sake.

"It would have been for you," he said after examining Billy on one of his worse days. "This is a big diamond he has given you to wear around your neck," he added, referring to Billy's sacrifice. "Wear it proudly."

"He's deteriorating Doctor," Ceci whispered urgently. Dr. Murdoch paused in the doorway.

"Do you pray?" he asked.

"Hardly," she replied.

"So let us be a little patient," he said, leaving.

Walking down the street, Dr. Murdoch had wondered if he should have been more frank with her. He could have offered his opinion but opinions were after all only opinions and he had often seen hope make men well again. In fact the man *could* live another ten, twenty years, so who was he to contradict possibility with an opinion?

Watching him from the doorway, Ceci wondered how much longer it would take before there were signs of an improvement in Billy.

Chapter 40

The plight of the women of Grevillton, more particularly Ceci whom she knew, moved Mrs. Jephcott. Though her husband assured her the women would get help from Churches and from Lodges their husbands may have joined, her eyes told her differently. She began to gather groceries in a basket.

"You'd do better giving a hamper of your potato peelings to the church," Jephcott said unkindly. "You won't make her popular going around there!"

"That is not the object of the exercise," Mrs. Jephcott snapped.

"Her husband'll sort you out."

"From what I hear he's positively ga-ga."

Ignoring Jephcott, she set off for The Hexham and made the difficult journey through town. Scarce was there a sight that did not cause pain. She had, however, a proposition she was sure Ceci would not refuse; a proposition instrumental to both their purposes, which cheered and gave her new confidence. Climbing the wooden runners before The Hexham she tapped on the door. After a pause it opened a crack and a thin face peered out.

"My dear—" she began.

Ceci looked wanly back at her through a veil of hunger. Mrs. Jephcott held out the basket.

"I was wondering if you'd reconsider—just two hours a day—May I step in?"

But the door was pushing in on her.

"I must respect my husband's wishes," came the weak voice.

Closing the door Ceci tiptoed upstairs to sit with Billy.

"I don't know what to do!" she confessed.

"Sue," he said in a weak voice.

"*Sue*?" she repeated. Billy nodded. After a while Ceci spoke:

"*You* weren't working for the mine. William was no relative."

"William loved you," Billy said weakly.

"*How* do I sue?"

"Marie," he whispered up at her.

Standing before Marie, her unspeaking children lining the walls, grey circles round their eyes, Ceci tried to persuade her.

"Am I to be messing with bits of paper when we've none of us touched bread to our lips these five weeks?" Marie burst angrily.

"And you, your husband—the grace of God alive—coming in here telling me what to do?"

"It's me as'll be slapping *your* face for hysteria, Marie O'Shea," said Ceci firmly.

Remembering the words Marie hung her head.

"Thank you," she said quietly.

Powered by a determination to do something for themselves, Ceci and Marie dressed up as best they could and jumped the barge to Greymouth. Although their mission was serious, there was no denying the element of childish delight that accompanied the adventure.

"I'm surprised at you!" Marie said as Ceci urged her to wait for her signal then run forward and make the jump. No sooner were they aboard, however, and hidden under the tarps than the barge man, who had heard the loud rustling of their skirts, came straight back and peered in at them.

"Be a lovely man!" Marie smiled up at him.

Gently he let the tarp drop.

They walked the streets of Greymouth, exhilarated to be there, enjoying its atmosphere and sense of energetic bustle. Unlike Christchurch which seemed to have been thrown together for a purpose *because a purpose existed*, Greymouth had the feeling of having come into being spontaneously for reasons since forgotten and, now established, found ample reasons to justify itself. The sight of its buildings and pillars, wharves and new faces seemed to put Grevillton firmly in place and remind them they had no need to take the punishment the mine had been dealing out. There was a whole new world outside whose people would not think of suffering the indignities they had endured. Finding a building with the names of four law firms on a brass plaque they renewed their courage and entered.

By the time they left, so filled were they with vigour even hunger seemed a thing of the past. Young Mr. Nayfach had so convinced them of their "quantifiable assets" as he put it, was so enthusiastic about their case, and ready to take them on credit they could almost believe they had stumbled on a gold mine. Marie was to lead the action against the mining company, it was agreed, on behalf of the women of Grevillton and they were to return at once and list all the dead, all the hardship they had been caused and basically what they personally thought their men had been worth. Nayfach had made it all sound very simple. That night, he instructed them, they must call a meeting at The Hexham.

Despite Nayfach's confidence it proved harder than they had envisaged to explain to their neighbours what suing meant.

"If he's so sure we'll win, why didn't the Royal Commission—" Peg began.

"The Government Enquiry was just looking to find out what *happened*," Ceci tried to explain.

"We *know* what happened!" snapped Dot.

"Well why would the Court hear a case they'd be bound to lose!" asked Aggie pointedly.

"It isn't the Court dilly!" Marie gasped, her patience running thin. "Yev just been told! The *company* and the *government*'s different!"

"Well we don't want to cause any trouble!" said a woman who'd lost her husband, but still had two sons working yet was not remotely concerned that suing might improve conditions in the mine.

"I don't feel right about—about—" another woman stammered hesitantly.

"About being upstanding?" Marie demanded.

The woman nodded. So used were they to being on the receiving end of misfortune, to existing without rights even in their own homes, the idea that they *had* any was hard to impress on them. In the last resort it was the direness of their situation which won the day; the fact that they would starve anyway and, as Peg put it, might as well be hanged for a sheep as for a lamb.

"So we're agreed then?" said Marie, frowning around.

"What was it again?" asked Aggie.

"We sue the Company for damages for our dead."

Around her heads nodded, eyes said yes as the room slowly emptied of hungry women, ideas of a reckoning and justice beginning to glimmer faintly in their minds.

*   *   *

In some ways there was a lot to the expression "it's an ill wind blows nobody good," Mr. Jephcott told himself. Or was "every cloud has a silver lining" the one he wanted? Looking at the figures before him, to have weathered the situation and come out of it with half the population of Grevillton on the mine's side whereas before *no one* had been for the mine, was no mean feat. It had been said a hundred times and could be said again that as long as there was coal, there would be people willing to work it, people willing to manage them and people who would buy. The odd hiccup could in no way change this. The residue of women left over was unfortunate, especially as without men they seemed unwilling to leave Grevillton and tramp off over the hills but hung on waiting for God knew what! Jephcott looked up, his eyes passing beyond the window and across the tracks. A man was approaching on a horse, bending, asking directions. By rights he should not be on Mine Property, Jephcott thought, turning back to his papers. Suddenly there was a brisk knock at the door. "Enter," he called and saw the door open and the stranger stand before him.

"Mr. Jephcott?" he asked in a pleasant voice.

Jephcott nodded. The man delved into his bag and handed him a long envelop and something in the way he stood staring made Jephcott want to open it before his eyes. Before he could read it the man spoke:

"You have twenty-one days to file Answer to the Summons and Complaint herein served for and on behalf of Her Majesty's Government on you as officer and agent of Defendant in this action."

Hardly had the words sunk in than the man had departed and the foreman entered to find a horrified Jephcott studying the document.

"... did knowingly conduct operations... conditions likely to cause or contribute or lead to explosions to wit..." his voice faded in and out "... were improperly supervised... likely to enhance predisposition of the accumulated gasses... use of naked lamps..." He raised a whitened face to the foreman.

"So what difference is this one?" the foreman asked.

Controlling his voice with difficulty Jephcott answered:

"*We* have to prove that *we* were not negligent. Not that *they* were clumsy! It is *we* who are on trial!"

Tight lipped, he printed a short statement, strode past the foreman and posted it on the board himself:

Operations will be closed down pending duration of the matter before Supreme Court, Hokitika under Section 52 of the Coalmines Act.

Seeing Jephcott in person and reading the manner of his walk, miners began to drift over and look at it. As Jephcott re-entered the hut he heard one of them shout, "Look at bloody this! Now we're all bloody victims!"

Immediately his wife noticed his changed frame of mind. Where previously she had seen the absurd bluster, the brinkmanship she knew so well when he was up against the odds, now there was desperation.

"I don't know what the Company want me to *say*," he whined, voice rising to a squeak.

"Say at that time—No. *Since* then you have examined the site of the accident several times and have to conclude there *could* very well have been gas."

"There *was* gas!"

"Well you can't pretend you don't know what gas is!" Mrs. Jephcott snapped, pleased to see him unsettled at last yet finding him very wearing in these moods. On the whole she preferred him strong.

"Miners themselves testifying—" he complained to her. "It's going to be—*untidy.*"

"Not if they want to be taken on again!"

"I can be got for coal dust, gas, the kind of lamps and explosives, supervision—"

"You've always won before," she said, thinking it time he pulled himself together.

Jephcott continued to pace and growl.

"I'll bet my bottom drawer," his wife went on, "that the *instant* word of this—this—*ingratitude* comes to the public notice, all those who have contributed to the Disaster Fund will promptly demand their donations back! You'll see, George. Those women'll back down!" she said confidently.

As word came to Ceci and Marie that the Big

Industrialists who were contributing to the public Disaster Fund had asked that all monies be returned to them, they began to look with trepidation at what they had done. Passing the wives of would-be working miners, lounging in the doors of their shanties with arms folded, they had to run the gauntlet of remarks like: "How does it feel to have brought the town to a halt?" As they turned the corner to walk back to The Hexham a cake of mud hit Marie and looking up Ceci saw someone had painted "Let us work!" on her pub door and "Non-Miner!!" under the window.

That night Billy chaired the final meeting of those wives who were going ahead plus those few sons and miners who were prepared to testify to conditions below. Gradually the excitement rose.

"You don't call out! You don't interrupt and make remarks, you just answer the questions," Marie said, anxious they should all understand. "If it's not a remark as'll do us good, you don't say it."

One of the men stood up: "It's made it very difficult with the lads, me coming here."

"Do it for William," Ceci said softly.

"Unless you testify to conditions—" Marie went on. The man nodded. He knew what she meant. He was surprised how she had changed since Jonas. In some ways she had become quite a person. At the head of the table Billy occupied the place of honour, people always turning to him when they spoke—needing his nod of reassurance. Though they respected him deeply, they were a bit afraid of him, now pale and shaky, but he was still a man, still the leader of miners at that. Though Ceci had to translate much of his speech to them it diminished his dignity not one jot and they felt it a privilege he would deal with "women's business" ... Tomorrow was the big day. Tomorrow they were off.

"This is the first time I've been away since I were married!" Marie confessed, squeezing Ceci's hands on the doorstep.

"Good luck!" Ceci whispered. They embraced then Marie turned and hurried off into the darkness leaving Ceci bristling with hope for them all.

* * *

With Marie gone and a virtual exodus of the women who had taken on the mine, Ceci confined her journeying to a morning trip—more a habit than gainful exercise—to the fish trap and an afternoon walk to the mass grave beyond Grevillton's bounds. No more was the hooter heard or the clanking, shunting and shouts of the working men. Never had silence seemed so awful. She was conscious of people watching her all the time as she moved about, could feel their hostility and was not really surprised one morning to find her fish trap smashed to pieces in the bushes, a lump of coal in it. Deciding to leave it lie she continued on by the river bank till she was opposite the spot she had first met Billy. There she sat for a long time thinking. At midday she returned home to care for Billy and in the afternoon, as was normal practice, visited William's grave. Thus she was not in town when a conspicuously well dressed man rode into Grevillton on a chestnut horse, its coat shining. Those who saw him thought him a healthy man, a man who ate well. They noted a hope which buoyed him up, a sprightliness which positively shone from his eyes. Slipping from his horse the man knocked on the door of The Hexham and when there was no reply, opened it, put his head in and called. Sensing people watching from their shacks, he glanced around then went to enquire at the store.

"She's at the grave," Mrs. Evans replied flatly.

Ginger headed there.

How harmless Grevillton now looked when its very name for so long had caused him pain, even accidentally overheard. That last visit had been *extremely* painful. It had marked a second turning point in his life. The first had been that moment with Ceci before Hexham's grand fireplace. It was amazing he had not been wise to himself 'til then! Amazing he could not have recognized what it was that had made him leave Hexham previously, his meal untouched on the table! Up until that time he'd been confused, perhaps angry at the upsurge of feelings both unexpected and to his mind unaccountable; feelings that *ought not to have been there*. Indeed, the idea that anything should happen to him that did not befall all others in Moke was quite unthinkable! Had he not seen himself as the epitome of the mundane? Yet instead of recognizing these feelings for the blessing they were, he had tried to crush them, beat them down. Time had proved them enduring. And at last Time was being kind! Oh the *timeliness* of his good fortune! Never had he forsaken her as his enduring goal! Rather he had poured into his labours the passion she had rejected by spurning him. Slowly, he saw the object of his quest lingering on the edge of the mass grave—sad—beautiful. So precious was the moment he could hardly breathe. Part of him wanted to shout out, raise her name in a great cry, that name he had carried in his heart over the Alps and down the divide to the West Coast! Cherishing each moment he stepped slowly through the grass towards her, marvelling that she did not hear him and turn around. Her head was immediately before his hand: so easily could he touch it. Before the obelisk Ceci glanced at the open grassland beyond the small fenced area, then returned to running her finger across the great peel of names cut in it: "Parish, McDowell, Maillart, Anderson..." Their ages ranged from fourteen to seventy-six. Leaning on it she looked at the nearby graves:

> In loving memory of Jack,
> the beloved husband of Alice Pickles,
> who was killed in the Grevillton mine
> explosion of June 15 1892.
> Native of England,
> aged 44

She did not sense Ginger coming up behind her.

"Ceci," he said.

Casually she looked round, then almost choked. Instantly he was on his knees, holding her, hardly able to keep back the tears which surged into his eyes, puzzled as she pulled back.

"What are you *doing* here?" she demanded, struggling to free herself, her tone, the words she had chosen, worrying him.

"I stayed away because you were married but I can't stay away any longer," Ginger confessed. "I read about it—"

Suddenly it dawned on Ceci what he was saying.

"My husband is still alive," she said slowly.

A myriad of expressions crossed Ginger's face. That he could not say he was sorry was evident, yet he wasn't glad either. He, who had come intending to tell her how heartbroken he was *on her behalf;* intending to lavish pity and compassion and comfort on her; to *win* her with it, use it, spend it like money to buy her *because her husband now was dead!*

"There was a Bill, with a pub address," he stammered.

"That was *William!*" Ceci burst, uncomfortable on his behalf.

How simple he had expected it to be, telling her she should come back with him! Why, he had even thought she would be grateful! What she was saying could *not* be true! Unwilling to accept what he was hearing, he clasped her to him but she leapt to her feet.

"Come—come home and meet Billy."

He looked distinctly put out.

"How are you Ginger?" she asked tenderly, knowing he loved her as much as he had ever done and was deeply hurt.

Because they were on the move, walking back to Grevillton, Ceci dared to relax. A sense of fun stole over her as, laughing and chatting, they forced from their minds the essential shortness of each other's company. Hearing a laugh tinkling out, a wife moved to her window. No one laughed in Grevillton. Who were these people enjoying themselves? So tangible was their pleasure she did not recognize Ceci, the scene before her eyes being so utterly foreign she could not put thoughts to it. But whoever they were, they did look good together, she told herself, turning away from the window.

As they went, Ceci ducked down to grab up handfulls of greens hoping Ginger would think it an affectation on her part. She did not realize he had noted her thinness and was not deceived into believing the greens were for arranging in a jar! It would mean using the last of the dried fish too, Ceci realized, that half she had been saving for just such an eventuality.

Making her explanations to Billy, Ceci helped him downstairs.

"Billy, this is Ginger. Remember?"

Billy remembered.

"How are the children?" he heard Ceci ask, preparing their food in the kitchen.

"Lizabeth's married—ran off with her sweetheart!"

"She did not!" Ceci gasped. From where did she get this enthusiasm, Billy asked himself. She sounded years younger.

"Well so's Olwen married," she said lightly. "She's over here now! You ought to meet her!"

As Ceci came into the room with the fish and greens broth Billy looked harder at Ginger. Why had he come? And why now? He saw the look of interest spread across Ginger's face as Ceci talked, serving the food. They were like two children together, chattering on while before him his broth got cold. Not that he wanted it now! Ceci turned and lifted some to his mouth on the spoon and Billy caught Ginger looking at her as if thinking: "So this is how she feeds him!" He knocked the spoon away, tried to push himself from the table and fell. Instantly Ceci was kneeling, leaning over him whispering:

"Please Billy! He's come *so* far and he's leaving directly!"

Billy struggled to get to his feet. He wasn't hungry and though he knew it was the last of the fish, didn't want the meal. But he felt ashamed. "Sorry," he murmured to Ceci as she helped him to his chair by the grate. Sinking into it his arm flew out involuntarily catching her in the stomach, heightening his embarrassment. Ususally they laughed at these muscle spasms but now he was overcome with confusion, by the idea of a stranger in their home interpreting and misunderstanding their behaviour. Glancing past Ceci he saw on Ginger's face a look of utter horror. Ignoring Ginger Ceci sat and tried to take another mouthful but hardly was the spoon to her lips than Billy began coughing. Quickly she picked up his glass of water and hurried to him, putting an arm around his shoulder, helping him drink, watching the water trickle over his chin and into his vest. She leant over him trying to shield him from the discomfort of Ginger's eyes which she could now feel staring. Behind her Ginger saw Billy's glass fly out and smash on the floor as his body jerked forward and the feet shot out.

"We have *hundreds* of glasses," Ceci smiled, trying to make light of it.

Yes, thought Ginger, and no one to drink from them!

"Don't bother with me Ceci. Go for a walk," Billy murmured, ghastly shame on his face. All Ginger heard was: "Doh boh tha wih me Shesh—Go foh woh." He saw Ceci shake her head.

After she had helped Billy upstairs, Ceci stood awkwardly in the bar room, uncomfortable to be in an enclosed space with Ginger.

"It's the lack of oxygen which damaged his brain tissues," she said, explaining with her hands. "A sort of spreading incapacity in the limbs."

"Come back with me," Ginger pleaded. "We'll take him too."

In reply, Ceci stared evenly at him.

"Dear *God* Ceci," he urged coming to stand behind her. "I can't *bear* to see you knocked around, shouted at by that bully."

"How dare you—" she began.

"Can he love you now?"

"Don't you understand 'till death do us part'?" she demanded.

"*Bring him! Come with me!* I'll pay for a good doctor."

"*This is his home.*"

"So you're happy?"

"If you love me Ginger—you'll pay for a doctor to come here."

"He'll be a vegetable soon!"

"Then I'll see he's well watered!"

"*Why?*"

"Ginger!" she exploded. "I owe you nothing. You were married, now I am."

"But I could *love* you," he insisted, as if somehow he could do it *better* than Billy, more completely.

"I don't think I could sit still and be loved." Ceci shook her head. "My happiness is not how you could love *me* but how *I* could love."

As they stepped on to the duckboards Ginger struggled with his thoughts.

"If I am to respect your wishes—" he began.

"Not wishes. *Choices.*"

"So you're sending me away," he said, hoping she would deny it. She nodded. Ginger turned and walked. He had come to Grevillton to get her. As he mounted his horse, behind him Ceci looked mortally sad.

* * *

Dragging herself on hands and knees up the inaccessible gorge, Olwen paused to look back at the sparkling sea and the clear blue of the sky above. She took a long swig from her water canteen, shook a little into her hand and smoothed back the fair hair from her face. Summoning her strength she continued, scrambling up the gulley, getting a good grip on the branches and boulders previous storms had piled up, clambering around and over rocks in what now resembled a dried out waterfall. As her hands grasped at roots she noticed her knuckles were flecked with blood, grazed where she had skinned them, white chalky slashes marking her wrists. Wobbling for balance she finally made out some stretched tarps guyed over saplings, indicating a place between fallen logs where a hobo had made his stand. By the look of the course rising above her, next winter's storms would certainly wash him out. Picking her way forward she noted out a couple of blackened pots on sharp sticks wedged under the awning and the feet of a man, visible as far up as the knees, moving about behind them. This she had been told, was the place "Legs" had staked out. Crouching by the rocks she tried to get a look at him, this man they said was her father. In the silence his billy can made a chinking noise. Some way off a bird started to hammer. The man moved to the edge of the awning and began to whistle, scratching his head at the sky.

Never had Olwen seen such an extraordinary fellow. Dirty, content, very much a loner. The sort of man she had passed countless times on the road chewing sticks, not going anywhere. If it rained they sheltered. When it stopped they moved on. Men of the hills: "fossickers" people called them.

Reg picked at a tooth—sent a belch crashing down the gulley and turned back into his tent. Slowly Olwen came forward.

"Papa?"

At once he knew who it was, and before even turning, straightened his back and tried to put dignity into this new role he must play. That voice had been a musket ball in his back.

"How are you?" Olwen asked, unable to believe they were related.

"Famous. Don't it look so?" Reg frowned. Why'd the girl come climbing all the way up here anyway? By the looks of her she'd do good running a grog shanty. He cleared his throat and frowned some more as Olwen, uninvited, stumbled past him into his lean-to and sat on his planking bed across rocks under which a stream trickled. She looked at him—waiting for him to say something but Reg stood straight as a pillar.

"What are they?" she asked, nodding at a tin in which things were moving.

"Cockabillies," he replied. "No need t'look at me like a yard of pumpwater."

Shrugging Olwen took her eyes off him and let them wander round his shanty.

"So you done married that fellow," Reg observed.

Olwen tossed her face in a closed mouthed way which struck Reg as curiously his own.

"Saw you an' your mother snivellin' up there," he went on, thumbing his head in the direction of Grevillton and wondering if she liked him enough to overlook his deliberate rudeness.

"So you were up there?" she asked, looking directly at him. In a rush of confidence he thumbed the area around them as if in the midst of London.

"Most of us *here* went on up. Too hard t'be diggin' that grave theirselves."

"Have you got any money?" she enquired.

He shifted on his feet.

"Might have," he said feeling her observing him. "Then again I might not."

"Well," said Olwen standing. "We need money."

Reg nodded to the corner of his lean-to. "Me pick's over there."

At that Olwen took a good look at it till Reg thought she might actually take it, rush out into the gorge and start thrashing at the rocks with it.

"You may choose to forget I was *your* bastard," she said calmly, as if getting ready to deliver a sermon.

"Thought you was averse to that word," Reg said, colour rising.

"You diminished my mother's marital prospects," Olwen continued.

Aha! Now he knew what they were talking about.

"Came on us like a fire cracker, your mother. Fair blew the place up."

"Are you saying I was *her* fault?" Olwen enquired.

"Not sayin' nothin'. Know better."

The girl shrugged, dismissing him like a badly designed piece of fretwork. Then she looked back at him.

"Can't you unbend a little?"

The appeal in her eyes was so familiar, so piercing. That look he hadn't seen since Moke, so long ago! He let out a long sigh, all his accumulated guilt slipping with it.

"Money, is it?" he asked. Olwen nodded.

"I bin chawin' on this a long time," he began. "And I'm not so sure as that piece of land that went to Hexham shoulda done. It was *our* banns, me and Ceci—what my father married on. Had me birth date on 'em."

He explained, and Olwen nodded, following the drift. "And he was well into 'is dodderage, my father."

"So you're saying their marriage wouldn't have been consummated?"

Reg went scarlet. He'd never heard the word before but sure as hell knew what it meant now!

"Hhrum," he cleared his throat.

"Did they sign a Register?" Olwen enquired.

"Wasn't there meself. Me brother—bein' a idiot—*if* he was there—coulda been witness. If she got the land—your mother—on account she was the old boy's wife—"

"I see," Olwen nodded, sparing him elaboration. "Why didn't you do something about this before?" she asked imperiously.

"Didn't 'ave a clean shirt."

Olwen shrugged.

"Well if it's yours—it's mine," she said.

"It's yours girl," Reg nodded.

Reg was relieved to see Olwen frown. That was a lot better than her running at him and flinging her arms around his neck. Obviously a thinker, this one.

"Could muddle a Judge's mind . . ." he offered, "a girl like you."

"If it's part of the law to post banns—"

"Don't set your hopes too high—It was a good bit of land though. Had water."

For a long time Olwen stared. Suddenly she looked up at him:

"Will you come with me?"

Moved, almost to the point of tears, Reg drew from his pocket the thing his hand had been curled around since she entered his tent. His lucky nugget. Smiling, he began to flick it up and down.

In Grevillton Ceci knew Olwen had found Reg for an ancient tramp who at once put her in mind of the Old Timer had knocked on the door of The Hexham to pass on the message that: "Alwenn had found her father and was with him."

The man's bird-like eyes had been pecking behind her into the shadows, wondering if there were ale or a meal to be had. When she'd told him he'd have to wait half an hour to eat he'd clacked his gums and said he was "in a right hurry!"

Now, waiting for Marie to come back, time dragged heavily and doubt gnawed at her mind. The river was so full of fish traps which were daily raided by small children before first light, she had taken to angling but her old sack on a stick refused to apprehend fish. If she had only the *tiniest bit of money,* she told herself, she would have purchased seed and cleared some land beyond Grevillton and gone into vegetables. The longer Marie stayed away the more she found herself worrying about what they had done. Returning past the store with her empty net she was surprised by a shout from Mrs. Evans:

"Did you hear they won!?" she yelled, setting a sign in the window which read: *Generous Credit to Award Winners.* "It was on the telegraph—Doctor heard."

"How much did they get?" Ceci asked running towards her.

"More than £7,000! Have a tin of salmon!"

Amazed Ceci reached out to take it.

"Bless you and about time too!" Mrs. Evans beamed.

"Billy! Billy!" she shouted, turning and rushing back up the street. She burst into The Hexham calling his name.

A grand party followed hard on the return of the victors, elated with their news, thrilled with their triumph, invigorated by the spell away from Grevillton and the kindness and attention the people of Hokitika had shown them. Because of the credit, food was plentiful, even punch.

It seemed as if they could not stop repeating to each other over and again those bits of the proceedings they could remember:

"—then 'e said what was it now Oh yes Any Fool would know—"

"No 'e didn't say Fool," said Peg, newly a respecter of accuracy.

Looking at the women they seemed to stand taller, to have become ennobled by the public affirmation of their rights as people. The men who had testified came over to clap Billy on the back. Happiness radiated from him. He positively shone.

"Marie got £940," Ceci whispered, scarce able to believe it herself. "Because of the children I think. Aggie only got £325. That Mrs. Drew got more because her son was her sole support—I *think* that's how it works..."

A flushed Marie came over and hugged Ceci.

"I'll never forget!" she burst out. "As long as I live." Tears spilled over her red face. "And you Billy," she bent, kissing him on the head.

Chapter 41

£940 was a sum beyond Marie's wildest imagining. Even the simple elements of her schooling told her it represented more than six years' wages. Yet she would not consider Ceci's suggestion that she take it and leave Grevillton. Mining folk they were and mining folk they'd stay she insisted. Her eldest boy was nearly ready to "go down" now, she pointed out, and while she did not feel she "owed" it to Jonas to send him, there was no other way for a youth in their community to obtain manhood. Grevillton was where they lived, she added. It was where

Jonas was buried. The idea of moving without him was unthinkable. Like the other wives, her first action had been to buy as much food as she could and fill Ceci's larder, then her own.

"It's a wonder Mrs. Evans isn't getting in new sheets of roofing tin and chimney pots!" Marie said as they passed the store for the umpteenth time.

Though confined to the recently bereaved—and this was a new cause of fricton—spending in Grevilton had reached a level never encountered before. Even passing the store women would automatically go in to see what was new to be had.

"Come on," Marie said, pulling at Ceci's sleeve. "Shop on the way back. Let's go and gloat at the mine!"

The two women stood on the river bank peering across at the mine, savouring their victory. Now that they had a judgment things would surely change. They might even win back the friendship of the wives of the miners who would now return to work under safer conditions! Why, if the mine improved, they would even open the pub again! They crossed the bridge for a closer look. Nothing seemed impossible!

"What a victory!" Marie sighed. From the gates of the mine they watched the familiar figure of the foreman retreading his route between the Administration Hut and the Notice Board. He was posting a notice. So the changes were to begin already! Emboldened, Marie and Ceci dared to run across the open site and read it.

> During the months of April and May this mine will remain closed pending Hearing of the Appeal . . .

"I don't know what they'd appeal for," said Marie. "The judge was very certain things weren't as they should be."

Well, it was beyond her too, Ceci thought, unless it was a face-saving exercise. Perhaps they wanted to offer some kind of explanation for the bad way they had done things . . .

Unbothered they turned to retread their steps and pay the visit custom now decreed be daily to the store. In view of their decisive victory and the force with which the Judge had come down on the Company, even the sign:

NO MORE CREDIT

in the window did little to ruffle their complacency, or
their new found faith in the invincibility of The Law. Idly
curious they went inside, Marie picking items at random
to put in her basket. Suddenly Mrs. Evans ran out from
the back and began to wrench the food out and replace it
on the shelves. Marie gawped at her open mouthed. The
woman looked to be under great pressure.

"Credit?" she exclaimed. "I can assure you Mrs.
O'Shea if 'n I'd knowed they was goin' to appeal you
wouldn't 'ave 'ad none t'start with!"

"Well there's a marvellous citizen you are for not
trusting of the Judge!" Marie replied. "I've £940 coming to
me!"

"And when you get it," Mrs. Evans snapped, "you be
sure and hurry in here and settle up!"

Marie and Ceci left the shop together. Obviously poor
Mrs. Evans was going through a "patch."

"Better not tell Billy about the Appeal," Marie advised. Whatever it meant, there was no reason to worry
him with it.

"Dr. Murdoch keeps saying he'll outlive me!" Ceci
smiled, turning into the yard. "Unless it becomes difficult
for him to breathe."

"And why should it?" Marie asked.

"If his chest muscles aren't strong enough to lift his
rib cage..." Her voice trailed off as she pushed the
kitchen door.

"Well we'll tell Billy when we've won!" Marie said,
following her into the kitchen.

"Oh, Dr. Murdoch's always telling people they're fit
as a fiddle," Ceci laughed. "If he's told me once—ugh!—"
she trembled violently "—that Billy'll outlive me—ugh!
—he's told me a dozen times!"

Marie looked across at her: "Are you taking cold?"

Ceci turned to Marie, her arms round herself and a
look of bafflement on her face.

"I felt someone touching me!"

Marie's expression stopped just short of "Well aren't
you the silly!" for something in the way Ceci stood bothered
her. Quickly she looked around.

"Alright!" Ceci said, as if replying to someone, but no one had spoken!

"He's calling me!" Ceci gasped, running from the room.

In her head the voice of Billy thundered, urgent—not with fear but with great imminency. Bursting into the room she saw him in bed, eyes fastened on her—voice coming to her distinctly, though his lips were not moving:

"Ceci! Ceci! Ceci!" his eyes shouted.

There was such thundering, receding love in the voice which filled her mind though no sound came from his throat, no air passed his lips. Running to him, she grasped his hand, knelt by the bed, her face next to his on the pillow. With an effort Billy managed to turn his head towards her; a thing he had been incapable of doing in weeks—the beginnings of a smile on his face. With supreme effort she saw the ends of his mouth curl as he moved his face, his lips closer to hers, as if to kiss her. Torn between the emotions of caring for one who was dying and responding to his need to kiss her, she offered her lips. Her face tilted, her eyes closed. And at that second he went. Waiting, she opened her eyes and saw with shock he had gone! "Billy!" She flung herself on him, sobbing. In the doorway behind her Marie, who'd witnessed his passing and the look of fulfillment and total commitment to what he was doing as he forced the muscles of his mouth into a kiss, shook her head slowly. His eyes had been so concentrated they were almost devout. If ever a man loved . . . She saw Ceci spin to look up at her, wanting her to say it was not true. She said nothing.

Crossing the room, Marie lifted Billy's arm from under him and laid it on his chest.

"He ran the race to the finish," she said in the plain voice of one who had seen death often.

Ceci rose and stood silently in her arms.

"He fought the fight, he ran the race," Marie repeated the words she had heard so often. "He didn't tire, he kept running."

Standing there enwrapped by Marie, Ceci let her thin body be shaken by grief. In her mind the words "I *loved*. I have *been loved*," repeated themselves over and over. She now knew it to be the greatest, the only success.

"Our days are vanished like smoke; our bones grown dry like fuel for the fire. We are smitten as grass, gone like the wind that blows over it, our hearts withered," she heard the Minister say. "Through groaning voices our bones have cleaved to our flesh. We are become like pelicans of the wilderness; night ravens in the house . . ." Softly she looked up at the Minister who was drawing this picture of desolation the newly bereaved recognized so well. "I have become as a sparrow alone on the house top," his voice sung out in the wet cemetery. "I am spent as spilled water; all my bones are out of joint. I eat ashes with my bread, my drink mingled with weeping . . ." How his voice rose and fell mellifluously, hypnotizing the listeners, taking their grief with him. "My days have declined like a shadow and I am withered like grass . . ."

Having understood their mood his words became more uplifting, giving hope and ending on the note:

"Then they will shine out, these just souls, unconquerable as the sparks that break out now here, now there, amongst the stubble."

How well that quotation had been chosen, Ceci told herself. A spark in the stubble. One honest man amongst the many. Withered like grass, gone down into her memory and become a part of her.

Against the loss of Billy, the matter of the Appeal seemed pathetically trite, yet Marie and Ceci felt they owed it to him to see the matter through. Now they had only each other, they told themselves, setting off for Greymouth in answer to Mr. Nayfach's letter. The quietness, the lack of boisterousness that had come over them was to do with the awareness that they were without a man to turn to and must rely totally on each other. The change weighed heavily for although in effect they continued to do as they had done before, the fact of being ultimately entirely answerable to themselves was sobering. More so than with their husbands, they understood the limits of the bonds which held them; knew with certainty on what they could depend. Both sensed the loss of their men had strengthened their relationship and that had they been younger or exposed to better circumstances they might never have known this new strength they had acquired. The time of thinking of men in any respect had gone from their lives leaving them a great freedom to commit themselves. Concentrating on getting to Greymouth, they set out for the road.

Since the disaster the women of Grevillton had been allowed free access to river barges between Greymouth and Grevillton—not with Jephcott's consent of course—more the secure knowledge that no barge man would turn them away. Since the mine had closed for the Appeal, however, coal barges had ceased to run but there was always the coast road with its coaches sweeping down towards Greymouth or Hokitika: they would stop if they had room and for a woman of Grevillton to be charged passage in these days was a thing unheard of. Walking towards the road they were afraid of nothing. What was there left to fear?

In the coach, despite their recent sadness for Billy, the feeling of being "recognized" and admired returned to envelop them. They felt the travellers from the East Coast acknowledging them as survivors of the small town which had suffered a disaster, then taken on the Coal Company. No longer were their poor clothes a cause for shame. They could be proud of the lines of suffering engraved on their faces. As they bumped along the road they felt people looking at them, wanting to talk. But as soon as they reached Greymouth the same heads turned away, their clothes again seemed poor and they knew people would not want to be seen on the street with them. Briefly they lingered before the quay letting the sun warm their bosoms then with difficulty dragged their minds back to Nayfach.

The minute they entered his office he noticed they were better fed and was pleased for them.

"Sit down," he began, the sun shining off his earnestly smoothed hair.

Though in his early thirties, he would have difficulty lifting a shovel, Ceci found herself thinking.

"The good news first," he beamed at them. "You won the Appeal!"

Glancing up he saw Marie and Ceci flash grins which made them look years younger.

"And now for the—less good news," he continued. "The Company took advantage of the lapse of time between the Judgment and the Appeal to file for bankrupcy. The debenture holders—with first claim to the assets—"

Marie was a jump ahead of him:

"Are you saying they have no money?" she shouted.

Nayfach looked straight at her.

"I'm saying they no longer exist," he stated flatly.

Picking up a piece of paper he read:

"Loss of earnings due to extensive closure of mine; bad publicity inhibiting investment; damage to plant; litigation expenses—" he paused, frowning at Marie as if the whole thing were indirectly her fault.

"Do you mean to tell me," Ceci interrupted, "that while we were sat here going over the whole thing a second time—"

"A lump sum of fifteen hundred pounds has been settled on," Nayfach continued matter-of-factly.

"More than seven thousand was awarded by the Supreme Court!" Marie shouted but he was already reading from another sheet:

"Re allocated sums thus: Mrs. Jeannie Thorpe—Original settlement six hundred pounds. New offer eighty-five."

"You needn't think you're getting anything!" Marie hissed, getting to her feet.

"Minus sixty pounds lawyer's fee," Nayfach continued, "equals twenty-five pounds. Betty Hawkins. Original settlement one hundred and twenty." His voice faded in and out. "New offer thirty-six—minus lawyer's fee—will be *twenty-eight outstanding . . .*"

To Ceci, who had already spent her emotional strength in mourning, the shock registered as mere information. Indeed had another person died, she would have been empty of tears, not from callousness but the simple lack of capacity. Marie, well recovered from Jonas, took the full blow to the stomach. Once they were outside the room she seemed to fall apart. The last straw for her had been to hear that pompous young man say that the section of the Coalmines Act under which they had brought their case was to be amended in favour of the employers . . . In the light of this crushing defeat, her confidence crumbled. How *could* they have been so stupid! How *could* they have put the whole town at risk! How *could* they, on the strength of an idea of a principle! No wonder Jephcott had been so rarely seen! Why, he was probably in England by now, laughing behind his hat at them! How could they return to Grevillton and tell the people who had depended on them, not to mention those who hadn't, that while the Supreme Court in Hokitika had been going through the Appeal with a toothcomb making it clearer than ever that they, the Women of Grevillton had won, men were sitting in another Court in another country, contriving to prove they were bankrupt?! It was too terrible to bear thinking.

"I know we did the right thing," Ceci said softly.

"I—I think I'll go for a walk," Marie replied, squeezing her elbow.

Letting her go, Ceci glanced up and down the corridor at the doors letting off into offices, the faint shape of figures beyond the bevelled glass suggesting activity. *"Registration And Deeds,"* she read, passing a door, moving on and beginning to descend the staircase to the street. She did not see the door open after her and two figures, flushed with excitement, emerge into the corridor.

Reaching the street Ceci paused at the entrance, almost too afraid to touch the pavement with her feet, to reenter the world of people whose lives were so well ordered. She looked up and down at the sea of heads. Marie had already vanished and before her forms flowed in a river of grey and black, sounds, moustaches, laughter. Cautiously she let go of the door lintel and stepping out began to move faster, intent on losing herself in the crowd.

As Olwen stepped out of the Registration And Deeds office Reg closed the door behind her. She smiled up at him, patting the long envelope under her arm then walked briskly along the corridor and began to descend the stairs. Although not strictly necessary she was heartily glad they had taken the trouble to register the deeds locally. Arriving at street level they glanced up and down, their work behind them and time to fill before the afternoon coach towards Grevillton.

"Look!" exclaimed Olwen, pointing after Ceci.

"Well I'll be jiggered!" Reg murmured, beginning to walk briskly after her.

Up ahead of them the bent head hurried away. Quickly they ran through the crowd.

Arriving on her their elation was not reciprocated by
her humour which at first they put down to the recent
death of Billy. Though bursting to share their own news
Reg took off his hat and Olwen indicated a small ice
cream parlour where they might sit. Privately she was not
surprised at the news and assumed her mother had come
to Greymouth to settle details of Billy's Death Certificate.
Reg dragged a small marble-top table away from the wall
while Olwen set about ordering ice cream for three.

Gradually distracted by their company and pleased to
see them together, Ceci pushed the unfortunate business
of the Appeal to the back of her mind. Reg, she noticed,
seemed very taken with Olwen and she quite relaxed in
his company. When the ice cream arrived in little silver
dishes, Olwen began spooning hers up as if she had it
every day while Reg made cautious stabs at his, the spoon
flying in one side and delivering its load on to Olwen's
lap.

"Careful!" she snapped at him. Ceci watched Reg
lean forward, pick the ice cream from her lap in his
fingers and throw it out the door ino the street where a
dog ran and licked it up. She was surprised Olwen had
been so annoyed about this. She did not know the ice
cream had nearly landed on The Official Envelope.

"Who's paying for this?" Ceci asked nervously, her
mind returning to the realities of daily life. Reg frowned at
her to indicate the honour was his. Slowly she began to
explain about the Appeal, barely conscious of the ice
cream she was eating and not a little surprised at their
virtual indifference to the misfortunes she was relating.

"Well that's what becomes of having ideals!" shrugged
Olwen, the edge of truth to her voice. "You've closed the
town down!"

Ceci bit her lip. Joke or not, those words were unkind.

"Oh don't *worry*!" Olwen went on. "The mine'll be
reacquired. Probably the same people will buy it back at a
better price! Evidently they kept their money! You did
them a favour!"

"I'm glad Billy didn't live to see this," Ceci observed.

Olwen grinned at Reg as if she had found her mother's small concerns quaint.

"Shall I do it now?" her glance said. Reg gave a

barely discernible nod and carefully Olwen lifted the big
envelope and pushed it across the table to her mother.

"What's this?" Ceci asked sharply.

"Deeds to the old place." Olwen grinned. Next to her
Reg swelled with pride.

If they had been expecting a reaction, they were
disappointed. Without opening the envelope, Ceci held it
but carried on talking about the Appeal:

"Do you think I've been too idealistic?" she asked
earnestly.

"Well, everything in your life has been the result of
pursuing ideals." Olwen shrugged patiently.

"Has it?" Ceci said directly at her.

Olwen flushed. Her mother couldn't *surely* mean *her*?

"Or wanting others to conform to your ideals," she
added.

Was there truth in Olwen's assertion? Seeing the
troubled look on Ceci's face, Reg stepped in.

"If your mother's what comes of taking ideals too far,
young woman—you're what comes of not having any!"
He leaned back pleased with himself. Olwen turned readily on him, amazed that as he learned to talk in public he
should leave himself so terribly open.

"Let's begin by looking at *you!*" she returned, conscious a family at the next table turning to peer at them,
the children sucking their fingers and staring.

"What did you say this was?" Ceci asked, waving the
envelope.

"My *birthright!*" Olwen said beaming.

Chapter 42

As the future spread itself before her, Olwen could
not understand her mother's nonsensical reluctance to
leave Grevillton and come back to the High Country.

Amazed, she watched her cling to the back of Billy's chair as if it were the centre of the universe.

"I—I don't think I ought to leave," Ceci said uncertainly. "This place is very important to me."

"But you don't need to *be here* any more!" Olwen protested.

"I *earned* my place here," Ceci replied, knowing it was not the reason she wanted to stay.

"We'll sell the piece of land, go to a big town and do something. We'll *work*. *Both* of us."

Ceci shook her head:

"I—I'm not ready."

Exasperated, Olwen waited for her mother to wake up to the fact of their completely new life. Perhaps she should ask Marie what to do.

"*Why*?" she demanded suddenly.

"This is my *home*," Ceci reasoned. "*Here* I loved. *Here* I was loved."

Though there was no point in staying she would *not* be moved.

"*Please* Mother," Olwen pleaded tenderly.

Finally with help from Marie the decision was made and Ceci sadly stacked the chairs and tables in the kitchen again, spread sacking over them, swept out the larder having passed on the remainder of the food, closed the windows, put a lock on the door and stepped out of The Hexham for the last time.

The whole town knew she was leaving.

"I wish you'd leave too," she whispered to Marie.

"Coal's me life," Marie shrugged. "*And* me eldest 'll be in the pits before you're settled!"

She saw Ceci withdraw an envelope from her coat.

"I want you to have the pub," she said, handing it to Marie. "For when things pick up."

Marie rolled her eyes across the sky at the idea of being a publican with *her* notorious record!

"Visit Billy's grave for me," Ceci pressed her hand.

"And William's," Olwen called.

"As the women embraced, Reg helped Olwen into the coach. She bent down and kissed the top of his head.

"Papa," she said, meaning goodbye.

Lowering his eyes, visibly moved, Reg quickly took

Ceci's elbow to help her up before anyone should see how he felt.

"Giddup!" shouted the driver and the coach took off with a great rattle, the last view the departing had being Marie's red tear-filled face, running, waving by the window and in the background Reg, stiff as a poker, turning his hat in his hand.

Climbing up the mountains, leaving the West Coast behind, Ceci was filled with doubts. She looked across at Olwen. That accusation about her idealism had gone deep. In truth it *had* been idealism that had made her leave England, had made her expect Reg to treat her responsibly and had, in the first place, given her that belief in men. Did her idealism consist in not seeing for what they were facts which were glaringly obvious? Had she simply seen what they could or she would like them to be? Had she wielded this idealism like a war club, reading Calvin's silences or non-committal remarks the way she had wanted? If so, she had trespassed on people. Was it herself she had been fighting all the time? Her idealism? Her idealism that had scorched Reg and burned Grevillton. Yet for the lack of it, Olwen had been branded. Had her idealism at the outset been a handicap or an asset. Though she did not know, even now she could not part with it!

Her mind fled through the corridors of Hope and Belief in the innate Goodness of Man which had enabled Marie and her to believe they could win. Olwen, she remembered, had said at the time she was hopelessly naïve; that the sort of sacrifices she had expected the shareholders to be prepared to make on their behalf were totally ludicrous! Yet was it not unthinkable that, at the time their funds were so desperately needed, they had withdrawn them? Surely they could not have known the extent of human suffering and misery their money could have allayed. It was true that she, like all others of Grevillton, had come there of her own volition and without the investors' original money would have been free to starve that much earlier for there would have been nowhere to come to! It was also true *she* took no chances with *her* pennies; *she* generated no work; so who was she now to complain? If she had a few pennies to rub together today she'd hope and pray not to meet someone else's disaster! Yet *still* the feeling that the outcome had not been *right* nagged. And what could be causing that other than unreasonable idealism she could not let go? Nayfach must have asked for too much! That would account for it! The newspapers had not been lax in pointing out the climate of opinion amongst those classes which had contributed most to the Disaster Fund. None had been surprised when their subscriptions had been publicly withdrawn because of the "lack of understanding and base ingratitude of the mining community towards the Company." The vastly reduced fund, already held up three months with the Public Administrator, had then been delayed to the extent it was only now beginning to make available tiny widows' allowances of twelve shillings a week per family... "twelve shillings a week per family..." she repeated to herself, feeling ashamed. Look what they'd asked for.

She let her eyes pass out of the window and over the deep punchbowl of the Otira Gorge. Towards the top, clouds lingered, caught on the luxuriant foliage. Everywhere was the sound of water rushing, plunging, sometimes even louder than the coach's rumble.

Now they were coming to the bare rocks she remembered from the High Country. There they stood at the pass, poking fom the windswept scrub like the ruins of an abandoned town. Now Grevillton surely lay behind her. Behind her it lay! Before her she sensed the dusty plain of Christchurch...

Descending into the plain, without entering Christchurch they linked with the main Christchurch/Otago trail south and after many hours and coach changes began to rise to the hills in the local trap. Olwen watched her mother's eyes pass over what must have been changes in the countryside since last she was there, the new fences and trails sloping inwards, the increasing signs of human activity. Olwen felt proud of what she had done and had proprietorial feelings already towards the piece of land which was her birthright. She saw her mother begin to get nervous looking this way and that as if afraid of missing something but having been there so recently herself, Olwen knew exactly where they were going.

"Stop!" she called out and the trap stopped. They got

down, Olwen with her valise and hat box; Ceci with a small cloth tied bundle. The coach rattled off, leaving them in the wind in silence. Ceci looked about. Was this actually the old gap Calvin had once cut in the wire to let her through? Had there not been a new gate there last time? Now all was overgrown and difficult to identify...She fingered the wire, frowning.

"Come on," said Olwen as, like a trespasser, Ceci slipped through behind her.

The two women struggled up the hill in the wind, their skirts lashing about them, almost torn away. They paused at the top, silhouetted against the vast sky.

"We haven't got much," murmured Ceci.

"Got each other." Olwen smiled, her eyes sweeping down the furrowed incline towards the scattered stones of the old place lying like spat out teeth in the deep green, the previous burn marks now washed away. Weeds poked over the low walls, waved in the wind. Ceci strained her eyes towards the dip in the land, disappointment on her face. She was not about to run down the hill towards it. Olwen, who had taken a few steps onwards, turned and reached out for her with her hand.

Ceci could not believe it! There it was, the ruined dwelling. This harmless seeming place—a few pieces of rock on some grass—had signalled for her the most formative parts of her life. Her first job in the Land of Hope! The rape! The loneliness of Olwen's birth! Dear Jock! Finding Calvin looking at her over the wall; Mrs. Laird's arrival; the return of Reg...Sighing she sought the marks of Old Bowen's grave and Jock's and *little Else's*...! It was all *too much*! She covered her face. All these things that had happened! Could that be *her life*? These things and timers—gone. Mute witness, some stones and grass. She heard Olwen calling and looked up to see the girl standing on the half-buried lintel stone as if there was a door frame still around it!

"Come in!"

Lamely Ceci stepped in. Now Olwen was kneeling, her back to her, lifting a rolled tarp from the corner.

"Take an end of this," she said. "Reg marked out the holes." As they guyed the tarp down to form a shelter, Ceci saw in the corner that remained standing, blankets, water jugs, a dried ham wrapped in a cloth.

"He has money you know," Olwen went on conversationally.

"He keeps it in a hollow stick! He doesn't trust banks!"

Ceci did not return her jocular mood.

"I never thought I would finish here," she said in a weak voice.

"Finish! We are starting up!"

"I couldn't *possibly* start again!" She shook her head.

Olwen brushed ants from the food and set about building a fire with the sticks Reg had left. She saw her mother sitting on a fallen stone. Slowly she laid out the blankets for them and made all ready for the night.

As they lay under the stars, Olwen looked across at her mother. Gradually it came to her that in her way, the woman was happy to the extent there was nothing left in life she wanted or was seeking. How amazing, Olwen thought, examining her own idea of "Happiness": an essentially ephemeral, perhaps shallow, probably temporary euphoria. Clearly it was a different thing. Was it possible that her mother could know the kind of happiness she personally wanted and sought; more than that, *expected* as a *right* from her life? In her sleeping hand Ceci clasped a slip of paper. Carefully Olwen reached over and tweaked it away.

Number 22		
When married:	August 11, 1891	
Where married:	Union Church, Grevillton	
Name and Surname:	Billy Manseell	Cecille Laird
Age:	42	33
Profession or Occupation:	Miner	Publican
Conjugal Status:	Bachelor	Widow
Birth Place:	Whalton, Northumberland	Macclesfield, Cheshire
Usual Residence (in full):	The Hexham, Grevillton	The Hexham, Grevillton

What was the significane of this, Olwen wondered, looking at the utter stillness of her mother's face, the peace which

had returned to it. In the morning she must tackle her
mother about this. And about living in the present. And
Happiness...

The marriage certificate had gone when she awoke,
replaced by a look of nostalgia and earnest thought.

"Go to him," Olwen suggested, handing Ceci her
breakfast. Ceci gave her a wry look.

"Well go on. You must've been thinking of him..."

It was amazing how she pieced things together!

Ceci shrugged: "You can't send a person away and
then go to them," she murmured.

Olwen gave her a level stare:

"Don't be frightened of happiness," she said. "You
have a right to it."

"I wasn't," Ceci began, meaning to excuse herself.

"We need tools! Go and borrow some!"

Drawn inexorably on, Ceci arrived at the weak crossing of
tracks. Was this right, she wondered? The tracks were
even more faded since that leading to Bowen's Gully was
no longer used. Why precisely she was going she was not
sure, other than that Olwen had urged her to and they
did need tools... This much she told herself, for want of
an alternative, moving on in a dream. Coming to the
more-than-ever dilapidated Nolan signboard she stopped
as memories and awareness came flooding into her mind.
Leaning forward she touched the signboard with a hand,
unable to believe she was standing in a spot she had once
dreamed of returning to. As she drew back her hand a
strip of dead paint curled off, making her fear the board
and the house beyond it might vanish. Feeling a little
nervous she positioned herself in the Nolans' entrance-
way, clenched her fists and willed herself to move bodily
up their driveway. As the stones tapped under her shoes—
stones of the High Country—she felt the fields falling
away beside her as, drawn by the dwelling at the end of
the path, she moved on. This stretch before the house
became visible was like walking a dark place as a child.
The path reached the bend, wound round and there,
finally, she saw the house—fondness for its dilapidation
leaping to her eyes. It was *exactly* as she would have
remembered it had she had time to think.

Run down. Quiet. Too quiet. There was no sound anywhere.

Running the last few yards to the door she listened, then with worried face brushed the door with her fingers. It swung open before her... She stepped into the silent house. The boards squeaked. It was without furniture. The leg of a doll lay in the grate; a bird had nested in a lamp bracket; the door to the room where she had first come upon Ginger amongst his brood lay wide ajar, its bare floorboards painted around the sides where a carpet had stopped. She wandered from room to room. They had gone away.

With head down she hurried back towards the road. _Now_ she knew pain. This time her heart had found her out and she knew herself to be bitterly disappointed. More than that, feelings which she had ever admitted to having suddenly rose up to accuse her. These feelings that she had denied, were _they_ what Olwen meant by happiness? That was _romance_! Was she now, at thirty-four, still clamouring for romance like a simple child? Surely she had reached the stage of being able not to care! It was _Love_ she had known—not romance. Who could deny the service she had rendered Calvin and Old Bowen, service which called for no gratification, had been _Love_? She had loved them not because of what _they_ were but because of what _she_ was. Even with Billy whom also she had decided with her mind to love before being drawn to there had been no "romance." And now she wanted it! And it was too late.

Romance! A fleeting thing and probably a severe complication to Love, she told herself, leaving much room to be hurt. Had she indeed been cowardly in choosing with her mind and not her heart the adventures of her life? Feeling she had at last discovered herself she surveyed what lay beyond the horizon she had never crossed. As she had walked up the driveway to the Nolans', she now realized, she had thought the door to romance stood open and with considerable trepidation had been prepared to step through.

Now, for the first time in her life, a real bitterness descended. Though it be impractical, perhaps even wrong, she knew what it was she wanted and what she had lied to herself about.

"They've gone away," she said, coming upon Olwen. Olwen looked up, alarmed at the tone of her mother's voice, then her face. She felt terrible. Here she had been, virtually playing "camp," designing her "kitchen area," building with branches and stones and so very pleased with her efforts. She had even been *congratulating herself* on doing her mother a favour and had now caused insuperable pain!

"We'd better get on with selling this place before winter," she heard Ceci say in a harsh voice.

"Do we have to sell?"

"Don't let it dominate your life as it did mine." Who was this talking?

Looking up Olwen saw a hard face she did not know. "We'll sell as fast as we can and get out," Ceci snapped.

Olwen nodded.

It was decided they should start by approaching the Big House—given that as the land had belonged to them until so recently, though they might resent paying for it, they would be glad to have it back. They seemed to have interfered with the river already, and stood at least to be charged for water.

"I don't want to sleep here another night," Ceci said.

In their faded dresses, trying not to catch their skirts on the wire, Ceci and Olwen squeezed through the gap in the fence.

"Have you no feelings for the old place at all?" asked Olwen, unable to believe her mother's sudden hardening.

"It'll go to the highest bidder!" Ceci snapped, eyes boring ahead of her. "We'll put a notice in Moke and advertise in Christchurch."

"I hardly think it's big enough for that!" Olwen said grudgingly. After all it was *her* land.

As they hurried towards Hexham, it was clear the original great mass of land that comprised it had been divided and subdivided many times. New roads ran off to the right; there were names on the fences. Suddenly Ceci paused, allowing Olwen to catch up. The old road had split, heavy cart tracks indicating the traffic went right as if the Big House, lying ahead, commanded little respect. Continuing on, Ceci noted the fences in such poor repair that by the time she came on Hexham's grand entry gates, it was no surprise to find the place ill-kempt and the victim of many changes. In poor repair the great house brooded beyond the gates, sombre, unloved. Ignoring all, Ceci strode firmly ahead in a brisk manly way. It was the first time in her life Olwen could ever remember having detected the slightest hint of this bitterness in her mother. As she saw her rap loudly on the front door she almost reminded her of Miss Robertson.

"Don't!" she whispered, wanting her to knock with more respect. Ceci turned her back on the door to frown across the weed-covered lawn. It had not been cared for and gave the sense of many owners having come and gone. But there *was* someone there because a curtain was blowing from an open window.

"Does it make you feel funny coming back here?" Olwen whispered. Ceci shook her head. She gave the door another sharp rap. Nothing. Turning the handle she stepped into the hall.

Moved almost to tears by the sight and memory of it, Olwen could not speak. So little had changed, the carpets, hangings, ornamentation that were auctioned with the house had obviously remained part of it even through subsequent sales. In all probability it would have been the land not the house the average farmer wanted.

"Oh I remember! I *do* remember!" Olwen gasped.

"We're here to do business," Ceci said. "Anyone here?" she called in a loud voice.

"I really thought I'd forgotten," Olwen murmured, turning on the spot.

Crash! The sound of a small glass item shattering came from the drawing room.

Olwen looked at her mother, frightened. Ceci tutted, strode towards the drawing room as if she still owned the place and pushed open the door. There, the billowing blowing curtain had swept a glass statuette off a table which now lay in pieces on the floor, its crystal fragments reflecting the light. Ceci paused to glare at it, then leant out, pulled in the curtain, closed and firmly latched the window.

"Come out of there!" Olwen called in a whisper from the doorway.

But Ceci remained where she was, merely turning her back on the window before speaking loudly:

"This is the room where Miss Robertson read *Pilgrim's Progress* to you. Do you remember?"

Before Olwen could reply, the tread of someone hurrying down the stairway was heard. In an instant, Olwen was behind the sofa, beckoning to her mother. Quickly Ceci joined her as the feet entered the room, passed them and moved towards the previously opened window. They heard the glass being gathered together, then silence. Olwen felt uncomfortable. They could not stay where they were indefinitely. Had the person in fact gone? She indicated this by a sign to Ceci who shrugged hopelessly back at her. They were caught in a ridiculous situation but trespassing nonetheless. What was the person at the window doing? Slowly they eased themselves into more comfortable positions. Time passed. Ceci began to wonder if the person had in fact silently reopened the window and climbed out! Cautiously she raised her head and peeped over the sofa to see a man standing, his back to them at the window. To Olwen's utter horror, began to stand and stood quite upright, staring over the sofa towards the window, her hands gently gliding along the sofa's edge, making their way along as if her feet could no longer find parts of the ground.

Ceci saw the man at the window shift slightly on his feet. She took two steps sideways to get his profile while behind her Olwen looked cautiously over the sofa believing her mother had finally gone mad and was creeping towards this man in whose house they were trespassing with the intention of assaulting him. But as Ceci turned, by the look on her face, Olwen could believe she was actually seeing a ghost!

"I am looking at the profile of a man who has come to terms with the fact he will never have what he most wants in life." Ceci told herself. It was a face which had suffered. They said suffering either made or destroyed a man. The set of his chin, his shoulders, were different, ennobled. Where before there was desire, now there was dignity. As the man half turned his face, she knew he would never push her again, would never seek to take what was not his. And that he was waiting for her to come to him. She knew fear.

Hearing her breathing Ginger stood absolutely still. These last few weeks had been a time of measured waiting, a time when he had daily reminded himself that whether he got her or not, he must continue on and not let external matters decide his behaviour or diminish by one jot his new found gratitude to Life . . . He could sense Ceci getting closer and dared not turn lest the appetite on his face should cause her to catch her breath and step away. How events may have changed her he had no idea, nor was he presuming on any affection she might have for him.

Standing upright now, Olwen saw her mother breathing like a trapped animal, hovering behind the well-dressed man who did not turn to look at her yet must surely know she was there. Something about him was familiar. Wasn't this the man who had come running from the blacksmith's shanty? The man who had visited her mother in Grevillton and written to her and who she had gone over to see that morning? If this were the case no wonder she had met with no objection when she claimed back Bowen's Gully! He must have watched her every activity with mounting joy unable to believe his sheer good fortune! All she had been told about him said he was "persistent" . . .

"I tried to tell you about here last time," she heard Ginger say to Ceci who remained speechless before him. Would he have waited for ever Olwen wondered? Had it been so obvious to him Billy was failing? Perhaps, she decided, she had better leave the room and make a noise about it to let them know. Deliberately she knocked over a chair.

"Excuse me. I'm going outside."

Turning, they saw her go. Ginger looked fiercely at Ceci, so still, so afraid. He touched the edge of her shoulder.

"Stop!" she said instantly. "I can't stand it!" He let his arm drop and moved to stand a few feet away. Beyond them through the window Ceci saw Olwen crossing the lawn towards the summer house as from it a child of thirteen or so came, waving and running.

"Myra," said Ginger. Myra turned, shouted something back towards the summer house and twins Michael and Kevin too emerged, followed by Faith who stood staring at Olwen, then began to run.

"They like a new face," Ginger murmured.

Ceci looked at him with caution. After her previous uncertainties and recent wisdom she was afraid that the greatest adventure of her life was about to unfold itself.

"Let us love each other, shall we Ceci?" Ginger said solemnly, his hands remaining hanging at his side. "It is right."

She moved to stand next to him, this man she would now call "Vincent."

Beyond them on the grass the children were punching each other's shoulders and joking. All feelings of guilt slipping away, Ceci carefully slid her roughened hand into his. In that moment she realized that, at the age of thirty-four, the life she had waited for was about to begin.

ABOUT THE AUTHOR

ELIZABETH GOWANS has lived throughout Asia, South America, and the United States, earning her living as (among other things) a teacher, a psychiatric nurse, a court interpreter, a legal adviser, and a Buddhist nun.

Experience all the passion and adventure life has to offer in these bestselling novels by and about women.

Bantam offers you these exciting titles:

Titles by Jean Auel:

☐ 25042 CLAN OF THE CAVE BEAR $4.95
☐ 25053 THE VALLEY OF HORSES $4.95
☐ 26096 MAMMOTH HUNTERS $4.95

Titles by Cynthia Freeman:

☐ 26161 DAYS OF WINTER $4.50
☐ 26090 COME POUR THE WINE $4.50
☐ 25433 FAIRYTALES $4.50
☐ 26092 NO TIME FOR TEARS $4.50
☐ 24790 PORTRAITS $4.50
☐ 25088 WORLD FULL OF STRANGERS $4.50

Titles by Barbara Taylor Bradford:

☐ 26534 A WOMAN OF SUBSTANCE $4.50
☐ 25621 HOLD THE DREAM $4.95
☐ 26253 VOICE OF THE HEART $4.95
☐ 26541 ACT OF WILL . $4.95

Titles by Judith Krantz:

☐ 25917 MISTRAL'S DAUGHTER $4.95
☐ 25609 PRINCESS DAISY $4.95
☐ 26407 I'LL TAKE MANHATTAN $4.95